To the missus, it means as much to put you at the front of the book now as it did that first time!

To my beta readers who helped immeasurably, Kimberly Sansone, Vix Kirkpatrick, Misti, and Jeff Shoemaker. Thank you!

To my editor Sheila Shedd, who works tirelessly to make these books as polished as possible.

To first responders and the men and women of the armed forces you always have and always will have the respect and gratitude of the Tufo clan for all you do.

And lastly you - yeah I'm talking to you. The person that bought this book and is as much a part of the process as I am. I love you guys and I mean that wholeheartedly, thank you for your continued support!

W0006421

Prologue 1

DENEAUX WAS HALFWAY through Indiana when whatever hell's angel was tasked with looking out for her took the morning off. She'd stopped at a rest stop just outside Indianapolis. Apparently, even demons hell-bent on misguided revenge and retribution need sleep. Her head was thrown back against the seat rest, a burned-down cigarette with an incredibly long ash firmly planted in her mouth. When the heavy rapping came on her window, she started awake and the residue fell onto her lap. She lifted her revolver, expecting to find a zombie at the window, but what she got was worse.

"Put it down," the man said with a gap-toothed smile. A thick, brown beard covered his face and the old acne scars he'd developed in his youth. An orange hunter's cap adorned his head. Deneaux could recognize evil in another, and his grim smile was unnerving.

"I won't say it again." He pointed to the front of the truck, where a man with a wicked looking assault rifle was aimed straight at her. "And in case you have a Jesse James complex..." He pointed to the passenger side, where another man had a large caliber handgun directed at her.

Deneaux did her best to remain calm. She placed the gun on the seat beside her. "There, all better now. I mean you no harm," she said evenly.

"Unlock the door." The man's grin faded almost immediately.

"We're all in this together. I'm just trying to get back to my family."

"We're in it together," he said, pointing to the men with guns. "You're just a resource. Unlock the door. I won't say it again so kindly."

Deneaux looked around the cab. The truck wasn't even started. There wasn't a chance in hell of her warming up the glow plugs and getting the truck out of there before she was riddled with bullets. She popped up the door lock.

Once it clicked, the man flung it opened and wrenched her out. She smacked onto the pavement hard, wincing in pain. The man leaned down.

"The next time I tell you to do something, I suggest you hurry up." The man roughly patted her down. "Get up."

"I'm…I'm hurt." She held her hands out to show the road rash she'd suffered.

"Not yet, but you will be."

"Please. Please—it doesn't need to be like this."

"Fuck, Wember. What is she, like, a hundr'd and twelve?" The man with the assault rifle had come over. He'd shouldered his gun and was moving to look inside the cab of the truck.

"Quit your bitching, Veeral. At least she's got a pussy."

"Are you sure?" Veeral laughed. "Thing prob'ly fell out from disuse."

"Naw, when they're this old, the things fill with dust and scab over," the third said.

"Fuck, Jolly. You're gross. I guess we'll find out soon enough."

"Just this piece and a shitload of cigarettes," Veeral said while he put Deneaux's gun in his waistband.

"Can…can I have a cigarette?"

Wember took one step over to her and punched the side of her head hard enough that she blacked out. She heard laughter as her head bounced off the ground, then nothing. When she awoke, it was hours later. Night had settled. Her head throbbed, but that wasn't the worst of it. She was propped up and tied against a decent sized oak, her arms pinned behind her. Her breath hitched when she realized her boots and pants had been removed. Her panties were torn and pulled to the side. Blood coated the inside of her thighs. She saw Veeral's back as he approached the fire. He was fumbling with his zipper.

"Bitch is as dry as a funeral drum," he complained.

"Like that's ever stopped you," Wember said, handing him a piece of cooked rabbit.

"Please," Deneaux croaked. Her shoulders threatened to pull out of their sockets. Her head swam from a concussion. Her genitals ached from the abuse. But it was the siren call of the nicotine that she begged for.

"Haven't you learned bitch?" Wember said, arising from his log around the fire. He grabbed a burning switch and smacked it along the side of her face. She screamed out in pain as the switch left a charred strip across her cheek. "You talk when I tell you to." He turned back and tossed the stick back into the fire. Deneaux whimpered, the pain momentarily making her forget about her addiction, but only momentarily.

"She smells better than she looks. Maybe we should just eat her," Jolly said.

"Nuh uh. I ain't doing that again. That boy tasted horrible, and I was sick as shit for like a week."

"I told you before, Veeral. It wasn't the boy that made you sick. It was the damned crushed can of beans that did you in. Botulism or some shit. How many times do I have to tell you? You can't eat the damaged cans. Bacteria gets in them."

"I was hungry."

"His calf wasn't enough?" Jolly smacked Veeral's arm good-naturedly.

"I'd rather have cow," Veeral said sadly.

"We all would. The chewers aren't leaving much behind, though," Wember said, turning the spit. "At least now we can play with our food and not get in trouble!" They all laughed. Deneaux shivered.

She didn't believe in karma. This wasn't about things coming full circle for all she'd done. This was a current bad situation from which she needed to extradite herself. She slept in fitful spurts; every time her head hung low, it would pull against her shoulders, jerking her back awake. More times than not, she would awake to have Veeral standing over her. Her mouth was parched, her cheek stung, she would have just about quit smoking for a glass of water right then. She thought her pleas had been heard when she felt water raining down on her. That quickly changed to disgust when some of the broccoli smelling saltiness of urine entered into her mouth. Her spitting and retching noises were met with Veeral's laughter.

"You like that?" he asked as he shook the last few drops free. "Don't want to get any in my pants," he said as he kept at it, making sure the clingers departed as well. "Gotta admit, you're not much to look at, but you fuck nice enough." He leaned down and stroked the side of her face. She did not flinch; a smoldering coal burned red and hot in her eyes. Veeral slapped her. "Don't you look at me like that. Don't you ever!" He smacked her again, hoping that would stop the shiver that had niggled into the base of his spine.

"Be nice to her. Don't you know who she is?" Wember asked as he untied her.

She again cried out as her shoulders slid back into place. She hated herself for being so weak.

"What do I give a fuck who this dried up hag is?"

"You're just about giving it to royalty."

"She's the Queen of England? Are you fucking kidding me?" Veeral got down to get a closer look at her. "She don't look like the Queen. What was that bitch's name? Eliza or something?"

"Elizabeth, you idiot, and I said like royalty. Naw. This here? This is Vivian Deneaux, if her license is right."

"Do know what?"

"No—Den-oh. Damn, you really are an idiot. If you weren't my brother's best friend, I would have shot you by now."

"Fine, Deneaux. So what?"

"Her husband was a senator or something. She comes from money. Or has money. Or more likely, knowing those rich fucks, stole money. Why ain't you riding this out in some super-secret government bunker?"

Too lost in her own pain and misery, Deneaux didn't answer immediately. Wember shook her back to reality quickly when he smacked a switch across the bottom of her bare foot. Pain rocketed up her legs and spine and flared at the base of her neck, where it radiated around her entire skull.

"So is you is or is you ain't?" Jolly asked coming up. The three men were standing over her.

Her tongue burned with a verbal acidity that she wished to spew, but it would do no good in this situation. They'd already proved they would hurt her, and the killing would come soon enough at this pace.

"I am Vivian Deneaux." She tried to hold her head high, but it pulled on her shoulders.

"So what?" Veeral asked. "She was a rich bitch once. What's that mean?"

"Isn't this about the time you tell us you can get us money?" Wember laughed.

"I could, but we both know money is no good. What about gold?"

"Where am I going to use gold?"

"Smart man like you has to have this figured out by now. Don't you?"

"Why don't you go ahead and let me know what my plans are."

"This has to end sometime. And you're right, regular paper money will be useless. But gold has always been valuable, ever since the first man dug it up. Thousands of cultures and civilizations have perished and fallen, yet gold has always remained a valuable commodity. The people that have it will always rule over the people that don't."

"And you'd just hand this gold over, that right?"

"I'd be willing to trade some of it in exchange for my life."

"What if I just take it all?" Wember asked.

"Yeah, what if we just take it all?" Veeral asked, not realizing the minor discrepancy between his and Wember's words.

"Where's this gold? I'm going to need to see it." Wember pushed Veeral out of the way.

"Do you really think I carry my gold around with me? Could I have some water, please."

"Where's the gold, bitch?"

"I need some water."

Wember raised his hand.

"I'm no good to you dead or rendered unconscious. I need some water. And a cigarette."

Wember's hand wavered in the air. He turned and smacked his brother on the arm. "Get the hag some water."

"And a cigarette," Deneaux added.

"And a cigarette."

Wember lit the cigarette. Deneaux took two long drags from the stick before she even spun the lid off the water bottle.

They watched her every movement as if she had just become fascinating; once you know who they are, somehow the rich and elite do the mundane things differently.

"Why ain't you in your bunker with all your gold and the other douchebag government types?" Wember asked.

She took another long drag. "We were on a mission of mercy. Bringing supplies to those in the greatest need, when we were attacked by a horde the size of which we'd never encountered before. Five of us escaped; two were bitten. We cared for them as best we could."

"The only care you could have given them was a .45 caliber aspirin."

"There's a vaccination."

"Bullshit."

"I've seen it."

"There's a cure?" Jolly asked.

"Not a cure, dumbass. It prevents you from ever becoming a chewer," Wember told his brother but looked over to Deneaux for confirmation.

"There's something like that out there?" Veeral asked.

"Well, if we're to believe Hagatha here."

"Civilization is closer to being restored than you know. That's why we were out there helping those people. The more that survive now, the more there will be to rebuild."

"Yeah and you rich fucks need the little worker bees to do it. Don't you?" Wember sneered.

"I'm offering you a chance to be part of the ruling class. You won't be a drone anymore. We can have the planet back in a year, maybe less."

"I like the way the world is now," Jolly said. "We can do what we want to whoever we want whenever we want."

"You can do that when you're rich and powerful, too," Deneaux said, smiling. "But you can do it while you're living in the lap of luxury. People will actually bring the things you desire right to you."

Deneaux could almost see the thought bubble form over Jolly's head as he dreamed about sitting on a couch, being fed grapes by nude women.

"Where's this bunker?"

Deneaux did not hesitate. "Maine."

Prologue 2

"CRONOS, THERE HAS been a fracture. The woman yet lives," Beleden the Messenger said, his head bowed in reverence as he spoke to the god.

"That is impossible. Who has assisted her?" Cronos demanded.

"That, I do not know," Beleden answered.

"What is her destination?" Cronos stood up from the bench he had been sitting on to walk around the vast white chamber.

"She travels toward the Ones."

"THIS CANNOT BE!" Cronos thundered.

"There have already been deviations in the line of time laid out before them," Beleden informed.

"I have carefully been maneuvering my pieces for two thousand years. I will not tolerate a usurper changing everything now! What is the projected outcome if she cannot be stopped?"

"There is nothing written; all will be forged in the present."

"Preposterous! No fate? No destiny? I will allow no such thing on my watch! You will stop the woman and you will find the one who has attempted to thwart my plans. If she makes it to the Talbot household there is no telling the irreparable harm she will cause to my campaign."

Beleden bowed as he left the great chamber. He would not

be able to stop her; in fact, he would not even try. He was playing a dangerous game, one which could have him thrown out of the great hall. But if it succeeded...if it succeeded, he would himself be considered a god. And that was all that mattered.

Prologue 3

IT WAS ALL a dream. Every last aching, shitty, skull crushing second of it. Tommy, Eliza, zombies, Tracy, the kids, even my beloved Henry, all fucking dreams. Mad Jack, Gambo, Trip—all just extensions of my fucked up psyche. Just dreams, illusions, mirages, mental break downs or lapses. I was in a room, and it did indeed have padded walls. My arms were locked tight to my side and behind me in a heavy cloak of white, respite with belts and buckles.

"How fucking cliché," I said as I looked down at my toes. A red crayon was gripped tightly in between my big toe and the this little piggy stayed home toe. I wonder what the fuck was his problem that he couldn't leave the house. Probably had a severe case of agoraphobia; or maybe he knew exactly what "to market" meant. And the stupid crayon! It wasn't even a Crayola; it was a knock off brand. Is there really a profit margin for that? I mean how much less could a Friend-O crayon be worth?

"Time for your medication, Talbot." The largest man I had ever seen in my life said as he stepped into the room. He was black, which honestly made no difference to me, but he just made such a stark contrast to his completely white outfit. White shoes, white socks, white pants held up by a white belt, and a fresh white shirt.

"It must be a blast going clothes shopping with you."

"Oh, we're friends now? The straight jacket making you feel a little more compliant today? I bet your shoulders feel like they're going to pop right out of their fucking sockets. I've never seen anyone wear one of those for more than seventy-two hours; looks like you're going for a record. Does it hurt?"

"Well, it didn't until you said something. What the hell man, why are you being so hostile?"

"Are you fucking kidding me? You're lucky you're not dead. Not three damn days ago you flung your shit at me like you were a fucking zoo monkey."

"No way man. There's no way I flung shit at you."

"Just shut up man. I don't like being around you anymore than I have to. Open your mouth. I'll give you your meds, and if you're a good little psychopath, I'll see if I can get your restraints off in the next day or two. Maybe you'll learn something. Odds are you won't, but I guarantee you won't feel like throwing feces for a good long while."

"What's the medication?"

"What the fuck do you care? Just open your damned mouth."

"I don't like this reality. I don't like it at all."

"Yeah, I don't like that your momma kept dropping you on your fucking head then tried to call it s.i.d.s. but it's what we've got. Now let me give you these meds. I got other, less crazy people to deal with."

"BT, just overdose me, man. Please just kill me." I begged.

The big man stepped back, shock and confusion on his face. "What? How the fuck do you know my name?" He shook his massive head. "Doesn't matter. One of the nurses must have slipped."

CHAPTER ONE
MIKE JOURNAL ENTRY 1

IT WAS SIX a.m. and I was standing on the deck looking out over the yard. Normally I avoided getting up this early, but I'd been doing it more and more. At first, I was able to blame it on the very real threat that the vampires or zombies would come back, but the real enemy was even more insidious. I was sneaking cigarettes. One to be exact. I had to have it like a supermodel needs her celery stalk. I know it's idiotic but of all the things that had great potential to kill me, this fucking stick was pretty low on the list. Even so, I snuck them; they somehow tasted better that way. Not sure who didn't know about it by this point, though. When you live in a house with, like, five hundred and forty-two people, there are very few secrets.

Trip and Stephanie had sex every night. I mean every fucking night. I've heard quieter howler monkeys. I don't know what she was doing to him but Trip seemed to be a mighty big fan. I'd asked him to keep it down one day but by the third attempt at telling him why, I'd given up. Ron cried his way to sleep; these were the times Trip's howls were welcome. Gary hardly slept, pacing the floors looking for trouble. I appreciated the gesture, I really did. I just wish he would wear more than his tighty whities and black dress socks as he went out on patrol. Our newest person, Tiffany, fit in fairly well, since she was just as damaged as the rest of us.

It was going to be a good long time before the kids, Sty, Ryan, and Angel got over the death of their friend, Dizz. Nicole was adapting to motherhood as best she could under the circumstances. The only problem was she was running herself ragged. She was too paranoid to let the baby out of her sight, and as such, was not getting much sleep. The baby that Justin and I had rescued was doing well. Or at least, I thought she was. Babies and teenagers freak me out and I try to have minimal contact with both. It's amazing that I was somehow able to raise three of my own. If not for Tracy I...my thought was cut off.

"Give me a hit of that." It was Tracy.

"You know about this?" I asked as I handed it over.

She looked at me like she knew everything about me, which was probably true. She took a long drag but did not hand it back. She leaned her elbows on the deck railing.

"You're going to bogart that aren't you?"

"What do you think?" She took another drag. "There's something wrong with that baby," she finally said, after a moment of introspection.

I immediately got alarmed thinking Wesley was sick or something. "What's wrong with him?"

"Not him, her."

"What?"

"Have you ever watched her?"

"She's a baby. They don't do a whole hell of a lot and you know I avoid them."

"She hardly cries and she's always watching—like she knows what's going on. It's unnerving."

"You're saying a week-old baby is giving you the willy-nillys? Don't look at me that way. I'm not giving you a hard time, I'm just trying to get down to what is going on. We already know the baby is different; just look at where she came from. Not in a million years would I discount something weird happening in this day and age. Putting blinders on and hoping for ignorance...that attitude will get you killed."

"God I hate these things," she said as she snubbed it out and threw the butt in a trash can.

"Didn't stop you from smoking the whole damn thing."

"Get another one and stop being a baby."

"I can't—two makes me an addict."

"This coming from the man that says he snorted lines of coke off the table at the local Papa Gino's."

"I was eighteen."

"So what about the baby?"

"What about her? Not like we take her to a doctor and have an MRI done to see if she has evil inside."

"She's going to have teeth sooner or later," Tracy said. As she stood back up, she was looking at me.

We'd talked about this before. Even if Avalyn was not a zombie, there was a good chance she carried zombie-infected blood within her. The chances she could infect someone were pretty high.

"Tracy, I don't know what you're asking of me. Do you want me to get rid of the baby?"

"If she's a threat, Michael, we can't have her here."

"Yeah, I get that. But how do we determine if she is or is not? Certainly can't ask for volunteers."

"Mad Jack thinks if he had the right equipment he could test her blood and maybe even be able to look at some slides."

"Let me guess. The stuff he needs is at the hospital?"

"Sort of. There's actually a lab about a mile away that has everything he would need."

I let my head bow down a bit. Going out on runs didn't usually work out all that well. "I guess before dawn we could..."

"HELP! HELP ME PLEASE!" It was Trip, but his shriek was so loud and high pitched— he was definitely in intense distress. People were converging from all around the house, rifles at the ready. We were a well-oiled killing machine, that was beyond doubt. We had converged on the living room when the next blood-curdling scream came.

"Bathroom." BT said.

There were now easily ten guns pointed at that closed door.

I put my hand up and addressed the aimed barrels. "Nobody shoot me. I'm going to open that door and then step back." I knew I was in trouble the moment my hand got near that door. A thick wet stench was leaking out and around the doorframe. Something had mostly definitely died in there. I twisted the handle; it was locked. Ron wasn't going to be thrilled, but it sounded like Trip was in a fight for his life. I kicked the door in. I don't know if the door was just solid enough to push me back or if it was the malfeasant emanation that bounced me to the ground. I thought I was going to be sick as what looked like green fog rolled out.

"I can see! I can see!" It was Trip. He was in all his naked glory sitting atop his throne.

"What the hell are you talking about crazy man?" BT still had his handgun up looking for a threat. Knowing BT like I did, he might just pop a cap in Trip for the hell of it. It was safe to say the big man was not a fan of the Tripster.

Trip had huge tears flowing from his eyes. "I was cracking off an oily mud hen when I heard a loud pop and that's when I thought my eyeballs had burst!"

"What the fuck is an oily mud hen?" I asked. I was still on the floor.

"Goddammit! What is that smell!" It was Gary; he immediately turned away and started to gag.

"It's the damn lightbulb, Trip." Stephanie had got closer and flipped the switch a couple of times. I could only think about how many Trip shit-molecules were on that thing. I wouldn't doubt if her fingers were sticky now. "The light burned out."

"Kind of like him," BT said in disgust before turning to head outside.

Folks started to dissipate pretty quickly, unlike whatever

bio-hazard Trip had sprayed. I understood why no one took the time to help me up; in situations like this, it truly is every person for themselves. I could blame none of them. It's just, I mean, there're some things you can never truly un-see, or un-smell, for that matter. Steph had stepped away. Apparently, even she needed a fresh breath or two. Trip stood up, I got the joy of being able to gaze upon his manhood (please tell me you know that's sarcasm), but that's not the worst of it. In fact, his glorious joystick didn't even register on the scale after what I saw poking out of that bowl.

First of all, it was blue. No, not the water or some sort of chemical Tydee Bowl. His fucking turd was a fluorescent neon-blue. Yeah. And if that wasn't bad enough, you need to remember I was on the floor, some ten feet away. Want to know how I saw it? Sure you do. The thing was up and hanging over the rim like he had coiled a fifty-foot rope in that bowl and left enough outside to attach a grappler. How is something like that even possible? It was like he'd rented out a few surrogate colons to help birth that thing. I scrambled backward on that floor like the toilet monster was going to come out after me.

"Gonna need a little help here," Trip said when he turned to gaze upon his creation.

It's amazing how fast you can move in an emergency situation. I nearly took out BT when I crashed into the backs of his legs.

"Shut the door!" I was referring to the sliding glass doors that led back inside.

BT didn't hesitate when he saw a nude Trip walking toward us. He just shook his head back and forth as he slammed that thing home. "Go find someone else!" BT shouted.

Trip walked straight into the door like he hadn't just watched BT shut it. Now I got to add pressed junk to the nightmare image file I was creating today. And even after he finally got the hint that BT wasn't opening up and left, the clear imprint of Trip's pork and beans clung like an oil portrait painted on the glass.

"I ain't cleaning that," I said as BT reached down and pulled me up by my shoulder.

"Maybe five percent of the human population is alive...maybe. And he's one of them, Talbot. How does that kind of thing happen?"

"Got nothing for you. He's good for comic relief, if nothing else."

"That's funny to you? Forget it. I forgot I was talking to a man with the mental capacity of a six-year-old."

There was a silence between us, a relatively uneasy one. Things were very much up in the air and no one knew when they would settle or what that would even look like. BT was taking it hard. Hell, everyone was.

"I know you've got something cooking in that head of yours, Mike. Let's hear it," he finally said. We were both looking out into the yard.

"Nobody's going to like it," I said after a moment of deliberation; I wasn't sure I even wanted to say anything at all.

"Spill it. Not like anyone else is beating down the door." We simultaneously turned our heads to make sure Trip hadn't returned. "See, now that shit is funny." He smiled.

"We need to move. Like, away from here." He still wasn't getting it, but that had more to do with how unclear I was being than how dense he was. "All of us, every single one of us, needs to leave this house, to find someplace else to be—and this is where it gets really hinky—wherever that is, Tommy and I can't be there."

"The fuck you saying?" He looked pissed.

"They know we're here. We in agreement?"

"This one of those arguments where you're going to make me agree with every point until you get to the end? I hate those kinds, man."

"Yeah, me too." I was remembering back to a time I went on a job interview. I hated my current job, shocker. So I found this start-up company that was hiring; figured I'd give it a shot. I'm sure my boss knew something was up when I came to work that morning in a suit. At lunch, I went on the interview. The receptionist looked like she'd spent every spare nickel she had on plastic surgery and unfortunately, she'd gone to cut-rate doctors. It's okay to have surgically enhanced breasts, I'm alright with that, but these were so uneven as to be unsettling. Whatever—that's not what I was getting at. The man doing the interview came out to greet me; his suit was nearly as shiny as his greased back hair. Is it like a trademark of shady people to oil their hair? You'd think they'd do more to disguise themselves. Already I was not feeling great about my future job prospects.

"Hey, Mitchell! My name is Dan."

"It's Mike."

"Sit, sit. Can I have Candy get you something to drink? A Perrier, perhaps?"

"I'm good, thank you."

"You working, Mitchell?"

"It's Mike."

"Of course you are, a sharp guy like you. But do you like your job? I mean do you love it? You don't, and that's why you're here. Am I right?"

How the fuck else could I answer that but with a "Yes."

"Do you like to make money, Mitchell?"

Again I said, "Yes," because to do otherwise made me look like an idiot.

"I see you have a ring on. You're married, right? Wouldn't you like to be able to get that special lady in your life everything she ever wanted?"

The anger meter was beginning to peg. I felt like a donkey being pulled down a path.

"Of course, you do. Happy wife, happy life. Am I right?" He was talking like we were best buds and also like I didn't want to break his fucking nose for wasting my lunch hour.

"Do you like clean water, Mitchell?" He was reaching

under his desk; I was already moving to stand as he pulled out a water filtration system. He had a confused look on his face.

"You're a fucking idiot," I told him. Fingers of red were traveling up my neck. "I hate being dragged around by my nose. You can take your little water-filter Ponzi scheme and shove it up your ass."

"I'm sorry you feel that way, but this is no Ponzi scheme." He put the filter on the desk.

"Okay, so let me guess how this goes. I sign up and work for you and part of the money I make goes up the chain, to you, to Candy out there, to the asshole you signed up with. Then it's my job to go and find people that come in below me and their job is to sell more water filters which I make money from and also some of that money keeps trickling upward. Is that the gist of it?"

"Pretty much," Dan said.

"That's pretty much the definition of a Ponzi scheme, dumbass."

"Mitchell, Mitchell, Mitchell! I need people like you. You could sell the hell out of these things."

"Do they even work? Is there even a filter in that stupid thing?"

"That's the beauty of the scam—I mean scheme. The filters are only good for a month and then they have to keep buying them from you for $29.99."

"I cannot believe I wasted my time for this. Your ad looked so professional." I walked out of his office.

"Wait, wait!" It was Candy. She was standing up from a five-gallon water bucket refilling a Perrier bottle. She was screwing the cap back on as she jiggled her way over. "I have your water!"

"You don't even trust your own filters in the office?" I asked, not taking the bottle she was trying to hand over.

"We have to pay for them if we use them and they're real expensive...I should know—I have five at home."

"You have five faucets?"

23

"No, silly." she giggled. "I put them on my toilets as well."

I just shook my head and left. I was still shaking my head, thinking about it all these years later. "Sorry," I told BT. "I won't do it again."

He nodded. "You can keep going."

"We can't stay here—none of us, I mean. They'll be back. There's no way they are going to forget the damage we inflicted on them. Even if Tommy and I leave."

BT "ahemed".

"And whoever else came with us," I amended. "They will still destroy everything and everyone left here."

"Your brother is never going to go for that."

"I know that, BT, but you're going to have to convince him otherwise."

"Me? Why me? I get scared dealing with any of you Talbots."

"We're hardly getting along. He'll do the opposite of whatever I suggest and probably not even realize that's why he's doing it."

"You get scarier when you make sense. The problem is, I don't know if you are truly making sense or I am just slipping down into your realm. You know things didn't work out so well when we split up, right? You already forgetting about your pickle juice incident? Sometimes when you walk by at a certain angle or the wind is just right, I can still catch a whiff of dill and vinegar coming off of you."

"I've always hated you," I told him. "How is it that I'm the one trying to be serious?"

BT shrugged his shoulders.

"Just hear me out and you can beat me about the head and shoulders afterward."

"Fair enough," he responded.

"Tommy and I are beacons; they, or she, can lock on to us. Either we kill them or they kill us. Otherwise, we're always looking over our shoulders."

"We whipped their asses, Mike. The one that could

command the zombies we cut into twelve different pieces and burned in separate piles. I don't think she's coming back."

That had been a particularly bad experience. Dismembering a body is one of the singularly most disturbing things I have ever done. "Yeah, she's not." I had to swallow down a little bile threatening to say hello. "Still, leaves two."

"Maybe. Tiffany said she popped one in the head."

"Not a confirmed kill, though."

"She shot her in the head."

"How many times did the bad guy's henchmen swear that they had killed James Bond?"

"Making sense with a spy movie reference? Damn near brilliant," he said, raising his meaty hand. We fist bumped. "Okay. One, two, who gives a shit. I can't imagine they are going to want to have anything to do with us."

"Revenge is a pretty powerful motivator. We can't just stick around here wondering and waiting for the next time they come. This one will be a lot sneakier, quicker—lightning strikes. Next month, someone will be out planting tomatoes and they'll just disappear. We'll be on edge for months...extra vigilant for a while, then a year, maybe even two goes by, one of us will be in the woods collecting berries and..."

"Yeah—I get it," he stopped me.

"They have until the end of days to hunt us. Striking when we least expect it. We're like a human Costco superstore sitting here. You don't go overly often but it's always stocked high and waiting right where you left it."

"Did you just equate me to a family size pack of paper towels?"

"Better than a double case of malt liquor."

"Now you're just being racist," he laughed. His eyes grew wide with a thought; he seemed pretty excited about it. "What about a ship!"

"Huh?"

"We go find a cruise ship or something and just take it. We sail the high seas for a few years until they forget about us."

"You want me to start at the top with all the things wrong with that?"

"I'm listening."

"I'll start with a personal one. I hate the fucking water."

"Hold the phone...Michael Talbot has a ridiculous phobia. I think the rest of us will be able to overcome that one."

"Jerk. Fine. Okay, here's a good one...do you know how to drive a ship? I'm pretty sure it's a little more involved than driving that scooter you had."

"You said you weren't going to bring that up anymore! Man, you put me on that thing!"

"I mean, I don't know for sure, BT, but I imagine it takes at minimum twenty to thirty highly skilled people to operate a cruise ship. If it fails or we run out of fuel...hell, I don't even know what kind of fuel we'd need. I don't want to spend the rest of my days drifting out in the open water where I'm a hundred percent positive we're going to encounter the Kraken."

"RV then," he hadn't skipped a beat. "We get a huge RV and we just keep traveling across the country, see? That way they can't get a lock on us."

"Have you been hanging with Trip again? Are you listening to yourself? You've met the same assholes out there that I have. The world is chock full of them. It's like God's reckoning; he took all the good people and left us shadier fucks behind to determine our own fates."

"Yeah, I'm pretty sure God's plan wasn't to turn the good people into zombies to make the bad ones suffer. That doesn't make sense."

"Well, not when you use that kind of logic," I told him.

"Mike, if you use this against me, I will bury you. Are we clear?"

"Crystal," I said as he shook his huge fist in my face.

"I love these people, hell I love you. I don't want to be apart from any of them. This is my...this is our family now and I want us to be together."

It was a given that I had a comment all ready to go. I decided to let it pass unsaid. He was being brutally honest and besides I felt the same damn way. Why go on if there's no one around to care about?

"Fuck," I said as I rubbed my eyes then pinched the bridge of my nose. "There's no easy answer."

"What about a Sam's Club or a Costco superstore?" he asked. He was reaching and he knew it.

"Every prepper with a modicum of knowledge will have holed up in one. It'd be like trying to break into a bank vault, and for what purpose? We'd have the same problems there as we will here."

"What gives?" Tracy had walked out onto the deck.

"I don't even know what you're talking about, woman," BT said brusquely.

"That right there tells me all I need to know," she replied.

"See, Mike? This is the stuff that makes me wonder how she ever put up with you for all these years."

"What the hell are you talking about?" I asked him.

"She knows things before they even happen; there's no way you're going to get anything past her."

"The key, my friend, is inundation. She can only track so many issues; some are bound to leak through the cracks."

"That's what you think." She was smiling. "Spill it. When the two of you are together and you look all morose I know something is up."

"You want me to tell you what morose means?" BT asked me.

I appreciated what BT was trying to do which was throw Tracy off our scent. Wasn't going to work—she had far too much experience and knew all our ploys. I sighed heavily before I told her. "We need to leave here and we need to split up."

She didn't say anything for a few moments, took a couple of sips of her coffee, and leaned against the railing, much like BT was. "I was wondering when you were going to bring that up."

I looked over to BT with a surprised expression, I hadn't been expecting her to say that.

"I don't know how to do this, Tracy." I pleaded. "The only part of me that wants to split up is the part that wants to keep all of you safe, but the more selfish part cannot imagine life without you all. What's the fucking point?"

"It's settled then," she said as she stood up.

"It is?" BT asked.

I put my hand on his arm. I wanted to hear what she had to say.

"Sophia is dead, right?"

We both nodded.

"Charity may be as well; at worst, she's injured. They are on the run; we cannot give her time to heal and bring the fight back to us—we need to go to them. Hunt them down. Make them wish they had never fucked with the Talbot line."

"You want to pack up the entire clan here and go out on a war party?" I asked.

She didn't skip a beat. "Yes."

"Whoa," BT said backing up. "This is different. Mike is usually the one going bat shit crazy.

CHAPTER TWO
MIKE JOURNAL ENTRY 2

I NEEDED TO hit up Tommy first before calling a family meeting. The success of Tracy's pitch was going to depend completely on what the boy had to say.

"Can you find her...err, them?" I asked. We were in the basement; Henry had opted to take the most comfortable chair for himself. I noticed Riley and Ben-Ben were on the far side of the room. I didn't need to get any closer than fifteen feet to realize why. "Oh come on, Henry, that's not even right." I blocked my nose, he lifted one eyelid and snorted before resuming his slumber.

"They're hiding."

"So Charity is still alive?" That was a blow. Payne was a formidable enemy all on her own; she needed no help.

He nodded. "She was, at least."

"Tommy, some very difficult decisions have to be made in the next few days." I could hardly believe the next words I was going to say. "The best course of action we have right now is to hunt those two down and chop off their miserable heads."

"It's not like they're wearing GPS locators, Mr. T. They have a psychic imprint like everybody does, but they're aware of it, and when it suits them they can mask their scent."

"But masking doesn't mean disappearing, right?" Looks

like I was reaching too.

"I could dream walk."

"Dream walk? Like astral projection?"

"Pretty much. I don't think they'd feel the need to hide there."

"That's possible?"

"It's merely another plane. There are rules that are different, there are rules that are the same. I'm going to need help."

This was where the conversation started to turn south. "Uh-huh…" was all I managed.

"I'll need your help."

"I'm not a fan of other planes, Tommy. I barely have a grasp on the things I need to do here. I think I'd be a bigger liability in a place where I have no idea how to respond."

"Mr. T, you're more powerful in ways you don't want to admit. They can kill me easily enough over there if I don't have your help."

"Wait, wait, wait, one." I put my hands up. "Everything I've ever read about astral projection says that you can't be harmed while you're out and about."

"You didn't read the fine print."

"What the fuck? Did a lawyer write the rule book?"

"In the vast majority of walks, that is the case. Take for instance a person walking in a wonderful, flower-strewn meadow. Almost always, nothing is going to happen, right? But sometimes there is a confluence of events and a Siberian tiger escapes from a zoo and just so happens to be hunting in upstate New York when it wanders across someone out for a beautiful spring stroll."

"Poor bastard."

"It doesn't end well."

"Wait, this really happened?"

"You're the one that makes things up Mr. T, not me."

"Can we bring weapons into this other world?"

His lack of response said it all.

"It gets worse."

"Oh do tell." I prodded.

"Only thought can travel into this realm."

"Okay?" The other shoe was hovering high overhead, I was pretty sure I could see it already beginning its descent, figured it would hit terminal velocity the moment it struck my head.

"Usually, not much in the way of higher functioning makes the journey, either."

"Well, you should be fine." BT had taken just that moment to come and see how everything was going. I'd told him I was going to talk to Tommy. "Mike like food, Mike like sex, Mike like gun. That's somewhere around eighty-five percent of his thought process." He sat down heavily next to Henry. He got up as if the chair had an eject button and it'd been activated. "What the fuck?" He was grabbing his nose.

"Serves you right," I told him.

"I'm going to kill Trip!" BT was looking around for the stoner.

"What the hell are you talking about man?" I asked him.

"The crazy fucker keeps making egg salad sandwiches. He takes one bite and then throws it to the dogs. Then he says he can't stand eggs and that he wishes people would stop giving them to him to eat. You know man, it's not like your dog smells like daffodils to begin with and then you throw mayonnaise and eggs into the mix and it's...it's just fucking gross, man. I've been in overused Porta Potties that had a better bouquet. Kick him out of the house until he takes care of some business, will you?"

"Henry doesn't like to be moved when he's sleeping," I told him.

"He's always sleeping, Mike!"

I shrugged my shoulders. "Naw...he eats sometimes." I held my breath and went over to rub Henry's head vigorously. "Don't listen to the big mean man," I pinched out. I headed out of range before I had to breathe again.

"Can he find them or not?" BT asked with a disgusted look on his face.

"He's right there." I pointed to Tommy. "And the answer is 'sort of'. We need to astral project to find them."

"Astral project? Come on man, we don't have enough shit going on we're going to travel into dream realms?"

"Can he come?" I asked Tommy. The boy's head shook from side to side.

"Why the hell not?" he asked indignantly. "Is the dream realm whites only? You think honkies invented trance travel?"

"Are you serious right now? You can't possibly be pulling the race card."

"Is it working?" BT was looking over me, mean-mugging Tommy who seemed slightly bemused.

"He's right there, man."

"It's not because of who you are," Tommy told him, "but what you are."

"A proud black man?" BT asked.

"Mortal," Tommy said flatly.

"Oh, well that makes more sense." He calmed down.

"Yeah, and I'm the fucking crazy one," I said.

"The first step is admitting you have a problem," BT said. "So how dangerous is this plan?"

Tommy laid it out. The more information I got, the less I liked the idea. But for right now it was the one that kept the majority of us safe and that was really all I needed to know.

When Tommy was done he excused himself, said he needed to prepare.

"How you feeling about this, Talbot? I'm not liking the part where you can get killed while you sleep."

"It won't come to that. We're merely heading out on an expeditionary quest."

"How many people do you think died trying to discover new things?"

"You're ruining this for me, man."

"Yeah, because I bet no one died finding the new world,

or climbing Mount Everest, or even crossing this country."

He went on talking about all the famous explorers, got to Amelia Earhart by the time I walked out on him.

About an hour later most of the adults were in the living room going over what Tommy and I had discussed. Ron took a skeptical position; he'd never been one for the occult. Most had anecdotal stories about times they went out-of-body, some with fear, some with awe.

"So you're telling me you're going to dream-battle two vampires, otherwise, we have to move and split up? That's just fantastic, brother. I love how you come up with these most awesome ideas."

A big meaty paw fell on my shoulder—it was BT. I looked up at him; he shook his head almost imperceptibly. This was Ron's new thing. Whenever I was around, he would bait me, looking for a fight of some sort. I'd been pretty good about just moving away and biting my tongue; he was grieving and his way of dealing with it was by lashing out. But not at multiple targets, just at me. As if I were the root of all his evils. With how much vitriol he directed my way, I was beginning to think that maybe I was. Until I had shown up, he'd not known his daughter was dead and his wife, Nancy, was most certainly still alive.

"The floor is yours, big brother, in fact, the whole house is yours. Maybe we should hear what you have to say. Maybe you could even be a man and stop this passive aggressive attack against me and just tell me what you want me to do. If it's leave, just say the word. There're enough enemies out there—I don't need any more in here."

Ron held his chin high, I figured this was it. The confrontation I'd been waiting for. It wasn't. He acquiesced. That I hadn't been expecting. Kind of sputtered over myself: I'd been gearing up for a fight of some sort and when it didn't happen...well, I mean, picture yourself bracing to pick up something you think is in the thirty-pound range and then you come to find out it's just an empty box so you lose your balance and the force of your momentum makes you canter off a few steps. Just like that, only not physical. So close. So fucking close to making it out.

CHAPTER THREE
DENEAUX

"I WOULD NOT suggest driving up as if you own the place," Deneaux said as a swirl of smoke encircled her head.

"What the fuck do you know, bitch?" Veeral asked.

"Do what you want, then." She took another long drag.

"Veeral there's a tree stand," Wember said.

"So, what do we look like? Deer?"

"Stop in the name of the law," Gary delivered in his best Sylvester Stallone / Judge Dredd voice, and with Mad Jack's electronic box, it sounded pretty convincing.

Jolly put a round into the side of the stand. Gary had ducked down, thrilled he'd listened to Mike and put in the quarter inch steel plating.

"Fool," Deneaux said.

A burst of gunfire blew through the hood of the truck and slammed into the engine block, instantly rendering it into a large piece of trash.

"Any of you move without me telling you to, and my large friend here with the RPG resting atop his shoulder will disintegrate that truck. And I'm here to tell you, this isn't like the movies. You won't be able to run fast enough to clear the blast zone. Sure...it's one thing to be shot by a rifle, but to be torn apart by shrapnel? Well, holy fuck that's just a whole new level of hell."

"Who the fuck is that?" Wember asked angrily.

"Michael Talbot." Deneaux took an extra long drag, snubbed out the cigarette in the coke can she had, sighed heavily and slowly got out of the truck. "Hello, Michael," she said.

"Shoot her, BT. Shoot her now," Mike said.

"She's just an old woman," BT said, trying to convince himself to ease up off the trigger.

"Old woman my ass. There's a legion of demons hiding under that sallow, saggy skin bag. Come on man! You know she's evil—even the cigarettes can't kill her."

CHAPTER FOUR
MIKE JOURNAL ENTRY 3

"IT JUST CAN'T be," I whispered.

"Mike, I feel like I should just let this rocket loose."

"Yeah you have no idea how close I am to telling you to really do it. Can't you just have a minor epileptic seizure or something?"

BT grunted.

"Deneaux, what the fuck are you doing here?"

"She told us there was gold!" A man that looked like he stepped out of Redneck Quarterly said as he stuck his head out of a truck window and then opened the door to let himself out. The problem was he had not pulled his head back out of the window; he'd moved with it, so when he stood he gave himself a solid thunking.

"Where does one go to get plaid pants?" BT asked me.

"Squeal Like A Pig country store I would imagine," I told him.

BT snorted. "Fuck, Mike, you almost made me pull the trigger."

"That was the idea."

"Jolly, you're a dumbass!" someone shouted from inside. "He ain't just gonna give us the gold."

"Your brother sitting on some gold?" BT asked.

"Fuck if I know. Probably has the federal reserve under this house."

"No, seriously, man."

"Do I look like I'm laughing?"

"This bitch said you two were friends and that you'd pay gold to get her back."

"Get out of the truck, slowly," I told him. "Keep your hands in front of you." By now there was a small contingent of people on that deck.

"Travis, Justin, go make sure nobody is trying to get into the house from a different side," Tracy told the boys.

"Look at you getting all tactical and shit," I told her. "Military women make me hot. You thought any more about that camouflage outfit I asked you to wear?"

"What the hell is wrong with you, Talbot?" she asked. "And it's camouflage. How would you even know I have it on?"

"That's the point," I told her. I think she blushed but I didn't want to turn away from our newest threat.

The man got out of the vehicle warily. He'd fiddled with something in the truck and I was pretty sure he'd tucked a gun in his waistband.

"Take your pants off," I told him.

"What are you, a faggot?" he shouted back.

"Yes, yes I am. I am a very, very cautious faggot. Now take your pants off or I'm going to put some new holes in you that I can fuck."

"Mike," Tracy said.

"Sorry, I wished you hadn't heard that."

"What about the rest of us?" BT asked.

"What do I care what you think? I'm not asking you to wear camo lingerie for me."

"TMI, Uncle." It was Meredith.

"I've have got to remember I'm not always the only one in the room."

"I ain't gonna do it," the man said.

This one looked dangerous—the black knit cap, the long beard, the tattoos on his neck and arms just gave him an appearance of malice. He didn't move when I put a round a couple of inches from his foot. He glared at me as he undid his belt, the pistol fell to the ground as soon as he pulled down.

"Aw man," BT groaned. "He doesn't have any underwear on."

"Well, there's another sight you can't un-see. At least it's covered in filth...can't see so much."

"Whoa. Who's the dude with the fro?" Trip asked; he was licking mustard off his fingers. I'd like to tell you that some had dripped off the sandwich he was eating but that wasn't the case. He literally just had mustard smeared all over all of his fingers.

"Pull up the damn pants," I told him.

"Mike you don't know if he's hiding anything...in that thing," BT said.

"You want to go check?"

He grunted a no.

"What's your name?" I asked once the man had stowed the stuff that should never have seen the light of day. Think I saw a couple of birds nesting before he was done.

"Veeral," he said, as he looked to his side where the gun was lying.

"He's a horrible shot," Mrs. Deneaux said. "You should go for it."

I don't know what lines of shit she'd been feeding him or if he was already so close to the edge he just needed that final nudge, but he did just that. Well, tried to, I mean. He was hardly twenty yards away. He'd barely turned before I shoved a bullet in his sternum. I could hear the air rushing from at least one of the punctured lungs. Blood filled his airway and spilled from his mouth as he dropped to his knees and fell over.

"You fucking shot him!" Jolly shouted at me.

"Yup. I'm not overly thrilled with that fact, but give me a reason why I shouldn't shoot the rest of you."

39

"What? Because...because we're friends of this Deneaux broad!"

"Oh man, that is probably the worst excuse you could have for me not killing you where you stand. Deneaux is friends with no one. I think the best you can really hope to achieve is a temporary alliance. I'm not completely sure, but I'm pretty sure her actions led to the demise of my good friend. I'm definitely to the point where shooting her wouldn't cost me any sleep. Fuck, maybe even sleep better knowing I'd given him some small measure of justice."

"Michael, I don't think you're going to want to shoot me," she said as she bent over and fished around in Veeral's pockets to grab a lighter. She stood and lit another cigarette, not even blinking that she'd pulled her flame from a dead man.

"Blow the fucking truck up, BT," I said.

"Are you sure?" he asked looking over.

"Mike?" Tracy asked.

"Come on, we all know how this is going to go down, don't we? She's definitely going to have something we could use or some knowledge that's pertinent to our safety. So we'll strike an agreement with her that she can stay and then when a better offer comes around she is going to do her damnedest to make us all look like Veeral over there."

"You can't just kill her outright," Tommy said.

"I don't need a conscience right now."

"We take a vote," Mad Jack said.

"Michael, do you want to know what I have?" she asked casually.

"Hold on a sec, we're trying to determine if we should kill you."

"I'll wait." She waved her hand. "The two with me are murdering rapists, though. I wouldn't leave them to their own devices too long."

I was about to ask her if that was true when the third man answered it for me. "You fucking two-faced bitch, you liked my dick. Everyone likes my dick!" He was coming out of the truck, rifle in hand. Gary lit him up; the first bullet pierced his shoulder, the second came pretty close to his world-beloved dick.

"Filthy pig," Deneaux said without ever looking over to him.

Something the size of a bowling bowl got caught in my throat.

"Mike, man, please tell me what I think happened didn't really happen," BT said.

I involuntarily gagged, that was about all he needed to know. The front of Jolly's pants stained dark as he wet himself.

"I ain't moving. I ain't moving." He raised his hands higher.

"It would be so much easier if he did." That from Tracy.

"I can't just kill him?" I looked over to her.

"Unfortunately, that's not who you are and you know it. He may indeed be scum, but we can't go by Deneaux's word. Is there anybody she wouldn't throw under a train?" Tracy asked.

"No. She'd probably put herself under one if it somehow benefited her."

"So what's it going to be? I don't have all day." Deneaux interrupted us deciding the fate of her kidnappers.

"You got a litter of puppies to set on fire or something?" I asked her. "You can wait."

She sniffed.

"The vote isn't going well; can you give us a hint of this information you possess?" I asked.

"Tell them, please tell them!" Jolly whined.

"You're pathetic. Deneaux elbowed past him." She turned on a phone she had in her pocket. She held it up and faced the screen toward us.

"Great. You have a phone. Call someone who gives a shit," I said.

"Good one," BT said.

"It's alright. A little dated, but it works in this situation," Mad Jack elaborated.

"Hey, thanks for that," I told him.

"You are most welcome." He seemed pleased as punch.

"It's what is on the screen that matters," Deneaux said.

"What is it?" I asked her.

"Satellite imagery," she replied.

"Great. You have Google earth."

"It's real time." She pulled the phone back to her.

I paused, letting that sink in. "You're full of shit."

"Am I? Don't you think this would be technology housed at the now-defunct Demense group building?"

"Don't go anywhere! I'm coming down!" Mad Jack said excitedly.

"Whoa! Hold on there, killer." I reached out and grabbed his shoulder.

"I am not a killer; I am a scientist," he explained, a confused look on his face.

I didn't tell him that among scientists were a fair amount of the most infamous mass murderers of all time. "MJ, we're still in a little bit of a volatile situation here. Why don't you put that big head of yours back under a hat and you can whip it out when it's safe."

"That a dick joke?" BT asked.

"Sort of," I replied.

"You've done better."

"Sorry. I haven't had a lot of time to come up with new material."

"I'll allow it," BT said.

"Are you two serious right now?" Tracy asked.

BT shrugged.

"She's just a little old lady. Shouldn't we help?" Tiffany asked.

"I know—I do feel bad for the guy," I said.

"I was talking about…"

"Oh, I know who you were talking about." I'd interrupted

her. "That woman down there is one of the most lethal people, man, woman, zombie, vampire you will ever come across. She's got more kills under her belt than everyone on this deck put together." Maybe...maybe not. But if we switched out "kills" for "murders" then yeah, she was the winner hands down.

"What about the man with her, Mike? We don't really have a jail. We're already stretched thin on regular guard duty," BT said.

"Him? I'm more worried about someone watching her full time." I said truthfully.

He grunted that he felt the same way.

"What do we do about him?" I asked Deneaux. "We don't really have a way of watching problem children."

"You could just let me go, man." Jolly nervously licked his lips. "I'm gone like I was never here. I get away from this crazy bitch."

"You're just going to walk away after two of your friends were killed here and not seek some sort of revenge?" I asked.

He hesitated. "They weren't no friends of mine, man. I got caught up with them when this all started. I stayed because it was safer, that's all. I'm happy to be rid of them."

"He's full of shit," Deneaux said. She was leaning against the car, her head slightly tilted up as she smoked her cigarette, a look of sheer ecstasy on her face. It almost looked like a damn sexual experience and now there is another moment of imagery I will never be able to burn from my memory. Dammit. Not enough vodka in the world to scrub clean that etched-in thought. "He was an active participant in all their debauchery." Smoke poured from her mouth along with the words.

"Shut up, bitch." Jolly half turned to talk to her.

"He has friends," she said.

"Listen, man, she's lying. It was always only us three. I swear it!"

"These three wanted the gold I told them about. You let

him leave, he'll go back and get the rest of them. And they have heavy equipment, Mike. They figured they could do this little detour, ransom me off, and then stash the gold before anyone would be the wiser."

There was no way I could tell if she was lying or not. More than likely she was; it wasn't even fair to call it second nature for her. That was just the way she operated continually. But it could be true as well, and if he went and got his buddies we could be dragged into another battle.

"How stupid are you?" BT asked Jolly. "There're zombies, and you're looking for gold? What are you planning on buying?"

"This one here said that the zombies'll be gone soon, then the government will make things right and that the ones with the gold will have all the power. She said that civilizations have been collapsing and rebuilding ever since, like time started, and that us smart ones should be the ones to rule when we was back up and running. That's what she said," Jolly said.

"Fuck me if that doesn't sound legit," I said aloud. "Shit, Deneaux, even I might have bought that."

She nodded her head slightly in acknowledgment.

"Whoa, man." Trip had gone back in the house for a few minutes before coming back out in a rush. He came to a skidding stop by the railing. He was looking up in the sky.

"What the hell are you doing, you damn fool?" BT asked.

"I'm looking for Auntie Em's house, man."

"What in the fuck is he talking about, Talbot?" BT asked.

"Wizard of Oz, man." Trip said, still peering intently up. "Isn't that the Wicked Witch of the West?"

Deneaux took one final drag, dropped the cigarette by her foot and with a very practiced routine, ground it out. "You can't hold him and you can't let him go, Michael. You know your choices. Do not let your pesky morals get in the way."

"Yeah, I hate when I act all human and shit."

"Why start now?" BT asked. It had come out so effortlessly; he had not even looked over to gauge my reaction.

It was not even meant as a barb, just a truism.

"The bigger they are the meaner they are," Trip stage-whispered to me.

"Deneaux, if I lacked morals I'd be more inclined to save Jolly and blow your ugly head off."

"Oh, I simply cannot take too much more of this. The suspense is killing me," she said dryly. She reached into the truck.

"Hold on, Deneaux," I said as she came out of the truck holding a revolver. At least four rifles were trained on her. She was a crack shot but there was no way she could kill all of us before someone drilled her. Now with that being said, I was fond of all the people on this deck, myself included, and I didn't want to see any of us doing some bullet catching.

Jolly jumped as if he'd been goosed as Deneaux appeared to have shoved the barrel between his ass cheeks. Before I could get her to drop the weapon or Jolly could get away, she pulled the trigger. The devastation to the man was immediate, and graphic. The front of his pants bloomed in a bright red. He was in such shock he never got the chance to bring his arms down to cover the wounded area. Deneaux dropped the gun.

"Asshole," she said to him as he fell over. She then stepped over his body.

"You can't let her in here," Tiffany said as she was looking over to the man who was crying out. There wasn't a medical team in existence that could have saved him. Even at society's best no one could have salvaged his now hollow tip injected junk. There wasn't a guy on that deck that couldn't commiserate with the pain that man was feeling. It was Gary, after a healthy retching, that put the man out of his misery.

"Hmm," Deneaux said turning and looking up at Gary. "Have a little more of that Talbot blood in you than I originally thought. I'll have to keep an eye on you." And with that, she winked at him and walked towards the deck. A shark with a chainsaw would have looked more inviting.

If there was some nerdy way for a geek to jerk off using

45

nothing but his mind, Mad Jack would have been spewing brain cells all over the device Deneaux handed him. He hooked it up to a series of monitors, and in a few moments we were looking at what he told us was the CDC building in Atlanta.

"Not sure how that's going to help us," Ron said.

"I have access to the satellites...I can direct them where I want to! This is amazing!" I was thinking MJ might need a little alone time; maybe this was a good thing—keep his mind off of the damn fission bomb he was so diligently working on.

Ron had told Deneaux a half dozen times "no smoking in the house" and she'd ignored him each and every time. It got to the point where Ron just left the room whenever she lit up.

"We need to talk," I told her, grabbing her arm and steering her out to the now empty deck.

"Is the rifle necessary?" she'd asked as I sat her down at the deck table. I sat across from her.

"Oh...I'm going to say yes. Now, we're going to have a little discussion, you and I, and listen, I realize that speaking the truth is not something you're overly familiar with. I think you might just get lost in your lies; you've traded money for lives for so long it's just who you are."

"I want amnesty," she said, as she fished a cigarette out and lit it.

"Look around, Deneaux. This ain't the good old U.S. of A. anymore."

"Even so, if you want the truth, something it seems you desperately need, then I have to have some guarantees for my safety.

"What the fuck makes you think I won't kill you anyway after you give me what I want?"

"Please. You won't," she smiled. "What's done is done. It cannot be undone. We move on. I seem to remember those being words of your speaking."

"In a different context, but sure."

"Am I safe? And before you answer that, the satellite

receiver requires the input of a new password every twenty-four hours and without the master key stored in my head..."

"The device locks."

She exhaled. "So?"

"Give the truth your best shot and I promise not to kill you until you force my hand."

She looked long and hard at me. "Fair enough. I sent Paul away without a rifle."

She'd said it so matter-of-factly, calm, cool, collected, and all that shit, like it was the most natural thing in the world to send another to their death.

"He was my best friend." Anger wanted to come to the surface; instead a wave of sadness washed over me.

"He was not made for this new world, Michael. You knew that. So ill-prepared he almost got your boys killed. How would you have felt about him, had that happened?"

"I'm not a big fan of the "what-if" game. Way too many variables. Why did you send him out?"

She took a little longer with this answer, I was having a hard time figuring out why, though. She'd just admitted to having a hand in killing my friend; what more could she heap on something already so heinous?

"Brian was injured. Broken collar bone and gut shot; we were hiding in the woods while Paul was searching for supplies. I'd fallen asleep, and when I awoke, I realized we were surrounded by zombies." She took two long drags. I think the physical exertion of actually telling the truth was taking its toll on her. "Brian wasn't going to make it; he was already bleeding out. I certainly couldn't carry him away from the danger; I gave the zombies incentive to find him over me."

I squeezed my rifle—not the trigger mind you—oh that I wanted to do, very much so. She was the enemy I knew. If I didn't watch her vigilantly, I deserved to have her knife blade dragged across my neck. "At any point in that long, winding life of yours have you ever placed anyone ahead of yourself?"

"Why would I? There is no one more important in my life

than myself. The question should be, why do you do it all the time?"

"Okay...just continue. We view the world through such vastly different eyes we are never going to see the reasoning behind the other's motives very clearly."

"When the zombies attacked, I left. I found Paul and we got to the safety of a house. When Brian showed up a little while later, he'd been bitten a few times. He'd not had the good graces to die, though. The bastard had killed them and escaped."

"What a dickhead for wanting to survive," I said.

She didn't take the bait. "He's walking down the street, cursing at how I had betrayed him."

"...And Paul was there; makes sense now. Paul knew you were a back stabber and he would have told me."

"I could not take the chance that I would be thrust out from your group, Michael. My chances of survival were greatly improved under your umbrella."

"Why didn't you just kill him? The way he went out—" I swallowed hard. "No one should have to die like that. Why take the chance that he somehow makes it back to us and now you have two strikes against you? I can almost see the point with Brian. In a twisted sort of way, I get it. With your back pressed against the wall, you did what you thought was necessary to survive. But kicking Paul out? That's tantamount to murder."

"I suppose, I did not believe Paul to have the skills necessary to survive on his own."

"No part of me thinks that you would have a problem with getting your hands dirty—unless you just didn't want to have a crime scene. If you'd shot Paul, it would have been difficult to hide the evidence of that crime."

"I let this brutal new nature take its course. Survivors survive, all others don't. Where does that leave us?" She was looking at me intently.

"Well, I'm going to be brutally honest. You are indeed

under my umbrella and I will keep you safe as long as that is in line with keeping everyone else safe. Should you stray, I will not make any extraordinary measures to save you. My days of risking my life for yours are over. If I have to choose between any other person in this group and you, you're on your own. And I want you to listen very carefully Vivian, hear this. If I feel like you are a threat to anyone here or are somehow seeking to harm anyone here—if I even suspect you of harmful intent, I will kill you. No questions asked. Do you believe me?" I did not waver as we looked at each other.

"I do," she said, finally breaking eye contact and snuffing out her cigarette. "It's exciting to see this new Michael Talbot."

"Whatever floats your boat. Oh, and another thing, no guns for you," I said as I got up.

"How will I defend myself?"

"I really don't give a fuck, Vivian." And I left her there.

"How'd that go?" BT asked when I walked back in the house.

"I'm sure she's figuring out how to kill us all in our sleep right now."

"About how you expected then?"

"Pretty much."

"You should see what MJ pulled up."

"It's not a sex robot is it?" I asked.

"This is me pretending I didn't just hear you say that."

"Come on, you know it could be true."

"Follow me and try your best to keep your mouth shut." BT led me to the garage and MJ's makeshift laboratory slash sex robot assembly line.

Mad Jack was clacking away at his keyboard as if he was penning the sequel to War and Peace. Three monitors of varying size had been hastily set up on his desk. Didn't need to get abundantly close to realize I was looking at a high aerial picture of Cain's pond. He clacked away some more and the camera started panning in.

"How old is that?" I asked, moving closer.

"It's right now!" Mad Jack said excitedly. "There are some holes in the viewing windows—not all of the satellites are operational. Their trajectories haven't been corrected in too long or they missed scheduled maintenance...that kind of thing. But I think I can get us fifteen minutes every hour in our general area."

"Fuck me. Is that Deneaux sitting on the deck?"

MJ did some more keyboard wizardry; I jumped back as her face took up the entire monitor. She was as clear as if I were still sitting across the table from her.

"Where the hell was this tech when I was a horny fifteen-year-old?" I asked.

"Really, Talbot? We have game changing abilities here and the first place you go is your dick?"

"Oh, like you aren't thinking the same thing. You're fifteen, okay? Now think of the hottest girl in your neighborhood out in her backyard, tanning...topless."

"Oh...I see your point."

"What point is that?" Tracy asked coming down with some soda for MJ.

I played it off smoothly but BT looked about as guilty as if he had cookie crumbs rolling down the front of his shirt before dinner.

"We can see the enemy coming," I said to Tracy. She seemed dubious only because BT looked like he was choking on that fucking cookie he stole.

It was not lost on me that Deneaux looked up at the satellite flying high overhead. She definitely wasn't praying to the heavens; her spidey sense must have been going off that she was being watched.

"Pull back out. I've seen as much of her for the day as I can stomach."

"This thing is amazing. It even has infra-red."

"Let's see that," I told him. The Maine woods were thick enough to hide an army.

"Going to have to wait," he said as the image got static-laced and then cut out.

"Deneaux said something about a password key every twenty-four hours. Is that something you can hack?" I asked.

"I could try, but this government stuff will have fail-safes. I start tinkering around there's a chance that I shut it down completely instead of open it up. Why would you want me to do that?" he asked.

"Just to be safe. You never know what could happen to her. She dies, splits, or I just kill her, and we lose this advantage."

"Makes sense," Mad Jack said as he started scanning around the States.

"Send for me when we come back up," I told him.

"What are you thinking, Mike?" Tracy asked when we three walked away from Mad Jack's station.

"I'm thinking we need MJ to hack that thing and get rid of Deneaux. I feel like we held a crazy Ouija session and let in all manner of demon. She needs to go." I didn't tell them about Paul because I figured their verdict would be swift and I couldn't take the thought of having to argue in favor of Deneaux staying, even for a short time. The satellite imagery was far too important to let slip through our fingers.

An hour later MJ came and got me. We both watched as he changed over to infra-red, and I almost had a heart attack. The woods lit up like the army I feared was hiding there had suddenly been exposed.

"It's okay Mike," he informed me. "It's just the cameras finding their balance. Just a couple of deer, maybe. These look small." He was pointing at the screen. "Fox maybe...could be a fisher."

"Will the zombies be warm enough to show?" I asked. The zombies weren't dead in the traditional way. They were undead, if that makes sense.

"They do have a heat signature, if that's what you're asking. It's considerably cooler than a human's, but it will show. Instead of the whites and the red," he pointed to his animal registers, "they'll show as blues and purples."

I scanned those three monitors repeatedly looking for any sign of the enemy. There appeared to be about a half-dozen some five miles away at the grocery store and little else.

"This is fucking amazing. We can map out runs and know exactly where they are."

"I think you need to think on a grander scale, Mike," Mad Jack said.

"You got the fission bomb to work?" That was my first guess.

"Humanity, Michael. A settlement, I mean. There has to be a place out there where people are regrouping—making a stand, a community."

"We went down that route once. It didn't work out so well." He really couldn't argue that things were different now. In fact, they were probably worse. We had maybe two vampires chasing us, and the zombies were far more intelligent than they had been. We held some responsibility for what had happened at Camp Custer, sure. But how could I have ever fucking known Eliza was going to lose her shit and destroy the entire place? How could I? If not for our presence, she would not have had any reason to show. Knowing what I knew now I could not run that risk again. When we lost the feed, he started scanning around the country again. Apparently, MJ wasn't a huge fan of my stance. I had the egg of an idea, but who knew what horrors were going to be conceived in that yolk, or what monster would hatch.

"That thing pick up vamps?" I asked before leaving the room.

"Have Tommy stand on the deck, I'll look for him next hour."

CHAPTER FIVE
MIKE JOURNAL ENTRY 4

"HAVING FUN WITH your new toy?" Deneaux asked. She was sitting in the living room on the couch. Uncharacteristically, she was without a lit cigarette.

She'd startled me. I was not accustomed to having a sworn enemy this close without action being taken. "I think the less we talk to each other the better we're going to be able to deal with this proximity."

"Oh Michael! I do not mind this at all. By the way, has your sweet Mad Jack had any luck with the encryption key?" She cackled as I walked out of the room. "Wait!" she called to me. I slowed but did not stop nor turn around. "I once read that smoking cigarettes can reduce the risk of Alzheimer's Disease. Could you be a dear and get my pack? I would hate to forget such a lengthy string of numbers, letters, and symbols."

"I'm going to be hearing that cackle in my sleep," I said as I got out onto the deck.

"Why did you want me out here, Mr. T?" Tommy asked.

"Just making sure you don't do the old mirror routine on me. Don't move—I'll be right back." I hustled down to MJ's lab; the satellite was just coming into view. Tommy was still looking at the doorway I'd vacated, probably trying to figure out what the hell I was talking about. "Infrared," I said, letting my hand rest on MJ's shoulder. I could feel his body tense up from the contact. I could not help myself from smiling. I wonder what women thought when he did this in bed. Then it saddened me to think that this had most likely never happened in bed.

"Oh you poor bastard," I said aloud. I then brought my other hand up and rubbed his shoulders, digging my thumbs into the tense muscles.

"I'm not really comfortable with you touching me," he said, slightly turning, trying to wriggle free of my hands. "Well, with anyone touching me, really."

"I know," I told him as I continued anyway. "Switch to infrared."

"The moment you stop manhandling me, good sir."

"Good sir? Okay, okay." I was smiling as I put my hands up. We could see Tommy as clear as day, I think I could have read the embossment on his buttons if I'd a mind to...then nothing. Well not nothing, exactly, but rather a black hole. One moment he was a normal looking kid and the next he was a faceless black blob, an infinity of darkness upon the screen. I thought maybe it was a mistake with the satellite software or something. I had MJ cycle back and forth a half dozen times, to make sure. The people around him showed as reds and whites; he did not. I didn't even want to know how I would show up. At least now we knew what we were looking for when and if the vampires came back. Just had to keep out a gander for a soul-sucking darkness among the heart-eating shades of purple. Perfect. Just perfect.

"I found something, Michael," MJ said.

"An open Denny's? Because I could really go for a Grand Slam Breakfast."

"There's something up in the Seattle area. I found a few smaller ones dotted around the country, but this one is nestled in the mountains. Seems to have a natural barrier against zombies."

He knew how I felt about settlements, but this was

something more, and I had an inkling of what it was. "Mad Jack you're not a prisoner here. You're free to go whenever you choose. I would hate to see you go, but if you want to try and get there then, by all means, I won't stand in your way."

He said nothing, but he was thinking about it. Couldn't blame him; he might not be super comfortable around people, but up there he was likely to meet more like-minded folks and even the ability to garner a much larger facility with more access to resources for his experiments.

"Do you think anyone else would want to come?"

Sure, I'd said he could go, but a cross-country excursion on his own was not a savory thought. He was generally oblivious to the dangers around him but that didn't mean he was suicidal. Had to figure he was doing the odds of a successful run in his head and wasn't liking the numbers that kept popping up.

I sort of liked the idea of him taking Deneaux along as a bodyguard, just to get her out of this house, but I felt as if I'd be sealing MJ's fate, like hiring Gacy to do your kid's birthday party. The rest of the house was all Talbots for the most part. Getting the fuck out of here held sway but for the above-mentioned reasons we couldn't go. Ron wouldn't. Really the only people without any true tethers were Trip and Stephanie and a bunch of kids. If I could be a hundred percent sure they'd make it, I'd feel good about them going. They'd be missed for sure, but they'd be safer upon arrival. Maybe that was the play. Maybe I could deliver them to safety. There were some serious logistics to figure out, though. Like who was staying to guard the fort and where was Deneaux going to be during all of this. There was no way I could leave her behind to be someone else's burden.

"Are there any significant population centers closer to here?" I queried.

"I have the satellites programmed to search for them; haven't completely mapped out the country, but it's not looking good for any other place."

55

"How do we even know they're on the right side of the good-slash-evil divide? What if you got all the way out there and found out they were all assholes? He punched something into the keyboard.

"I recorded these snippets over the last couple of hours." He played them back letting the video speak for itself. There were people walking dogs, couples kissing. Parents playing with their children. Sure, there was a heavy military presence, but they were manning the walls or patrolling the streets. I didn't see one thing in there that would lead me to believe those people were under duress.

"ABSOLUTELY NOT!" BT said when I brought my idea up to him. "We stay together. No splitting up."

"We're just holding on here, BT. I've come to terms with that, but what about the kids? They deserve better."

"I realize you're talking about Sty, Ryan, Angel, Porkchop, and Zach, but what about your own kids? We're going to risk everything to travel across the states so these kids can have a life and then you're going to leave yours behind? How the hell are you going to reconcile that in that thick melon of yours? Sounds to me like you want to dump your problems off. And speaking of which, if we're planning on ridding ourselves of pests, you'd better make sure Trip goes."

"I didn't make up the shit about Mad Jack. He's ready to go. How about I ask the kids and see what they say?"

"Mike, don't ask Trip; just tell him that's what's best for him. My world would be just about perfect if that crazy stoner headed to parts unknown."

"That? That above all things would make your world perfect?"

"I'm not like you, Mike. I'm low maintenance."

"Yeah, you keep telling yourself that. I seem to recall just two days ago you lost your shit when Gary poured too much syrup on your pancakes and it bled over and God forbid touched your bacon."

"That's different! Bacon is savory, pancakes are sweet, and never the two should meet."

"Sounds like a poem from the third grade. Everybody knows bacon dipped in maple is one of the best things ever."

BT did his best to hide it, but I could see the reflexive gag in his throat. He tried to disguise it, but I'd been witness to that little throat spasm enough times with my brother. "We live in a world overrun with zombies, and maple bacon grosses you out?"

"Be careful man, I was bigger than you when I was in the third grade."

"Maple bacon, maple bacon, maple bacon."

I was chasing him around the room.

"Shut up!" He'd placed his hands over his ears and kept going. It got real interesting when Trip came in and mimicked BT's actions. He was a step behind the giant, screaming maple bacon as if this were some sort of game. Long after I stopped, Trip kept it up. "This is the shit I'm talking about!" BT picked Trip up and placed him out of the room.

"Hey man, can I take my hands off my ears now?" he questioned loudly. "Wait, I can't hear anything! Stephanie, I'm deaf again!"

Stephanie came from down the hallway and gently moved his hands away.

"Oh, I can hear again." He started to sob. "It was horrible, I was imagining never being able to hear the Grateful Dead again."

BT could do little except shake his head. "He has to go," he whisper-shouted.

"I'm not forcing anyone."

"What are you going to do if the kids refuse?" he asked.

What would I do? That was a dilemma. Odds were they

weren't going to want to go. They'd made attachments here; they loved us. We loved them. That didn't even take into account Zach, Ben-Ben, Patches, and Riley. Henry and Riley went everywhere, but would Riley leave Zach? How could I justify risking everything to get one person across the entire country?

"Just driving, with no problems, I could make it there in four days and then the same coming back. Hardly over a week."

"Are you listening to yourself?"

"What?"

"In what world do you live in that you think you could make it across the country 'with no problems'?"

"We could carry enough gas, food, guns, and ammo that we won't need to stop. We get one of those RV's you were talking about. There's a dealership out in Bangor has rows and rows of them—saw it when we got the fireworks."

"Don't make me slap you back into reality."

"Fuck no man. You slap me and the last thing I'm going to see is reality. Listen, BT, maybe we can get out of here. Maybe there is a better life for all of us. We get the family to safety. Then me, you, and Tommy, we hunt Payne into extinction. We kill the last threat—shove a stake right through her."

"You're bordering on fairy tale, Mike."

"What the hell else do I have, BT? This is a waiting game here— a stalling tactic, nothing more. Listen, we both know I'm not a big fan of people."

"What?" BT looked shocked.

"Kiss my ass. But you're right. My kids deserve a chance too. We pack everybody up and we head out."

"What are you possibly going to get that can fit twenty-eight of us plus the dogs?"

"Bus. Screw the RV...we'll get one of them comfortable casino buses. They have plush seats, small monitors, we can play movies. There's tons of storage for food and fuel underneath. We can do this, man. If nothing else, just think of how many fewer nights you'll spend on guard duty."

"Keep talking."

"Maybe there's some women there into circus acts. You could love again, my friend."

"You get so close to me liking you and then you throw it all away."

"I'm serious though, BT. There're things all of us could gain from being around more people."

"Yeah. Trip could get that psychiatric help he's been putting off. That's all I really need to know, that is the deciding factor for me. Ron's going to be the tough sell," he said, getting serious. "I think everyone will fall in line behind you except for him."

"I'll talk to him."

"You want me to be there?"

"Listen, man, this is nothing personal. I love you like a brother, but you intimidate the hell out of me and we're besties. I don't want Ron thinking I'm strong arming him."

"I thought I probably intimidated you. Is it the right arm?" He flexed. "Or the left?" He flexed that one as well then he did the traditional power muscle making move. "People have to apply for a special permit to climb these mountains. Hire Sherpas, even. Some have even known to get altitude sickness at the top; some have never been seen again."

"How come no one else is around when you show just how nuts you are?"

"I saw it." Trip had come into the room.

"Oh, man, please," BT said putting his arms down. "What exactly did you see?"

"Don't I know you?" Trip asked BT. "You were a cop once." Trip got a far away stare into his eyes.

"Yeah, I probably busted you a dozen times. Surprised they didn't lock your ass up for life."

"She lived." Trip said without missing a beat. It was easy enough to see he was traveling in other planes or at least across other levels of his head.

BT's smile couldn't have vacated his face any faster if it were on fire.

"No…she…did not!" He looked pissed off and about to go Twin Peaks on Trip. "I buried her!"

"Whoa. Mike, man...why is this mad dude all up in my personal space?" Trip asked, returning from orbit. "Western culture dictates at least two and a half feet of personal frontage space. I wish we used Native American proxemics of four feet, but right now he's going the Chinese route and it's freaking me out."

"Come on, BT."

"She didn't live, Mike." BT had a panicked look in his eyes.

"BT, you can't take everything he says seriously. You know that right?"

"There you are," Stephanie said as she came into the room. You would have had to have been Trip to not realize there was a strange vibe going on in that room. "Everything alright?" she asked, looking from me to BT.

"Uh yeah," I said, looking at BT, who was clearly remembering something distasteful from his past. "You might want to grab Trip."

"Come on, Trip. It's time for your bath." She gently grabbed his arm.

"Again? It's spring already?"

She smiled weakly at us. "He'll only take showers in the spring so I, um, have to tell him it's spring all the time."

"What about when it's snowing?" I had to ask.

"Pollen."

"Of course."

BT had sat down, or rather sunk to a sitting position. I stayed with him for a few minutes; he never said anything.

"You can go, Mike. I'm alright. It happened a long time ago. I won't dwell on it too long. Go talk to your brother. The sooner we can head out of here and do other stuff the less I have to think."

"Yeah I get that."

He started laughing. "Oh man, thank you for that."

"What the fuck are you talking about?" I asked.

"Just the idea of you stopping to think—that's one of your better ones."

I flipped him off as I left the room.

CHAPTER SIX
MIKE JOURNAL ENTRY 5

RON AND I were better; we weren't back to normal, just...better. He'd said some things that you just can't ever come back from. It wasn't that I was holding it against him, but rather he was maybe beating himself up for saying them. A measure of guilt, perhaps. It was enough that our relationship had shifted on a fundamental level. Strained might be a good word. He tended to be less combative, so if anything good could come out of it, that was a plus.

"Leave? You just want to leave?"

"Want? Whatever. I guess I do, as a matter of fact. At first, I was thinking it wasn't such a good idea. But I've had a change of mind and heart. The things I love are here. My family, my friends...a twisted sense of safety and security. Leaving is not high on my list of things I want to do." I stressed the "I" part. "But we both know it's not just about me." I waited, half expecting him to throw something out there along the lines of: "Oh really? Now you've finally come to the conclusion that it's not all about you?" That he hadn't taken the opening spoke volumes to the new parameters of our relationship. "It's our kids, Ron. It's BT, it's Mad Jack...they deserve more. They deserve better. Maybe not better; maybe there is no 'better,' but a chance at real happiness. All we can offer here is more time. Sure, it beats the alternative, but it's not really living, either."

"And you just want to grab a bus and trek across the country like we own the joint?"

"Flying would be better, but I've already been up in the air with the only man qualified to fly and I'm not fucking doing that again."

"This is my home, Mike."

"Yeah, I get that, but maybe both of us can leave the ghosts behind. I hate to say it, but I get the feeling this place is haunted. Not in the traditional 'there are monsters in the closet' thing, but rather the ones floating around in our skulls."

He was surprisingly compliant. I had not been expecting it to go so easily; I figured this meant Tracy was going to be the most difficult to persuade. We had a meeting that night. This wasn't a dictatorship; we'd think aloud, throw our ideas out there, kind of get a feel for where everyone was—and then take a vote. Plain and simple. Yeah, you'd think that, maybe in the abstract, it was. I'm not going to go into details, but did you ever watch YouTube before the zombies came? If you did, I'm sure you saw some of those Australian legislative sessions where punches are thrown and furniture is tossed. It was a lot like that, actually. Resistance to the ideas came from some of the weirdest angles. Stephanie was all against it, and because she was, so was Trip. Though, to be fair, he thought we were trying to move from the lawn to some crappy seats for the Phish show. "No dancing in the stands, man."

Gary was a big fat "no" because he'd lose his beloved tree-stand hide out. Justin didn't want to leave the last place Jess had been alive. So when he'd said that, Angel had said the same about Dizz. When the dust settled and the blood was mopped up off the floor the decision to head to Washington State won by a measly two votes. It had almost been a bad idea to let the kids vote at all, as they had single-handedly almost thwarted the attempt. Then I started to wonder about that whole "out of the mouths of babes" thing where maybe they knew something more than we did and that staying was the right thing to do. But second guessing myself lead nowhere. The decision was made.

We weren't going to head out for at least a little while. Mad Jack was going to do some serious reconnaissance on the place first to make sure it really was going to be an ideal location for us and that it wasn't some sort of barbaric human barbecue pit set up to process people meat for the black market or some other weird shit. We had to also be very deliberate on what we took to make the journey, plus we still needed to find a good bus. And even when we got one, we planned on doing some serious retrofitting to make it a lot sturdier, should we run into any trouble.

"I said should," I mumbled, and then shook my head.

"What, Mike?" Tracy asked. We were laying in bed; I was looking at the ceiling, now totally stressed out that I had fought to leave with so much vehemence. If things went wrong on the road, it could all be traced back to me. I would trace it back to me, anyway.

"I was thinking to myself and I said should something happen while we're on the road. Like there's really a chance that something won't."

"You don't know that."

"Now you're just patronizing me. Am I doing the right thing?"

"This isn't all about you, Mike. We voted."

"Did you vote with me because you wanted to move or because I'm your husband?"

"I voted with you because it's the right thing to do."

"Yeah, but if I hadn't brought it up this wouldn't even have been a discussion."

"The moment Deneaux gave us a way to use satellites it was going to be an issue sooner or later."

"Yeah. That doesn't make it any better. Her being the source of the move, I mean."

"We'll make it, Mike. We always do. You have this innate

ability to always land on your feet."

"Please tell me that's not a cat analogy. And haven't you ever seen those investment commercials?"

"What...what are you talking about?"

"They always say that past events cannot be predictors for future ones."

THE NEXT DAY was a busy one. Mad Jack had spent the entire night finding suitable buses. We'd dismissed all the ones on the road; we had to assume they'd received some sort of damage in one way or another. There were two bus depots and a casino in Bangor, roughly forty-five minutes away. There were four bus depots in Augusta—but that added another twenty minutes to our drive time. More chances for a fully operational bus, but more time driving. In the end, I flipped a coin. Life was one big fucking coin flip anyway. Wasn't it?

"Heads," I said as it landed in my palm and I flipped it on to the back of my hand.

"Great. Was Bangor heads or Augusta?" BT asked.

"Shit. I forgot to designate one or the other."

"Typical Talbot—just start flipping away. You can't even properly plan a coin toss. Personally, I'd like to go to Bangor."

"Any particular reason?" I asked, pocketing the coin.

"I want to grab a slot machine," BT answered.

"You're kidding, right? Never pictured you as much of a gambler. Can't imagine many casinos letting you in any way."

"All right out with it. Let's hear your 'funny' explanation of why casinos won't let me in." He used air quotes around the word funny like I wasn't going to deliver.

"Well, I was going to say something about you being a cop once and how they probably hated seeing you since they had to pay you out protection money."

"That's the mob, dumbass. You got anything else?"

"Um, okay...maybe when you lost money you smashed machines like the Hulk." I made two fists and brought them down heavily on the table top. "BT break." I did in my best Hulk smash voice.

That got a smile. "Okay, that was alright. You want me to make you feel like an ass now?"

"Not really. I can do that all by myself."

"Linda and I used to go to Vegas once a year. We weren't big gamblers, it was just the fun and excitement of the place. I'd like to have a memento of those better times."

"How about a nice casino chip instead? Those machines have to weigh a couple of hundred pounds. I mean, I guess for you that's like a keepsake, but you do realize we're trying to travel light, right?"

"Man, I just want to play."

"There's the truth, hiding just around the corner. Did Linda even go to Vegas?"

"Yeah, for the shows. I'm telling you, man, I was addicted to all those lights and sounds."

"Monsters usually are; that's why they always attack big cities."

"See? That's pretty good, right there."

"Thanks, man."

"I don't know what it was; they were able to make me completely forget about the outside world. I had cases that still haunted my dreams, but no matter what was going on in my life or what I had seen, when I sat down with a one-armed bandit, everything else was blitzed over. I'm wondering if I could do that again."

"Fine...we'll find an extra seat on the bus for it. Not sure how popular you're going to be at four in the morning when everyone is trying to sleep and your bells and whistles machine is spouting off. But I'll let you deal with that."

I wanted to go very light: myself, BT, and one other...whom I was about to enlist right now. I found Deneaux in the living room; she was reading a murder mystery. "Haven't you had enough of that?" I asked pointing to the book.

"You read what you know." She smiled. "Is this a social visit? I've been feeling very secluded."

"Get your shit. You're coming with me."

"Where are we going?" She had not moved.

"We're rounding up a bus."

"Road trip? Under these circumstances? So you believe Etna Station to be the haven you hoped it would be?"

"You knew it was there?"

"Of course. When the Demense group was ready they were going to incorporate it into their fold."

"Any other secrets you think I should know?"

"Plenty."

"But you have no intention of telling me—am I correct?"

"You're getting smarter! Almost as fast as the zombies."

"Since this involves you as well, tell me: is the Etna Station a worthwhile trip?"

"They are people."

"Okay. Let's try a different tactic. Are they people like you, or normal people?"

"You're asking if they are survivors?"

"Sure. Let's call you a 'survivor' with maybe a tinge of 'murderer' in there."

I got a glare, but she let it drop.

"Well, it's very heavy-handed on the military side. Not sure how comfortable you're going to be with all that authority, especially with your penchant for rebellion."

"You wear one 'Fuck the Man' t-shirt and suddenly you're labeled as a conspirator. I can deal with authority if it means my family is safer. Let's go."

"To get the bus? I'd rather stay and finish the book."

"Not going to happen. I'm not leaving you behind without me here. You're entirely too treacherous."

"What good would murdering everybody here do for me?"

"I have no idea. But the fact you even thought to say that makes me think you've considered it in passing, which means you are, without a doubt, coming with me."

"No." She brought her book up.

I pulled my Ka-Bar from its sheath and pushed the top of the book down with the blade. "Do you believe that I would stick this knife through your eye? Then pull it out...would look like an olive on a toothpick."

She looked to me. "I do believe you might."

"Get up then," I said, putting the knife away. "We leave in ten." And I strode out. I have a feeling that if she'd had a gun she would have placed a round in the small of my back, neatly severing my spine. Keeping extra guns accounted for in the midst of a zombie apocalypse was not the easiest of tasks. I did a check every night, to make sure they were secured but handy. A time would come when she would be able to get a hold of one. I needed MJ to hack that password before that could happen.

"I'd like to come." It was Tiffany.

I wasn't big on bringing who I considered a kid. Tough to tell a woman who stood up to vampires that I didn't trust her out in the field, though.

"Sure. One thing, though...Deneaux is coming, and yes, she looks like a frail old woman, but I'm telling you she is the most dangerous one of us out there. You need to keep that in mind at all times. She will sacrifice you in a heartbeat if it gains her even a one step advantage over her enemies."

"I understand. Meredith told me all about her and I saw."

"How you doing? We haven't had much time to talk."

"I like it here. It isn't home, but it feels a lot like it."

"Is that why you voted against the move to Washington?"

"I'm not a fan of strangers, Mr. Talbot."

I smiled. "Yeah, neither am I. Wasn't before the zombies...less so now. Grab some gear. We're getting ready to go."

I shrugged at BT who glared at me when Tiffany came

outside and hopped in the car.

"Be careful out there," Gary called down.

I waved. This started out like our runs always do. Smooth sailing for a bit, then storm clouds form and a hell of a squall hits. In this case, it was a little more literal. MJ had said there was a potential for some weather and here it was. We were maybe fifteen miles from Ron's house when the front rolled in. It went from crystal clear blue skies to heavy dark rain clouds in fifteen minutes. It was too much to hope for that they would roll on out as quickly as they'd come in.

"Oooh...an omen," Deneaux cackled as the first fat drops splattered on the windshield.

"Witches melt, sweetheart. You shouldn't be so happy," BT said to her.

I hadn't thought about it when BT sat up front and Deneaux hopped in the back with Tiffany. I watched them in the rearview. It was after the second time I caught her looking to the girl's sidearm that I stopped the car.

"What are you doing, Mike?" BT asked.

"Sorry, big man. Tiffany, can you come up front please?" I asked.

"I'm not sitting back there, man. I won't fit. My head will be all scrunched over, I'll be eating my damn knees."

"You big baby. Tiffany, do you know how to drive?"

"Of course! But I don't know where we're going."

"I'll guide you. Let's switch."

"I know you want some alone-time with me, Michael, but is this really necessary?" Deneaux asked.

"Probably not; I'm sure Tiffany can hold her own. But the way you keep eyeing her damn pistol is making me nervous and if I'm nervous, my driving suffers."

"Son of a bitch. She makes it so easy to forget that she's a pit viper." BT now had his eyes glued on her.

"Yeah, now you look." Tiffany and I switched; we only got slightly drenched. "Stay straight for another ten miles or so. Miss me?" I asked Deneaux as I slid in next to her.

She lit a cigarette. I made a move to grab it from her and decided against it when she threatened to put it out on my face.

"How can you expect me to be out here in the wild without protection, Michael?"

I ignored her and she, thankfully, said nothing else...although she did make sure to send every plume of smoke my way.

"Alright—you have a turn coming up here." We were in the center of Hampden; I looked longingly at the shut down Dunkin' Donuts as we took a left. Got our first notion of trouble as we passed the Rite Aid drugstore; there were five people outside looking around. When we drove by, all eyes were on us.

"That can't be good," BT said.

"Mr. Talbot?" Tiffany had her eyes riveted on the people loitering in the parking lot.

"There's a turn up here, it gets us on the highway. Punch it a little, Tiff. Let's get the hell out of here." I'd mistakenly figured we'd at least make it to Bangor before the shit started. Now I wished I was driving, but I didn't want to take the time to switch out again.

"What do they want with us?" Tiffany looked panicked, I could see it in her eyes as she met mine in the rearview mirror.

"What people always want—power over others," Deneaux said. She seemed to be enjoying herself.

"Friends of yours?" I asked.

"I have no friends," she said evenly.

"They're following." BT had been keeping an eye out while I directed Tiffany.

"There's more ahead!" The car swerved violently as Tiffany struggled to keep her emotions under check.

"BT—you to the front. I'll watch our six. How many?"

"Three."

"Guns?"

"Two of them, yeah."

"It's a damn trap." We had no side roads to go down; our

only defense was speed, and there were sufficiently enough abandoned cars on the road to make that difficult. Plus the torrential downpour wasn't helping; at least it affected everyone. When we blew past the trio and they did not open fire on us I was confused...unless we were being herded into the final aspect of the trap, where we would be forced from the car and made to surrender our weapons for whatever nefarious reasons our waylayers had.

"They didn't fire!" BT felt the need to tell us, although I'm pretty sure we would have figured it out soon enough if they had.

Not long afterwards, we knew why. They weren't a part of the group that had been following us. The souped-up Dodge Charger, which had been catching up to us fast, came to a screeching, skidding halt when they spotted the easier prey. The three never stood a chance as four men and a woman emerged from the car; they were firing before any sort of introductions could be made.

"What the fuck?" BT asked, watching the entire scene. "Why would they just kill them like that?"

"Drugs, it's got to be drugs. That's why they were at the Rite Aid, probably as high as fucking kites on whatever they could find. Fucked up their minds."

"We need to help them," Tiffany said, trying to see what she could through the mirrors.

"It's too late," BT told her. "They're going to be coming for us next, we need to get the hell out of here."

We had just gone over a rise and were dropping out of sight when I saw the attackers go to the trio's car, probably hoping there was a kilo of meth in there or something.

"We killed those people." Tiffany cried. "We led those animals right to them!"

There were a lot of things I would take responsibility for in this world, but I didn't see how I could possibly be held accountable for this one. Just a shitty set of random events was all it was.

"Death comes swiftly for those that are ill-prepared for life. Isn't that right, Michael?" Deneaux asked.

Fuck if I wanted to agree with anything that woman had to say but in this, she was right. I grunted as non-committally as I could. We had just passed into Bangor; four zombies were hanging out by the town limits sign like they were the welcome wagon. I radioed back to MJ to get an update.

"MJ, this is Mike. You there?" I radioed the house.

"Where else would I be, Michael?" he asked. "And if I wasn't here I certainly would not be able to answer."

I wrapped my hand over the mouthpiece. "Sometimes I want to put him in thumbscrews."

"I don't think you have to worry about him hearing you unless you press the send button," BT said.

"Don't you start on me. Don't any of you ever wonder how a person that takes things so literally can survive? I mean, I'm talking about even before the zombies came."

"I thought he was kidding, but the other day I asked him how his day was going and he told me it wasn't only his day, it was everyone's. And then he just went back to work," Tiffany said.

"Can you give me an update, please?" I asked, doing my best to not grit my teeth.

"Weather?"

"Not weather, MJ, the only thing I care about is zombies. We just passed four of them." We'd been keeping a close eye on Bangor. It seemed a fairly decent zombie-free zone; there were a few deaders walking about, but nothing to worry over. Seeing four already was starting to fire off distress signals in my head like tiny little flares.

"Until that storm passes, Michael, I cannot see anything."

I stuck my head out the window, hoping to see something besides the black of storm clouds. "What about infrared?"

"The electrical discharges are making that impossible."

To the occupants of the car I asked: "What electrical discharges?"

"Lightning? Is he saying lightning?" Tiffany asked.

"What lightning?" I'd no sooner said the words when a flash as bright as a supernova illuminated the car. We all looked momentarily washed out under the intense glare. This was immediately followed by what sounded like an artillery barrage of thunder. "Holy fuck," I said, as it rumbled away. "Okay...weather report, definitely a weather report."

"I'm not a meteorologist, but I dabble in it," MJ said.

"The way he dabbled in virginity," Mrs. Deneaux chuckled.

"You smell smoke?" BT asked.

"That would be from my burn," Deneaux said. She was having a grand old time. "Oh, how I missed this."

"The storm sitting over you is huge, and with the way it's swirling, I think it's going to sit there for a while."

"So we're flying blind, then?"

"When did you become airborne?" he asked, concern rising in his voice.

"It's almost like talking to a sober Trip," BT said. "Your call, Mike. What do you want to do?"

"I hate to come this far and not have any success, but I don't like not knowing what we're up against," I said.

"We didn't use to know what we were up against before she brought her toy," BT replied.

"True, but that didn't always work out. We should at least take a look; the casino is only about three miles up. If it looks clear enough, we'll head in. It seems we lost our tail; stopping now makes sense."

My unease grew incrementally. It wasn't any one particular thing. We were seeing zombies but in very small groups and spaced far enough apart that it wasn't overly alarming. When I saw a half dozen of them together I was about to make the call to head back.

Just then BT called out. "There it is!"

A large sign that read "Hollywood Casino" dominated our view. A more misleading moniker would have been hard to come by. There was nothing Hollywood about it, and as far as being a casino…well, that was iffy. I'm not much of a gambler, but that was one of the saddest facilities I have ever walked into. It wasn't old or in need of repair; they could just never really attract a clientele. Money is not the easiest commodity to come by in Maine, and most folks aren't so willing to part with it playing games specifically designed to remove it from their pockets. The place was subjugated (and I mean by nearly three-quarters) by penny slot machines. Regular casinos would have laughed at this poor place, made fun of it even. Pretty soon they would probably start paying people to play. Now, I'm not saying you can't lose money there, but you could dislocate your shoulder pulling that machine's arm before you could blow through twenty dollars.

"Is that smoke?" I asked pointing off to the left. It looked like a thick plume of black, but it was difficult differentiating it from the backdrop of the sky.

"Must have been what I smelled," BT said, though he never turned to look. He was peering at that sign like he was hoping it would light up. I'll tell you, though, if that happened I would have told Tiffany to floor it. That sounded too much like the beginning of a Stephen King book for my liking. Frying ozone dominated my senses as multiple lightning strikes hit the city. It was usually a smell I loved; one of those things you remember from your youth. But right now I was afraid it could be masking the scent of zombies. The sound of the thunder and whatever was burning was awakening or gathering zombies from all around the general area. This place was going to be a hotbed of activity real soon. I was all for a good party, just not this kind.

"We going?" BT asked, although he was already opening his door as Tiffany pulled up to the curb.

"Should I stay with the car?" Tiffany asked.

This was a dilemma. Part of me thought she should, but if she got in trouble we'd never hear the sound of her horn over the storm or even through the thick walls of the casino. The smart play was for her to come with us and to leave the keys in the car, in case anything happened to her. But there were assholes afoot and they knew what this vehicle looked like. With the keys in it, they were bound to take it, or at the very least disable the car then wait for us to come out.

"Leave the keys and come on." I was opening my door when I noticed Deneaux wasn't moving. "Nice try. Get your ass in gear."

"It's pouring out."

"You didn't believe BT's comment about witches melting, did you? Get going or I'll drag you out."

"Fine way to treat someone who brought you the gift that I did."

"Fine lot of good that's doing us right now," I told her.

BT was halfway up the steps.

"You might want to wait for some back up there, buddy. Those doors are still intact." I don't know what had me more distracted, BT acting like Disneyland had opened up early just for him, keeping an eye on Deneaux, the blinding flashes and deafening sounds of the storm, or worrying about zombies and assholes. Why we didn't just drive that damn car into the parking garage behind the building is one of life's little mysteries. On two side notes, I was happy to see that Deneaux was wearing red—some of you sci-fi fans will get that, others might think bullfighting, either way she could maybe get a small dose of what she had coming. And if I ever do get the chance to sit down and write a book I think I'm going to call it Zombies and Assholes: How to survive when all those around you either want to shit on you or shit you out. Lengthy, but telling.

"It's open," BT said gleefully as he opened the door.

The first whiff I caught was of something like a seafood buffet table that had been thawed a few too many moons ago. That, and it was pitch black. Casinos are notorious for not having windows. Something about not wanting the betting people to know when it's past their bedtime. But since this place was generally filled with blue-hairs, I guarantee that they knew when four o'clock rolled around, as this was generally early bird dinner time, or at the very worst five o'clock, when Diagnosis Murder or Murder She Wrote came on one of those stations that perpetually shows re-runs. We all flipped on our rifle mounted flashlights, save Deneaux, who had a penlight. She wanted a baton style light but I told her no. I figured if she could strike someone hard enough to knock them out with a light the size of a standard pen then she deserved to take their weapon.

As we crossed over the threshold, the wonder of the place distracted me from our mission: we'd come for a bus, and most likely there would not be one parked in the foyer. Tiffany had kicked down the door stop to keep the heavy door open. When she looked up and noticed zombies in the distance, she warned us about them.

"Close it," I told her, reluctantly. Not that we were getting much light from outside, but it sure beat the compressed blackness we were now engulfed in. I remember playing a computer game called "Doom" when computers were relatively new. You wandered through these dark caverns and could not see more than a few feet in front of you and things would always show up unannounced at your sides. I felt like I'd immersed myself into that world, and as much as I was a fan of playing that game, I was not a big fan of actually being in it. We moved forward slowly—BT, Tiffany, and myself in a straight line, Deneaux right behind, her smoky breath striking my left ear. I had a feeling she was nervous; didn't know demons could get nervous—so that at least was a positive.

The entrance was large, fifty feet by forty at least. There was a staircase ahead of us that came from the garage—a place we should have been heading for. Instead, we went to the right, where a row of wide doors lead into the casino. Tiffany propped those open. There were four sets of double doors; I guess they were hoping there would be stampedes of people fighting to get in so they'd better make access as accessible as possible. What we were doing was stupid and unnecessary and still we moved through those doors. Cautiously, sure, but still. Whatever subliminal pull those casinos radiated when they were alive, it still works. Unfortunately, this casino was very much dead. The smell was riper inside. My flashlight glinted over a fair amount of spent brass and then the body of the security guard that had spent them. The first rows of machines had been obliterated by gunfire; four old women had been cut down in their seats, one zombie man at their feet, chips and nickels everywhere. The security guard was a dumbass; I wouldn't have let him guard buckets.

"Tiffany, can you get that man's gun, please?" I said, still scanning the area for threats.

"He's dead," she responded.

"Yes, yes he is. And if you don't want to be, your best bet is to get that gun before Deneaux does."

"Don't be silly," Deneaux said. "The gun is empty—the breech is open."

I spared a glance. "Fine. But I'm not liking that you looked that hard."

"It's instinct; it's what I do."

"BT man, stop moving so fast. We'll get your machine—we just need to be smart about this." Stupider words could not have been uttered. What we were doing was as far from smart as one could get and still use human speech to utter the words.

"I like the video poker machines. The ones with the 'double down'"

"You have to have a particular machine. Is that what I'm hearing?" I asked incredulously.

"When you went to the liquor store did you just grab the first case of beer you came across?" he asked.

"Fair enough. Let's just find the damn thing." We were halfway in; the stench was getting worse, yet we hadn't crossed whatever was producing it. It's a sad state of affairs when you hope for decomposing bodies as opposed to some other alternative. I turned around quickly when I thought the light behind us dimmed momentarily; I couldn't swear that I saw a shadow run past, but I could make a strong mention of it. "BT."

"Yeah, yeah...I know." He was looking around carefully. What had been child-like glee was now turning into grownup concern. We all turned when the light behind us was snuffed out. Yeah, I used "snuffed out." It has a much more ominous tone to it. "Tiffany?"

"It was secure. Somebody shut it deliberately."

"Shit, I thought you might say that. Dammit. Here," I said, handing Deneaux my revolver.

"A gun? I do hope I don't have an accident or something," she said as she opened the cylinder to check for rounds.

"It's loaded."

"Aaand I should trust you why?" she asked flipping her hand to close it.

"Because I'm not you."

"I could kill you all," she said from behind us.

"You could, but then you'd have three rounds to fight off the zombies." I think she was doing some math in her head.

"Has anybody seen how many zombies there are?" she finally asked.

"Good call giving her a gun," BT said doing a slow scan of the entire area.

"Relax, kids. If I was going to kill you I would have done it already."

"She always makes me feel so warm inside. She's like a fucking teddy bear," BT said.

"Yeah, with rabies," Tiffany added.

"See? Now you're starting to get it," I told her.

"I'm with the big man on this. I don't think giving her the gun was such a good idea."

"She'll prove you both wrong." I was looking off to the side, my flashlight caught the back of a running shoe before it was once again out of sight.

"What the fuck are they doing, Talbot?" BT asked. "Why aren't they just attacking?"

"They're looking for an opening," I turned to say. Just then I heard Deneaux's gun roar. I felt blood flow down the side of my face and heard the distinct thump of a body collapsing to the carpet.

"You should pay more attention. He almost had you," she cackled as she pointed to the zombie. His skin nearly matched the gray of his security uniform.

"You nearly shot me," I said as I tenderly touched the raw spot on my head.

"I barely buzzed you. And besides, it was the only shot I had. You should be thanking me for saving your life instead of whining about it."

"I'll make sure to send you a card every year." The zombies were beginning to make themselves known, flitting quickly through the shadows from light to light. Tiffany fired two wild shots; change clattered to the floor from the machine she'd destroyed.

"You're a flighty little thing, aren't you?" Deneaux goaded.

"That's just what we need," I said sarcastically.

"I'd rather be attacked. This shit sucks," BT said.

"The better question is: why are they still here? If they're intelligent enough to close a door they should be smart enough to open one. I'm thinking they live here," I said.

"Live here?" Tiffany asked.

"Like in stasis?" BT asked.

"I don't think so. They'd be covered in that zombie goo." This changed things on a fundamental level. A group of zombies—not only staying together, but having a central place to call home? Wasn't that how civilizations were born? I wanted to chuckle thinking about a thousand years from now when the first little zombie daughter sits at the table and says she needs a bump in her allowance and, oh, by the way, she no longer eats meat. Probably last as long as it takes mom to drop a fresh, ketchup-coated brainloaf on the table. But the topic will have been broached.

A zombie was already running full speed and straight for me when it appeared from the darkness. I pulled the trigger before my mind could even recognize the threat for what it was. The first shot was low, breaking open his exposed chest plate. I don't think the man was ever heavy in life, but now he was all ribs; his stomach was concave—you could see his backbone through what was left of his skin. Clearly, he was starving. Why this particular group had not gone into stasis was troubling. My next shot took most of his lower jaw off, and then fortuitously the bullet took an upward turn and exited through the very top of his skull. He collapsed no more than three feet from me. Tiffany's resolve was tested next. Unlike me, she only needed one shot with her much heavier-caliber weapon. She hit a female zombie in the neck, completely decapitating the thing.

I used to think that sexing the zombies wasn't worth it; they just were what they were. Like, if a shark was trying to eat me, I wouldn't care if it was a male or a female, and that had been true for zombies. But now I had to wonder with their advancements, would they, or even could they, procreate? And how long behind that would the first zombie porn film be made? There was someone, somewhere, that would jerk off to that.

Luckily, BT was tried next, distracting me from that horrific train of thought. We had formed a loose circle; I found it oddly telling that Deneaux was the only one that a zombie didn't charge, as if they knew just how lethal she was...or maybe it was that they identified more with her; I hoped it wasn't something more sinister than that.

"I'm sorry for getting us into this," BT said over the roar of his gun.

"Let's get our backs up to the machines." I figured that way at least we had one less side to defend. It was good for a moment until we heard zombies starting to climb up and over.

Deneaux turned to take care of them.

"I have one bullet left, Michael," she'd said as calmly as if she were talking about how many Biscotti cookies she had left at her tea party.

"Right side cargo pocket." I was carefully picking targets and eliminating them with extreme prejudice. Fucking Deneaux squeezed my damned ass as she reached down to grab the box of shells. Only supreme self control kept me from jumping forward, straight into the arms of the attacking zombies.

"Sorry. I'm just so nervous." Refer back to the not having enough biscuits tone.

Tiffany had dropped down to one knee to reload her rifle. At the moment, only BT and I were firing. The zombies pressed their attack. It was difficult to get an accurate count because of the darkness, and some of the fuckers were merely running back and forth just at the edge of our flashlights, giving the illusion of multitudes. Was this a deliberate ruse?

"Any day!" I shouted to Deneaux, who was methodically, but casually, putting rounds into her cylinder.

"Haste makes one's hands twitch. Not my hands, mind you, but some hands. And nervous hands drop shells and miss their targets."

I was yanking on a trigger for far too long before I figured out it would not depress because the bolt was open. I hit the release; cursed under my breath at Deneaux as I fumbled with the new magazine. Bitch saved me again when she brought her pistol up, the barrel inches from my nose, and fired off two quick rounds—obliterating the heads of the two closest zombies. Having to thank her was like kissing the ass of the boss you absolutely despised because he allowed you to keep the crappy job you needed to support your family. I grunted something that may or may not have stood up in court as a "much obliged".

"Oh...it's okay, honey. Now that we're intimate I felt it my duty to save you. Again."

Even through a zombie attack, BT had to stop everything he was doing to shoot me a quick questioning glance.

"Fuck off," I told him as I released the bolt and got back into the battle, making sure that I didn't need Deneaux to throw me another bone. The frontal attacks had stopped; there was a fair amount of gore on the ground. A few zombies were still running around but they seemed to have pulled back.

"Now what?" Tiffany asked.

"Now we get the hell out of here," I told her.

"I'll be damned," BT said. I turned to look at him as he was shouldering his weapon. He was wrapping his arms around a machine that was directly behind him. "This is the one!"

"You realize this is a hot zone right?" I asked.

"Well you'd better cover me then, 'cause this baby's mine." He grunted with heavy exertion. A loud crack of splintering wood exploded out as BT rocked that machine clean off its moorings. He yelled like an Olympic lifter as he wrenched it free and picked it up.

"Is that such a good idea?" Tiffany asked.

"You tell him, dear, that it isn't," Deneaux said.

"Alright. Let's get out of here before they hit the dinner bell for round two." We formed a cluster around BT. I don't think any of us took a decent breath until we hit those doors. The entire time we were moving I fully expected an attack. It wasn't until the doors opened and a sickly finger of sunlight broke through that I realized that this zombie family had taken some serious losses. Six zombies were about halfway across the casino peering out at us from behind machines; we'd dropped at least triple that number. Part of me thought going in after those six would be a good idea, but BT and the rest were almost to the stairs leading to the garage, and I'd be damned if I was going to be alone in that void.

The garage was four levels of emptiness; again it looked like the owners of this casino had been much more optimistic about the number of customers they'd draw. It was on the bottom most level that we found two large buses parked side by side. I went into the first one; it looked pristine, as if it had never even seen a guest.

"Clear," I said, coming back out.

BT had put his machine down and was checking the second. He had taken considerably longer to come to the conclusion that his bus was free of zombies as well—long enough that I went to see what the problem was.

"How's the bathroom in that one?" he asked when he stepped down off the stairs.

"Empty," was all I could think to tell him.

"How empty?"

"There were no zombies, alive or dead, no people alive or dead, no pets, nothing. Not even a decent magazine collection," I told him, trying to figure out where he was going with this.

"The toilet—did you look there?"

"What in the hell are you talking about? Why would I look in the toilet? It's a Blue Chem kind. I don't want to see old turds."

"Mine was empty."

"Perfect. We'll take yours, then."

"You don't understand. It was empty of everything; no blue stuff at all."

"Even better," I told him honestly. "That stuff smells horrible."

"It smells better than the accumulated waste of thirty people sloshing underneath us all the way across the country."

"Oh…oh. I get it now. Maybe I'll just go and check again."

"Yeah," he smirked, "that'd be a good idea."

I started to let my imagination run with this one as I went down the center aisle. I remembered a story I'd read on the internet once about chem toilets. I was hoping some Saran-wrapped pervert didn't click a couple of pictures of me from inside the hole. I approached with the barrel of my weapon. If I so much as caught the glimmer of a flashbulb I was shooting first and apologizing later. Any motherfucker that got his jollies from taking pictures of people taking care of business from inside a toilet needs to die. There is no chance I'm letting that aberration reintegrate into society. Seriously, man, how many things have to go off the rails for that to be something you're interested in? There's not enough medication, whether professionally or personally prescribed, to bring someone back from that.

I'm not going to admit it, but this thought had me more spooked than the zombies. I could see him. There was the fucker, a dull nightlight glinting off his thick, plastic-wrap suit, goggles cover his eyes and he has a snorkeling tube firmly entrenched in his mouth. Almost put a bullet in the phantom. Even when I was pretty sure he wasn't there I still almost shot just to be extra careful. Like BT's bus, this one was also empty. I wiped the sweat from my forehead and took a deep breath to compose myself before I stepped outside.

"Empty too. I guess we just start them up and see which one has more gas."

"You have the keys?" BT asked.

I popped my head back in to look at the empty ignition. "Only in Maine," I said, as I looked on the expansive dashboard where a small ring of keys sat. I wouldn't doubt it for one second if one of these went to the vault. My wife and I would joke when we visited Maine, that if we were to leave the keys in the ignition with the car running, someone would more likely turn it off for us than steal it. Not that this is a bad thing, just so vastly different from the other parts of the country I'd resided in.

"Keys are on the dashboard." I sat in the seat and tried to figure out all the buttons. "Like sitting in a damned cockpit," I shouted outside. "How the hell do I start this thing?"

"Get up." It was Deneaux; she was at the door, pointing at me with her gun. "Stop looking at me that way; I'm not going to shoot you. I just know how to drive a bus."

"How is that even possible?" I asked as I yielded my seat.

"There are many things about me you do not know, Michael."

"Maybe we should keep it that way," I said, as she started the engine.

"Three-quarters of a tank!" I yelled to BT and Tiffany. BT was already hefting his bounty up and inside once he heard the bus come to life.

"Do you mind if I drive?" Deneaux asked.

"Have at it," I told her. "I would like the gun back, though."

"I saved your life twice already today and still you don't trust me?"

"Trust? I don't think that's something we're ever going to be able to achieve. Let's just aim for co-existence. We'll try for some of them deeper relationship words later."

"I caressed your ass, Michael. We're almost lovers now," she rasped.

I dry heaved a bit. I got that "What the fuck?" stare from BT again. Tiffany did her best to completely ignore the entire situation.

"Let's just get this bus moving. The fumes are going to choke me out," I said, sitting a few rows behind Deneaux. I turned my head when I noticed she kept looking at me in the rearview mirror. If she was trying to unnerve me, she was doing a fantastically wonderful job of it. The bus jerked forward so hard that BT fell back into his seat, I bounced my head off the seat in front of me, and Tiffany was sprawled on her ass.

"Sorry! It's been a while," Deneaux said, I noticed she'd already put her seatbelt on.

"Horse and buggy while ago?" BT asked as he adjusted and braced himself.

I helped Tiffany up; she quickly sat. I heard her belt buckle snap shut just as the bus lurched forward again.

"It's not as easy as it appears. It will smooth out as this warms up." Looked to me like she was having the time of her life.

We'd no sooner left the garage when BT announced he had to "go".

"Really man? In a water-less toilet?"

"I ate your damn sister's pancakes. Now they're sitting like stones at the bottom of my stomach."

"What the hell is wrong with you, man? Nobody eats those things."

He was holding his stomach.

"Maybe go use it and we'll grab the other bus," I told him. "I mean, now that you're about to fill this one up."

He flipped me the finger and stood. I did my best to not think about what was happening at the back. Saran Wrap Man threatened to muscle back into my thoughts. Deneaux's driving was indeed smoothing out and she was cruising right along. We'd had a rough start, but things seemed to be getting better. That was right up until BT opened the lavatory door and a big steaming whiff of what my sister liked to pass off as food wafted up my way. Tiffany was hunched down with her jacket pulled up over her nose.

"Come on man!" I said to him as he shrugged and sat. It was not difficult to see the proud smile he tried to stifle for being able to stink out the entire bus. Deneaux had slid her window open. I thought maybe she was passing out from oxygen loss when the bus began to slow down. I looked up front, thinking I was going to have to take over driving duties, when I noticed the red and white Plymouth from earlier.

"Michael, I would very much like your pistol back," Deneaux said as she put her hand out. I placed it in her palm.

"Now what?" BT asked.

"Well, it's safe to assume we're not going to be able to outrun them. You comfortable with ramming them?"

Deneaux already had her foot floored before I could finish the question. It was a bus, so it wasn't like we dashed forward; the men in the car had plenty of time to open fire. The large windshield shattered as multiple rounds penetrated.

"Feel free to return fire," Deneaux said. "I would, but I'm a little busy." The pistol was in her lap and she was holding on to the oversized steering wheel with both hands.

"Mike—couple of cars coming up from the side." BT was looking at the main console which had a back camera view of what was going on behind us.

"One thing at a time I suppose." I braced myself against the railing that led down the stairs and opened fire on the men who were using their car to shield themselves. We were starting to pick up steam now and between the bus barreling down on them and my suppressive fire they were in a bit of a quandary. Better them than us. The car was parked horizontally in the roadway; Deneaux was going to make contact here in the next couple of seconds. One of the men had enough smarts to make a dash for it. Of course, he paid for his escape attempt with his life as I shot him through the side, most likely ripping his lungs apart, but hey, he got an A for effort.

I was just about to ask Deneaux if she planned on hitting the thing head on when I was tossed sideways as the bus pulled to the far side. The impact was jarring but I'm sure it was nothing compared to what the three behind the Plymouth got. For a brief second, they were exposed as Deneaux shoved the front of the car farther down the roadway while the rear turned toward the side of the bus. I had the most unfortunate angle when the hood spun and pounded into the men who hadn't even had time to act surprised before they were slammed. The first's head exploded against the quarter panel and then he disappeared under the wheels. The other two were launched by the impact. Judging by the force, they had at minimum a dozen broken bones between them. One lay still when he finally hit the ground on the other side of the road. He was either dead or paralyzed. In this new world, the former was a much better option. The other guy was rolling around in that extreme pain—the kind that makes it difficult to think of anything else.

Bullets were now pinging the sides of the bus as we were

catching gunfire from mobile vehicles. Glass was being blown out and the wheel was jumping around in Deneaux's hands, which led me to believe we'd suffered at least one flat.

"A little closer," Deneaux hissed as she looked in the rear view mirror. "That's it...come on dearie...you know you want it."

I personally don't think anybody at any time had wanted anything from Deneaux, but that's just me. Apparently, the car next to us had come looking for what she was offering. The bus jerked violently to the left; if the door had been open I would have been tossed out. As it was, I had the wind knocked out of me when I slammed into it. A trio of bullets whistled past my head. I turned to see that the other car had come up alongside us. They slammed on their brakes when Deneaux went to shoulder them off the road like she had their comrades.

"There're three more cars back there," Deneaux said as she pointed to the screen.

"Why in the fuck do they want us so bad?" I asked.

"I'm sure part of it right now is that we've killed at least four of them," she said.

"Wouldn't have been any if they hadn't started this shit," I said.

"Do you really believe they are going to see it that way?" she asked.

"It would be nice," BT said from behind me.

There was a heavy burst of fire and then the rear left of the bus dipped down. They'd taken out both tires. We slowed considerably.

"I'm going to cut their throats," Deneaux said evenly.

"I was sort of hoping we wouldn't have to get that close," I told her.

Another round of bullets and the right side dipped down; we were dragging our ass like a dog with worms.

"Going to be on rims soon, Michael. This should be the time you begin to root around in that bag of tricks you carry around with you." She looked at me far longer than anyone driving a bus should.

"I wish I knew where I put it down," I told her truthfully. The back facing camera was displaying a heavy shower of sparks as the shredded tires finally peeled away, leaving metal to grind on asphalt.

"Not going to get far before the wheels either seize up or fall off," BT said. "Seen it enough times with the spike strips we used to use. Gonna be fast, especially with something this heavy."

As if the bus were cognizant of BT's words, thick, nose-melting smoke began to drift up from below, and the bus began to wobble as if we were on square wheels. Then there was a horrible squealing as the bus began to fishtail. We weren't in danger of losing control or tipping over; I don't think we were traveling much over ten miles an hour by this time. Deneaux kept her foot down on the peddle for a little while longer, but all she succeeded in doing was getting the engine to rev louder. We were grinding to a halt.

"Get out of the bus!" was screamed at us.

We didn't say anything or move; we knew they were "kill first and talk later" type of people.

"That thing is basically a big soup can. Do you really think it's going to stop our bullets?"   We already knew it wouldn't; there was sunlight streaming through enough bullet holes to prove that point. The man, maybe wanting to make double sure we understood that, punched a slug through one side that traveled over the aisle and exited the other. Smoke swirled in its wake.

"Fuck," a collective response.

"We've got enough bullets to make that thing look like a cheese grater!" There was some laughter outside as he said the words.

"The bathroom," Deneaux said.

"That room isn't any safer than the rest of the bus," BT told her.

"The waste tank leads to the cargo area," she explained.

"We can lift the bucket out first, then someone is going to have to go down and unscrew the large nut that holds the flange in place for the drainage and cleaning."

"Good thing it's clean," I said without thinking.

BT looked sheepish. "I had to go, man. Remember?"

I stepped into the bathroom and took a quick peek down the hole with my flashlight. I don't think vomit is the right word in this situation. What punched me in the nose should have never been produced by a human.

"What the fuck man! Did you eat a pony?" I stepped back. "Not for nothing, Deneaux, but there's no way I could fit down that hole even if I wanted to, and BT certainly can't. You and Tiffany, maybe. At least you two will be safe."

"Women and children first," Deneaux said.

"Is that what they really said on the Titanic? I mean when you were there?" BT asked.

I wanted to smile over to him but refrained. "BT and I will hold your legs."

"Sounds pleasant...but whatever for?" she asked.

"We're going to stick your head in there so you can undo the screw."

"My hands are far too arthritic to turn that." She made her hands into claws and showed me for effect.

"Tiff?" I asked.

"Nuh-uh." She backed up. "I'll die of asphyxiation long before I can get that undone."

"It's not that bad," BT beseeched.

"The Hindenburg wasn't that bad. Whatever is going on down there is fucking epic," I said.

Deneaux pulled out the trash liner and handed it to Tiffany.

"What do you want me to do with this?" she asked.

"Well, I'm thinking your best bet would be to put it over your head so you don't have to smell BT's ass anymore," I said.

"Don't listen to that fool. Put it over your hand and arm like a glove; you won't even know you're touching it,"

Deneaux said.

"I'm not going down there," Tiffany reiterated.

"Don't be a fool, girl," Deneaux snapped. "Michael and BT are about to be captured or killed and that's nothing compared to what awaits us. We need to survive. If they are merely captured, it will be necessary to rescue them."

Maybe the bad guys figured Tiffany needed persuading; they took a few shots through the bus to hurry us along.

"I don't know about all she said, Tiffany, but I would at least like to see you live through this all."

She looked over to BT who nodded his agreement.

"This is so fucking gross," she said as we lowered her in. "Oh god! I'm touching it! I'm touching it. I can't feel a nut..." she said after a few seconds.

We began to pull her up. "Make sure you leave the bag behind," I told her.

Deneaux lifted the shell up slightly and pushed it to the side. "Looks like it wasn't screwed back in."

"You...you mean I went down there for nothing?"

"If we survive, we'll get you therapy," I promised her. I pushed the shit box out of the way leaving a decent sized cavity for the two women to go down into. They'd be able to move the box back in place and hide should anyone look in the toilet. "Try not to be too Deneaux-ish," I told Vivian as I was about to close the seat. She gave me a thumbs up like this was Top Gun or some shit.

"Haven't they already seen Deneaux?" BT asked.

"The witnesses are dead." She said softly.

"Bet she's said that a lot." I said.

"We surrendering or going out blazing?" BT turned to me.

"I'd like to give the surrender route a go first."

"Really? You?" he asked.

"My wife said there were some things about me that needed changing. I figured I'd start now."

"I'm not afraid of dying, Talbot."

"Neither am I, my friend. I'm just scared of watching you

die."

"Fair enough," he replied.

"We're coming out!" I shouted.

"We would appreciate it if you did not bring your weapons," came the polite reply.

I put all my weapons on the seat, as did BT. "You ready for this?" I asked. He nodded.

I opened the door and took the three steps to the road. I was staring down at least a dozen guns. Most of them had on camouflage gear or khaki pants and shirts. Military or survivalists or maybe both. Either way, they were well-equipped and at least moderately trained; this had been our only option. I noticed that grips on rifles tightened as BT followed behind.

"That son of a bitch has to be from Nebraska," one of the men said.

"Do they even have enough corn to feed him?" the other replied.

"Where's everybody else?" the man who I figured was the leader asked. He had close-cropped hair and a neat but fairly unremarkable beard and mustache, except for the bright red hue. He had enough freckles it could have been considered a tan.

"That's it," I told him.

He motioned for me to keep my arms up. "The two of you have a bus? For what reason?"

"Look at the size of him. It's the only thing big enough to give him some leg room."

"Be that as it may, I do think I'll have some of my men check the bus out."

Three men elbowed past us and went in cautiously. Not more than thirty seconds later they came back out shaking their heads.

"Open the cargo doors," the man said.

Turning to look would have made them even more suspicious than my profuse sweating. When one of the men

92

said "clear" I did my best to not act relieved.

"My name is Knox. Who might you two be?"

"Lenny and Squiggy. He's Squiggy," I said, pointing behind me.

"Are you fucking kidding?" BT asked. "He's Mike and I'm BT. My friend here doesn't do well under pressure."

"Well, BT, it is indeed a pleasure to meet you. You will be a welcome addition to my army."

"Army?" I asked.

"Have you never seen a post-apocalyptic movie in your life?" His eyebrows furrowed and he got angry; here was the insanity I'd been expecting. "There is always a man of greatness that rises and takes control of the world to bring order back to all that was lost. And I am that man."

"Have you never watched those to the end?" I asked.

"Mike—stop antagonizing him," BT whispered.

"You killed five of my men; you two are now my newest conscripts. It's almost a fair exchange, if we go by sheer weight."

"Do you offer dental?" I asked.

"You're a funny man. You like being dead, funny man?"

"Beats the hell out of being under your command."

"That can be arranged."

"Mike—stop it, man."

"Those assholes in the car we took out, we saw them earlier. They just shot a family up for no reason. Why?"

"Too old or too young; we don't want them. But the ones you're talking about were trying to go awol and we don't take kindly to deserters, especially in a time of war."

"In a world where people are as rare as dodo birds you just kill them?"

"Wouldn't you kill me if you had the chance?" He asked.

"Well sure, but you're a prick," I told him.

He started laughing then turned to his men, still laughing, until they all started laughing, I should have realized this wasn't gonna go well for me. The fire in my belly was intense—I'd not even heard the shot. I wasn't even sure what had happened; I didn't remember downing a bottle of tequila as the heat spread out. I'd moved my hand to the entry wound long before my mind could catch up to what was going on.

"Don't even think about it or you'll join him," Knox said to BT. I wasn't sure what he was going to do; I was heading down the road to shocksville and I'd caught a bullet train. "Not so funny now, is it?"

I coughed; a ball of blood fell from my mouth. I pounded my knees on the pavement as I dropped to them. Knox's men were still laughing as they watched me die.

"I don't think you would have made a good soldier anyway," Knox said. "You look like the type that constantly questions authority, and I just don't want that in my regime. Handcuff the giant and let's get out of here. I can't wait to watch this initiation."

I was slowly canting to the side, and then I fell completely over. Knox came over to give one final parting shot.

"Hurts like a motherfucker I'm told. Probably going to hold on for another few hours, too. I'd put you out of your misery but fuck you, I don't like jokes."

I wanted to tell him "I'd noticed," but the pain was so intense it was almost surreal; like it was happening to someone else. I watched as BT was pushed forward and into a car, then they took off. It was long moments before I heard movement behind me.

"He's shot! Help me!" It was Tiffany.

Figured this was the end once Deneaux got involved. She knew what I was and that there was a chance I could recover from this. If she put a bullet in my head, though, that would be it for me, and she sure did have the opportunity.

"You going to live?" Deneaux asked as she looked down on me. She bent and grabbed the extra shells for my pistol out of my pocket.

"He's been shot in the stomach. We have to get him back home."

"Don't have a car, dearie, and I don't think the two of us are up to carrying him."

"What are we supposed to do, just let him die?" Tiffany was on the verge of crying.

"How far is the car you sideswiped?" I managed to get out.

"Couple hundred yards."

"Bring Tiffany," I told her. The exertion to speak was all I could handle. There were some questions from Tiffany but I'd already decided to clock out for break.

I felt a rapidly cooling arm drape across my face; thought it might have been my own. I realized it wasn't when I started drinking from it. Deneaux was watching intently as I pulled the blood in—I could only hope Tiffany wasn't. It was maybe a half hour later that the bullet was forced out. It was going to be a lot longer before the pain released its grip.

"How come you never told me?" Tiffany asked after a while.

By now I was sitting against the front tire of the bus. "Not usually something one brings up in normal conversation...especially considering your experience with them."

"Tommy as well?"

"Yes."

"Anyone else?"

"Deneaux might be; nobody's been able to prove it yet. Speaking of which, where is she?"

"She's been smoking through her cigarettes as fast as she can inhale."

"I would imagine she's pondering whether she made the right choice or not in saving me."

"What happens now?"

"I need to heal up a little more. While we're waiting, please give MJ a call and tell him to track where BT went. Then we go and get him back."

"There's only three of us."

"Well, you two don't exist and I'm dead, so they'll never

see that coming. Plus, I'm going to ask for back-up."

CHAPTER SEVEN
BT's initiation

SHUT UP, SHUT up, shut up, Talbot, BT thought frantically as his friend harangued the gunmen. These guys are dangerous. He'd no sooner thought the words when he heard the gunshot. At first he'd thought it might have been a warning shot until he saw Michael go down to his knees. He did not think it was a fatal shot—painful sure—but it shouldn't be fatal. Now if his friend would just keep his damned mouth shut long enough for them to leave, he might just make it through this. BT felt the cold metal of a gun barrel press up against his temple.

"Hands behind yer back," Simpkins, Knox's second in command, said. At six three and two hundred and fifty pounds, he himself was a large man. He sized himself up with their newest acquisition.

"Gonna need another set of cuffs. This one's shoulders are too big." Pirelli had placed one cuff on and had attempted to pull BT's other arm into place but couldn't; even with the second pair on it had been a struggle. "This is one initiation I'm glad I'm not going to be a part of. Although I'm sad I'm going to miss you getting your ass beat. Damn, dude, you're huge. Making us mere mortals feel all inferior and shit."

BT looked back to see how his friend was doing as he was

shoved forward, his head forced into the side of the car. A large laceration formed over his right eye and blood flowed down the side of his face. The look of hatred he leveled on Pirelli made the man step back.

"Yup, pretty fucking glad I'm not in the initiation."

"Knox, we should just kill this one," Simpkins said as they trailed the car holding the prisoner.

"He could die during initiation; he wouldn't be the first."

"I'm more worried about how many of our men he's going to take out before we break him."

"We could use a little thinning of the chaff, don't you think? And just look at that glorious bastard. He will be a magnificent addition to my army," Knox replied.

"Where are you taking me?" BT asked.

"Shut up." Pirelli had turned from the shotgun seat. You talk again and I'm going to shoot you in the knee. BT had no way of knowing if this was an idle threat or not; if Pirelli was as loose with his trigger as Knox was, he had to assume it was viable. His head banged off the roof as the car hit a speed bump entirely too fast.

"Bet that felt good," Gordon, the driver, said as he looked in the rearview mirror.

"You in the initiation?" BT asked.

Gordon looked away nervously; BT smiled.

"Welcome to your new home. Although, I got a feeling you won't be staying long," Pirelli said as he opened the back door and waited for BT to exit. "Let's go. Inside."

BT looked up and noticed at least four people on the roof of the giant superstore they'd parked in front of.

"You live in Best Buy?" They walked in, leading BT by both forearms. BT had not been expecting the set up. The merchandise and shelving had been completely removed. Off to the far left were orderly rows of cots; on the other side were picnic tables, which he assumed formed the mess hall. Directly off to his right was what looked like a small recreation room with a caged ring dominating the center. A pit formed in his stomach. He wasn't entirely sure why, but he had a feeling that cage had something to do with the initiation—just something his old cop instincts told him. And those instincts had saved his life more times than not. People turned to stare as he was escorted in, men, women, and children. They looked well fed and well cared for. He wondered if they knew just how insane their leader was, or if they cared.

"Let's go." Pirelli pushed him in the back. "I've got someplace special for you." "Someplace special" ended up being a cleaned out supply closet with a heavy oak door. An even heavier wooden beam had been placed across the front to bolster the lock. The door shut behind him and he heard the cross beam drop into place.

"Don't bother with the fake ceiling," Pirelli shouted from the other side of the door. "Everybody thinks that's a way out. It isn't. A mouse couldn't fit through them openings and you ain't no mouse."

"I'm not just going to take your word," BT replied.

"Of course you ain't. I'm just trying to save you the trouble. Most people step up on the edge of the sink, but I'm telling you right now if you break that sink and I have to clean up the water, I will shoot you."

"I'll keep that in mind." The composite sink began to creak and bend as BT placed his foot on it. "Fuck him." BT jumped up and placed his hand against the rectangular ceiling tile. When it didn't yield, he figured maybe the man wasn't lying. The seal around the drain cracked and broke from his weight, but the pipe held. "Well, it isn't leaking." He looked for some sign of weakness or something he could use as a weapon in his enclosure. "Hurry your skinny ass up, Talbot," BT said as he sat down on the cold cement floor.

He didn't know how long he'd been asleep when he was awakened by a loud rapping on the door.

"Strip." Came the one-word command.

"What?" BT asked back groggily.

"Take off your motherfucking clothes, you stupid fuck."

"Fuck off," BT replied.

The beam must have already been lifted because the door flew open. Three rifles were pointing directly at him.

"Get your clothes off or we'll do it for you."

"You can try."

"We'll try this one more time. My name is Griffins; I am the Master at Arms. I have been authorized by Knox to come and collect you for initiation. If you don't come willingly, I was told to shoot you first in the shoulder. If that doesn't convince you, the next one is supposed to go into your elbow. Now I'll do it—I've done it before. If you look at the rear wall you can see where the bullet hit after it exited Johnson's shoulder. Show him the wound." Griffins stepped aside to allow Johnson to move closer, the man handed his weapon off and pulled his shirt to the side to show a pink and puckered wound.

"Hurt like a son of a bitch. I don't recommend it," Johnson said as he readjusted. "I'm a corporal now in Knox's army. I hated them all that first couple of months, but now, well, we're doing wonderful things."

"Yeah. The best things always come from those trying to take over the world," BT sneered.

"What's it going to be?" Griffins asked. "Please don't make me shoot you. Oh, it's not that I'm squeamish or that I have a fundamental problem with it. It's just that after I saw you come in I bet on you going twelve deep before you succumbed, and if I have to send you out all gunshot, I'm probably going to lose my money. There was only one man that ever went twelve deep—Moosey. We found him way up north, gutting a moose. Biggest fuck I'd ever seen until you. Couldn't talk, that one, so we just named him. He died in the ring. The doctor said his heart just exploded after the twelfth. Too bad, too. He would have been able to carry all the heavy equipment around. Now get up, take your clothes off, and before you start asking stupid questions, I mean everything. Your underwear, your boots, your socks, and any jewelry you have on."

BT stood slowly.

"Just shoot him," Pirelli said.

"You always say that," Griffins told him. Griffins pulled his sidearm out and flipped the safety. "One." He brought the pistol up and leveled it on BT's shoulder. "Two."

BT thought the man seemed as casual about it as if he were pouring a glass of lemonade instead of getting ready to shoot a man. BT pulled his shirt over his head, then bent over to untie his boots. In under thirty seconds, he was fully nude.

"Had my doubts, but thank you. Would have hated to lose an ounce of gold before it even started. Now come on out of there. This part is called the parade, where everyone in our community gets a chance to see you. It's more for the betting handicap, though, even if the boss says it's sort of like your rebirth into a brand new world. You know, all naked and screaming. Well, the screaming part comes soon enough anyway."

There were a lot of oohs and aahs as BT was led to the caged ring. The tables had been moved from the makeshift cafeteria and now completely encircled the ring. Knox was standing atop one.

"Welcome, Dragons, to this most special of nights! We bring forth a man who is sure to be a great addition to our rebuilding force! But first, like all of us had to do before, he must be born into this brand new violent world!"

There was a practiced cheer of "Dragons baptized in fire, death before dishonor!"

"He must come forth the way God intended! He will fight his way into our ranks, through the Initiation! Now we will bow our heads in prayer in the hopes that none of our brothers or sisters are gravely hurt."

BT looked around as every person bowed their heads and closed their eyes. If he wasn't directly in the middle of them he would have attempted an escape.

"Get him in the ring," Knox said, "and let him know the

rules."

"There aren't really any rules, other than there's no weapons," Griffins said as he got BT into the ring. "One person will come in that door. You'll allow them to fully enter, and then you both go at it until one of you can't. It's easy for the other person because they get to come out. You keep going until someone bests you. If you beat twelve and then take a dive I'll make sure you get some easy duties afterward."

"Tampering!" Someone yelled from the stands. "Griffins is trying to tamper again!"

"Shut your trap. I don't know what you're talking about, Kendall!" Griffins smiled as he got out of the ring.

"Hey, that ain't fair! There's not supposed to be any weapons!" Kendall again yelled out.

"What the fuck are you yapping about now?" Griffins asked, turning back to look at BT and making sure he hadn't missed anything.

"He's got a club!" There was raucous laughter at his joke.

"It's just a dick, Kendall. It wouldn't look so huge if you had one of your own!" The laughter got even louder.

A man came through the door. BT figured he was around twenty-two. He looked fit and strong, but also scared. He circled warily; BT adjusted to make sure he was always looking at the man.

"I'm going to fuck you up," the man said. The words would have had more force if there hadn't been a quiver to them.

BT raised his arms up at his sides and opened his palms in a "Here I am" gesture. The man charged; BT quickly made a fist and proceeded to explode the man's nose across the side of his face. Blood sprayed out onto the first two rows of spectators. The young man fell over, out cold.

"That might be a record," someone in the audience yelled out. Two men came in to grab their fallen comrade; as they did, BT noticed two rifles trained on him from the opposite side of the cage.

Next stepped in what BT could only describe as a robust woman.

"A woman? You want me to fight a woman?" BT asked the crowd.

"What's the matter? You afraid?" she asked. At five and a half feet high, she was nearly as wide as she was tall. But BT thought she might just be the definition of big-boned. "Name's Betsey, and I have personally ended three initiations."

Griffins sheepishly raised his hand.

"I've wrestled bulls bigger than you to the ground. If you underestimate me, I will make you pay," she said.

"I believe it." BT was acutely aware that Betsey was spending an inordinate amount of time looking at his genitalia, and not because it held any sexual interest to her, but rather it was his most exposed vulnerability. "Wish I could blame Talbot for this, but if I hadn't wanted that damn machine I've got a good feeling I wouldn't be here right now."

"What are you pussying on about?" the woman asked right before she lunged. She made a feint for his face but slid away, her eyes lingering on his knob and berries for a millisecond too long. She backed away a couple of steps. She came in again, much faster than BT figured she was capable of. She took a half-hearted swipe at his head, which he did little to block, knowing what she was actually aiming for. BT leaned to stop the kick she sent, realizing too late that also was not her full intention.

BT swiveled his hips to avoid the worst of it but that did not halt the gasps and cries of "Foul!" from the crowd when her meaty fist wrapped around his dangling manhood. She squeezed tight, then loosened, going for the more tender balls, where she had originally intended on landing. BT didn't even bother to think about it as he drove a ham-sized fist into the side of her head. She babbled something about being kicked by a mule and fell over onto the side of her face. BT bent over and covered up. His stomach roiled its displeasure at the pain welling up from his groin. Betsey began to convulse on the ground and then vomit as two men dragged her out. BT watched as a medic tended to the woman; he was not saddened when the man shook his head back and forth to signify she was not alive.

"Send them all in!" BT roared. "I'll kill each and every one of them!"

The next to come in was a man named Bryant, mid-thirties. BT thought he could have been an accountant, with his close-set eyes and thick glasses. It was clear by the man's stance he wanted to be anywhere but here.

"Please," Bryant begged. "I'm new here!"

"Consider this a favor then," BT yelled. "I'll make your stay short," he added as he thundered across the ring. It had all been a ploy though, as the man lashed out with a kick, trying his best to cave BT's knee in. He'd misjudged and hit low, causing BT's foot to slip and for him to fall forward. Before Bryant could get out of the way, BT dragged him down as he went. Bryant was gasping for air after BT's full weight came down on him and forced the oxygen from his lungs. BT pushed up off Bryant's chest and stood. He reached down and grabbed the man's hand and forearm while placing his left foot on his chest.

"What…what are you doing?" he choked out.

With a grinding sound, BT wrenched up and pulled Bryant's arm free from its socket. There was hushed silence from the crowd and then came the tortured screams from the man, somehow more poignant because of their lack of volume without the fuel to fire his voice.

"Next! I can do this all day!"

Knox, who had been enjoying himself, was quickly angering. Fights were one thing, busted nose, chipped tooth, bloody knuckles. Those were all the norm. But now he had two men with injuries that could keep them sidelined for weeks, and Betsey, his best armorer, was dead. The new recruit had fought three fights and had nothing worse than a little dick-pull. He didn't know how many people he dared send into that ring. The Pit Master looked up to him. Knox tersely nodded. The Pit Master sent the next one in. Knox noticed that the line to fight the big man had been twenty deep at the beginning. It was now fewer than five, as most of the volunteers had opted out. He was thinking sourly on this when he looked up at the ring and noticed BT was swinging his newest victim by the feet before flinging him in a wide arc to crash into the side of the cage. The fighter's arm audibly snapped in three places as he tried to brace himself from the impact.

"What about you?" BT looked straight at Knox. "Or do you just sit on your little throne while others do your fighting for you?" BT pointed to the man who would re-make the world.

"Two." Knox held up two fingers to the Pit Master.

"I can take him on my own!" Reggie, the next man in line, yelled out.

"Send in the two! That way I can be done fucking you all up sooner rather than later!" BT yelled.

The second man came in, but stayed mostly behind Reggie.

"Spread out, Vic. He can't get both of us." Reggie pushed the man away.

"Which one of you two is my bitch?" BT asked. "I'm thinking it's you, Vic." BT pointed a finger at the man who looked like he was trying to be invisible. "Saw a movie once, Vic. Had one of my favorite actors in it, Will Smith. What the hell was it called? He was a superhero...angel or some shit."

"Hancock!" Griffins called out from the audience.

"Yeah, that's it," BT said. "Anyway, there was a scene in the movie where he shoved one man's head up another's ass. Today I'm going to finally see if that's possible." BT moved toward Vic knowing he would shy away and Reggie, the aggressive one, would come in thinking he had an opening. BT wheeled, his fist already on the move as it collided with Reggie's jaw. Three teeth were sent hurtling out of his mouth, one was stopped by the chain link, the other two landed on one of the picnic tables. Reggie groaned, his jaw broken and hanging askew. When Vic saw this he turned back to the gate and tried pulling the door open.

"Let me out, man! Let me out! Come on! This shit ain't funny. He's going to kill me! Who's going to cook if I die?" he pleaded.

"Make this easier on yourself, Vic. If I have to come and get you I'm going to break your pelvis. I swear I will," BT said evenly.

"I'm just the cook." Vic turned to face BT when he realized they weren't going to open the gate for him.

"Not anymore." BT raised his leg up with a bent knee, he leaned back and front kicked Vic into the fencing, cracking three of the man's ribs as he did so. "Looking a little pissed off over there, Knox. Man, if I'd known how fun this initiation thing was going to be I would have come willingly. It's not often I get to beat men senseless these days."

"Tase him," Knox directed the Pit Master.

"What?"

"I said to fucking tase him. Then send the next one in."

"Don't you fucking dare!" BT said as the laser dots targets his stomach. "Dammit!" He shouted when the prongs embedded themselves into his flesh. The current running through was curling his arms up. His legs were trembling and wanted to go rigid.

The next man came in and quickly ran across the mat, punching BT repeatedly in the face until blood began to pour from a cut above his eye. "This will go better for you if you just go down!" The man was raining blows on BT's chest, stomach and head, yet BT would not budge. Blood splattered the mat as it sprayed around from the impacts.

BT slowly curled his fists; it took longer to stretch his arms down. The Pit Master held the switch down, sending as many volts into BT's body as he could, and incredibly, the man kept moving forward. BT slowly wrapped a hand around the leads and yanked them from his flesh. The Pit Master still had his hand on the switch when BT drove them down into the skull of the fighter sucker-punching him.

"Hope that fries whatever fucking brains you had in there!"

The man immediately went rigid, his eyes rolling back into his skull before he toppled over like a struck bowling pin.

"Got any other pansies I can plant for you?" BT asked Knox. The crowd had gone unnaturally quiet.

"Tase him again," Knox said as he stood. "Perkins, Girard, Griffins with me." He pulled off his shirt to show a latticework of scars which rippled from his muscles. "This is supposed to be a good time. We break you in to how things work around here. A little blood is spilled, a broken finger or two, maybe. Nothing horrible. We gamble, make bets amongst each other. When it's all said and done and the newbie is broken, they commit their loyalty to me."

"And if they don't?" BT asked.

"I shoot them," Knox said as he removed his sidearm and placed it on his seat. "We only want people here that want to be here. That want to make a difference in this new world. To become all that they can become. But you see—you're fucking that up. I don't think you're a team player. You're still a man, though. A big man, granted, but you'll fall. Everyone does eventually. No doubt you could have broken the record here tonight; you would have been a legend. Respect from the men, more love from the women than you could have imagined. When the last record holder, Dander, got eaten by the zombies, I thought he'd let it happen on purpose because he couldn't handle all the women chasing him. That could have been you, my friend. A giant among giants!" Knox stepped down off his raised platform. "But now, you're just a walking dead man."

"Get in here, asshole. We'll see who ends up dead. Maybe I should take charge of your little play army here."

"Get our other guests in here," Knox said.

"Are you sure?" The Pit Master asked.

"Do you think questioning my authority is a good idea right now, Bruce?" He spoke so calmly, but his eyes threatened to burn a hole through the back of Bruce's head.

"Harry, go get 'em," Bruce said. The men sitting by the cage door immediately stood and pulled their tables out of the way. Once that was done they went to the far side of the warehouse to grab some fencing material BT had not noticed earlier.

"You'll probably want to know what's going on now and I'm going to tell you. Not out of any kind of kindred spirit thing—I'm not trying to alleviate your stress—I want to elevate it. We're a community here, and in any community, you're bound to get your fair share of fuck-ups. People that just aren't right in the head. No matter how much you talk to them or discipline them they just don't get it. We had a situation just the other day where two of my people were fucking. That in itself is fine, I don't have a problem with that. What was wrong and intolerable was that each of them was married to another." Knox's mood went from explaining to exploding. "We cannot be a proper society if we do not honor our vows! Both of them made vows to their partners and then broke them. They also made vows to me and I will not, WILL NOT allow them to break those to me. They were standing in that cage, just like you, both naked. He cried; she glared at me the entire time. My wife—MY WIFE had the audacity to glare at me after she cheated!"

"You ever think maybe she wanted to get caught?" BT asked.

"Careful," Knox hissed.

"You can't make me more dead. I can't imagine this whole big build up you're doing somehow involves a gigantic pillow fight."

"Oh, in your case it's not whether you live or die; it's how you die. That's what you're fighting for now. There's a merciful way that includes being shot in the head, then there's the brutal way of going out one bite at a time. Build the tunnel!" Knox shouted.

Build The Tunnel...Build The Tunnel...Build The Tunnel..." became the chant of the crowd.

"This really is like a bad Mad Max movie," BT said quietly. "Mike might get a kick out of this. Speaking of which, buddy, it sure would be nice if your ass showed up here really soon. Got a bad feeling about what's about to happen."

A crew began to bring sections of fencing from the far side of the building, they were quickly lashing them together with ropes and chains, making a tunnel that stretched from the store room right up to the gate leading into the cage.

"Zombies." Knox was smiling as he looked at BT. "Whole shitloads of them. They're going to get one look at your huge-ass self and they're going to come blazing down that tunnel like they were shot out of an air cannon. A fucking zombie loaded air cannon! And there ain't a thing you can do about it. Oh, I'll give you a bat, not because it's more sporting, but once you're holding that thing you will actually have a glimmer of hope in your eyes and I want to be front and center when that light finally flickers and dies. I mean, it won't at first—you're going to put up a hell of a fight, I bet. But even you have to get tired, right? And even if you don't, the bat will inevitably slip from your grip from all the blood that's sure to coat it. Then it just takes one little nibble on a knuckle, maybe just a pinch of your forearm in their front chompers." Knox peeled his lips back and clacked his front teeth together in display.

BT looked around the cage and finally to the fence above him.

"You could try to hold yourself up there...might even make it a few minutes. Personally, I'd rather see you fight. You should feel lucky."

"Lucky? Why, are you joining me?"

"No, sorry. I have a world to run. We didn't use to give people the bat, but it was so boring; most just ran around in circles or held onto the roof. It was usually over too quickly; I didn't feel as if they had adequately paid for their transgressions, and it was disappointing to the crowd."

"Are you people listening to him? He's fucking insane. This is the United States of America. We haven't lost yet—we can still get our world back...but not with people like him!"

"Haven't lost yet? That's rich. Everyone here, including yourself, I would wager, has lost a great deal. We are here together because we are going to rebuild from these ashes something much purer."

"By feeding people to zombies? You're as bad as the Romans throwing Christians to lions. And that's it, isn't it? You keep them in line with diversion, distraction, and fear. You're sheep, all of you! Give me my damn bat. I've got some zombies to kill."

The Pit Master looked over to Knox before feeding the bat through a hole specifically designed for that reason.

"Open the door!" Knox yelled. The Pit Master opened the gate to the cage and tied it into place, completing the fencing on his side. Another guard on the far end opened the store room door and tied it off in a similar fashion. For long moments nothing happened. Then a ghostly face peered out and pulled back in.

"What the hell?" BT asked. The zombie once again stepped forward, this time a little farther. She looked down the long corridor to BT, then she peered around, her eyes finally resting on Knox. Then she snarled. "She even hates you in death. Smart woman," BT said once he realized the zombie was Knox's ex. Knox said nothing, but he looked a couple of shades paler than his normal hue. BT stepped closer to the gate and off to the side. "Always liked to hit the high ball," he said as he brought the bat up. The zombie woman once again stepped back, then it was as Knox had said; zombies flew through that opening, rushing to get a meal. BT hit the first one so hard all that could be heard in the store was the twang of the bat's vibration and the shattering of the zombie's skull. He sent it sprawling backward, which slowed the advance of those behind. Loud squelching and bone cracking dominated as BT sent tufts of hair, scalp, brain, tissue, blood, and splintered bone into those with ringside seats.

"I think he broke the record!" someone shouted.

"Not going to be able to tell until he dies," another said.

Knox's predictions were nearly right as BT's hands slipped more than a couple of times and a zombie chomped down no more than an inch from where his fingers had been. After twenty kills, the cage entrance was sufficiently clogged up with zombie bodies that the rest were having a difficult time making it in. BT had a chance to try and catch his breath. His chest was heaving from the exertion, his body was coated in blood, the fluid sluiced off him in thick rivulets. The pile was shifting as some zombies tried to push forward while others were trying to pull bodies out of the way.

"I've never seen them do that," one of the men nearby said.

As BT lifted his upper half, he noticed the lock that was holding the chain. It was a cheap import. He'd seen more bikes ripped off on his beat from people that didn't want to spend the extra couple of bucks for American steel. He raised the bat over his head and swung down onto the lock.

"Big dummy missed! Plus them ones are already dead."

BT swung again; the lock exploded into parts. The haft ripped through the observant man's cheek in the front row. He screamed, mistakenly thinking he'd been blinded. BT took two hard steps and lowered his shoulder into the fence. He yelled out as he strained to move the structure along with the dead bodies piled up by his feet.

"He's letting the zombies out!" someone screamed.

"Shoot him!" Knox yelled as he got into position to follow his own order.

BT made a three-foot separation in the fencing; the zombies, seeing the opening and the potential for more food, ran right through. Screams and gunfire erupted at about the same time.

CHAPTER EIGHT
MIKE JOURNAL ENTRY 6

WITH A BREAK in the weather, MJ had actually witnessed live our bus chase and BT's capture. I was doing better. My guts still felt like I'd maybe eaten something from my sister, but odds were I'd live. Ron had shown up with Travis. He'd brought with him five high-resolution pictures of the store we needed to break into to get BT back. When I talked to MJ earlier he'd told me that the store was a Best Buy and then he'd proceeded to give me a list of all the electronic equipment he wanted me to round up. I'd told him that sure, once I'd rescued BT from fanatical murderers and we were running for our lives, I would most certainly get the items he was looking for. He'd thanked me.

I'm not sure I could have responded with any more sarcasm if I tried. How could he not hear it? The words were practically dripping in it as if I'd dipped them in a huge, wet, sticky vat of it.

"Four towers." Ron pointed to structures at each of the store's corners.

"That's going to be a bitch to sneak up on," I said.

"We'll just wait until night," Tiffany said.

"You're right, but odds are they have night vision. We'll need to light a couple of fires, night blind them so we're on even ground. I just hope BT has that much time."

"If they wanted him dead, wouldn't they have just shot him when they shot you, dad?" Travis asked.

"He's got a big mouth. He's bound to use it to get himself into trouble."

"Sounds like someone I know," Deneaux said.

"Don't talk about Ron that way. He gets sensitive," I said, looking over. We weren't quite on stable terrain yet but we were working on it. Besides, this mission had nothing to do with me.

"Did you bring what I asked?" Deneaux was looking over to him.

Ron pulled out a suppressed twenty-two and was about to hand it to her.

"Whoa, whoa, whoa, man. You don't just hand a snake an extra fang or a cat an extra claw. Why are you handing her a rifle?"

"She asked."

"Since when is it that easy?" I asked.

"I only have the one," he said, ignoring me and handing it to her.

"Ruger...nice," she said around a cloud of smoke as she checked the weapon out. "What about the rounds?"

"Didn't think I had them, but I found a box buried underneath the rest of the ammo. Must be fifteen years old."

"What are you planning on doing with that?" I asked.

"Ever heard a suppressed, subsonic, twenty-two round?"

"Yeah...meaning no, not much sound except for the action of the rifle."

"Exactly," she said as she loaded the magazine.

"Great. So you kill one guard before they realize what's going on. So what?"

"I thought about that when he said he might only have one. We shoot all four with this."

"How are we going to pull that off before they realize something is going on?" I asked.

"It will have to be done quickly."

"I've seen you shoot; it's amazing, like sniper amazing, but I don't think even you can run those distances and get off well-aimed shots while you're trying to catch your breath."

"I'm not running anywhere."

"I've tried that shit, Deneaux, I can't do it either. Gun barrel moves all over the place when your heartbeat is accelerated and you're breathing hard."

"No. You, me, and two others will already be in place. We don't move."

"Oh," I said when I finally got it. "The gun is coming to us. We're going to have a gun runner."

"Mike, Travis is a better shot than I am, but I can't make those runs with any sort of speed," Ron said.

"Okay, I'll take the first shot, hand off the rifle, and shuffle to the fourth location. I should have caught my wind by the time the gun gets back to me. Still going to have to light a big-ass fire to distract them. One of you is going to have to shoot while the other lights the fire," I said.

"I'll take care of the fire," Ron said.

Tiffany looked like a deer in the headlights scared. Not scared to shoot an enemy, but rather that her lack of proper aim and technique could cause a catastrophic failure that could cost BT his life.

"I...I can do it," Tiffany said weakly.

"I'm hoping for something a little more optimistic, kiddo," I told her.

"Dad, what if Tiffany runs the gun? I can make that shot."

He was right—he was a decent shot. I didn't like the fact that he would have to shoot a man, but desperate times called for desperate measures and I definitely quantified getting my best friend back alive as desperate.

"You alright with that, Tiffany?"

"More than." She breathed a sigh of relief.

"Alright, let's go find a good place for Ron to burn and then we'll get close to the store. Only have an hour or so before dark."

There was a gas station right around the corner from the Best Buy; there was enough gas fumes left in the tanks it was bound to make a hell of a blaze. We did all that watch synchronizing shit like we actually knew what we were doing. As soon as Ron lit the gas station I would drill that first unlucky bastard and off Tiffany would go to tower two.

We were all looking at a long, gas soaked rag sticking out from the holding tank. "You realize that once you set that rag on fire you need to get the hell out of here as fast as you can, right?" I asked him.

"You realize, Mike, that I've done far fewer hallucinogens than you. Not everyone is fascinated by bright, shiny things."

"They should be," I replied, slightly hurt. "Alright. Give us a half hour to get into position, then light this sucker up."

"I was there when we planned this out. I think I can handle my end," he snipped.

"That was more for me than for you, Ron. I'm nervous as hell and that's BT in there."

"I'm sorry...I'm sorry. I get it. I guess I'm pretty worried as well."

"Don't forget to swing by and pick us up, too."

"Yeah—I think I can remember that part as well. Get going."

CHAPTER NINE
Ron

RON HAD BEEN carefully pacing the gas station parking lot, making sure to stay out of the line of sight of the Best Buy and not garner the attention of passers-by, should there be any. He'd gone over to the side of the station to take a leak, he dared not open the bathroom door. Those mostly looked like the dead had inhabited them even when the station was operational. He was finishing up just as he heard the crackle of his radio. He rushed over; very rarely were communications these days not extremely important.

"Dad. Come in, dad!" His heart thudded in his chest when he realized it was his daughter Meredith. She sounded distressed; he could only hope she was safe and that zombies hadn't attacked while he was away. He would not be able to forgive himself if something else happened to his family and he could do nothing to protect them.

"What is it Mer?" he asked, dreading the reply.

"It's more horrible than watching your dad pee," Meredith said.

Ron had forgotten that Mad Jack had trained the satellite on them and apparently this fifteen-minute window had been perfectly timed. "Is that the only reason you called?" Ron asked, embarrassed.

"You've got to get out of there. There's a zombie horde heading straight for you."

"How far?"

"Ten minutes—maybe less. They just caught the scent of something and have started to run. We'll only be able to watch them another couple of minutes...you need to get out of there!"

"Must be the gas vapors," Ron said as he looked over to the open tank. "How many?"

"A horde dad. How many does it take to matter?"

"Approximately three hundred," MJ said in the background. "More than he would be able to handle on his own," he said dryly.

"Dad, please leave."

"Just fifteen more minutes. They have to get into position."

"You don't have it."

"Losing satellite in four..three…" MJ was counting off in the back, "...gone. Tell him I estimated seven minutes—they were sprinting."

Ron looked around. When the wind picked up he began to smell the stench of the dead approaching. He had to hope that eight minutes was not going to make a difference. He'd hold on for as long as he could, but what good would it do to trade one life out for another? Or more importantly, make his three surviving kids orphans? He watched the time on his watch tick off super slowly yet frantically fast. His heart was racing and his mind was calmly running through possible scenarios. The smell was getting exceptionally pungent; Ron got out of the truck and stood on the side rail then climbed onto the hood and then the roof. The leaders of the horde were about a block away.

"Seven minutes my ass," he said as he hurried off. He started the engine then got out to hold the edge of the rag. He planned to light the rag the exact second he could spot a zombie from this angle. He'd looked down at the ground and back up—it couldn't have taken more than two seconds—and in that time three zombies had rounded the corner of the gas station not more than twenty yards from where he stood.

He flicked the lighter and was rewarded with a small shower of sparks, but no flame. He spun the wheel again with the same disappointing results.

"You're kidding me with this shit, right?" He would have been giving God a hard time if he believed. In this instance, all he could really do was give shit to the makers of the lighter, who were most likely dead already. There was another lighter in the truck somewhere but he didn't have enough time to find it and light the rag. He spun the wheel again. This time, he did not even get the sparks. The truck rocked as the fastest of the trio slammed into the rear bumper. He dove into the cab and shut the door. He quickly locked it, remembering that these smarter zombies probably knew how to open an unlocked one. Almost simultaneously, zombies came up on either side of him; he looked to the middle console where the extra pistol was and noticed the blue Bic right away.

He picked it up and spun the wheel, knowing without a shadow of a doubt it was going to light on the first attempt. As if to double the mocking, the flame was nearly twice the height of an ordinary one.

"Go fuck yourself," he told it.

More zombies were arriving as Ron tried to figure out what he was going to do. If he didn't drive away soon, he would never be able to. If he didn't light the station up, he was exposing Mike and the others to more danger than they were already in, and they would be waiting for his signal. Without a distraction, the guards were most likely going to notice one of their own shot, and with their superior position, they'd give them hell on the ground. Ron was horrified when he saw the zombies stepping on the rag wick, one even stumbling over it; soon enough one would get tangled up in it and either pull it away from the truck or out of the gas holding tank. Ron peeled off his shirt, he was going to use it to start the flame.

"Alright...what do I do with it once it starts to burn? I don't want to pull a Mike and have no plan whatsoever. I could see him holding this blazing thing and just waving it about the cab of the truck. Probably catch the whole truck on fire. But with his luck he'd escape through the broken out windshield and the flames would magically spill over to light the rag just at the ten-minute mark...that's just the kind of luck he has. Can't fault him for relying on that. Why buck a system that keeps working out in your favor?" He thought for a moment. "Should I give it a go?" He thought for a few more seconds. "Yeah, probably not." He started the corner of the sleeve, not happy with just how quickly the flames were spreading on the material.

"Great, I wear incendiary devices" He lowered his window about a quarter of the way. Two zombies tried to shove their entire heads in—one had gripped the edge and was attempting to pull the glass out. Ron blew the two closest away with the pistol. He'd not been prepared for the amount of gore that had blown back at him. He wasn't certain, and he was never going to think on it again as he spit it out, but he was pretty sure he had zombie brain in his mouth. "There's a turn I wasn't expecting," he said as he shoved his white, phosphorous shirt through the opening. The nearest zombies instinctively stepped back from the fire. Ron closed the window back up and watched the shirt, which had been threatening to become a huge conflagration, begin to flutter and whither as if he'd thrown it into a tub of water.

"Hell. That's not even right." The flame began to flicker in shades of blue. "Come on, come on." He urged. "I don't believe. We've both known that for years. But if you're there...err...God, just give me a little something," Ron beseeched.

The flame had become so translucent Ron thought it had gone out. "Wasted breath," he said, sourly thinking on his words to a deity he'd lost faith in some thirty years before. Until a slight stirring of the air billowed the bottom of the shirt and gave it the oxygen it needed to burn—and burn brightly. Now the next hurdle was that the wick had been moved at least a good foot away from the shirt. He pushed the door open and leaned down and grabbed the edge of the garment, doing his best to ignore the heat burning his fingertips and traveling up the length of his arm, sizzling and singeing the hair. He'd moved it enough that if it burned all the way down, it would be directly on top of the rag. He was pulling his arm back in when the door was slammed against his hand, pinning it between the door and the frame. He cried out in pain, the bones in his hand twisting, bending, and finally breaking under the assault.

The pain was intense and he didn't think anything would make him forget about it, at least not until the zombies pulled the door back off him. Ron reached over with his good hand, desperately trying to keep them from opening it completely and pulling him free of the truck. Two of the fingernails on his right hand were ripped free as the door was finally yanked open. Realizing he was fighting a losing battle, Ron let the door go and put the truck in drive. Almost instantly he felt hands on him as the zombies grabbed at him. The tires squealed as he jumped on the gas pedal in his haste to get away. Behind him, the rag fuse ignited and a flame shot to the hole. Ron's truck mowed zombies down like weeds as he tried to get away. A dead hand slid off Ron's shoulder and gripped the steering wheel, veering the truck violently to the right where the gas station wall loomed large. The crash of the front end hitting the building was quickly and loudly outdone by the concussive boom of gas fumes being ignited from below. The ground rumbled and shook. The metal discs on the tanks blew fifty feet into the air. A superheated cloud of fire and debris spread out from the epicenter, consuming everything in its wake before rising up into a mushroom cloud.

CHAPTER TEN
MIKE JOURNAL ENTRY 7

"HOLY SHIT RON, way to go," I said as I watched the fireball rise up into the air. I knew it was a damn fine distraction and I could barely take my eyes from it. I would imagine the bastards that were about to be shot couldn't either. The guard I was assigned was the farthest from the blaze. I got a good sense he wanted to travel across the roof to a better vantage point; he had completely turned away from me and was looking in that direction. Morally, I wasn't sure if I should have felt bad or not for shooting the man in the back. Dead is dead, after all. I did not move, nor did the barrel of the rifle as I fired. To be honest, I wasn't even sure I had fired, as all else was drowned out by the echoing explosion and all the aftershocks, I suppose, as other combustibles were consumed.

The man I was shooting at reached his hand up to his neck as if he were swatting away a particularly nasty deer fly before he fell forward. He was draped over the knee wall of his tower like a drunk over a park bench. I silently willed him to fall back as I handed the rifle to Tiffany, who was now running away from me. He didn't fall over, but he also didn't call out to his fellow guards. It was a victory. I moved quickly to my next shooting station.

I waited for the rifle to shoot again. It was one of those

things where part of me hoped that gun never came. People were such a rare commodity; killing them was not beneficial to us as a species. Maybe when we were grossly overpopulated war was a necessary evil. Nature's way of population control. Simplistic maybe, but effective to a point. But now that we were clinging to existence, this was tantamount to walking into an endangered species zoo and opening up an all-you-can-eat exotic meats buffet. Who does that shit?

It was Travis I saw sprinting through the woods towards me. I figured it was time to run—that something bad had happened.

"Tiffany?" I asked as he handed the gun off. You'll note: not then, nor ever did I ask about Deneaux. If she'd somehow found a Japanese restaurant still open and they served her an improperly prepared puffer fish and she died from poisoning...well, so much the better.

"Twisted ankle," he chuffed out as he blew hard a couple of times to catch his breath. My son was easily in the best shape of his life, even taking into account his football playing days. I'm sure he could run for miles without a problem, but those fucking sprints, they're brutal. You ramp up the body to perform a task it can only do in short bursts. I don't know if I've ever sprinted in my entire life where I haven't wanted to puke immediately afterward. He looked like he was at that point.

I brought my rifle up; my target was nowhere to be seen. I peered intently, now pissed off that I hadn't kept my eye on him the entire time.

"Left side, dad." I saw the top of his head peak up. Travis was pointing.

My target was aware he was marked. He was showing the bare minimum, looked like I was trying to shoot a damn yarmulke.

"I'm good...I'm not that good." He raised up maybe an inch more. I fired; my round careened off the steel he was encased in. I saw the barrel of his weapon come over the lip, he had an idea where we were and he was planning on returning fire.

"Get to cover!" I grabbed Travis. The man on the roof had a much bigger and a much faster gun. Dirt, clods of grass, and rocks sprayed all around us as he absolutely salted the earth with lead. Tracer rounds lit up the night like angry fireflies. I don't know if he had NVGs on but his rounds were getting dangerously close. We were trying to use a tree for cover that had taken that very year to go on a diet. I think he was shooting an AK-47, though it could have been an AR using .308 blackout rounds. Didn't matter because either of which, I was thinking, could very easily go through the tree. I was about to tell Travis we needed to make a run for it when more rounds started firing off to our left. It was Deneaux and her pistol, she was a crack shot; a real Annie Oakley (not even incarnate...like, maybe Annie was really still alive and had just changed her name to stay out of the public eye). But there was no fucking way in hell she could make that shot.

A magical elf riding a fucking unicorn would have to grab that round and guide it into that guard and even then it would be iffy. What was actually happening was so out of the realm of things I thought might happen that it almost hadn't occurred to me. Okay, that's a stretching of the truth. Ok, I lied. It didn't occur to me at all. Travis had to tell me that Deneaux was pulling the gunfire away from us. Oh...and I'd be lying again if I said it didn't cross my mind to let Deneaux hang out there on her own a little while longer. She was a perfect target standing there, gun raised at a forty-five-degree angle as she shot.

Rounds were now impacting all around her; tracers lit up her smiling, smoking face. She was having a grand old time, like she was in glass slippers at the ball listening to Pachelbel Canon in D, back in the seventeen hundreds when she was a teenager. I followed my way back to the exit point for the rounds; the man was indeed completely standing, exposed, attempting to get a better angle on her as he did his best

Stormtrooper impression. Most will get that reference, for those that don't, I mean he was missing with spectacular consistency.

There was a quick volley of errant shots as his rifle traveled upwards but it was over. I'd put at least two rounds into the side of his head.

"Took you long enough, Michael!" she shouted as she came closer. I could see Tiffany hobbling up behind her. "I thought perhaps you might leave me out there." When I didn't reply she only smiled wider. "A little more of this and you'll be just as dark as I am. The guards are neutralized. Phase two?"

"A good a plan as any," I told her. We'd raided the Home Depot just down the road, grabbed a thirty-two-foot ladder. I didn't want to come up short like we had at WalMart, seemingly fifty years ago. It was strange to think about how much had happened on that night, on that very first night. The problem with a ladder that big is just how damned unwieldy it is. I knew we had to move quickly; there was no way that amount of gunfire went unnoticed. I did not want to be on a ladder when someone poked their head over. We slammed that thing into the wall. Santa would have been proud of how much clatter we made.

"Watch your fingers," I automatically told Trav as I grabbed the guide rope and quickly extended the rungs up.

"Where's Uncle Ron?" he asked, looking around.

"Good question. Don't have time to answer it right now, though." I was five rungs up before the ladder stopped vibrating from the impact against the wall. My son was right behind me. I poked my head over the edge of the building quickly, convinced I was going to see ten heavily armed people looking around trying to figure out what was going on. It was empty, save the four corpses, and they didn't seem to mind that we were up there. Tiffany was supposed to have joined us for this part of the assault but she was injured and I could ill afford to have to look out for her. Trav and I raced across the roof to the access door that led down into the building. I had an irrational fear that it might be locked; I needn't have worried. Once I opened the door I found my answer as to why our little firefight hadn't been noticed.

Sounded like a stadium down there—like the Super Bowl was being played and the score was tight. I knew in my gut it had something to do with BT, but I still had to be careful. I was in the enemy's lair and I had my son with me. Every single person I encountered was a hostile; there could be no innocents. The stairwell was empty and mostly dark; I could see the door at the bottom—it had one of those small sidelights that let some light in.

"Clear," I whispered to Travis, though I could have yelled it and not been heard. We went down and I looked through the small window to the other side of a narrow corridor. I opened the door a crack and poked my head out; to the right was an immediate dead end. To my left, the corridor went down to the employee break room and then the bathrooms. Out beyond that was the main store where Thunderdome was going on.

"Murph! That you?" someone called out from the break room. "You're missing it, man, that guy was a fucking monster in the ring. Knox flipped and is about to execute him, you know, z style. You already done on duty?"

I quietly handed my rifle to Travis and unsheathed my Ka-Bar as I crept along the hallway.

"Yo Murph." The man was coming out to meet his friend. When he saw me his eyes went big. He dropped his snacks as I plunged the knife in and up into his lungs. I covered his mouth with my other hand as I helped him to the ground. What I had not noticed at first was the woman sitting at one of the tables, reading a book, sitting back in her chair, her feet resting on the table. She looked over at me and then to the tabletop. I was dead to rights. Travis came in and told her not to move.

"Make a sound and I will kill you," he told her.

She kept looking at that gun. "Don't," I warned her as I stood and moved closer. I'm sure the sight of me with warm blood dripping from my knife was very comforting for her. She leaned forward, pulled her feet off the table, and did what she felt she needed to. I absolutely could not blame her. It will be a long time before I forget the sound of that blade slicing the ligature in her neck as I slid it in. Maybe I should have tried to knock her out, but despite what you see in the movies, that's much more difficult than flat out killing someone. Sometimes you can hit a person hard enough in the head you think you split their skull and they just shake it off. There is no second guessing when a cartoroid artery is severed.

"Dammit." Killing a man in the heat of combat or in self-defense sucks but it's justifiable. Killing a zombie is a definite, no matter what my inclination. But killing a female reading a book? I think I've got to consider that murder any way you look at it. Travis was already looking the way we needed to go. Not sure if this phased him so he wanted to get out of there as fast as possible or if it mattered not at all and we just had more things to do than debate over whether killing her or not was reprehensible in the eyes of the Lord. I'm not going to lie, growing up Catholic can cause far too much baggage in the guilt department.

There was no sense in sticking around here any longer; she wasn't going to absolve me and if I didn't save BT, then what in the fuck had I cut her throat for? Is it weird that I didn't give two shits for the four men up top, but this one romance reading lass was going to haunt my dreams for years. Maybe I am a chauvinist...although this might be reverse chauvinism...but is that feminism? Can't say I'm one of those either. Shit. I lightly tapped my head against the wall as I headed out of the break room, snapping my psyche back into place. The crowd, in the meantime, had gone exceedingly quiet. And then the cheers rose again. I heard what sounded like a cloth covered bell being rung every second or two or more.

It was a hollow gonging that I'm sure I'd heard before, though I couldn't put my finger on it. Travis was at the end of the hallway now; he'd stopped and was poking his head around the corner to see what was happening.

"What the fuck am I looking at right now?" he breathed. I'd caught up to him. We were staring at the side of an octagonal cage with a fenced tunnel that led into it. It was completely full of zombies and rising head and shoulders above the crowd was BT, inside that cage. He was smashing zombies with a baseball bat while the crowd went nuts. My first inclination was to just come out from around the corner and start spraying the audience with bullets, but I held back. "Got any ideas?" I figured I'd run something by my son first and see if he could talk me down off that particular ledge.

There was a break in the action; I couldn't see BT anymore. I was moving around trying to get a better angle.

"He's fine," Travis said. "He's bent over trying to catch his breath."

"We're going to have to do something soon."

There was the sound of metal on metal once, then twice. BT screamed out, everyone went quiet—I'm talking crickets chirping quiet.

"What's going on?"

"He's broken a lock and is forcing the cage open. Go BT!" Trav said.

I knew these assholes weren't going to like that much. As soon as they were over the shock of what he'd done, someone was going to stop him before he had a chance to escape.

"We have to cover him." Now I did come out from the hallway. There was already a panicked expression sweeping across the faces in the crowd as people started to move away. Then I got it. BT wasn't trying to escape; he was letting the zombies loose. Well, that should make for a fun mixer real fast.

The spectators were between a rock and a hard place as I unleashed rounds. People were scrambling, falling over themselves in their haste to get away from the two dangers they were now faced with. Travis joined me and we just kept shooting. Fish in a barrel would have been harder to hit. Were they all bad? Of course not. Did I have the time to interview them and find out their individual true natures? Definitely not. That they were sitting there cheering while a man inside a metal cage fought for his life with a baseball bat against a horde of zombies was all the criminal intent I needed. Those that saw Travis and myself were attempting to veer off; those behind started to scream as they were dragged down and eaten.

The zombies were loose. It was only a matter of time before our position was compromised. Ironically, right now the safest person in the building was BT.

"We have to get to him!" I told Travis. That made as much sense as wearing a chum suit in a shark tank. We'd moved a couple of steps when I swore I caught a glimpse of the bastard that had put a bullet in my belly. He stood on the far side of the cage holding a large revolver out and it looked like it was aimed at BT—like he was going to make him pay for what he'd done, wrecking his little circus act.

"Don't think so asshole," I said as I sent three rounds his way. None, unfortunately, hit, but he got the message that he wasn't dealing with just the zombies. He looked around wildly for who had fired the shots. I hoped there was some fear and surprise when he finally settled on me. Tough to tell. Insanity burned so brightly in that one it had the tendency to overshadow all other emotions. He'd disappeared into the maelstrom before I could get another shot off. The arena had mostly cleared out of people by the time we got up to the cage; no one was even paying us any attention anyway as zombies were in hot pursuit of all living flesh. We were on the far side of the cage from where the zombies were exiting. I was happy to note we didn't seem to be on their meal plan. I'm still not sure if the people inside even knew they were being attacked from the outside as well as in. BT was coated in gore head to toe. Carrie would have looked upon him with disgust.

"Why the fuck are you naked?" was the first thing I could think to ask him when I got up there like I figured for some strange reason it had been his choice.

"Took you long enough."

I was having a hard time getting past the fact that he was nude. "Did you do any umm…strange shows in Mexico?" I asked.

"Don't make this weird, Talbot."

"Me make it weird? You're the one playing Roman gladiator in the buff."

BT did the only smart move available to him; he spoke directly to Travis. "I'm going to wait until the zombies have all cleared through and out, and then I'm running back into the storeroom. Meet me there. Bring your dad with you…or not."

"Not cool," I told BT as Travis led me away. We circled around the cage via the side that was fairly free of pandemonium. The Best Buy forces were now getting into defensive positions; they had obtained weapons and were firing. It wouldn't be long before they had the situation under control. Once that happened, Knox would be out for blood. I was never a fan of shooting at locks; bullets always did funny things when they hit steel, but I didn't have time to be cautious. Yup…I stopped when I thought that, too. It would be nice to remember a time when I had actually thought to be cautious. This would have been the perfect opportunity to give that a go. The careening bullet wasn't the main problem; it was the zombies at the end of the parade that were. They were watching as I made a new exit, opening up a whole new buffet lane. They'd moved to the front, instantly.

"Jumped the gun on that," I said as I raised my rifle to my shoulder and fired. The tunnel was not emptying fast enough. Travis and I were doing our best to usher them along. There was a chance Knox could rally before we had a chance to make good our escape. "We need to go in the storeroom—shut the door behind us when the zees are gone."

Travis looked about as sure of that as I had felt when I said it. The back room was a dark void. If there were any malingering zombies who had been taking their time, we were about to shut ourselves in with them, in absolute darkness.

Even I had the ability to recognize a bad idea; doesn't mean I would not implement it, I'm just saying I could see it. I shot two more zombies as Travis shouldered past me and into the warehouse section. He clicked his flashlight on just as I stepped in behind him and pulled the door shut. From what we could illuminate by our flashlights it looked much like what you would expect a large room once inhabited by zombies might. And by that I mean it reeked. There was dried blood and fresh blood stains everywhere. It looked as if the zombies had been painting the floor in the crimson fluid.

Large slabs of old skin and incidental body parts were mixed into the fun, giving it all a very surreal, movie-set feel. I was doing my best to convince myself this was just where the studio stored all its props. Wasn't working; maybe it was the stench. We stuck real close to the door, first off to secure BT when he made it here, and secondly to escape if the need arose. This place was big enough I was convinced that not all the zombies had made it out. There were a couple of thuds against the far wall and what sounded like keys jangling.

The battle was still waging on outside, and as of yet, nothing was trying to eat us inside. I opened the door just wide enough to get an idea of what was going on. Once I was convinced the zombies had shuffled off, I yelled: "Move!" to Travis, slamming the door wide open in my haste to make way. BT, in all his magnificent glory, was barreling down on our location. Something was chasing him, but it was like trying to peer around a Winnebago to see the sub-compact car following. BT blew past us and I got a quick glimpse of the squad of zombies fast on his heels.

"Shut the door! Shut the door!" I shouted.

Travis had the "make up your mind" look, but did as I asked. It whistled past my face by not more than an inch—I felt the large whoosh of air as I nearly became de-nosified, if that's even a thing. I leaned my shoulder into the door just as the zombies collided with it. Light spilled in as they pushed me back. Travis joined in and we were able to reduce the crack of light to a sliver. Once BT had stopped his momentum and turned around, he was able to help and we got the door shut again. I had no idea how we were going to keep them from coming in. It was just a swinging door. Sure, the other side had a cross beam to keep it shut, but we were in no position to slide that into place. But then, maybe we were.

"You got this?" I asked BT. He nodded. I looked over to the right of the door; there was a large, flat piece of steel with a handle on it. It was the same as on the other side of the wall. It made sense. The zombies were smart enough to know about a door that could open both ways; they would need to prevent that from happening. I grabbed the steel and pulled it along until it slid through the small handles specifically retrofitted for this device. It should keep them out for a while, at least, until they figured out all they needed to do was slide the bolt back on their side; we didn't have the capability to lock it on our side.

"You alright, man?" I asked BT

He looked down at the blood coating his skin. "Most of it's not mine, and thank you for coming to get me. I should be asking you how you're doing."

I pulled up my shirt to show that I barely had a scar where I'd been shot.

"Must be nice," he said.

"Not so much. Listen, I love you like a brother, but you being all naked like this is freaking me out a little bit. How about we find you a Best Buy smock or something."

Didn't have to go far. There was a small metal desk that the employees used to mark off inventory, and there was a set of hangers with a row of clean, blue smocks. I couldn't help but laugh when BT put one on.

"What the fuck is so damned funny, Talbot?"

"You look like a damn baby with that thing on. Like it's a bib or something."

"I've had a rough night, man. Do you think it's wise to further exacerbate the situation? Wouldn't you rather be decent to me?"

"Oh no, my friend. I don't think you're getting it. Kicking a loved one when they're down is that much better! You've been around long enough to know that."

"It's true," Travis chimed in, nodding.

I knew the man had been through hell, so when we fashioned some crude pants from the remaining smocks I didn't have the heart to tell him that they looked like diapers. Plus I think he would have killed me. Everyone has their breaking point.

"Now what?" he asked once he figured he had enough of himself tucked away.

"Well, there should be another way out of here—a truck access, and I'm hoping our ride is waiting and that Deneaux hasn't bailed."

"She's still here and a part of this rescue?"

"Yeah. Integral, as a matter of fact."

"That's not good, Mike."

"Yeah, tell me about it. I'd rather buy pharmaceuticals from a snake oil salesman."

"You probably have."

"Don't judge," I told him as I started to go deeper into the room looking for the way out.

"Do you guys have an extra firearm for me?"

Travis handed him a small pistol. I smirked when I realized he was going to have to use his pinkie finger to pull the trigger.

"I wish I had my boots," BT lamented. I looked down to his feet as he shuffled them through all manner of organic material I did not want to identify. In the span of two heartbeats from me looking down and looking back up, I felt hands wrap around my waist and a fetid breath brush up against my ear.

"Watch out, dad!" My son was pointing his rifle right at my head. The zombie was holding a pinch of skin from my neck between its teeth, almost like a mother cat will its young as it's moving them. If the zombie had wanted to chew through, it had ample opportunity thus far. As Travis moved to get a better angle, the zombie spun me to stay out of the way.

"I can shoot her, dad," Travis said with the gun up to his shoulder. All I could see from my angle was down the bore of the barrel.

"Everyone just hold on a second." I had my free hand up.

BT had his pistol up. "Mike, talk to me man—what's going on?"

"You tell me," I said nervously. The zombie pulled me in tighter and released my neck. Before I could make any sort of counter move, she whispered a word. It wasn't the word that froze my blood, it was the fact that she spoke one. "She said 'Knox,'" I told them, not moving an inch.

"She said something?" BT looked more concerned than me. "She's a zombie. You sure?"

"Plain as day."

"Knox," she rasped again, this time, more audibly. I was glad I didn't have to try to convince them I hadn't lost my mind.

"Whoa. That must be his ex-wife. She cheated on him and he had her turned into a zombie."

"Yeah...now what?" I asked.

She struggled with the next word but damned if she didn't put a sentence together. "Want Knox."

"I think she wants us to let her out, dad." Travis had not lowered his weapon.

My mind was racing. If she bit me, if she just nipped me, the shit fest would begin. I was open to any options.

"BT?" I asked.

"I can take her."

The zombie growled.

"What about me?" I asked.

"You could be collateral damage."

"Yeah, that's not going to work." Terrified was a pretty good word for how I was feeling, petrified, maybe. Shit my pants nervous. Is that too far? You have a zombie breathing on your neck, whispering in your ear. Now, tell me how you feel. Loose bowels would be the least of your concerns. "We'll go to the door; I'll let you out. You let me live; they let you live."

She did not answer but she began to pull me in that general direction. I went with the flow. BT and Travis stayed tight, firearms raised, aimed and at the ready. I was not at all thrilled to be in the middle of this.

"What if this is a trick, man?" BT asked.

"A trick?"

"What if she just wants us to let her friends in?"

"I'm not sure what you want me to do here? She could have already killed me. Let's just let her go and hope for the best." She obviously understood the conversation; there was nothing I could say that threatened her that wouldn't also threaten my own well-being. I wanted to get her sewer breath off of me. Apparently, the dead don't believe in Listerine. She pressed her back up against the door and gave me a little shake, I presume so I would pull back on the crossbeam, I did just that. I was not too thrilled to be on the front lines. If zombies were still on the other side, I was going to be ground zero. I opened the door a crack; the battle for Best Buy had moved to the far end. Mrs. Knox's grip on my waist loosened, as it seemed I was no longer at the forefront of her thoughts. When I could tell she had turned to look, I broke free from her grasp. She looked at the three of us as we looked at her.

"Mike?" BT asked.

I raised my rifle thinking on the strange zombie girl I had let go in that field seemingly years ago. How much easier might survival have been if I'd just killed Eliza back then? I blew Knox's wife's head clean from her body. I've made mistakes in my life, sometimes even the same one multiple times. This was not going to be one of them. I lowered my weapon just as Travis moved forward. He pushed her body the rest of the way out of the door before closing it.

"Hardcore, man. Hardcore," BT said.

"I'll get over it," I told him. "Who do you think she'd eat once she finished off her husband? Let's get out of here; I don't think I can take any more weird things happening today." I made sure that he knew I was looking at him. Found the exit without any more fanfare, which was just fine. We were behind the big store and we were absolutely alone. No Ron, Deneaux, or Tiffany.

"What's the plan now?" BT looked around.

"To be honest, the idea of getting you out seemed so remote I hadn't solidified this part too much."

"You're kidding, right?" He seemed genuinely pissed off.

"Yeah, because I fucking knew you were going to be doing MMA in a fucking cage, naked, and that we were going to have to escape through a gauntlet of zombies, then into the storeroom where we would be taken hostage by the Mrs. Woman Scorned of zombies. I had all those contingencies planned out because it's about what we expected. But hey man, you're fucking welcome for the rescue."

"That's not what I meant. I'm sorry. I'm tired, I'm scared and I'm dressed like a homeless baby-man."

"You wish you were dressed like a homeless man," Travis told him.

"Nice one." I fist bumped my son.

"Fuck you both," BT told us.

"Let's go. Staying here isn't an option. Knox is going to come looking for us soon," I said as we headed to the corner of the building closest to us.

We'd no sooner made it to the edge of the building and were peering around the corner when we heard the throaty roar of a throttling engine behind us. A black muscle car was rocking slightly as the driver kept pressing on the gas pedal.

"Now what?" I asked, almost resigned.

A thin, ancient, wrinkled arm stuck out from the driver's side window. A yellow, tobacco stained middle finger arose, just as she laid down a patch of rubber in her haste to get to us.

"Should I shoot her?" BT asked in all honesty.

"It wouldn't be the worst thing you did today. Let's just wait around the corner and see what trick she's got hiding in her wrinkles."

The car fishtailed as she tread-marked the pavement with her heavy-footed stop. Deneaux was looking at us, a cross between sadism and ecstasy on her face, I'm pretty sure a common expression there. Tiffany was in the passenger seat, looking about as pale as a snow drift in a blizzard.

"She's fucking crazy," Tiffany said without turning to look at us.

"Get in." Deneaux nodded her head to the back.

"Ron?" I asked as I got in.

"Nothing." She peeled out. I was forced into my seat like we were being launched into orbit. "That's a new look for you, Mr. Tynes," she said as she looked in the rearview mirror with a bemused smile on her face.

"Fuck you, Deneaux."

"Testy testy."

"You have no idea." I was echoing her words. Without being asked or told, Mrs. D. was heading to the gas station to see if we could pick up Ron's trail. It was bizarre having her as an ally. It was like riding on the back of crocodile as he paddled you across a river; you could not navigate without his help, but you knew, you absolutely fucking knew, that once you were at your most vulnerable, say in the middle of the fast moving current, that the fucking reptile was going to flip you off its back and drag you down into the icy depths where it would do a death spin on your ass. Nothing personal. It's just the nature of the thing. It was exactly like that with Deneaux; it wasn't a matter of "if." The best thing to do would be to pretend she was like Knox's ex and put a bullet in her head. And maybe I would have if she hadn't come to the rescue, like, three times already today.

My thoughts were pulled away from Deneaux as we got to the gas station. Well, close to, anyway. It was still burning; the fire had been so hot that the asphalt in the parking lot had started to melt. Black slag flowed away and down the street heading to the storm drain.

"Mike." BT had tapped my shoulder and was pointing to the far edge of the lot by the station itself.

We were all looking at the husk of a truck, Ron's truck. There wasn't much left of it and we couldn't get close enough to tell if anyone was in there. My stomach clutched up in that painful panic one gets just before being presented with very bad news.

"Stop the car."

She was rolling slowly past. She didn't stop.

"Deneaux. Stop the car."

"I can't. Look behind you."

I turned to look out the rear windshield. Hundreds of zombies, thousands maybe, were hauling ass down the street right for us.

Another one left behind. I thought. "I'm sorry, Ron," I said as I put my hand up on the window. Deneaux pulled away quickly and was heading back to the casino.

"What are you doing?" I asked as she pulled into the parking lot.

"What's changed? We still need the bus."

"BT almost died by those crazy fucks and my brother is dead. I'd say plenty has changed."

"Big picture, Michael, big picture. There are still over twenty people in great need of safety and security. If anything, today proves that more than ever."

I heard her, but I was on auto-pilot. Another Talbot gone on my watch. BT and Travis went and checked out our new ride. I pretended to keep a look out. Was going to be difficult to see much with my head hanging down the way it was. What the fuck was I going to tell his kids? They were orphans in a world where they needed more protection than ever. Tiffany got out of the car when the bus's motor cranked over.

"Come on, Mike." BT had put his hand on my shoulder.

I stood up from the car I'd been leaning on. Deneaux was

still inside her beefy ride.

"I'm keeping it," she said as she lit a cigarette. "I'll follow you."

I got onto the bus and took a seat. Travis had asked me a few times if I was alright, but it was like I was at the bottom of a pool and they were all shouting to me from the surface. Sure, I could tell people were talking, but it was so distorted, unintelligible, and it was so peaceful here on the bottom. As eventful as the first bus ride had been, it seemed we were getting a free pass on this one. Seemed like someone actually gave a shit. We rolled up to Ron's house an hour later where I burst into tears that wouldn't stop until I'd fallen asleep some four hours later.

CHAPTER ELEVEN
MIKE JOURNAL ENTRY 8

THREE DAYS LATER and I'd not done much except stay in bed. The house had been a whirlwind of activity for those of us not completely enshrouded in depression. They worked to get what we would need for a cross country expedition. Meredith, Ron's oldest surviving kid, had come in to assure me that what happened to her dad was not my fault. Fell on deaf ears. Melissa, his youngest daughter, mirrored my actions, I mean, she stayed in her bedroom with the lights on for the better part of the week. Mark, his son, was morose, but at least he was walking around and doing things, although he seemed to be more on auto-drive.

"Talbot, you need to get up and check over what we've done," Tracy said smacking my foot.

"I'm sure you've got it handled," I told her.

"I know we do. I'm trying to get you up and active, to feel like you're a part of this family again. And before you even open that trap of yours, don't go into that crap about how you shouldn't be part of this family or that you only get people killed."

I couldn't say anything because that was exactly what I was going to say. She'd pretty much cut me off at the knees. I did the only thing I could—I got the fuck up. Tracy hung around the door making sure I put some clothes on and didn't just fall back into bed.

"Mike, can you help me?" BT appeared at the door just as I was finishing up with my belt.

"Tracy send you up here?"

"What do you think?" he asked back without really answering my question.

"Is this a real emergency or a fabricated one?"

"Follow me and you can judge for yourself."

We'd made it to the first floor and were halfway down the basement stairs when I heard Trip shouting.

"This is a travesty of justice, man! This is just like Saigon! You can't leave them behind!!"

"What the hell is he on about?" I asked as we headed to the storeroom.

BT said nothing as he pushed me forward. I looked in. Trip had handcuffed himself to a box, and not like a heavy crate full of iron parts, but rather a half empty box of Ho Ho's.

"Ponch man! Ponch! Help me, man, we've got to rally the people. Join my sit in!" He was sitting cross-legged on the floor, an ocean of cupcake wrappers around him.

"Trip; what the hell are you doing?" I asked.

"It's the Man, man! Well, in this case, it's a woman. She's telling me I can't bring all the cupcakes to the show! Who goes to a show without all the cupcakes? When did we leave America and move to Sweden, man?"

"Sweden?" I asked BT.

"Apparently, they're a cupcake-free country," BT shrugged.

"Makes sense."

"Is he still in here?" It was Stephanie; she was coming up behind us.

"Could you maybe fill me in on what is going on here?" I asked.

"It's Deneaux," she whispered after looking around. She spoke the name like it might summon the bogeyman, which in this case was more real than not. "She told him yesterday there wasn't enough room for all the snack cakes and he's been down here ever since doing his best to eat them all before we leave.

"All of them?"

She smiled weakly. "I've already thrown a large trash bag of empty wrappers and boxes away."

"He's going to catch diabetes," BT said.

"Is that possible?" I asked.

"You can't just eat bags of sugar and not have some repercussions. Will you do something with him? It gets really bad when he starts chanting. And oh yeah, be careful—he's been awake for all that time and he periodically rides his sugar highs and then crashes." With that, BT left.

"Thank you, Mike." Stephanie rubbed my arm and left as well.

"Yeah, that's cool," I called out to them. "Hey, Trip. Hey buddy...how you doing?" I was talking like I was approaching a wild animal and I didn't want it to attack me.

Trip hugged the box of Ring Dings he was motoring through closer to his chest. I think he growled; bare minimum he bared his teeth at me.

"It's gonna be alright," I told him.

"Is it man? Because it doesn't feel like it's going to be alright. Shit's going sideways in a hurry. This isn't the right timeline for Ron to die."

I was floored by that; we'd got real serious real fast. "What are you talking about?"

"He's supposed to be here, right now, man. A point is coming where you have two roads to go down. And you, you're going to choose the wrong one. And Ron? He's supposed to make you change your mind, man."

"How can you know these things, Trip?"

"It's the high fructose corn syrup, man. It really attaches to the 'sight' receptors in my brain."

"Trip, I need the serious side of you now. Tell me which

road I'm supposed to avoid and I'll do it before it ever happens."

"That's the thing, man." He looked at me, extreme sadness surrounded his eyes. "None of us are going to realize it was a choice until it's too late. People are going to die."

He didn't say who, but I had a feeling he knew. And if the look on his face was telling a story my guess Stephanie was included among those lost.

"Is that what this is all about?" I asked, regarding his sit in. "Should we just stay here?"

"Do we have any milk?"

"Dammit." I knew I'd been close to the well-spring that was Trip. Someday I was going to get the whole story out of him. The burned out hippie façade, while entertaining, was far from the entire picture. Like the boy Tommy we'd initially discovered on that Walmart roof, Trip walked around with a veneer. Sure, it smelled burnt and was smoky colored, but it was a veneer, nonetheless. The problem was he was not able to control it in any useful way. It was not a disguise like Tommy's had been. Trip's was more of a self-defense mechanism, a hiding place.

"I don't trust that one," Deneaux said to me pointing at Trip. The stoner had moved from the floor and was loading another small pallet of snack cakes onto the bus. We'd made an agreement; after some great self-sacrifice I took off a case of paper towels.

"Trip? You don't trust Trip? Relax. He smokes things but certainly not cigarettes; he's not going to raid your stash." I told her. "Anyway, that's like a polar bear not trusting a baby seal," I told her before walking away.

"We have to go!" It was Mad Jack and he was much more animated than I'd seen him in a long time.

He was holding the only reason Deneaux didn't have a bullet in her skull.

"Zombies?" I asked, looking at his face.

He just nodded. He turned the display so I could see; the

screen was on infrared or something, didn't matter, it just looked like a huge blob of zombie colored goo.

"We're done! Whatever you're doing it's as done as it's going to be! On the bus!" It went agonizingly slow. We were as wieldy as a wet carton of eggs, and yes, I know that makes no sense. Sometimes I wished for the discipline and strength of my old Marine Corps units. I was ushering kids on to the bus; Tracy was helping Carol, whose hip was bothering her. Ben-Ben was freaking out about something and was being a pain in the ass about getting on the bus. Of course, the fucking cat was one of the first to find her way on; was not at all surprised to find her sitting on Deneaux's lap. Apparently, demons can sense their own.

"Tommy, do you know what's going on?"

He looked at me and shook his head. "It's not Payne."

"Well, that's something."

"Knox?" I asked BT.

"Maybe...if he followed us here," BT replied.

"Tracy, how are we doing?"

"We're ready to go, save one."

"Well, get them on the bus. We don't have time for this shit."

"I think you're going to have to take care of this one." She nodded to the house. Henry was sitting on the deck, patiently looking down at us.

"Shit." I climbed the stairs and sat down on the step next to him. "I know, I know, big guy. We're leaving another home. I forget sometimes how much you hate change. We're definitely birds of a feather in that regard. But we don't have a choice; not if we want to do better than we're doing now. You get that, right?"

He barked, I wasn't sure if he was agreeing or disagreeing.

"I love you, Henry. I have from the moment I saw you in that litter. There were three other pups there, but you were the only one that wriggled your little ass up and came over. You remember that? You licked my finger, bit it, then backed up and took a crap nearly half your size at the time. Kind of crazy, huh? I was smitten at that point; you were showing your true colors and you didn't care who knew it. A pretty much 'love me the way I am' kind of persona. I could empathize with that, and I still do. Listen, pup, I have reservations about this whole thing too; is it the right thing to do? Am I exposing all of you to more danger than necessary? What good is making a better life if only half of us survive the journey? Yeah, I have those kinds of thoughts running through my head. So, my big furry friend, if you don't think going is such a good idea, then I'm inclined to stay with you. And if I stay, there's a good chance Tracy will as well. I mean not a definite chance she'll stay, but a decent one. Who knows, this could be the opportunity she's been looking at for years to get rid of me. If she stays, though, there's a good chance this whole thing unravels. Then we're here. We'll stay; for better or for worse, we stay. Your call, Henry."

He swiveled his large head to look at the house first, then the bus, then his gaze settled on me. I'd love to say I knew what was going on in that head of his. He stood, moved closer, and licked the side of my face before starting his strange, patented hop down the stairs. He didn't so much walk down steps as bounce down. He sauntered onto the bus, throwing a definite 'fuck you' to all dangers past, present, and future.

"That's my dog," I said as I followed him on.

"Bout time," BT said from the driver's seat. "And no, you're not driving. Everyone's seen firsthand what you do to your vehicles." He closed the door and just like that we were underway. Some, like myself, looked to the house we'd left. I won't swear it on a stack of bibles, but I swear I saw Ron wave from his bedroom window. I waved back. Tracy turned quickly when she saw what I was doing. There was a tiny gasp from her as maybe she saw the same thing I did. The curtain fluttered as whatever was there moved away or maybe a breeze had stirred it. I sat down next to MJ to get an idea of our present predicament.

"Where are they all coming from?" Tracy asked.

MJ had to hit the pan-out button twice so we could see more than just a horde.

"I've counted. There are fifteen thousand, four hundred and twenty-seven zombies," MJ told her.

"You counted the zombies?" I asked, wondering how the hell something like that would even be possible.

"Well, the software did. It would be much too time-consuming for me to do it."

"But you could?"

"Well...of course."

"You could pinpoint individual beings from a tracking satellite?" I asked.

"Why wouldn't I be able to? It's only in the tens of thousands."

"Forget I asked."

"How could I? I have an eidetic memory."

"Tommy, any idea?"

"I don't know," he sighed.

"How could it be Knox?" I was thinking out loud. "BT, when you get out to route 1 you're going to have to take a left."

"That doesn't get me to Augusta."

"Gonna have to take the long way around. I don't think we can fight through what's coming."

Belfast, which was about six miles from us, was completely overrun with zombies. I watched, fascinated, as they were streaming past houses like refugees. Occasionally, groups would stop and chase down the few survivors that still called that place home. Dozens of people were being slaughtered. Screechers were pushing them from their hiding spots and into the waiting mouths of the hungry horde.

"Losing feed," MJ said. I don't think he could have uttered better words. I'd been watching the screen intently. Rage had been building up in me for all those that were being murdered. The horror was somehow magnified—being able to watch it and to do absolutely nothing about it. I'd been looking for some sort of driving force behind the mass movement and as of yet, had not discovered it. Unless this was just a massive hunting party, out doing what deer hunters of old would. Get a line of men, then make an abundance of noise to shepherd the deer into hunters already waiting in position. If this were a campy television show, a red alarm klaxon would have gone off over my head. As it was, I thought my ass may have puckered up a bit. That too much information?

"Stop the bus!" I bellowed much louder than I needed to, considering I was only two rows from the driver.

"Fuck, Mike!" BT roared back after the bus did an impromptu swerve.

"Oh, thank goodness." Trip said coming up the aisle. "We going back, man? I forgot one of my lighters. Maybe I can grab the rest of the snack cakes, too."

"No more!" Stephanie said. "I've watched you eat thirty since we started."

I was about to talk to BT, but I mean, I couldn't just ignore that. "Thirty? You ate thirty damn snack cakes? We've been on the road for less than fifteen damn minutes, Trip. How do you have any teeth left?"

He smiled. You can already guess that I was looking at a grill dominated by chocolate. The bus had slowed, and now stopped. BT turned to ask me what the hell I wanted him to stop for.

"How much time until the feed is up?" I asked MJ.

"Forty minutes, twelve seconds."

I didn't know what to do...must have shown.

"Mike, talk to me. Tell me what you think is going on," BT said.

"I'm wondering if we should go back. I think this is a trap."

Yeah, that got everyone's attention.

"For us?" Tracy asked.

"Not us specifically. I think the zombies are driving food. My guess is there's another horde somewhere off to the other side of us, even now approaching at a run." There wasn't one of us that didn't look off to our left. It didn't help there was a small hill blocking the view, another ten thousand zombies could be cresting the side right now and would be coming down in droves within the next few minutes.

"They could be miles away, though," Tiffany said.

"Or only a few hundred yards," Justin added.

"This road could be flooded with them soon and there is nowhere to turn off."

"Fuck. What do you want me to do?" BT asked.

"I don't know. I don't know." I repeated myself for effect, shaking my head and running my hand through my hair. "If this is a trap and we stay here and wait until the satellite comes back up, there's a good chance our escape route will be cut off from the zombies coming from Belfast. If we go back now, there's a more than good chance we'll end up in a battle against those very zombies."

"I think you've answered that part, Mr. T," Tommy said. "Either way, going back is not a great option."

"Moving forward blindly is not the greatest idea either," Carol said.

"We didn't always have the satellite," BT said. "We shouldn't allow it to dictate what we're going to do now."

"I don't think I've ever loved you more than I do right now," I told him. "You want to move with no plan and half the information available to us. A man after my own heart."

"This is serious." Tracy felt the need to remind me.

"I know hon, I'm terrified. I honestly don't know what to do." I was sincerely hoping this wasn't the fork in the road Trip had alluded to. Seemed entirely too soon for that kind of foreshadowing to come to light. The bus started moving.

"Decision made," BT said pointing to the rearview mirror. Two zombies had stepped out onto the roadway and were now coming our way.

"I hope I didn't fuck us by making you stop." I was standing behind his seat holding on to a railing.

"Don't go down there. I don't like the second-guessing

Talbot. Just go with that sick, twisted gut of yours and we'll find a way out after the fact. You hear me?" He was looking at me in the oversized mirror that was used to spy on unruly guests and teenagers necking in the back seat. Although, I don't know how much it was needed with the geriatric nature of the previous riders. Although who knows? Maybe Howard Lipenstein, wearer of many golden chains and unbuttoned shirts with thick chest hair poking free, likes to sneak hooch on and play a little slap and tickle with the ladies' knitting club.

Like our bus was a huge zipper tab and we were opening the most disgusting pair of pants ever, zombies were spilling out into our wake. We were staying ahead of them, barely, they were coming up on our left side at full sprint mode.

"Faster," I told BT.

"It's a bus. How fast do you think I can get it?"

"I don't care how you do it but you should go faster. The road curves heavy to the right coming up."

He got it. If the zombies were in a line, we'd be steering literally straight into the teeth of them. The bus lumbered forward as BT stepped on the gas. I wasn't feeling too good about our chances when I saw a trio of cars blow past us going the other way. They were obviously trying to get away from something. I watched as the lead car fishtailed and spun around when it encountered a thick cluster of zombies. Whoever was in the car blew out the side windows as they opened fire on the zombies. Can't imagine the driver was overly thrilled with the loss of that added layer of protection. All three cars had turned around and were now following close behind us. Much like World War II foot soldiers hiding behind a tank as it blazed a trail.

"If they get any closer they'll be able to use the bathroom," BT said.

"Tommy, are they doing anything we need to be concerned about?" I shouted, he had his head out one of the rear windows.

Before he could respond we drove into, through, and over our first set of zombies. Blood sprayed up the front of the bus and smeared heavy fluids all over the windshield.

"I can't really see them that well, but it doesn't make any sense for them to fire on us. We stall out and they're done for," Tommy said.

"Allies for the time being. Alright, keep an eye on them. Gary, Justin, can you two keep the older kids occupied?" I asked.

"There's too many, Mike! I can't keep using the bus as a battering ram," BT said.

"Yeah, you can."

"Imagery is back up!" MJ shouted.

"Find us a way out...now!" I yelled back.

I could hear the whir of his fingers pressing buttons. "Ooh," he moaned.

"That didn't sound like a good, 'ooh'," I told him.

The bus started to slow down, BT was trying to save our front end. I'd not been expecting the heavy caliber bullet to rip through the roof of the bus from behind.

"They shot at us!" Tommy announced.

"Yeah I figured that out." I knew why. If we slowed down, so did they, and they apparently had paid extra for the fast lane pass. BT hadn't slowed any more, but he hadn't sped up either. They shot at us again, fairly close to the first round. At the angle they were shooting we weren't in any danger of being struck, but let's face it, any bullet coming in your general direction is totally unwelcome. And if they got spiteful they could easily put one in our engine compartment and that would be about all she wrote. The stakes were too high.

"Move," I told Tommy.

"I will not. You cannot shoot them."

"The hell I can't. You know something I don't?"

He said nothing.

"I like it a lot better when that radar of yours is telling us stuff. Now get the fuck out of the way. If they incapacitate this bus while you delay me I'll hold you personally responsible for all the lives we lose."

"What about their lives?"

"Not my problem. I pulled them out from under the umbrella of my protection the moment they aerated our ride."

"Move boy." BT had come up behind me.

"I appreciate the back-up BT, but who the fuck is driving?"

"Driving this bus, high on...hey, what rhymes with bus?" Trip called out from the front. he was singing to the much more famous Grateful Dead tune.

"Trip? You really let Trip drive?"

"Relax. You looked like you needed help and we're going like, four miles an hour."

BT caught me as I fell backward.

"We're off road and he's heading for the water!" Mad Jack, sitting three rows behind Trip, had his face nearly embedded in the screen of his satellite toy and was watching the whole thing from above.

BT lifted me up and tossed me slightly forward, back to the front. "Trip, what the hell are you doing?"

"Funkies don't like the water. That's why they smell so bad."

"Trip, you put this bus in the water and we'll never get out. This bus doesn't like water."

"Isn't this, like, one of those Duck Boat Tours they do in Boston?"

"No. This thing most definitely doesn't float." I pulled him up and away from the seat. He stayed in the same position as if he were still sitting and holding the steering wheel. I ended up putting him gently on the floor that way before I could get behind the wheel. Tracy had helped Trip up before she stood next to me.

"There's a footbridge up ahead."

"And?" I asked trying to find a way to get the bus back on the road. We were beginning to bog down in the wet ground as we approached the Penobscot river. I was certain that within the next few seconds my wheels would begin to spin in ever-deepening holes of mud and slippery plant life.

"I thought you should know," she said a little miffed.

"Can the bus fit?" I was doing my best to scan the ground ahead, looking for potential tire sucking holes. The cars up ahead were a little off to our left, firing from all sides like pirate ships in high-seas combat with a flotilla of zombies. Just as the trailing vehicle was coming to a complete stop, the sunroof popped open and a man came through. He looked around and jumped out, heading in our general direction. I wasn't so sure I'd let him in, even if he had a prayer of actually making it.

Maybe he was with those quafftoddles, but what happened to him next should only be reserved for the most depraved of us all, child molesters, rapists, and cat lovers. The zombies swarmed in on him immediately, even though he was firing his twelve gauge shotgun to great result. At first, it seemed to be a decent tactic; the zombies closest to him were dead, and were being forced upon him like his own version of bubble wrap, protecting him from the others. But finally the press of so many bodies began to take effect, he became immobilized—his arms stuck over his head as he tried to keep firing, though I think by this time he was out of ammo.

The zombies couldn't get in close enough to bite, so they did the next best thing: reached over the true dead and grabbed a hold of anything they could. Hair, jacket, ears...it was all torn at and eventually ripped off or out. Then fingers began digging into his cheeks, lips, beard. His face was being stripped of meat one stringy piece at a time. His cries continued long after he was recognizable as a human. I don't know why I couldn't resist continually looking in the side view mirrors to check on his fate; it wasn't like he was going to get out of it. And my bouncing view tended to add to the nightmare quality of what I was looking at. So, we were going to make it to the footbridge. Then what? Just vacate the bus? And go where? Certainly not back to Ron's.

I pulled up parallel to the bridge, as close as possible. Ah, who am I kidding? I scraped a swath of paint off from the headlight to the end of the door. The torturous squeal of metal on metal was as grating as it sounds. BT looked over at me harshly.

"What? It's not like it's a rental and you signed the agreement." I told him.

"The door opens outward," he said.

"Shit." I realized that I'd pinned the door against the bridge, effectively sealing us in. There was more grinding and the bus lurched up and down, back and forth, as I repositioned it. "Happy now?" I asked once I got it moved.

"Yeah, ecstatic." He really did seem pissed off about the whole thing. One by one the occupants of the bus turned to me. None of them looked pleased.

"Fuck if I know what to do next. MJ, talk to me." I was thankful that at least in this one instance he did not need an abundance of clarification to understand what I was asking. Normally this would be when he asked what did I want to talk about.

We were going to be encased in zombies on all sides except the river, soon, making us the Florida of food. You know…a peninsula. The bus, once again, began to rock as zombies smacked into it at full speed. There were going to be a lot of broken noses, jammed fingers, and smashed knees in their camp tonight. Driving out of this was about out of the question; the ground was already suspect, and if I got this thing stuck in the mud and we were completely surrounded we wouldn't even have this small window of escape. Although none of that was going to matter if the zombies started crossing this bridge from the other side.

"They're coming from the Stockton Springs area. You're…" he paused, hesitated, swallowed some bile back, and spoke again. "You might not believe what I'm about to show you."

Unless it was grizzlies flying in on winged pigs, I was pretty open to a myriad of things he was about to show me. Deneaux was first on the scene.

She looked for a second; I might have seen her right eyebrow upturn in a momentary flicker of surprise. "I believe the egghead has discovered where the zombies are coming from," she said before sitting back down and lighting up.

"There're children on this bus," my sister said, referring to Deneaux's smoke.

"Perhaps you should let them out then," Deneaux replied.

We were surrounded by flesh eating monsters but my sister, worried about the kid's lungs, looked to me to do something about it. Now, Deneaux would listen to me as well as she listened to anybody else, which was not at all. Obviously we were going to be pretty lucky if second-hand smoke became a concern.

"Is that a…" I started.

"Cruise ship," Deneaux finished. "The Neapolitan, as a matter of fact. Largest cruise ship to ever sail the seven seas. Wonderful amenities, as long as you stay in first class. You start to rub elbows with the coach classes if you're not too careful."

"Yeah wouldn't want that to happen," I said on auto pilot. I was having a hard time believing what I was seeing. An impossibly enormous ship had beached itself in Stockton Springs, which is not really known for its cruise tourism. "What's something like that hold for passengers?"

"Twenty-five hundred, possibly three thousand if they have a season-end sale. Apparently, even peasants are allowed on ships these days."

"It's absolutely impossible for you to speak without belittling someone isn't it?" my sister asked.

"Not the time sis, and don't worry, you get used to it. If you filter through the elitism, she actually has a lot of things to say that are worthwhile."

Deneaux grinned at me with this thing I think she thought was sincere but basically just scared the hell out of me. It was a lot of yellowy teeth surrounded by thin, pulled back lips.

"Even at the high end, that doesn't explain all these

zombies," BT said.

"I think I can," Mad Jack said as he hit more buttons. A line of ships was up and down the coast of Maine.

"What the hell is going on? This isn't for us, is it?"

"You cannot be so naïve, can you?" Deneaux let a plume of smoke go. "There are a dozen large ships carrying tens of thousands of zombies, crashed within twenty miles of here. And they are converging in Searsport. How on earth could you think this is for you?"

I took note that she used "you" while referring to the group. My guess was she was going to try and find out who was responsible for the assemblage and see if she could join up with them. Maybe get in on the bottom floor. Evil internship or something. Although that wasn't really her thing; she was more of a top-level type. Maybe she'd apply for C.O.O. or something.

"Tommy this has got to be too big for Payne right?" I asked.

He shrugged.

"Shrugging is not going to work right now. Going to need a little more, bud."

"She's closed off, Mr. T. You know I'm not as powerful as I was when my sister was alive. I don't have the ability to force her to show herself."

"Does it really matter who is doing this, if anyone? Hell, there could have been a huge storm out at sea that forced them all aground," BT said.

"You keep telling yourself that. Coincidences are for the ignorant and ill prepared," Deneaux said.

"I don't know how or what happened here, but BT, you're right. It really doesn't matter at the moment. What we need to do is get away from here." We all looked down the length of the footbridge as I finished saying my words. It was still empty, and near as MJ could tell, the hill and woods beyond were a zombie-free zone, too. But for how long? The bus was moving back and forth as zombies smacked into it, but we weren't in any immediate danger. The question now was: did we pull the parachute and jump from a perfectly good vehicle? The majority of the zombies were farther away from the action, but would eventually get bored and move on to more fertile grounds; at least that was what happened in theory. These new zombies were about as predictable as a rabid, menopausal, female yeti. Not even sure if something like that could even exist, but holy shit can you imagine the rampage that thing could go on?

"I think we may have a problem," Mad Jack said.

"You think?" Gary uncharacteristically asked. He was keeping an eye on the kids, and to him, well, to all of us, the idea of taking them outside was pretty unsettling.

"Well, I do think or I wouldn't have said anything," MJ replied, clearly confused.

I looked down to the screen; it was pretty easy to see what was going on. "Everyone out, let's go."

"Mike, most of the food is down in the cargo holds," Tracy said.

"Where it's going to stay. We'll come back, hon but for now, we have to go. There's a line of bulkers coming this way; they'll crush this bus like a beer can."

We were about as awkward an escape team that was ever produced. We had babies, young kids, old dogs, and Carol, who was relegated to a cane. If we could move faster than two miles an hour I'd be amazed. We could outpace a snail, a turtle, maybe an armadillo, possibly a porcupine, but in terms of the animal kingdom, that was about it. That didn't even take into account stamina. Henry was as strong as a bull and a fierce fighter when he needed to be, but even on his best days, a mile was about all he could walk. There'd been more than one occasion where I'd had to carry his ass back to the house or call for a ride if one was available. Basically, we couldn't move fast and we couldn't go far. Things were looking fucking stellar.

My hope was that if we vacated the bus, maybe the bulkers

wouldn't see the need to smash it up. The zombies would leave, we could get back on the bus, and we would drive away as planned. That was the hope anyway. I waited until everyone was nearly off, I scooped up Angel in my arms, and was about to head down the steps when I caught sight of the bulkers moving through the ranks of zombies. We had a minute, maybe less, to make some space. I know we're only as strong as our weakest link; that was part of my decision to let Carol off first. I thought she could get a head start while the rest of us packed up. She was about three-quarters over the bridge and the rest of us were backed up like a New York City traffic jam.

I wasn't more than five feet from the bus when the ground under me vibrated. The bulkers were thundering like a herd of water buffalo.

"Not good," Angel said in my ear.

"You got that right," I told her. "BT, pick Carol up, man. We're going to have to make a run for it!"

I might have heard a slight protest from her saying she could do it on her own. That was drowned out by the mangling of our bus. The thing was starting to resemble a huge horseshoe as it was bent in at both ends around the structure of the bridge. The bridge, which had been designed with pedestrian traffic in mind, was beginning to shudder and sway as the bulkers repeatedly nailed the bus. Nicole had nearly pitched over the side with Wesley in her arms. Odds were she'd survive the fall, we were only fifteen feet above the water, but this was Maine. That water was freezing and there was a current. Retrieving her before something awful happened was slim. Deneaux. It was damn Deneaux that reached out and kept her from hitting the railing and teetering over.

How do I reconcile this shit? I have to thank her, right? Then the cynic in me hit full stride. Nicole, carrying a baby, was slow—slower than Deneaux. When we had to make a run for it Nicole would be in the back, where she would delay the zombies for a few precious seconds. That had to be it, right?

No fucking way Deneaux did a one-eighty. I got a clue what the old bat was up to when she turned around to make sure I'd seen what she'd done. I nodded a thank you to her, even if it was all for show...my nod and her moment of altruism both. We were moving a little better now; I had just stepped off onto the other side when a support cable on the bridge snapped. The bulkers had pushed the bus over, so it was resting on the cables. It was still effectively blocking the path, but I didn't want to hang around to see if they figured that next problem out. Bulkers and zombies were falling over the edge and into the water. A few, upon seeing us, tried to wade over, but were dragged away by the current.

Angel and I were about to catch up with the rest when Jess, Lyndsey's son, came up and tapped me on the shoulder, pointing back the way we'd come.

"Fuck." I handed Angel to him. "Get Tracy, Gary, and Meredith." I unslung my rifle, did my magazine check, slammed it back in and ratcheted a round into the chamber. Speeders were scaling over the upturned bus, presumably using the drive train and tires as a ladder. They were coming up over the top. Most were being jostled off to the side and into the drink, but not all, and those lucky few were now doing what they do best—speeding along toward their dinner.

"Not on my watch." I got down into a classic Marine kneeling position and pulled my sling tight, giving me a rock-solid firing position. "This is just like bowling," I said as I fired my bullet down the bridge lane into my lead pinhead. Tracy and Meredith were first on the scene.

"Tracy, find the most secure house you can. We're only going to be able to hold them so long." I fired again. Meredith braced up against the bridge and started firing. "You stay to the right, I'll stay to the left," I told her. "Tracy, get them out of here. When you find someplace decent, send someone back to let us know where you're at."

Gary came next, dragging two ammo boxes.

"Alright brother. There's only room for two shooters; you

take over when one of us is reloading. Or would you rather hand magazines?"

"These are loose bullets, Mike. Most of the magazines were in the cargo."

"Fantastic. I love a challenge. Tracy, we don't have as much time as I thought. Get them out of here!" The bulkers would occasionally slam into the bus, sending the speeders atop it sprawling, flinging them forward like they were being launched from a slingshot. It was close to a stalemate. Actually, we were doing a little better; they were having a hard time getting a foothold on the bridge. We lost a little of our advantage as I dropped my spent magazine out and put in my only other full one. When Meredith ran dry it got worse, as she only had the one.

"Uncle! Give me your bullets!" she shouted impatiently with her hand held out, her fingers moving rapidly in a "come hither" motion. He quickly handed the magazine over and started jamming rounds into the empty ones. We once again pushed them back. But when both of our bolts held open at the same time, we gave up almost a quarter of the bridge while Gary fumbled with the rounds.

"Breathe, brother. I'd rather you take your time and get a round in than rush and drop them."

"Okay, okay," he said repeatedly as a way to calm his nerves. He kept looking up to see the progress of the zombies.

"Stop looking up. We'll tell you when it's time to go. Give me what you've got, Gary."

"It's only ten rounds."

"Don't care." He handed it over. I took well-aimed shots, doing my best to make sure that the zombie going down would tangle up those behind him. Either Gary was getting better or he'd only given Meredith a short magazine, but she was shooting just as I was ready for more. I wanted to tell her to slow down and make every shot count when I spotted her strategy. Instead of head shots, she was shattering knee caps and breaking femurs. The zombies would crumple and completely disrupt those behind, and because they weren't dead, they would also reach out—further screwing up the chase.

"I always knew you were smart," I told her.

"No shit."

"They make it to the halfway point and you have to go, Meredith."

"Won't be enough time for the rest to get away. And what about you?"

"I can run faster than you. I'll hold them off until they're almost here."

She didn't fight me on this; she knew I was right.

"Gary, that means you, too," I told him as he handed over a magazine. "You head out with Meredith."

"What good is that going to do Mike? You'll have maybe ten or fifteen rounds, then they'll be on us all. I can stay and keep reloading."

"Just enough to give you a head start, man. I've seen you run. You can do a lot of things well. That ain't one of them."

"I won the hundred yard sprint in school," he said indignantly.

"It was the third grade and most of your class was home with the stomach flu. You raced Mrs. Garley, and she was like, a hundred and two."

"Seventy-three, and she was very spry."

"You barely beat her, man."

"I've still got the trophy."

"I'm sure you do." I noticed the calmer I kept him, the better he was able to load. Meredith and I almost got full magazines our next go around. We were holding them just short of the halfway point, but it was a lost cause as a tidal wave of the damn things were flooding over the bus. This was something like the three hundred Spartans holding back the Persians. I wondered if, sometime in the far future, there would be a tale of the Three Rednecks holding back the zombie horde on McKinley's foot bridge. Although it was my sincerest hope that we did not go down like the noble King Leonidus. I'd like to live long enough to write my own history. Fuck that revisionist shit. In the movie, I'd be wearing a kilt or something. Nothing wrong with a kilt, but with my proclivity to go commando...things could get embarrassing mighty quick.

Fate sent us a nice big "well how do you do?" just as the first of the zombies was straddling that midway point. My head was turning to yell at Meredith to haul ass when I got a stove-piped round, basically, that's when the expended brass gets stuck in between the chamber and the bolt. I screwed with it long enough that Gary jerked my shoulder to get out of his way as he took up my spot. Now I had to think of how long I wanted to mess with the jam or just start reloading.

"Shit." By the time I cleared my weapon and got Gary back to fill duty they'd be at least three quarters over, if not more. I slung my new paper weight over my shoulder and got down to grab the magazines. Had to be down to about a hundred rounds. I wondered when Gary was going to tell me that pretty important fact. I was having a hard time steadying my fingers and hands as I put rounds in. It was entirely less nerve racking to shoot than it was to load. Shooting, you're active; you have that control. With loading, your fat fingers are playing pegs-in-holes against time...who is eventually always going to win.

"Going to need some rounds, Uncle," Meredith said impatiently.

"Working on it," I answered, not daring to look up.

"Pretty much now," she reiterated.

I decided to do the unthinkable and look. I handed her what I had. I didn't have four rounds in Gary's when he asked for it back.

"You're better at this than I am," I told him honestly.

"Not as easy as it looks, is it?"

"Not so much." I shoved another six or seven in to at least make it worthwhile. We fought on like this, layering zombie on top of zombie. I was hoping to make an impenetrable wall.

There had to be a pile of fifteen or so zombies not more than fifty feet away. At first, the speeders had been climbing over and adding themselves and their genetic material to the coagulating puddle of decayed mass, and then it just stopped. It took us a few seconds to notice, as it was so out of the ordinary.

"Gary, you load up the rest. I'm going to get this jam removed. Meredith, keep an eye on that pile." We were all working frantically, Meredith even grabbing some rounds to load. None of us took more than a second or two from what we were doing to take a look at the pile. When zombie bodies started splashing into the water below, Meredith figured out what they were doing. I was apparently too dumb-founded to figure it out.

"They're clearing the bridge," she said.

"Yeah, but why?" I asked as I finally popped that stupid piece of brass free. We got the answer less than half a minute later as the ground we were on began to tremble. The bridge itself groaned in protest of the onslaught it was receiving.

"Bulkers," Gary said with reverence and a healthy dose of fear. "Last magazines." He handed them to us. "Twenty-five rounds each."

"You two first. When you're done you make a run for it. I will hold them off until my magazine is gone. You guys ready for this?"

"Of course I am. I'm a woman," Meredith said.

"Yeah...what she said," Gary replied.

I let it alone. A bulker hit that zombie wall so hard he splintered bodies as he sent them hurtling in all directions. I mean, some of them literally shattered like a Mack truck driving into a table loaded with fine China. True to form, Meredith immediately starting sending rounds down range. Gary and I were a little too stunned maybe to do much more than catch flies with our mouths wide open. Five rounds in and my niece had done little to slow the behemoth down. He was thundering along like a runaway train and here we were, trying to stop him with bicycle chains tied to fishing poles pulled taut across the tracks. Gary used Meredith's tactic and aimed for the knees; it seemed the only vulnerable part of the beast.

I lost count of how many rounds it was until he fell over; his giant head and face scraped against the path as he slid even farther along. He wasn't dead, but unless food came to him and stepped into his ugly maw, he was going to have a difficult time getting something to eat. The next bulker through finished the job we'd started. When its left foot came down upon the fallen beast's head, it exploded outwards like an egg under a hydraulic press. If I live to be two hundred, I don't think I'll ever get the imagery of that exploding brain out of my head. Gray material spurted everywhere—all over the bridge supports and cables where it hung there in thick wet slabs of glop, occasionally dripping down to pollute the waterway.

Like the first, the knees were the key, but it wasn't going to matter that we knew their weakness. They were making too much advancement and we didn't have the means to keep them at bay. A line of bulkers were in position to overrun our perfunctory defense.

"Go Meredith—GO!"

"I'm not out!" she shouted back.

"GO!" I moved in front of her. She may or may not have given me a look that could turn steel to slag, I don't know—I wasn't paying her that much attention. I just needed her to be safe.

I fired five more rounds. "Gary."

"Kiss my grits," was his exact response. "I run when you run and we'll see who's faster."

I had a couple of more rounds and I wanted to give Meredith as much of a head start as possible; that didn't mean I wanted to watch my brother die, though. Even if he did tell me to kiss his grits...who the hell actually says that? It was time to go, that was the material point. There was a line of lumbering giants coming and odds were good Gary could stay ahead of them, but the speeders behind were fast and deadly.

"Let's go." I smacked his shoulder and was turning to make a go at it. Bumped right into Meredith. "Mad" didn't approach how I felt. She'd lost her chance to run, and now Gary and I would have to stay longer to give her another shot. Before I could release some choice expletives, she spoke.

"Brought some help." She was smiling; I swallowed my words.

"This shit is like babysitting. If I don't keep my eyes on you at all times you're bound to stick a fork in the electrical outlet." BT strode past and started firing the much heavier 7.62 round. The bulkers didn't seem overly happy about that, as body parts flew off with each hit.

"Mike."

"Steve," I replied to his nod and acknowledgment that he was here to help. Known the guy for like, twenty years. I'm not sure if I'd heard more than five complete sentences from him. Tommy was bringing up the rear, hefting more ammunition.

"Let's get this party started," I said as I helped open up the ammo boxes. I think I sighed when I saw the plentiful rounds.

"Only you would call this a party," BT said as he looked over at me.

Within five minutes we had a bulker logjam. It wouldn't hold, but right now the mangled, twisted, and disfigured dead were doing an admirable job of keeping us safe.

"Everybody else?" I asked Tommy when we started loading magazines again.

"There's a small hill about a half mile away. Good sized house sitting about midway up. They're getting it defendable right now."

"How defendable is it?" I asked the question because Ron's had been a damn fortress and it wouldn't have stood up to this assault. Not sure how the expression, all things being equal, works here, but I was using it. I figured this spot was a much better place to keep the enemy at bay. Couldn't march

on Athens if you couldn't get there. I had fully adopted the
Spartan theme for myself.

"It would be better if they never found us," BT answered
when Tommy gave me a look like he'd just eaten a whole
block of habanero pepper jack then realized he was lactose
intolerant and hated spicy food.

I almost told Tommy to spill it, but I wasn't sure which
end it might come from.

"There's more," Tommy said.

"Yeah, no shit. We need to play poker some day."

"A large group of zombies is circling around."

"Around where?" I spun.

"There's a bridge a couple of miles back; we have maybe
another ten minutes. We're just here to bring you guys to the
house."

"How are they damn doing this?" I asked, more to myself.
No one really had a clue. "Let's get out of here, then. King
Leonidus wouldn't have left, though."

"He was betrayed by one of his countrymen, surrounded,
and slain. Do you really want to give Deneaux the opportunity
to be Ephialtes of Trachis?" BT asked. "Let it go, man."

"I really hate talking to people who are smarter than me,"
I replied. Realized just how far I'd stepped into it right after I
uttered the words.

"Surprised you're not a hermit then," rolled instantly off
his tongue.

If you're going to serve them up on a silver platter
someone might as well hit a home run. I was stewing with how
bad the day had started off and for how bad it was likely to end
when we came up on the house.

"Real logs?" I asked. Steve nodded. It looked stout.

Justin waved from a second story window and poked his
head out.

"How's it going?" I asked.

He yelled down like he was listing off his Christmas
presents. "You're going to have to come in from the other side.

We have a rope ladder set up. The bulkhead has been chained shut from the inside. Travis and I ripped down the small porch and deck for the front door—just tore it right off! The weakest part is going to be the back... French sliding doors."

"Dammit." I was thinking back to Little Turtle and how little they'd done to keep the zombies out; hell, they barely kept mosquitoes at bay.

"There were cement stairs there; we were able to pry them a little ways away with BT's help."

BT and I checked out the perimeter of the house as Gary, Tommy, Meredith, and Steve went up the ladder.

"This isn't going to work," I told BT as we looked at the toppled over steps. They weren't much more than three feet from the entrance; a speeder would have absolutely no problem using that as a launching point and crashing through the glass. Or trying to—it looked like those inside were trying to piece together enough boarding to cover the entrance.

"Do you want to roll them farther away?" BT asked.

"Nothing about them says 'roll' to me, but yeah."

I may have popped a goiter helping BT get that thing away from the house and I'm not even sure what a goiter is. The zombie would have to be a world-class Olympian now to span that distance, but those doors were still a weak point. When I walked up to them I was nearly waist high with the bottom of the door.

"If we had more time, I'd love to dig a huge trench."

"Yeah, well, unless you have a backhoe I don't know about, we can't. Let's go." BT was heading for the ladder.

"That thing going to hold you?"

"Gonna suck for you when I get to the top and pull the thing up behind me."

"Not funny."

"Didn't mean it to be."

I made sure to grab the bottom and pull myself up before he could make good his threat. Like so many places in Maine, this residence looked to be used primarily during the summer months, maybe as a rental or maybe when the owners came back up from Florida. Snowbirds, they were called in this part of the country. Usually took off for warmer climates around late October and came back at the beginning of May. Not a bad deal I suppose; avoid the mind numbing cold up here then avoid the body blistering heat down there.

I wanted to do a quick once over of the house—get an idea of the weak spots, where the zombies were likely to get in, and inevitably, where we would make our stand. I hoped it didn't come to that, but that was looking less and less likely. I took a glance at MJ's display and noticed the zombies were making a straight line for the bridge we'd been defending.

"I'm going to be out of battery life soon."

I didn't even need to ask him. I knew the spare batteries were in the cargo hold or on the bus somewhere.

"Don't worry about it. Pretty sure we'll know where they are soon enough," I told him.

"How are we going to do that without the satellite feed...oh," he said when he got it.

The basement looked strong, though it wasn't without weak points. I wondered if bulkers jumping up and down could cave in the thin steel bulkhead doors. And the windows were the traditional small ones, but little zombies could sneak in. Besides some boxes labeled "Halloween," there wasn't much down here. A couple of old work benches with a smattering of basic tools and a couple of long forgotten tennis rackets.

"Get rid of the staircase," I told Travis and Justin. "Just make sure you're on the first floor when you do."

"What's with you and staircases, dad?" Justin asked.

"I'm thinking a lot of tripping. Mom told me Dad was real clumsy when he was younger," Travis replied.

Justin made a mock bottle with his thumb pouring into his mouth.

"Dude, can I get a hit of that? My mouth is parched," Trip asked.

"Just get it done. I'm out of here before this goes to where I can see it's going," I told them.

The dismantling started before I could even get up the stairs. When the zombies came I knew where they were going to make entry through the path of least resistance. We knew they could climb, and those French doors just screamed "Free Lunch!" with a flashing neon sign.

"Let's stack everything we can against them." Wasn't much: a half filled hutch, a couch, a love seat. "Could possibly keep a wayward vacuum salesman away, but not if his quota was down. Certainly not then. Have you ever listened to their pitch? They're some pretty pushy people. When your livelihood depends on selling somebody something they most likely already have, you've gotta be."

"How many have you bought?"

"What are you talking about?" I acted aghast.

He arched an eyebrow at me.

"Two—but one of them was because of Tracy."

"Don't you dare blame that Kirby on me!" she yelled down from upstairs.

"How the hell did she hear me?"

"Don't change the subject. What the hell are you doing buying two vacuums?"

"Tell him the damn truth!" Tracy reminded me.

"One salesperson was a woman, and the other had been a former minor league pitcher for the Pawtucket Red Sox. I couldn't help myself. I got a signed baseball from him."

"Yeah? How much that baseball cost?"

"That's beside the point. Come on we've got to shore this house up."

"Uh-huh," BT said following me into the kitchen.

"I hate to say this, but I think the stairs to the top floor are going to have to go too."

"Hate to say it, my ass. You think that's the best idea you've ever had. I'm surprised you didn't take them out of your brother's house."

"You're right, I am pretty proud of that one. But honestly, man, I don't know how we're going to defend this place for any length of time. They will get inside."

"You know Alex isn't going to ride in for the rescue this time, right?" he reminded me.

"I know man. But these are the cards dealt to us. Can't play somebody else's. Hey, Tracy, we need all hands on deck. We need to grab anything even remotely useful or that can potentially be used as a weapon. We're going to make the upstairs our base."

"It's the damn stairs thing all over again isn't it?" she asked, coming down.

"You didn't hear that one?" I asked.

"Busy with Nicole and the baby. You ever think you should patent your idea?" She smiled.

When the breeze shifted just the right way, we could catch the stench of zombies in the vicinity. As of yet, none had stumbled across our hideout. We kept the noise down to a minimum and even did our best to pry those stairs up quietly, using as few hammer whacks as possible to get the crowbar in position. We moved the rope ladder to the staircase, though I hoped I would not find myself hunkered upstairs anytime soon. It was pretty big up there as far as homes go. Three bedrooms, two bathrooms, and a study, but we were still thirty strong and that was a lot of folks on one floor. We put those that absolutely had to stay upstairs there—the kids, Carol, and the animals. The rest of us took turns keeping an eye on things on the main level. Travis sat at the top of the basement stairs to make sure nothing tried to sneak in that way.

CHAPTER TWELVE
MIKE JOURNAL ENTRY 9

DAY FOLDED INTO night and the night was about as quiet as it could get. Remember how much fun you used to have playing hide and go seek when you were a kid? Yeah, this was nothing like that. Hiding for hours on end, afraid for your life, just plain sucks. Conversation was kept to a minimum. We had no lights on when it got dark; really, the only thing to do if you weren't on guard duty was sleep. We had little food and even less water; we would not be able to stay in siege-mode for too long. I'd stopped staring through the window a while back. Really no point to it now. The night was so dark that unless the zombies were bio-luminescent, I'd never see them until their faces were plastered on the glass, and, um, yeah. I didn't want to see that.

"This sucks," BT said as he came over. We were using flashlights with red lenses, other than that, inside the house might as well have been like a black box in a cave.

"It ain't fun," I replied.

The heavy, oak farmhouse table I was on creaked when he sat down next to me. "Want a digestive?" he asked, I could just barely make out a thin, wafer-like cracker.

"This like ex-lax or something? Because the thought of having the torrential shits while I'm locked in a house doesn't sound very grand."

"Yeah, 'cause that sounds good to me too, asshole. It's an English cookie, you uncouth slob."

"You keep telling yourself that. I'd rather stay hungry."

"Your loss," he said as he took a bite and almost as if by magic, Trip showed.

"I smell Tam-Tams," he said as he sidled up to BT, who was doing his best to move away.

"If I give them to you will you go away?" BT asked, holding the package out.

Trip snagged the package and disappeared as quickly as he'd come.

"I really wanted those," BT said, saddened.

"Did I ever tell you about the time Paul and I tripped?"

"Was there ever a time when you didn't party?"

"When I was young? No man. I don't know why I hit it so hard. Maybe a part of me knew how fucked up my adult life was going to be and I'd better do all the crazy living early."

"You don't call this crazy?"

"Yeah, but that was crazy-good, this is crazy-sucks."

"I'll have to give you that," he said.

"You want to hear the story or not? I'm trying to distract you from losing your diarrhea enabling crackers."

"They are not diarrhea enabling…oh, forget it. Just tell me your story."

"I don't remember dates well—I lost swaths of time back then. Have you ever partied so hard on a Friday that you didn't wake up until Sunday?"

"Mike, I'm pretty sure you had a problem."

"Damn right I did. You have no idea how pissed off I would get when I woke up only to realize I'd blown completely through a weekend night. When you're in high school that's a pretty big deal."

"Not necessarily what I was referring to. What did your parents think?"

"Not around much by then...probably why I did it. No

chance of getting caught."

"Ever hear of self-restraint?"

"Sure. I didn't eat your shit cookies, did I? And I'm hungry, too."

"How am I going to forget about the damn cookies if you keep bringing them up?" BT asked.

"Fine. So it's fall in New England, maybe a week before Halloween. Air has that clean, crisp feel to it. The leaves have all changed; they haven't fallen yet, but they're dry and when the wind blows they rustle around...sounds a little like cookie wrappers."

"Asshole."

"Sorry. So anyway, by this time Paul's family had moved. He's like, a half hour away in a town called Stoneham."

"Fitting."

I stopped swinging my feet. "Yeah, kind of is...never thought about it. So it's the weekend, and I had gone up to his mom's house. He'd picked up some acid—or maybe it was mescaline, we did a lot of the microdot back then. Ever done it?"

"Do I look stupid?"

"Right, I'm not touching that one. So we pop the dot—takes about twenty minutes from ignition to lift off, if you know what I mean."

"Yeah. I get it."

"So we're at his mom's house and I'm not sure where she's at. It sometimes amazes me to think about how wrapped up in our own lives we are during our teenage years that we have damn near no concern for others."

"Not every teenager is like that."

"Really? I'm honestly hoping you're wrong, because back then I couldn't have given less of a shit for the welfare and well-being of others. Does that make me a bad person?"

"I'll return the favor and defer from answering," he said.

"This next part man—I honestly still don't know if I hallucinated it or it actually happened. But Paul's mother was taking care of her own mother who was suffering from the early effects of dementia, or possibly Alzheimer's. Anyway, the buzz starts. A pressure forms around your eyes; vision begins to elongate and redefine objects with sharper definition and brighter colors. Your brain reroutes your thought patterns into new and interesting avenues. You should maybe have tried it. It's never too late, you know; you'd probably be less mean."

"I like me; I don't need drugs to realize that."

"I'm talking about for everyone else, man."

"Just finish your damn story."

"I just fucking started it," I told him.

"Then get on with it. I swear you only tell me this shit when there is absolutely nowhere else I can be."

"Duh. So like I said, it's fall. It gets dark fairly early, so we were gearing up to head out—denim jackets packed with weed and beer."

"Acid wasn't enough?"

"You grow up under a rock BT? No, it's not enough. Sometimes you need a little weed to smooth out a particular high spot and you drink the beer to keep an even keel and stay hydrated."

"Seems like a lot of maintenance for a high. Maybe you should have thought about staying sober."

"You are wrecking my story talking like my damn parole officer. You have no idea the incredible adventures we used to go on, and sometimes we never had to leave the basement. A 'journey to the center of your mind' type of thing. Pretty fucking liberating. You know, I kind of feel sorry for you now."

"You're lucky you didn't end up like Trip."

"Maybe...but right now Trip's eating a box of English cookies, enjoying watching an unlit candle burn while I'm sitting here with a true cynic, deathly afraid for the lives of my entire family," I said as I reached up and grabbed his shoulder to know I meant him included.

"Yeah, I get it. Keep going, maybe we can both forget about what's outside for a few minutes."

"Right. So we're just about ready to go and Paul gets the idea to bring some snacks with us in case we get hungry."

"I get the reason why you might want to bring snacks."

"I'm being thorough. If you're going to give me shit about everything I did on a trip we're going to have some problems." BT just nodded so I kept going. "So Paul has these doors leading into the kitchen that have those two-way hinges so you can open them either way."

"Uh-huh."

"Fine...you know what two-way hinges are. Anyway, he freezes in the doorway half in, half out from the kitchen and he's like, 'Yo, Talbot. You have to come over here.' So I open the door a little wider and his grandmother is at the fridge. No biggie, right? Normal stuff. Until I look at what she's doing. She had a squeeze bottle of mustard and was squeezing it so mustard was squirting up and out like a tiny condiment geyser. And then she was lapping it up in mid-stream like a cat might. She's getting mustard all over the floor, the fridge, and her night shirt. Paul and I are transfixed. What are we supposed to do? We both backed out of there like we had stumbled into our parents' room while they were fooling around."

"Have you ever?"

"Oh fuck no." I almost gagged. "I would have needed a lot more drugs to burn that out of my head. Oh, I'm sorry. That's what happened with you, isn't it? Is that what went wrong?"

"Shut the hell up, man. So I take it you left his grandmother in that state?"

"Dude, what part of two stoned-off-their-gourd teenagers seems capable of dealing with a senior citizen in the throes of a psychotic snap?"

"Yeah, she was probably better off on her own."

"That's what I'm saying. So we head out of the house without the snacks."

"Oh, the horror," Trip interjected, he'd showed back up.

"Trip gets it," I said.

BT merely grunted and would not budge an inch when Trip tried to squeeze in between the two of us. Eventually, he sat on the floor right in front of us. Almost immediately, he peeled off his sneakers and socks and started digging dirt and debris from underneath his toenails.

"I think I'd rather see the mustard fountain again. Okay, so Paul and I head out. The wind is blowing hard and the trees are rubbing against each other, sounds like old bones scraping at their coffin lids. It was pretty fucking creepy. We walk down the street maybe a half mile or so and we're in the center of Stoneham. Not really much there, a few small shops, all of it closed up at this particular time of night. Even the one store we were hoping was open, was closed. It was called Treasures and Trash. For most of the year it had small, handmade local crafts—candles, bath shit, that kind of thing. But come Halloween they had costumes and this huge display of masks that took up an entire wall."

"People use masks all the time to hide their identity." Trip pulled his big toe out of his mouth long enough to say.

"Please tell me you're not biting your toenails?" BT asked.

I just kept going on with my story, the alternative was to be completely grossed out by Trip's grooming habits. "We stared through that window for at least an hour. They had Jimmy Carter, Nancy and Ronald Reagan, Freddie Krueger, Jason Voorhees, it was unreal. I swore they were moving. It's a pretty surreal experience to be in that condition while also looking at an entire wall of faces—of real and fictional characters. When they started to meld into each other we both kind of figured it might be best to move on. It was a weird night for sure. Stoneham isn't the center of the universe by any stretch of the imagination, but it's also not a secluded little villa either. That night there was no one out, no one driving by, everyone was buttoned up like there was a storm coming."

"Dad," Justin said from the kitchen. "I think the storm is here."

"You didn't hear that whole part about me tripping did you?" I asked as I got off the table and joined him.

"Naw...not a word. Who cleaned up the mustard?"

"I was thinking the same thing." Trip had stood and hopped into the kitchen with us; he was holding his left leg up and dipping his head down trying to get at the hangnail he was causing.

"That's it? That's the story?" BT asked in a huff. "You have this whole build up and then you stare at masks?"

"Of course that isn't it! There was all sorts of mayhem and super juicy parts! But I think maybe we should deal with this first."

"What if you die, though? How am I going to find out what happened?"

"I told Tracy the edited version once. You should be able to tell where I toned down the story a bit and you can fill in your own thoughts. If you really stretch the limits of your imagination you might just start to hit on some of the things we did that night."

"You suck, Talbot. Make me listen to your lame ass stoner story and then don't even have the good graces to give me a satisfactory conclusion."

"One of the most intense nights of my entire life."

"I reiterate my last point," BT said quietly as he looked out the window with me.

A couple dozen zombies were shambling into the yard through the thick, overgrown brush that surrounded the place.

"Everyone upstairs." I was walking around, tapping them on the shoulder and pointing to the ladder. "Shut off your lights and go—quickly and quietly."

"We can take them," BT said, following me around.

"Probably, but this is just a hunting party. We kill them, the main force comes. They don't discover anything here, and maybe they leave."

"Look at you going all thinky-think."

"Thinky-think?" I questioned him.

"This is your fault. Listening to your stories about getting fucked up is screwing with my mind...like a contact-high."

"Sure, whatever you say. Justin, when you get upstairs have your mother put the babies and the kids in the pinger room."

"Okay," he said as he climbed.

The zombies had a new weapon—echo locators, or the terrifying tweeters—whatever you want to call them. It was all anyone could do to keep from pissing their pants when those zombies broadcast their signal. It was brutal when you knew what it was. For babies and kids, it was beyond their ability to not react. We figured the pingers would come and had set up the only defense we had, a room where the crying of babies might not be heard. Off the master bedroom was a large walk-in closet. We had hung sheets all around it and used every mattress and chair cushion in hopes of creating a natural sound barrier. The signal would still get to the babies, but the idea was they would not be able to send a response the zombies could detect.

Carol, Tracy, Nicole, all the kids, both babies, Justin, and eventually Trip all made it into the closet. I'd no sooner heard the mattress slide in place over the door when I almost screwed everything up by screaming out. The ping had rocketed inside my brain cavity, threatening to drop me to my knees or put me on my ass. There was more than one of them out there—it was a continual barrage for maybe seventeen days...or the longest minute of my entire life. I had to wonder if this assault was causing micro-hemorrhages in my brain. Like it was getting stabbed repeatedly with those little plastic cocktail garnish swords. Got to figure that would be a pretty bad way of going out. When I looked around, there were more faces with gritted teeth than I had ever encountered at one time. Looked like a constipation festival in full swing.

"What the fuck is that smirk for?" BT managed to push through clenched teeth.

"I was thinking that everyone looks like they've been

eating blocks of cheese for a week and is now paying the price. Too bad Trip ate all your cookies."

I think BT wanted to punch me; then as he looked around at everyone, his arm relaxed, as did the clenching of his mouth. Eventually, his mouth upturned in a smile.

"See?" I asked.

"Fucking Talbot. The only guy I will ever know who, while we're being actively hunted by ravenous monsters, can still make me laugh about it."

The babies were crying, that was for sure, but it seemed sufficiently muted that the sound should have no way of reaching the zombies and the babies certainly weren't going to be startled to run like jackrabbits. After that horrifying brain quivering minute, the pinging stopped. It was like having the sun break through after a tornado had just destroyed the entire town. Hopes rose with its ending and just as quickly were swept away like the smoky mirage that hope was. First one window broke downstairs, then another. There was a distant tinkle of glass; I had to think the basement windows were being broken out as well.

"Why?" Tiffany asked.

I was with her on this question; we'd given them no reason to think anybody was here, and still they looked. We could clearly hear them; it was a vocalization of groans and growls. There was enough pitch and inflection that it was a logical step to believe they were communicating. Mad Jack had been sitting at a table, I think trying to figure a way to get juice to the satellite device. When the zombies began to break through, he had a change of heart about where he wanted to be. That was all well and fine until he knocked the corner of the table and sent one of the knick knacks rolling off the side. Fate couldn't have made the previous owner of this domicile a cubist, nope, this person seemed very much into spherical objects. It was dark, but not dark enough. I watched in agonizingly slow-motion as the baseball-sized piece of crystal rolled to the edge of the table where it would drop to a sudden, spectacular end. The moment it struck the floor, we would be exposed. I was on the move; wasn't going to matter, I was sure to be woefully short of the mark.

It approached the edge of the desk and hadn't thought twice about letting gravity be its dictator. Two inches...just close enough to make it a game, but one with a fixed outcome—like, yeah, I'd rallied late in the fourth quarter during garbage time, but corporate bets had been laid against me. The ball dropped. I dove. One inch—one inch from the floor a wizened, skin-cracked hand shot out in front of my nose; bony fingers cupped the ball before it could strike. A fucking miracle play. I looked up the arm and right into the face of Deneaux who was smiling at me like she'd laid a flush over my full house. I think I finally got what people mean by "my blood ran cold."

"Shh..." she said as she raised a finger to her mouth.

I felt like a child that had been given a reprieve from the monster in the closet as it had returned from its rampage of slaughtering and sating its bloodlust with the neighborhood kids. I pulled up short, was lucky I didn't rupture an Achilles' tendon and maybe an ACL and MCL for good measure. There were monsters outside, that was for certain, but they were also inside, as well. After my heart stopped threatening to break through my rib cage I thought about smacking MJ up the side of the head for putting me through that. He was still holding his clenched fists up high and his face was pinched, as he waited for the resultant crash of the globe. When it didn't happen, he comically opened one eye to look around and see if he could figure out what saved him and maybe take a peek to see if anyone had laid witness to what he'd done.

Deneaux took care of lightly smacking MJ in the head before thrusting the ball into his hand.

"Dumbass," she'd whispered into his ear loud enough for me to hear.

He looked as mortified, as you'd expect. Once our little round of excitement was over we hunkered down for the real terrifying part. We waited as the zombies began their assault on the house in earnest. They were banging against the outside walls, the doors, and smashing every last panel of glass. Nobody dared move or say anything, though we were all wondering why they were doing this. As far as any of us knew, zombies weren't known for their sense of smell. They worked primarily on eyesight and none of us were in view. Tommy shrugged when I looked over to him.

The babies had stopped crying, but I could hear Angel whimper a couple of times as the glass broke. There were some thuds, and I had a hard time figuring out what was going on until Travis came over.

"I think they're in the basement."

That sent chills up my spine. That added a new wrinkle as they were going to be trapped there. There was a possibility the zombies would stop attacking what we hoped they would come to believe was an empty house, but now we had at least two, maybe more, trapped zombies in the basement and they could communicate telepathically. Not far, was the general consensus, but we also weren't sure. Killing them before they could get a distress signal out was going to be tricky. One problem at a time, though. We weren't anywhere near crossing that bridge just yet. The noise around the house began to ease, subside, then it just about stopped. I thought I was going to be able to catch a breath, then I heard what could only be described as a bull elephant in full-on attack mode coming through the brush.

Trees were snapping, the ground was shaking, footfalls as loud as thunder were approaching on the gallop. There was no need to say anything; bulkers were coming. At what point were we going to have to fight? Still didn't know if they knew we were here or they were just bored and on an exploratory mission. I don't know if that made what was happening better or worse. Food was scarce for them and having to find new and unique ways to attain nourishment was how brain power has developed in predators since the dawn of life. There was no reason to think this was not going to happen with the zombies as well. What clever and frightening methods would they evolve over the next few years, after the earth was basically scoured of human life?

Add to that, the problem that the evolutionary rate of the zombies was parallel to that of the virus they housed; they evolved so quickly. Not only had the shit been produced, it had been stepped in warm and then smeared across a priceless, irreplaceable Persian rug. The first shuddering impact shook the house to its very foundation. I wouldn't have been surprised if the bulker had actually shifted the entire structure. More cry outs from the kids in the closet...or maybe it was me. Those of us that had not been sitting down were now basically on all fours trying to keep a semblance of balance as another impact shook us. When I almost teetered over from the next hit I figured getting on my ass was warranted. Dust and plaster rained down on us as the house was tortured; wood splintered and groaned as it was twisted out of shape.

Windows on the second floor imploded as the house was warped enough to force them out of shape. I had to wonder if they were destroying this place just so humans couldn't seek shelter in it some time in the future. Other than that weak argument I couldn't figure out their motivation. There was one final smashing by the bulkers and then all was quiet, I mean except for the house, which was trying to find a new balance with itself now that it had suffered a significant amount of structural damage. Anything that had still managed to stay on the walls up to this point finally let go; sounded like all of the kitchen cabinets with their full complement of dishes shattered across the tile floor. I didn't think any more fear-adrenaline could have been squeezed out of me up until that point. Yeah, I was wrong.

I could only hope the zombies thought the sound was a result of their actions and not people, otherwise, they would certainly resume their activities until they had us. I blew out the gust of air I was holding when one final ping pierced my skull. I would not have been surprised in the least if I had brains leaking out of my nose. Then there was quiet again. Nobody moved, nobody coughed; even though there was enough dust floating around to clog up a coke-head's nostrils. The silence was heavy, like a wet woolen cloak. It was not welcome in the least. The zombies were doing nothing except waiting for us to show ourselves, but fortunately we were on to them. Not sure how long we held that frozen standoff. We were the rabbit hiding in his hole while the wolf waited at the mouth of the warren. It was every bit that picture. If I thought about it hard enough, I could even imagine the long ribbons of drool dropping down and onto that poor rabbit's face, too scared to even wipe them away.

Finally, imperceptibly at first, the weight of the hush began to lighten. It had to be an extra-sensory thing, because at no time did we hear them leave. When Travis shifted to look through the broken window, he told us they were gone.

"What the fuck?" BT asked in a hushed voice, as he stood, then reached out to help me up.

I knocked lightly on the closet door. "It's over." By this time the sun was beginning its journey up the eastern sky. Figuring out how the hell and where the hell we were going to go was a pretty big decision, yet everyone here looked exactly like the refugees we were, none had slept in over twenty-four hours: hungry, thirsty, uncertain. We had to move; there was no way we could stay here, but trekking an entire troop this slow and unwieldy was not going to work. Some were going to have to stay behind while we secured a new ride. We checked out the basement, something had been there but it must have gone out the same way it came in. There was no sign of it, save the slimy blood trail it had left.

"Ten miles, Mike. We didn't make it ten miles," BT said to me as we looked out over the landscape we needed to cover.

"That's one way to look at it, but just imagine if we had stayed at Ron's." I gave him that one to think on, though I really had no idea how that place had faired. MJ's magic box was out of commission. I don't know if it was fate, kismet, or just bad fucking luck but we definitely needed to know if those cruise ships just washed up on their own or were they steered here by some, as of yet undisclosed, enemy. Talk about overkill. Sort of like the nuclear option. Sort of like my wife I suppose. Tracy wasn't much into fighting. Well, back that up—she wasn't much into losing. And I would tell her that because she would go straight for the nuclear option. Imagine coming into a fight with a knife and your opponent has a thermo-nuclear device. That's my wife, and apparently our newest enemy. Stood to reason that she was more than likely of the female persuasion.

"Where are we going to get another bus?" he asked, breaking my reverie.

"Might have to go down to the school and get one; less comfortable and no bathroom but we certainly can't risk another jaunt into Bangor."

"You think this is Knox's doing?"

"I don't. This is something different. It smells of Payne, though I'm not even sure how she could have pulled it off. I'd say, Eliza, if I hadn't seen her die."

"When are we leaving?"

"I'd like to give the zombies a little more head start—I have no desire to run into any of them. Has to be soon, though. The babies and the kids are going to need supplies."

"Yeah, I'm hungry too."

"Sure you are. I'm sure it takes a buffet to keep you going."

"Fuck you, Mike."

"Can you imagine if you were a zombie? No one would be safe, you'd be like that chicken wing eating champion—what was his name?"

"Kobiashi!" Trip chimed in.

"Yeah Kobiashi. You'd be shoving people, whole people, into your mouth and stripping them clean of meat, just pulling the skeletons out intact. Sure, it would be disgustingly gross, but on the other end of the spectrum, it would be fascinating and comparatively tidy. A zombie cult would probably form around you, deifying your prowess to eat."

"You done?"

"I'm getting there." I'd pretty much petered out by now and BT looked like he might be ready to physically shut me up anyway, so when Riley came and barked at me, I figured that was as good a time as any to withdraw. "What are you doing, pretty girl?" I asked as I petted the side of her muzzle. I saw a concerned look on my sister's face as I followed Riley around the corner. Lyndsey was holding Zachary, the baby Jess had brought with her.

"He seems flushed," my sister said.

"Is he sick?" That was a concern; not only for him, but for everyone else as well. It's one thing when an illness runs through a household. Mom and dad might miss a day or two from work, the kids miss some school but get to watch plenty of daytime television, by the end of the week it's usually business as usual. In an apocalyptic world, being sick could get you dead much easier. "Is it a cold or a fever?"

"I don't know, Mike. I missed my medical degree by this much." She held her pointer just away from her thumb.

"Sucks growing up in a family that runs completely on sarcasm," I replied.

"Keep him as far away from the others as you can. We're so jammed up in here we have to do our best to contain it."

"New plan," I told BT when he came to see what was going on. "We're heading out now."

"I'd like to come," my sister said.

"Are you sure, sis?" I wasn't keen on this new development. She was untested in this shitfest and I just wanted to secure a ride and get everyone to a semblance of safety as smoothly as possible.

"If she goes, so do I." It was Steve, her husband. Super nice guy, but about as handy as an earthworm. That make sense? Alright, I'll go for a practical explanation that will kind of show you how his mind may or may not work. If you are holed up in a facility with a kitchen, please go to it now. Walk over to the sink and open up the cabinet below it. That poor piece of plywood on the bottom shelf is probably exposed to more leaking water than any other place in the entire house. Now in Steve's home, that's more than usual because that's what happens when you use chewing gum as plumber's putty. Don't ask me why; I couldn't give you an answer. So suffice it to say that shelf got waterlogged and began to bow. It got so bad that the shelf looked more like a bowl and was resting against the sub floor.

A normal, fairly competent homeowner first fixes the leak. Steve did not. Second, a normal homeowner removes the completely obliterated piece of saturated particle board and replaces it with a brand new one, after making sure that there is no accumulation of mold anywhere near the area where water has been sitting. Strike two. Now you're sitting there trying to figure out what Steve did. Well, I'm going to tell you. He took a five-gallon bucket of drywall spackling, which he bought specifically for this task, and filled the hole in. Yup. You heard that right. He scooped out great big globs of the compound and did his best to fill in the hole. Now in some weird form of logic, this makes sense, I guess. But...and yes, there's a but, he didn't even smooth it out. It went from a meteor crater to what could only be described as a diorama of the Swiss Alps under there.

When an actual plumber was finally called in to fix things, he had to get a helper to remove cabinetry so they could remove the board that now weighed in excess of fifty pounds. And—oh yeah, he also had to get a mold mitigation company in there. Steve had figured if he just covered the problem up it would go away. So, let's see. Three dollars for putty, six fifty for a piece of plywood, a buck or two for some bleach...the job wound up costing him four and a half grand (plus the money for the chewing gum and the spackle), and he still doesn't see what he did wrong. So yeah, I was a little hesitant to bring him along. The chances he would stick gravel in the magazine well when he ran out of ammunition were pretty high. Oh, and just so we're clear, Steve is a highly intelligent man. He's an engineer, more book smarts than any person I know but he just skipped the common sense-issuing line; probably hit the men's room then got a smoothie.

BT and I gave a sidelong glance at each other. This wasn't exactly an assemblage of the A-Team. In hindsight, I wish I'd done things differently and told them to stay, but she's still my older sister and I'd spent years suffering her telling me how things were going to happen. Old habits die hard...unfortunately, it's not so difficult for people.

Mad Jack came to me with a very detailed hand-drawn map of the area.

"What's this?" I asked him.

"That's a fairly accurate representation of where we are, within a ten-mile radius."

"You drew this?" I asked, amazed at the level of detail.

"I admit it's not my finest—and some of the scale is off...but I am ninety-five percent confident that everything on there is where it should be."

"Only ninety-five?" I was giving him crap, obviously his map was invaluable.

"I regret that. Another five minutes of battery life and I could have had it up to ninety-nine, because, well, no one is perfect no matter how hard they strive to be."

"No worries, MJ I'm thinking ninety-five is going to be fine. Want a kiss?"

"I most certainly do not."

"Just a little one, it won't mean nothing. Just the start of a wonderful bromance. I won't even say anything to Tracy."

"Won't tell Tracy any what thing?" my wife asked. "Are you making the poor man uncomfortable with your overt gestures?" she asked. "Did you know, Mad Jack that I had to marry him because he pestered me so much with his advances? I've seen less aggressive sharks during a feeding frenzy."

"Or possibly a honey badger as it suffers through hundreds

of bee stings for a little drop of honey," Mad Jack said getting in on the Mike bashing, but I think it may have been his idea of a compliment to Tracy. "They are commonly known as the most aggressive animal on the planet, almost stupidly aggressive, as they will even take on a full-grown lion for a meal."

"Wow, that flipped fast—even for you, Talbot," BT said, taking the map out of my hands. "There's a construction yard not more than three miles from here."

"That beats heading to Searsport High School by five miles. Gonna suck for those that have to ride in the back of a truck, but it will only be until we can find an RV dealership or something. I'm done with buses. Let's get this show on the road," I said.

It was the four of us: Steve, Lyndsey, BT, and myself. We had to make it three miles—that was it. I didn't even bother asking myself "what's the worst that could happen?" One or more of us could die; one or more of us could be captured. The house we were leaving could be attacked, fucking Somali pirates might come ashore after raiding the valuables left on the cruise ships. Who the fuck knows these days?

We'd gone a good mile when I got the thought to ask Steve if he'd brought extra ammunition. There were just things I didn't think I needed to ask people, not nowadays. I wouldn't ask a mountain climber if he brought rope, or a scuba diver if she'd put oxygen in her tanks. These were things that people should already know. Our first indication of trouble was his response.

"Extra?"

I was about as close to railing on him as I could be, especially since the sink fiasco was fresh in my memory. Was going to use the whole "This ain't the fucking movies, dumbshit! You do not have an unlimited supply of rounds in that one magazine." But what was the point? It was too damned late now.

"You want to turn around?" BT asked.

"No. We're too far in now; let's keep going." I'd been presented with another open door to walk through. Instead, I closed it.

Besides walking all that way with clenched butt cheeks, it was a fairly enjoyable walk. At least we were out of that dark house. I was that close to being able to take a full breath when the first ill breeze rankled across our noses.

"How far you think we are?" I asked BT, doing a quick scan of our immediate area.

"According to MJ's map it should be right around that small hill, so, half a mile at the most."

"Time to pick up the pace," I said.

"Mike, I have bad knees." Steve took this exact moment to refresh my memory.

I wanted to punch him in the head, I really did. That was the first and strongest impulse I had. It's not that he had bad knees, those things happen. But why in fuck's name would you volunteer for a foot mission with a high degree of probability that you're going to have to run? My sister must have seen my less than poker face.

"We'll bring up the rear," she said.

"BT help me. We'll support him so we can get moving. They're close."

Steve made a modicum of protest. "I can do it, I can," he said when we were just about to get into position.

"Let us help you, Steve. This isn't a man-pride thing is it?" I asked.

"Like you're one to give anyone shit about that," BT snorted.

"I'm fine, Mike. I'm fine." He had his hand up as if to ward us off.

I wanted to ask why the hell he'd brought up his knee problems if he was "fine." I kept a close eye on him as we headed off. He had a bit of a gimp in his stride, but there was no telltale wincing with his steps and more importantly, he kept pace. It wasn't five minutes later that we were staring at a huge, rock quarry pit. A front-end loader and a dump truck were sitting at the very bottom.

"Not a fan Mike," BT said as he reacted to what I was thinking.

There was one way down; the walls weren't quite sheer, but close, and the loose shale made climbing down, and certainly back up, out of the question.

"What if they don't work?" Steve asked.

"Yeah, that would suck too," I told him. I seemed to be stuck in this continuous loop of looking at the truck, back to the scree-lined walls, around the surrounding area, repeat. It was my brilliant sister that was actually walking the perimeter of the pit to find the trail leading down.

"I don't think we should all go down," BT said as we stood at the top.

I looked over to Steve who was bent over rubbing his knee. Lyndsey had stopped to see how he was doing. Climbing at that pitch, down, back up—the exertion would be extreme on everyone's knees. If we were unsuccessful landing a ride, it would make the five miles back excruciating for him. It was up to BT or myself; one of us had to stay to watch over them and the other had to check the truck.

"I got this," BT said when he saw me struggling with what to do.

"We've got your back."

"Well you do, and that's all that's ever mattered," he said quietly.

Everything was going fairly well as I watched BT wind his way down. I'd randomly catch whiffs of zombie but as of yet, none of us had spotted any. Steve seemed to have worked out whatever kink was ailing him. I was noticing that my sister was looking relatively fierce. She'd always been sort of a girlie girl. With three older brothers to look out for her, she'd very rarely had to worry about outside threats and she'd grown up a bit sheltered. Nothing wrong with it; she'd always worked hard for the things she had in life. She liked shoes, purses, all that stuff, she always looked like she was getting ready for a gala—again nothing wrong with that. But right now she looked like she could have been a guerrilla fighter; a rebel kicking ass in the jungles of Cuba. She had on a green military jacket, hair in a messy bun tucked underneath a Cardinals baseball cap, I would have to ask her about that at some point. She was wearing camouflage cargo pants cinched with a web belt and boots. I don't think they were military standard issue, and they had ragged pink laces, but they were perfectly acceptable for fighting. I hoped it wasn't all for show.

Then the turn for the worse came. Far distant explosions. In and of themselves? Nothing to overly worry about. They weren't in the direction of the house we were at, and nowhere close—the problem was the damned noise attracted all manner of predators.

"Fuck." I looked up to a small rise to our left, a lone figure was looking down at us. I looked into the pit, BT was roughly three-quarters down. "Company!" I shouted down. He looked around but he didn't have any line of sight to see much more than us. He started picking his way down a little faster. Wasn't sure if that was the direction I would have had him go. The one figure became three, then five. They were all just standing there looking at us, five became ten, each one of them that showed increased the fear in my belly. At this point, all three of us were staring back. When ten became twenty I knew we had to do something.

"BT—we're going to be in real trouble up here...soon."

"Zombie?" he asked.

"I'm thinking so, but they're too far to tell and they're just standing there looking back." The acoustics in the bowl were pretty damn good; I was happy not to have to yell and my message was still being received without any distortion.

"How many?" He was now chugging along to get to the bottom.

"I'm gonna say thirty."

"Go, Mike. Make a run for it!"

"I'm not leaving you here."

He stopped and turned. "If you come down here and neither of these machines works we're all dead. If you take off, they'll probably follow you. None of them are coming down here, and I'll be hiding."

"You son of a bitch. You figured this all out."

"Of course. I'm not you. Now get the fuck out of here—get safe. I'll meet you back at the house."

I waved. We had to go. He was right; they wouldn't go down the hole if there was no reason to.

"Steve, we have to run again."

He didn't give me a smile and a big thumbs up but he also didn't complain about it. It's the small victories you have to take.

We hadn't gone far when I decided to take a look behind us. The zombie numbers had swelled. They took up pretty much the entire top of the hill they were standing on. A couple had started coming down; the pursuit was on.

"Steve, we're going to have to burn in another gear."

He turned to look where I had and to his credit, he notched it up. We played run, hide, and evade for most of the day. The idea was to keep the zombies from flanking around and surrounding us. No matter how many times I deviated off course, they followed like a Sidewinder missile. The thirty that initially started the pursuit had swelled in numbers up into the hundreds, maybe more—I'd not gotten an accurate census. We rested when we could but those breaks were getting fewer and farther between. Our only chance involved the woods. Our going would be slower, but so would theirs. One thing I knew, we couldn't lead them back to the fort.

It was twilight outside, so within the confines of the forest, it was much closer to night. A ground fog swirled around our feet, leaving eddies as we ran. Steve was off to the right, my sister was straight ahead of me. We made separation from the main group and were now running for our lives, to stay ahead and away. Lyndsey was breathing heavily, she was in great shape and had even run for fitness back before. Things are different though, when you're running for your life. Adrenaline can be your friend, but after a while it begins to become an enemy—calling in too much, too quickly on its loan of strength and endurance.

I was under the belief that the zombies were trying to separate us. Divide and conquer shit. They were assuming top-predator qualities and I was not a fucking fan. The pursuit was heaviest from behind, but I would periodically stop and give them a few rounds...something to think about, perhaps. The problem was the runners creeping up on our sides. There was no doubt in my mind that eventually we would be surrounded. My sister could go on a while, but the real problem was Steve. He'd had knee replacement surgery the year before the zombies came. Running around like a track star wasn't really in the cards for him; another stellar decision, letting him come along.

My sister was small enough that when the time came I could pick her up and run for, I don't know, at least a little ways, but not while her husband lived. She would never leave him behind. I don't know if I was more pissed that he kept hobbling along or not. There was a strange translucent color to the woods as we ran. There were distant gunshots as some other group fought; they would be no help to us. Our drama would be long over, one way or the other, before they could find their way to us, and then what? Would they be another foe to battle? The fear was palpable; it was a demon in its own right, one that threatened to overtake us.

"Mike...." my sister said it all in that one word; that she'd labored so hard to issue the utterance let me know she had pushed to her limits. For a good long while there was only the sounds of people running through the woods, leaves rustling, fallen branches breaking, grunts and growls of those chasing us, our curses hissed through clenched jaws as uneven ground threatened to turn an ankle or hyperextend a knee. Either would be a fatal injury right now. I'd stop again and give her some more running room, but that would not slow the ones already abreast of us. I whipped my head to Steve, his .45 sounded explosively loud in the relative silence of our flight for life. A zombie had come dangerously close to dragging him down.

His limp was much more pronounced, in a couple hundred more yards, he'd be dragging his bad leg behind him. He'd always said that training for and running in the Boston marathon had been among his biggest achievements and biggest regrets in life. He'd finished that grueling race, but at the expense of the health of his knees. Steve was six feet tall and built more like a lumberjack than the prototypical whip strong long-distance runner. The cumulated effect of running those distances with that much weight had worn away his cartilage; for a few years he had actually been bone on bone until his surgery. He was only two months away from having his other leg worked on when the zombies threw a wrench in those plans.

If it had been a little quieter I probably could have heard the grind of his bones like seeds in a mortar and pestle. He didn't want to die, and he wanted to protect his wife, but the longer he lingered the less likely he was going to be able to do the latter—the former was damn near a foregone conclusion. We'd kept on for another half an hour; it was getting difficult to navigate. My face was a criss-cross latticework of cuts from branches scraping across my face. The time would come when I would run eye first into a branch and scramble what little brain I had left. There was a loud "oomph" from Lyndsey, as her shoulder took the brunt of the impact from an unyielding tree. That was compounded when I ran up on her heel; I'd had to reach out and grab her by the arm before she fell over. I was half dragging her as I kept moving.

"Where's Steve?" she asked breathlessly.

"Side," I said tersely. "And behind," I finally added.

"Save him." She'd put her hand on my arm and was pulling on it when we heard him scream out. I turned just as four rapid shots came from his weapon. He'd taken three zombies out but at least two had gotten to him. I didn't need to actually see them bite; I'd heard that high-pitched keen before. It was the only proof I needed that they'd broken through skin and into meat.

"Run, Lyndsey. Run and keep running." I told her. I left her and headed back. I could not save Steve, but I could save my sister from hearing the final death cries of her husband. I went through ten rounds, blasting the zombies that had begun to feast. All manner of zombie debris flew up and away, more than one round found its merciful way to Steve. His screams cut short, I turned to catch back up to his wife. An armbar nailed me right across my Adam's apple. If I had been running full speed, the zombie would have crushed my windpipe. As it was, I was going to have a significant bruise. Getting the rifle up was out of the equation as he came out from behind a tree and we began to grapple. I dropped my weapon, letting the tactical sling hold it against my chest; this afforded me the opportunity to reach down to my leg sheath.

"How about a little Ka-Bar for your troubles," I grunted. His head dipped as he watched me reach down, he was following my hand. He knew what I was doing. My first inclination had been to shove that steel serrated blade straight into his temple. But this one had other ideas. He faced the blade, making that strike more difficult. I was running out of options; the bastard had plenty of back-ups; I was on my own. I drove the point of that black blade into his right cheek where it skittered across his cheek bone and then popped over and into his orbital socket. I had about two inches in—his eyeball was a jellied mass of a mess. The serrations had got caught up on the delicate bones that surrounded his eyes, keeping me from pressing it in deeper and into his brain. I'd nearly lost my thumb to his crunching teeth as I leaned in farther and shoved. There was a small snapping as if I'd broken the wings of a sparrow then the blade slid easily in. He was falling away as I pulled the knife free.

I had a sense I was surrounded, but last I checked, their night vision wasn't any better than a normal person's. I should be alright. The thought hadn't even had the opportunity to get dumped into my economy-sized short-term memory bin before I thought my ears drums were going to bleed. A shrieker was out there and he was actively seeking food. When Justin and I had first come across them we'd thought that perhaps they had some sort of echo location system like the others, but this seemed a more base, but insidious hunting tactic. They had the ability to send a debilitating sound straight into a mind, causing their victims to panic and run, giving the speeders the chance to hunt their quarry down.

For the time being, zombies were only able to use their most rudimentary, God-given natural weapons to hunt. Without bows, guns, knives, or any other deadly instrument, they'd begun to adapt. Human eyes and noses would only take them so far to locate food from their rapidly diminishing supply; like all species, they needed to keep coming up with new and creative ways to learn and adapt. Tomorrow's zombie would look nothing like today's and that was terrifying. The spike sound in my head was threatening to make me shut my eyes, although with how dark it was getting, it wouldn't make much difference. I was up and running by this time. I'd slowed down out of necessity and I had my hands out in front of me so I didn't clock a tree like my sister had. Zombies were all around, there were low groans, as maybe they were communicating with each other. But they'd slowed as well, and I didn't know if that was because they realized they had me in a snare, or they just couldn't track anymore in the dark. A bright half-moon was on the horizon, I wasn't sure if I was elated or dismayed at its showing. For now, the field was leveled; we were all stumbling around in the dark.

My foot went through a rotten tree, or possibly a corpse. Everyone nearby stopped due to the resultant sound. I held my breath, not trusting myself to not sound like Darth Vader. A hand slapped against my face, dropped down, and clutched the front of my jacket, pulling me closer as he leaned in. I turned my face away just as his mouth bit on my head. The zombie towered over me; I was being attacked by Wilt Chamberlain. In addition to his height advantage, he was strong, not stronger, but strong. He spit what instantly became my lucky hat out and I knew where he would attempt to lodge those teeth next. All I could do was lean away, down, back, and keep dodging his mouth because I could not break his vise-like grip on the front of my jacket. He was moaning/messaging our location as he did his best to do me in. I thrust my knife blade completely through his lower arm and twisted, using his bones as leverage to force his arm away.

It wasn't the pain that caused him to let go, but rather the damage I'd inflicted. What I did next was done purely for survival mode. I gutted the lanky motherfucker. I stuck the blade, hilt deep into his midsection and then ripped up. He didn't really care so much as lengths of ropy intestine spilled out—he was still trying to bite through my cranium. My mother always told me I should wear a helmet. Right now a suit of armor sounded like a pretty good idea, but it would have to wait. I reached inside him with my left hand, not even believing what I was doing. I plunged deep enough that my thankfully gloved fingers scraped up against his spine. I wrapped a fist around that bone stick and pulled him down by it. I brought my right hand up and repeatedly started stabbing him in the face and head. It was the sixth or seventh strike when I finally got the response I was looking for. His body went slack and we crashed down onto the ground with him on top.

A zombie's foot came down less than six inches from my face. The white swoosh of a Nike sneaker clearly visible. The moon was indeed making its presence known now. I couldn't ever imagine a time when I would like the moon less than I did at that very moment. I could hear him sampling the air with his nose. If I thought I could smear more intestine over me without making any noise I would have. He was looking around and now leaning over. I could see moonlight glint off the milky gray cataracts that completely covered his eyes. My body went rigid when he sent a shriek through me. The rest of the zombies had gone still as they waited for the brushes to be beaten and the rabbit to start fleeing. My heart was pistoning like an overtaxed engine—that scream pressed directly on my adrenal gland; prickles of heat flared through me. Without a doubt, I knew to run meant death, yet I desperately wanted to. These screaming zombies had nailed some primal part of human psyche that demanded flight.

Fighting against instinct, I stayed put. The Nike zombie took a step or two down the length of myself and my zombie-stench covering. He leaned down again. Scanning, sniffing...he got down onto his knees. I almost reacted again when he leaned in and took a small sampling bite of the zombie on top of me. I wonder if his slogan was Just Eat It, probably signed a multi-million dollar contract with the shoe company; I can't imagine a tiny apocalypse infringing on the shoe giant's business permanently. This one knew something was here, he just hadn't wrestled the answer out yet. I would have sat up and shoved my knife into his temple if not for the dozens of his teammates streaming past. I imagined they were following the sounds of my sister's hasty retreat. My panic, which was already at a pretty high threshold—red-lining even—was ratcheted up a notch. I was not sure how much more I could ask of my circulatory system as it force pumped my blood at rates of speed that I didn't think my heart capable of handling.

Nike zombie was moving my cover, the zombie above me was rocking back and forth. I had gripped his sides trying to keep Nike from flipping him over and off. The movement of my hands, or maybe a whiff of the new scent as they came out from underneath, seemed to pique his interest. He stopped; the air sampling began again. This one was not going to get bored and leave.

"Just fucking great." I thought. "I have to get a zombie

with OCD."

There were still the flat footfalls of zombies all around as they stumbled past, looking for us. What I'd first figured to be dozens seemed to more likely be hundreds, this was an impressive horde. I don't understand why they were assembling in such great numbers. With their food source so scarce, I couldn't imagine that when they finally did land something that many of them would get more than a morsel. The only thing saving me from zombies right now was a zombie. Nike finally stood; I mistakenly thought he'd got sick of this game and was distracted by something. Nope, not this one. He was like a damned pit bull—he couldn't let go, like his damn jaw had locked on to a hand and nothing short of a crowbar to the skull was going to make him release his grip. I'd not been expecting the next maneuver, so when he grabbed the dead zombie's leg and pulled down, I was exposed, at least my head and the top of my shoulders, before I could grab the zombie's head and keep him from being yanked completely off me.

Those walking past seemed to slow, but I couldn't honestly tell; I was a little preoccupied. It could have been that everything was speeding up inside of me so much that all else slowed in comparison. Nike was apparently content with his work; he'd stopped pulling. In the pale burgeoning light, I could tell he was looking at me. Damn near saw his thought process, too. No other zombies knew I was here. Telling them would be tantamount to calling your buddies to a chicken wing party before you'd had your fair portion. If he told them now, he would have to share his boon with all of them; he'd be lucky if he got a phalange to eat on his own. Nice to see zombies weren't above greed; it meant their humanity was in there somewhere. He didn't even look around to make sure he wasn't going to be busted. He just went for it, pitching forward like he'd been shoved over. One of the most bizarre strike attempts I'd ever seen—good enough he'd caught me by surprise and almost got to eat some cheek meat before I could thwart him. I'd got my arms out just in time to absorb his fall; the weight of him had pushed my arms out and we were close enough that when he stuck his tongue out, the blackened appendage dragged across my lips.

Eliza's kiss had been a welcome, tender filled moment in comparison. His tongue was rough, like a cat's, and the smell—well, you can probably imagine. Although, when you would have ever had the opportunity to stick your nose in week-old skunk roadkill is beyond me. After his sampling, I can only assume he liked what he'd tasted. He growled as he tried to push closer, I involuntarily turned my head as he got abundantly nearer my nose. Seems Nike zombie was big into 'roids, he was stronger than he should have been. Either that, or zombies in general were increasing in strength, another weapon in their expanding arsenal. Of all the evolutions, that required some of the easiest changes—just a synapse break in the brain, apparently. My understanding is that sane humans are their own strength inhibitors. That's why crazy fucks are insanely strong, although, I don't know how much weight that theory holds. If it's true, then I should be able to lift cars and Trip, well, Trip should be able to juggle elephants.

I moved my left hand so it was close to centered on his chest and pushed back; with my right I felt around for the knife I had put down. Nike got an idea of what was about to happen as he caught the glint of the blade out of the corner of his eye. Maybe he wasn't too keen on dining with others, but he liked the idea of permanently dying even less. He had just started his shriek when I so rudely interrupted him. The extra energy juice I'd got from the scare shock he'd sent through me, forced my strike harder and deeper. The hilt of my knife was actually inside of his skull; when I pulled it back out, large wet pockets of brain and blood fell on me. My guess is it saved my life, but ewww. Just fucking ewww. Globules of matter rolled down my face. I did my best to keep it from my mouth...I hate to admit my success was limited. Trying to gag, retch, and spit quietly was not among the easiest things I'd ever done. A small troop of zombies were dangerously close; they knew something was going on. I sat back slowly, taking Nike with me. His mouth and teeth rested against the side of my face. I shivered with revulsion; I could not control myself.

A blood-curdling scream, far off in the distance, was my savior. The zombies started moving off. That someone else's distress worked out in my favor was not lost on me. At least it was not a feminine scream; for that, I was thankful because it meant that it wasn't my sister. Sure, a guy could reach a high falsetto given the right set of circumstances, but I'd yet to hear a woman go low for a bass sound when screaming. As far as I knew there were only two of us wandering around from our group now that Steve was long gone and BT was hopefully still in the quarry. So whoever was in trouble right now was low on my priority list of people I needed to help. I was going to count until twenty-five after I heard what I hoped was the last zombie to pass before I got up. I made it to eleven and a half.

The moon was up by this point and the zombies were now illuminated in a ghostly pale. The vanguard of the horde probably was a mile or more from my current location. I would not be able to fight my way up to the front, though that was exactly where I needed to be.

"Think, Talbot," I said in a whisper as I snuck up on one of the slower zees. I stuck my blade into his temple and eased him to the ground. A sea of zombies was in front of me and it was at least fifty feet wide. If I went too deep forward I would be surrounded on all sides again and I'd lose more time—and possibly my life.

"Around it is." I went back about ten feet and then cut across a hundred yards; now I needed to make up speed and try to get ahead of them. With the moonlight, I was afforded more speed, and in theory, able to avoid most trees. I ran with my hands up in the classic old school fighter approach. What I wouldn't have done for a world class pair of goggles; odds were at some point I was going to send a branch straight into an eyeball. Had to think that would seriously fuck my night up. I was far from quiet, but as long as I didn't make "human" sounds there was little chance I was going to be heard over the running feet of the zombies. I was so focused on moving forward and protecting my eyes I had no good chance to check my flanks; should have guessed at some point there would be stragglers outside of the imaginary boundaries I had created.

The zombie that hit me was at a full sprint. If he hadn't slammed me up against a tree I would have been completely bowled over. The only reason I didn't lose my knife was a bit of good fortune. I'd been running with my hands up and the knife blade pointed outward. He'd run nasal cavity first into my Ka-Bar—he was dead before I had the wind punched out of me by a hundred twenty year old aspen. Okay, so we all know I don't know what kind of tree it was. Suffice it to say it was huge and infinitely harder than me. Running became more difficult, as I'd for sure bruised or possibly cracked a rib. I moved another twenty yards out in the hopes I'd got to the farthest peripheries of the zees. The problem I had not taken into account was the sound of their stampede was bound to draw in others from at least a mile radius.

There had to be a reason they were amassing in such numbers, but I didn't know what it could be. Hadn't seen a mess of them this big since the very beginning when prey was abundant and still very ignorant of their status. Not many were ready to believe that they'd been so easily and thoroughly booted from the top of the food chain. Gunfire off to my left...no telling who that was, maybe the man I'd heard screaming earlier, or more likely, his friends exacting a measure of revenge. Great, fine...gunfire pulled zombies away from me. They could shoot those guns all night long for all I cared. There was a frenetic burst and then silence. I was hoping for reloading but when it didn't start back up I figured he, she, or they'd been overrun. I'd been running for fifteen minutes when I guessed by now I was halfway through the group, so, in theory, I'd be at the front in another fifteen. Then what?

Charge headlong into the front lines to find my sister? That would put me be back on the menu so even if I found her, we'd be in the same kettle we were before.

We'd be repeating a vicious circle, and we would not get a third try at this. By now my sister had to be flagging; I was winded. I ran a little faster, there were no other options. I didn't have time to find a vehicle that could navigate in the woods; the odds I could find a Star Wars landspeeder were slim. As far as I knew there was no help in my general vicinity. No, my sister and I would live together or die together; those were the two scenarios I faced. Now I just had to figure out how to make one happen or not, and preferably the former. Suddenly there she was. I'd caught up to her faster than I should have; she was leaning up against a tree, possibly a poplar, catching her breath and checking over her rifle. Here was where she wanted to make her stand.

"Keep running!" I urged her on, motioning with my right arm.

"Tired, Mike," was her reply, though she was doing what I'd told her to.

I shot a three round burst—dropped two zombies with thigh wounds, not dead, but not running either. Right now that was just as effective. We'd had a slim, twenty-foot lead as I caught up, it was shrinking fast. I grabbed her by the elbow and half-propped, half-dragged, half-carried. That's a lot of halves, but the combination of them kept changing.

"Wicked bad stitch in my side," she hitched.

"Better than teeth in your head," I replied. She kept moving, one hand pressed deeply into her left side.

"Left hand above your head. It will help." I wanted to turn and fire on the zombies, slow them down a bit, but I was afraid my sister would collapse if left to run on her own. Fuck, I was exhausted; I don't know how she was still running. And before those of you with a feminist stance think I'm being chauvinistic, I'm a way better runner because I have vampire blood, not due to my having a penis. Is that clear enough? In real life, my sister was a fitness freak. She could have run the old me into the ground, done a little victory jig, and then continued on her way. The beer I liked to drink before the zombies came wasn't overly conducive to healthy living. Darkness began to encroach again, I'd thought that maybe we had run through the night, the next day, and were coming back up on nightfall. Everything was beginning to blend. When the first fat droplets of rain hit my face I thought maybe myself or my sister had been caught and I was being sprayed in blood. A soft glow rose around us as the dawn began to emerge; soon we were soaked through and through, as the drops became a torrential rain that wouldn't stop. It had done nothing to slow our enemy.

By this time, my sister had puked once...me, twice. The zombies were a couple of feet closer. What we had left was no longer measured in miles, maybe not even yards. Up ahead was a break in the woods; maybe we could make it to a house, barricade ourselves in a basement and wait for the cavalry to come. That all sounded like a wonderful plan until we stepped out of those woods and onto a large roadway. The landscape was dominated by its nothingness. A large sign signified the future home of The Guardians Mansions, a fine gated community starting in the low 1.2s. It literally said "the low 1.2s," like that was fucking pocket change. I wouldn't be able to afford to get my lawn mowed in this place, had it ever been built. So much for holing up in a house. I was pissed at Mr. Romero for even suggesting it. The area had been so deluged with water from the storm that it was coursing down the roadsides, running along the cobblestone berm and down the storm drains.

"Storm...drain..." I barely got it out. Didn't really need to tell my sister; she was about as close to being passed out on her feet as one can be. I was mostly dragging her at this point. "Stay with me, sis. I'm going to take the cover off and you're gonna go down. Got it?"

She nodded. The timing on this was going to have to be

better than a precision crafted Swiss Time Piece, performed as smooth as German Engineering, greased as well as the pockets of American Politicians. Too much? I'd be happy if it worked like a piece of clunky post revolution Russian technology as long as we were safe. I more or less flung my sister forward past the grate, bent down, and wrapped my fingers around the heavy cast iron bars. For two agonizing seconds, I strained, cords stood out on my neck, muscle in my arms bulged, my back cursed in protest, my knees threatened to blow out sideways. I didn't think it was going to budge, until it did. I yanked up and sideways, nearly dropping the beast on Lyndsey's foot.

"Down—" I labored.

She looked dubiously into the darkness but otherwise went without uttering a word. It took a second to stretch my fingers out, they were still bent into claws from their previous strain. I brought my rifle up and emptied the entire magazine; the last shot had my barrel pressed firmly up against the belly of a zombie. I was bowled over by falling zombies and went down under a heap of bodies—I cried out in pain as I was being trampled. If not for a protective zombie covering I would have been mashed into the street. I turned over and reached out to the lip of the drain and dragged myself towards it. The zombies behind had yet to determine where their food went.

Lyndsey popped her head up to see what was happening, she reached out and grabbed my arm, straining to pull me in. My legs were tangled up in two bodies; when I got free I fell through the hole head first. Would have cracked my skull on the concrete below if not for the torrent of water sluicing through the pipe. Lyndsey saved my life as she reached down and grabbed my foot, although my head was underwater and I was unsure as to how I was going to twist up to grab something without going for a ride like a flushed turd. Ended up being a zombie that rescued me. Weird how that crap happens. One had stepped neatly through the hole, narrowly missed my sister, but was a big enough douche to drive his foot into my crotch. Swallowed a lungful of water as I yelled out in misery. Fortunately, he was kind enough to accidentally knock me away from Lyndsey's grip and twist me violently upright from the blow. I was choking on water, my nuts were screaming in agony, but I had the wherewithal to use at least one hand to reach out and grab ahold of a ladder rung. The other was clamped down on my newly injured nether region. The zombie took a fleeting snap at me then was sucked away as swiftly as if we were unbuckled on a jumbo jet flying at thirty-thousand feet when a two by two foot hole was ripped through the fuselage. He went that quickly.

What little light would have trickled down to us was being blocked out by zombies, another of which had fallen in halfway. One leg had dropped through. If he still cared about his privates we would have been able to commiserate—the way he smacked whatever junk was left to him up against the lip of the opening. I had to get up and past my sister before more started dropping in. One would eventually get lucky and get a bite into one of us or pull us off our perch and into the jet stream below.

"Pull in close," I told my sister. She hugged the ladder tight. I crawled over and past as she went down a couple of steps. I rested the zombie's foot on my shoulder and climbed, pushing him free of the hole. Fucker didn't even say thank you. The tricky part now was going to be popping up, grabbing the cover, and pulling it back over the hole without letting any parasites latch on. Where the ruptured zombie had been was now a flood of water pouring onto my face. I was pretty sure this is what waterboarding felt like. I had to keep turning my head so I could get a proper breath. Without us in sight, the zombies seemed hesitant; not sure what to do. They'd been hunting us for so long and they knew they had been right on top of us. As far as they were concerned, we had simply vanished. Replacing the cover had been easier than I thought it would be, and I hadn't garnered any attention until it dropped back into place. The scraping sound as I dragged it over had been completely masked by the torrential downpour; none had taken notice until the loud clanging sound as it reseated, almost like a dinner bell for them, though I'd still not been spotted. We were out of immediate danger of being eaten, but far from being safe in general.

The water in the hole had risen almost a foot just since we'd been in. The maintenance ladder had fifteen steps that dropped down into a small square opening; on either side was a large pipe that, in theory, was supposed to channel the water away. Either the rain was coming down too hard for the channel to keep up with or there was some sort of blockage down-pipe that was damming up the water. If the horde above would just move on, we could escape a potential drowning, but they were just loitering around now that there was nothing worth chasing. I hated to admit it, but I wouldn't mind if a fascist rally had just adjourned nearby, sending the attendees exiting this way. I don't have any personal grudge against fascists, just needed a diversion and it seemed way worse to wish for a Lamaze class to have just finished. The zombies were milling, while we were nearly swimming.

"Mike...I'm...I'm getting tired."

I looked down to my sister; I'd seen drowned rats that looked less water-logged.

"Climb up," I told her, giving her the room to do so. I went down, her feet were right in front of my face. I figured if she slipped I'd have ample opportunity to halt her descent, provided I could hold on myself. I looked down to note that my boots were completely immersed, as was half my calves. Water from below, water from above. Of all the ways I wagered I would leave this world, a watery grave seemed pretty unlikely, considering my aversion to deep water. After another half hour under that barrage, the physical pounding and the leeching of body heat from the cold water was taking its toll on both of us. When the water was a few inches from my crotch I climbed a couple of rungs higher. Lyndsey said nothing. She had one arm hooked over a rung, her head hanging low. She looked as miserable as I felt.

Her teeth were chattering. She looked to me and held eye contact for a heartbeat or two.

"He's dead."

I nodded curtly. She wasn't asking and there was nothing I could really say to make it any better. I tried anyway. "He died to give us a chance to live, sis. We have to honor his memory by doing just that."

She nodded in response, or it might have been a shiver. Either way, she didn't say anything else. Another ten minutes, another rung. The water was not abating. Near as I could tell given the current state of affairs, we had about an hour left.

"How you holding up?" I asked as I finally came abreast of her.

"When we were kids I never really liked you all that much. I feel bad about that."

"Whoa—hold on sis. Nix the disclosure. We're not dead yet."

"You were the baby; I just remember mom making me do stuff for Mikey—get Mikey's breakfast, wash Mikey's clothes, pack Mikey a lunch for school. I felt like I was your personal servant sometimes. It wasn't until I finally moved out that I cared much for you. I mean, I always loved you...I just couldn't stand you."

"Is right now really the time you want to do big reveals? I was perfectly fine with the status quo. I always thought I was a pretty good younger brother, and I'm really starting to hate these confessions and what I'm discovering about what my siblings truly thought. I'm not sure if I can take any more, especially if Gary feels the need to get something off his chest, too."

"I didn't want anything bad to happen to you...I just wanted you to get adopted or something."

"Oh okay, that's not so bad. Just have me ripped from my family."

"It wasn't like that! I was the youngest for five years before you came into the picture. I got all the attention, all the pampering. I was not a fan of having to step down from my throne."

"You moved out when you were what, eighteen?" She nodded. "Thirteen years is a hell of a long time to hold a grudge, sis."

"I got over it. I guess I really didn't mean to start there. What I meant, Mike, is that I love you as only a big sister can. I've watched you stumble and fall and yet you always get up, dust off your knees, fix your crooked smile and march on. It's something I've been proud to witness all these years. It was the same even during my difficult years; I had a gut feeling that you were going to do wonderful things in this world. Didn't expect exactly this, but..." She hesitated. "I just thought you should know."

"Son of a bitch," I said after a guilt-wracked minute.

"What?"

"It was me that got you in trouble with mom and the whole diary thing."

"What about it?" She turned to look at me.

"I needed a piece of paper."

"And?"

"Well, I couldn't find any."

"And?" The look of defeat she had on her features just a few seconds ago was quickly transforming into anger. She'd been grounded for three weeks after my mother had got a hold of her diary and read some particularly incriminating passages.

"I picked the lock."

"You read my diary!?" She was hot and indignant.

"What nine year old cares what his fourteen year-old sister is up to? I was making a list of all my Matchbox cars and I needed a piece of paper."

"I had that crammed under my mattress. How did you even find it?"

"Come on sis. What kid hasn't thought that was the perfect hiding spot since the dawn of the mattress?"

"But mom said she found it on the kitchen counter top."

"Yeah that was me. I had to bring it downstairs so I could pop the lock."

"I was grounded for nearly a month, Mike! Lee broke up with me because he didn't want to wait until I got out again."

"Lee Brandle?"

"Yes!" She was nearly shrieking over the roar of the storm.

"You should be thanking me! He turned out to be a huge ass wipe. Last I heard he was still living in his parents' basement."

"People have to move back all the time," she tried to defend him.

"He never left."

"How do you know?"

"Because the ass kept in touch with me—always trying to catch up on what you were up to."

"Why didn't you ever tell me?"

"Well, first off because you were married and raising a kid. I didn't figure you were all that interested in an unemployed man that seldom left the sanctuary of his parents' cellar. And plus, you know what? Your number was listed, which I told him. If he was so fucking inclined, he could have called you himself and left me out of it completely."

"I guess that's one in the win column for you."

"Just one?" Without saying a word, we both climbed the last wrung afforded us. Our heads were scant inches below the grate. Not sure if it was wishful thinking, but the water pouring on our heads seemed to have let up just the smallest bit. With the water rising past our hips, my sister began to shake uncontrollably; I had no body heat to share. She was having a difficult time holding on to the steps. I pressed in tighter, hoping to use myself as a human clamp.

"I d...don't want to d..die down here," she said. I was worried she was going to bite her tongue off as her teeth clamped down hard between words.

I don't know if it was a moment of weakness or of strength

when I told her there were worse ways to go. I looked up. Thunder sounded off in the distance—no idea which direction. By the time it made it to us it was filtered through a hole and muffled by the running water. The only thing decent about the loud crashing was it gave the zombies something to hone in on. At least a few were moving away, but from what I could tell from our limited vantage point, not enough to make it worthwhile. I forced my sister higher when the water reached our necks; she was slack in my arms. I could feel her breaths against my chest; they were shallow and too far apart.

"Stay with me sis—stay with me." I peeked around to look at her face. Her lips were a deep, goth-girl shade of purple. Her face had a bluish tinge, her eyes were half open and threatening to roll up into her skull. "You remember that time when I was seven and Jamie Hollister was picking on me? When I saw you running to tackle him I felt like you were a Warrior Goddess; I'll never forget it. I don't think I ever thanked you for that; I mean, now I guess I realize you were just protecting me from someone else getting the satisfaction of beating me up."

She grunted a laugh.

"But back then it meant the world," I told her truthfully. The thunderous noises picked up. I was now pressing up against her hard enough that her lips were on the cold steel. The water was above my chin and sluicing into my mouth.

"P...pe...pen," she managed.

For a sec, I thought we were going back to the diary.

"P...pocket," she stammered.

"Pen in your pocket. Okay, so what? Unless it can pump water not sure what it's going to do." I had to cough out that last part after swallowing too much water.

"Bre...breathe."

I'm going to blame my slow faculties on the stress. It took a minute, but I put the pieces together. I fumbled in her pocket and pulled out a cheap plastic pen. Nearly lost it when I couldn't grip it quite right. I couldn't remember the last time

I'd seen a pen with a cap on it. Didn't trust my fingers enough to attempt to pull the cap off so I gripped it between my teeth and yanked it free. Got the fucking cap lodged in my throat. The thing I was trying to use to save us was looking more and more like it was going to be the source of my demise. I coughed hard three times before it dislodged and struck my sister in the back of the head. She didn't seem to take notice; compared to the Chinese water torture beating us around the head and shoulders this was nothing. I then gripped the tip of the ink tube tightly in my teeth, blocking it from going farther with my tongue. Odds were slim that I'd get something else stuck in my throat, but how far could this comedy of errors go?

Just a little further, I suppose, as my teeth slipped off and I chipped at least two of them and drew an inky line down my chin. I used my molars the next go around and pulled it out. I then handed it to Lyndsey, who was nearly underwater. I could feel her chest rise and fall heavily as she pulled in as much air as she could through the small tube, like she was hiding in a swamp and using a reed. I'd gone up as high as I could and made a duck face, my lips puckering up in between two grates waiting for a kiss but getting only a sliver of oxygen mixed with raindrops. I felt a tap on my shoulder. She was trying to hand the pen back. I shook my head; for at least the next few moments I had a place to breathe. I wouldn't be able to hold it long, though. I was straining and in an unnatural position.

Even with my ears underwater I could hear the rapid concussions of what I at first thought was thunder—the zombies were on the move. My sister slumped against me. I frantically searched for the pen but I couldn't see it, couldn't see much of anything with the white water cascading over my eyes. It was now or never. I climbed one more step and put my shoulder against the grate. It was frozen stuck as if it had been welded. I was not going to let my sister die in a fucking storm drain. I roared—water rushed into my mouth and down my lungs as I strained. Toppled two zombies that had been standing on it. The horde's attention was somewhere north of us where they were moving out toward. Except for the two that I had uprooted.

I was coughing out leaf and litter strewn water as I reached down and dragged my big sister free. I'd like to say I laid her gently down in the gutter; let's just say the least of her problems was going to be the few contusions she'd just suffered. I was trying to catch my breath—the zombies were trying to catch a meal. We hadn't been noticed yet by the rest, and our survival depended on it staying that way. Thankfully, the storm noise raged, now that I was outside, it sounded more like artillery, maybe mortars. Weather and some unknown force were my heroes right now. The first zombie to recover was a young boy, maybe around ten. Good thing too; anyone bigger and I would have been screwed since I was nearly choking as he came in. I wrapped my left hand around the back of his head and with my right, I grabbed his shoulder. I used his own forward momentum and collapsed my legs, forcing his head into the cobblestone gutter berm.

He struck mouth first. The sound of most of his teeth smashing was drowned out by the rain. His bottom jaw hung by a single hinge. I lifted his head and pulled him closer to the stones where I slammed his skull three more times until he was still. Hair, blood, and brain coated both of my hands. The next zombie looked as if it could have been the boy's grandmother. In terms of the feeding chain, these two ranked low—probably why they were at the back. Granny might have been old, but she still had all her teeth and she looked all business as she eyed me warily. Warily, I didn't need. If she felt threatened there was a good chance she would ask for some help. I didn't have time for that shit. I'd yet to hear my sister take that first, gasping breath. I needed to clear her lungs immediately.

"Naw...you ain't calling for no one, are you?" I was standing, knees bent, hands out in front of me in a traditional fighting slash wrestling pose. "You're hungry, Granny. You could have two squares right now...when's the last time that happened for you? I'm guessing it's been a while."

She growled. If I didn't know better I'd think she knew what the hell I was saying.

"Do it," I urged.

I had eighty pounds on the small woman, yet I had not been ready for the speed and ferocity of her attack. Well, that and I was pretty low on the reserves. That's what I'm going with. My journal—I'll write it any fucking way I want. Not going to come out and say Granny Smith was kicking my ass, that looks undignified. Bitch was, though. I was able to shift enough that the back of my head didn't come down on the very same stone I'd killed her grandson on, but I still scraped the side of my face enough that I was going to have a hell of a raspberry. For one horrifying moment, my hand had gone into her mouth. She chomped down just as I was pulling free, her top teeth scraping against my index fingernail. She slammed down; there was some satisfaction as one of her teeth cracked in half.

My hand slipped as I tried to force her away; instead she fell in closer, her mouth landing on my shoulder. I wanted to cry out as she bit me through the material. Felt like a snapping turtle had latched on. I could not get any stability or traction on the rain-slicked roadway; she was using her mouth to pull up to my more vulnerable neck. I tangled one hand around in her mop of blue hair and wrenched her up. Okay—let me clarify. I tried to wrench her up. The hair came away in great clumps; looked like I was auditioning for a part as a Muppet operator. I expected her next bite to be lethal.

Trust me, I was happy with the next series of events, but there was going to be a need for serious damage control. Blood and gravel pelted my face as Granny was knocked sideways and off me. My sister's chest was heaving; she had a broken piece of asphalt in her hands and had just caved in the side of Granny's head, sending her skidding off. Granny had watched her last episode of The Golden Girls.

"You're alright?" I was getting up.

"I'm a Talbot. I'm realizing we're exceedingly difficult to kill."

"We're not going to talk about this...her...to anyone, right?"

"Not right away. It's always nice to have something to hold over your head, though." She reached out to help me up, but she was barely standing herself.

"We have to find shelter; get our clothes dry. Warm up."

She let the chunk of road drop and we headed in the opposite direction of the zombies who were cresting a small hill not too far away.

"Wish the zombies had come a few months later. Would have been nice to take a rest in a house listed in the low one point twos."

"There's my sister." She was fighting back against the sadness that threatened to stop her in her tracks. A time would come when she could fully immerse herself in her loss; now was not that time. Pure survival mode has a way of crowding out all extraneous thought, which is any that does not revolve around: "How am I going to survive?"

Farther down the road there were some large excavation machines, a potential hiding spot if the zombies came back. I climbed up onto the large tank tracks and poked my head into the cab, opened the glove box, and pulled out a bunch of papers. A green lighter fell to the floor. I flicked the top and a bright steady flame lit.

"Fantastic." The problem now was if I stuck it in my pants pocket I would soak the flint and it wouldn't light again until it dried. By that time my sister would have succumbed to hypothermia. A brown paper bag was on the floor as well; that would do for the immediate, but the paper would soon soak through, too. "Unless..." I said. I opened the sack; there was indeed a plastic Ziplock bag inside; unfortunately it housed something that had once been food. Now it resembled a previously undiscovered alien life form.

"You have got to be kidding me." I was going to forsake the baggie until I looked over to my sister, she was standing in the roadway, her lips trembling in tune to the rest of her body.

"You owe me!" I yelled out to her as I opened the bag. Of course the thing stuck to the sides; I had to grab it and pull it out. My dad used to like to watch those country veterinarian shows and for some god-awful reason those vets were always sticking their entire arms up the ass of a cow. I felt a lot like that as I pulled that golden-green nugget free, only cow shit is like French perfume compared to what I'd just touched. I placed the lighter in the waterproof package and sealed the top.

"Come on." I grabbed my sister's shoulder. "I saw the beginnings of a house when I was in the cab." It had no windows, but it had to be dryer than where we were now.

"I'm not sure I like what they did with the place," my sister said. We were now staring at it from the dirt driveway. I was rubbing her shoulders vigorously as she chattered.

"Don't move."

"Can...can't help it." She was shivering uncontrollably.

"I mean stay put. I'm just going to check the house out real quick." I did a mad dash around the main floor, then upstairs. I was amazed at how much a house this small was actually going for. The location wasn't that good either; had a fucking infestation of zombies nearby, and a lousy storm drain. "You good?" I asked as I went past my sister, who had followed me in and was headed downstairs. One corner of the basement had a pool of water, but the rest was fairly dry. Plus it had a framed-out fireplace for what looked like it was going to be a hell of a man cave.

"Come on." I grabbed my sister's hand and led her into the cavernous room. In a few minutes, I'd made a decent collection of scrap wood. Another ten minutes, a fire was going. My sister started peeling off clothes; to stay in the wet ones spelled disaster, she knew that.

"What's the matter? Oh, that's right Meredith told me about your condition."

"My condition? What the hell are you talking about?"

"Your aversion to underwear." she smiled.

"Hilarious. I hate the fucking things but I swore I was

never going to let that happen again." We were as close to the flames as we could be without standing in the damn thing. Funny thing was I must have been so cold, I didn't start shivering until a half hour later in front of the blaze. Once the shaking started I wasn't sure it was ever going to stop. I longed for my clothes to dry; I wondered how long I could leave them on a burning log before they would be unsalvageable. I dragged over some large sheets of plywood and fashioned a crude bench atop some sawhorses so we could at least get up off the concrete. I didn't give a flying fuck if anyone could see the smoke we were making. I said that, but knew the moment a zombie popped in, I'd rue my words. Still, all things considered, I'd rather die warm.

At some point, I'd fallen asleep. The fire was still blazing; my sister was no longer next to me. I got a small start in my system until I saw her finishing up tying her boots.

"Clothes are dry. Mostly." She flipped a wet pocket out.

"Turn around," I said.

"Huh?"

"My underwear is still damp; I'm not putting nice toasty pants over them."

"I'm not sure why mom didn't get you some therapy." She turned.

"Why? Because I don't want my sister to see me naked?"

"No, because I bet they're as dry as mine were—you just have some sort of mental issue about having them on."

"Yeah, that one isn't even high on my list." I was pulling my t-shirt back on, rubbing the warm material against my skin. "That feels so damn good."

"Now what?" she asked.

My boots were still slightly damp but they were dry enough I'd deal with it.

"It's night now and it's still raining. I'm not in any rush to head back out there."

"What about the rest?"

"I don't know how to get there from here and I'm going to

imagine them safe and sound, BT included. I don't think stumbling around in the dark is a good idea. And even though we nearly drowned today, we are going to need some water, and a little food would be nice. We get caught out like that without refueling or have to run without fixing our energy stores, it's game over." I tossed some more wood in the fire.

"My son is still out there." She was staring into the flame. I didn't feel the need to remind her that my family was out there as well.

"We're not doing anyone any favors if we leave here now. I'm going to check those other machines and hope somebody left something behind worth eating."

"You'll get soaked."

"Naw, some of the windows on the top floor have plastic on them I'll use that to make a raincoat or something. Should keep most of it off."

Wasn't sure if there would be anything in the earth-moving machines or not but that wasn't the real point of going out. Next to the lighter had been a pack of smokes. Not sure why I felt the need to hide my one cigarette a month habit but fuck it. I did like to be alone when I cheated with one. I stayed in the cab and savored every inhalation of that stupid thing. When I finished I figured I'd do what I said I was going to. Had a pretty good haul between the two other machines...one breakfast bar, a whole sleeve of fig cookies, a diet coke, and an orange energy drink. None of it was optimum, but it beat eating bugs.

"Look what I found!" I said holding up my loot.

"Did you bring the smokes in with you?"

"I'm twenty feet away you can't possibly smell that."

"I went to see what was taking you so long."

"You haven't touched them in years. You sure?"

"I could use one right now."

We killed the rest of that pack before we opened any of the food or drinks. I felt a little green around the gills and somewhat high as a kite.

"We're not going to talk about this to anyone either, right?" I asked, the basement was a fog of smoke.

"Looks like a bar in here," my sister replied.

"I wish."

We sat there the entire night. Every once in a while one of us would put something in the fire. There was some small talk, but for the most part, we were both lost in our own thoughts. Together but alone. There's a connectivity between humans and even stronger bonds within families, but ultimately no one can know exactly what another is feeling. Even if that person wanted you to know, odds are they wouldn't have the ability to adequately convey it through words, and even if that was somehow possible, the one listening wouldn't have the knowledge or experience to completely understand. It was truly weird that we were so wired for communication but could actually accomplish so little of it.

CHAPTER THIRTEEN
MIKE JOURNAL ENTRY 10

I MUST HAVE dozed at some point. When I woke, the bright shiny sun was streaming through one of the window slots.

"Stopped a couple of hours ago," my sister told me.

"Did you sleep at all?"

"No. Went out and found more cigarettes, though."

My stomach turned a little thinking about doing one this early in the morning.

"I hope you didn't want any."

"I'll be good until next month," I told her truthfully. "You hear anything?"

"Nope. The thunder and the explosions stopped before the rain did."

"Well, I guess we go find BT and get back to the rest of the clan."

Had to squint and shield my eyes as I exited the house, the sun was shining so brightly and there wasn't a cloud in the sky. Hard to imagine that yesterday it had rained enough to fill storm drains. The roadway was completely dry; the fields off to our right still looked plenty water logged. As for the woods on our left, I had no desire to head back that way whatever their condition. While I was pondering which way to go, Lyndsey was already heading down the road.

"You do know that's the way the zombies went, right?" I asked when I caught up.

"I plan on taking a sharp left as soon as the road allows."

"I'm not so sure that's the best idea. I mean, staying in the open like this."

"Until I was sixteen years old and got my license you used to follow me around constantly. Without question, without my asking, even when I threatened to punch your lights out. And now, now you're going to be a pain in the ass about it? How about we just do this for old times' sake?"

"Well, when you put it like that."

She smiled and hugged my waist. I knew why she didn't want to go back in the woods. At some point, we would come to where Steve had fallen and she didn't want to. What more, what better, reason do you need? We hadn't gone more than a half a mile when we got our leftward traveling highway. I want to say it was Route 62 or something, but the sign was fairly shot up. There was only left or right as far as wheeled vehicles could go. The zombies were now traveling off-road to whatever the source of the noise had been. Didn't bother me where their final destination was going to be as long as it wasn't here.

The longer we stayed on this road, the more my nerves began to fray. It was open on either side of us for a couple hundred yards; if a car came, we would never have enough time to get to safety. I'd brought up finding a safer route to travel and my sister unequivocally said "no" each and every time; said she wanted to feel the complete sun on her body, to feel it wash over her and soak through, much like the rain had. She mumbled that it would take weeks of being in full sun to wash off the stink of that rain. I had that feeling to a point, but it was gonna be a bitch laying out in the sun if we were getting eaten by zombies or shot up by assholes. Another hour or so passed, we hadn't said much. I had my head on a swivel, constantly looking around for any signs of a threat. My sister was playing Sun God Rah every so often, by that I mean laying her head back and putting her arms out to her sides as if she could catch more of the beams that way.

Shit, maybe she could; she seemed fairly content. I had my concerns about where her head was. This really wasn't the time to pretend you were in Cancun on Spring Break. When I first saw the shimmering silhouettes in the roadway up ahead, I figured them for zombies—a couple of holdouts from the massive horde. Why wouldn't I? Normal people did not just walk down the streets anymore, regardless of how nice it was outside. Lyndsey seemed only mildly interested in our approaching guests.

"I never figured you for a worrier, Mike," she said. She calmly pressed the magazine release to look at her loaded bullets and then slapped it back into place. "There's only two."

"Only takes one," I answered, though I was happy she was coming back to a better semblance of vitality. The zombies did not start running at the point where they should have been easily able to see us. They did something far worse. They held up guns. "Well damn, that's something new."

"What?" Lyndsey asked.

"Zombies with guns. Now, that's bad news."

"Um, Mike, maybe they're not zombies."

It took longer than I'm willing to admit to take off my zombie-colored glasses. I was just so expecting them to be zombies I almost couldn't picture anything else. Two lone zombies were actually way better than two armed humans— leaps and bounds better. Meeting decent people this far into the thick of it was unlikely. Not as unlikely as, say, screwing a super model or winning the lottery, but the odds were clearly not in your favor. We all had our guns up in the ready position as we drew closer together. Was like the world's slowest game of chicken as we all walked down the center line and directly at each other. The way we were going, I wouldn't doubt if we collided and the entire troupe burst into flame from the contact.

"You should maybe not smile like that."

"Like what?" I asked my sister.

"You have this far off look and a lopsided grin that makes you look like you should be holding crayons instead of a rifle."

I was working hard on wiping the grin off my face. Weird how sometimes under really stressful situations that can be difficult. The more I concentrated on looking stern, the more I wanted to smile. Looking at the damn barrel of the .45 the man was holding should have been enough to fix that. Sun was glinting off the fat, chromed barrel. The man was tall, couple of inches over six feet, lanky...no, not that. Wiry. He had strength in that thinner frame. It was his eyes, those pale blue eyes, that caused me more concern as we got even closer. They were cold, calculating—I didn't read negotiation in them. If he felt threatened, his first call of business was to shoot. I was thinking that the only reason he hadn't was because of the reach of his weapon.

The woman with him had a hunting rifle, a much better tool to reach out and touch someone. In terms of firepower, though, the advantage was ours.

"That's far enough," I shouted at about two hundred feet. It was a damn near impossible shot with a pistol, whereas my sister and I could spray the entire area.

"What are you doing on this road?" old blue eyes shouted, his pistol still up.

"Wow, this one has balls," I said softly to my sister. Louder, I said to him: "Road construction crew. We're filling pot holes! What are you doing here?"

He looked over to the woman he was with. I felt we were a handful of heartbeats from slugging this one out with bullets.

"Following the herd," he replied as he looked back to us.

"Most people head the other way," I told him.

"Yeah, well, we have an interest in where they go."

"By all means then, don't let us stop you." I was motioning for him to get to the far side of the road so they could pass. "You might want to be careful. Whatever the z-pack was heading towards sounded a lot like artillery."

"Blanks," the woman blurted out before the guy could stop her.

"And you know that how?" I prodded.

"None of your concern," the man said.

"We actually might have a vested interest in this."

"How so?" I noticed that the man tended to punctuate each word by moving his head forward and the barrel of his pistol, though completely menacing, was extended far from his body and pointing somewhat to the ground as if my boots were deeply offending him. Now, maybe you don't know much about stand-off etiquette, but this is an unpredictable stance. My senses notched up and my grip tightened.

"We came across that horde; got separated from our group," I said.

"We're moving them away," the woman answered.

"Maggie," the man said, getting her to stop her explanation.

"Those zombies were pulled our way," my sister said.

"So all of those zombies herding, being drawn to the noise, that's all your doing?" I asked. I think he saw how pissed off I was getting; he said nothing. "My sister lost her husband, we almost lost our lives. You owe us."

"Owe you?" The man cocked his head to the side.

"You're starting to look mighty hostile, friend," I told him.

"I'm not your friend." He felt the need to state fact.

Again with the head tilting and bobbing. I know I'm a suit or two short of a deck, but this guy was playing with blank cards. I got a sense he would do just about anything to make sure he and Maggie were safe. I got the motive, I did. I just thought he might easily go down darker paths to get his point across. Shoot first, tell his adversary to fuck off, later.

"Put the gun down." I put my rifle up to my shoulder, I had him center mass. He started looking over to his companion. "Stop!" I yelled in an authoritative voice. "I've seen that action a hundred times, trying to distract me by looking away and by the time you look back you plan on shooting. I'm telling you right now, friend, I will put a three round burst in your chest before you ever have the chance to pull that trigger. I can hit a man from five hundred yards with this weapon; I'm pretty sure you are significantly closer than that. You manage to hit me with that pistol from this distance and I would have to think that God has a personal vendetta against me and is using you as the instrument of my destruction. So what do you think, friend?"

"It's Rick...my name is Rick."

"Okay, Rick, put the damn gun down. We go about our merry little way and you go yours. I hope you catch up to the zombie horde and they just gobble up your sweet disposition."

"I can't do that."

"How about I just blow Maggie away? Will that change your mind?"

"Mike?" my sister asked softly.

"Relax," I said to the side. "I'm not going to shoot her unless I have to."

"Oh, that makes me feel so much better."

"Keep your gun up on them. Just because we're not too keen on shooting them doesn't mean they don't want to shoot us. The ones that have survived this long don't take many chances."

"Apparently, they never met you," she said.

"Are you fucking channeling BT, right now?"

"Right now, I'm more scared than I was at any point yesterday."

"We'll get through this, Rick," I yelled down the road. "I'm two pounds of pressure from laying Maggie all over the highway. Put the fucking guns down. Now."

He put his hands up then leaned over to place the weapon on the roadway. Maggie did the same.

"Now take a couple of steps back," I told him. He hesitated again. "Fuck, man, if I wanted you dead we wouldn't even be talking right now." As he backed up I moved forward, always keeping the barrel trained on him. He looked at his damned gun a dozen times, weighing his chances of picking it up and firing before I could. Seen too many movies, this one. "I'd like to say it's nice to meet you, but you seem like a dick. Lyndsey, check his pack." He had a small beige backpack on. My sister went behind him and rooted around in it.

"Energy bars," she said, holding them up triumphantly.

"Grab his canteen." I was five feet away with my barrel pointing at his heart. "We're grabbing some water and a small meal, and yes, you do fucking owe us that. If not for your little zombie relocation plan, we wouldn't have had to run all fucking night and then almost drown in a storm drain."

"And you owe me this," my sister said as she pulled back and punched up, striking him in the chin. "Fuck! That hurt!" she said as she waved her hand around. "That's for my husband."

His lip split as she twisted his head to the side. His gaze, when it came back to us, looked as cold as frozen steel. My sister wisely stepped back.

"I'm going to walk backward until we get over that little rise, if at any time before I clear that hill you reach for your guns I'm going to consider that an act of aggression."

He put his hands down almost immediately as we left but he did not go for the gun. I do not think Lyndsey and I would have survived the encounter had we not had the advantage. I would wonder long and hard if the smarter thing to do would have been to shoot them on that road.

Later we stopped and stood in that road for a bit. Wasn't sure where the hell we were and wasn't like I could pull up Google maps. There were times, long ago, when I had wanted to toss technology into a fast moving stream. This wasn't one of them. We were miles from where we needed to be, that was all the information I had to go on. We needed to get out of this new development and back onto an established roadway so I could get my bearings. My sister looked exhausted, scared, and she was obviously suffering.

"I'm not sure I believe he's gone," she said as I looked

around.

Did I go with the syrupy sweet, semi-nauseating platitudes like: "he'll always live on in your heart?" or "as long as you remember him, he'll always be with you." Neither meant shit. They were words and they could only make you feel so much better. Anybody who's ever lost someone knows there are no words that can take the place of someone's smile, their warm touch; their eyes on yours. Those were statements that only comforted the speaker. They could not begin to unravel the tangle of devastated emotions and confusion that loss brings home. It hadn't hit her completely yet, but in a few days, she was going to be in pretty bad shape when she realized he truly was gone, that he really wasn't there. We'd be there for her, I'd be there for her, too, but in the only way one can be for someone that is suffering, for comfort. Unfortunately, there's just no way to crawl into someone's head and fix all that ails them. Modern science tried its best with a variety of pills, that's for sure. And then there's always the self-medicating route, which I traveled a fair way down when I thought I had real problems. What a fucking joke.

I wonder how that old Mike would have dealt? Would he have risen to the challenge or drowned himself in a sea of pills and booze. Has my supposed intestinal fortitude always been there and the Marines just shined it up and polished it a bit, or did they have to build it from scratch on an assemblage of battered, scavenged parts? Maybe it wasn't something I needed to worry about right now.

"You ready to move on?" I asked my sister. Sure, it had two meanings. She picked up on it.

"Yes and no," was her response as we started to walk.

"I'm sorry, sis. I truly am."

She reached out and grabbed my hand. "None of this is your fault, Mike and I'll never for one moment think that."

She was letting me know that unlike Ron, she wouldn't begin to harbor a bitterness toward me. I was grateful; I was. Didn't mean I wouldn't manufacture my own guilt, as usual.

I'll decide eventually that somewhere along the line I should have sent him back or that there was more that I could have done. Hell, maybe there was.

"I'll make sure Jess understands that, too." She squeezed my hand and we continued to walk. "You remember when we were young and I smashed that frozen pita bread over your head?"

"Not sure how I could forget."

"I'm glad I did that," she smiled.

"Here I thought I was going to get an apology thirty-something years in the making."

"No, I think it's the first time I stopped thinking of you as my bratty little brother. That maybe you were a decent person all along."

"You got all that from smashing me in the head?"

"Yeah, you know...you never called me on it. You never screamed at me or called me a name. That next week I snuck some of my friends into the house when mom and dad went out and we smoked cigarettes. Remember? You caught us, you and your friend...Eddie, right? That was his name?"

I nodded.

"I thought for sure you were going to tattle. I mean why wouldn't you? I was an asshole to you and had done my best to even hurt you a little bit. I'd told my friends I was going to get grounded for a month. Then nothing. You didn't ever bring it up with them or me. At first, I couldn't figure out why. I thought maybe you were going to make me do your chores for a while as a way to keep your mouth shut. But nothing, Mike. It was then I think I figured there was something special about you." She gave me a hug. "How come?"

"How come I didn't rat you out, you mean?"

"Yeah," she said.

"It was the brain damage from the pita bread. I'd forgotten about you, your friends, and the cigarettes the second I got my baseball glove from the garage and got out of that cloud filled space."

"Should have maybe hit you twice."

"I loved you back then, I love you now sis. I would never do anything deliberately to get you in trouble or harm you. You did a good enough job all on your own without me interfering. I didn't have to say anything anyway because the way you behaved you were bound to get caught eventually. You got busted the next week making out with Davey, if I remember correctly."

"I remember Davey."

"Yeah, he had that gig as the Clearasil before-photo poster boy."

"Shut up." She shoved me. "I've got something to tell you, Mike, and I hope you don't think any less of me."

"Would be hard to think any less of you, sis."

I know she was thinking about other things and hadn't been paying complete attention to what I had to say, probably was building the appropriate resolve to spill what she needed to say, so it took her more than a few seconds to realize that I'd just given her a little jab.

"Too bad it wasn't a roll of frozen dough. That would have done so much more damage. Are you going to listen or not?"

"I'm sorry, go on."

"The day the zombies came I had been coming back from my lawyer's office; I'd filed for divorce."

"Whoa, damn! I didn't know."

"No one did—not even Steve."

"What? What the hell are you talking about?"

"I loved Steve. He was a decent man, great father, and provider for our family. I just wasn't in love with him."

"A lot of people use that excuse sis. What exactly does that mean?"

"We could have been roommates for all the passion we had in our lives. We didn't even sleep in the same room anymore."

"I didn't know...you guys always seemed so happy."

"You ever seen him hug me? Kiss me?"

"No; I don't know...that's not stuff I'd be comfortable

watching."

"I'm not exactly comfortable with it either when I see you and Tracy, but you guys are practically oblivious to those around you when you do. Kiss and hug I mean; it's just something so natural and easy for you both. We'd lost that about five years ago. I tried so hard to rekindle it, but he was uninterested. I was done. Jess was ready to move out and I wanted to start over—maybe find someone, maybe not. I just knew I didn't want to live like that anymore."

"I'm so sorry sis. You could have talked to me, you know."

She looked at me strangely.

"Yeah, you're right. I would have told you to stop being so high-maintenance or something."

We walked in silence. Well, I walked in silence, mostly listening to my sister talk. I knew the chatter for what it was. A way to distract her from what was happening; what had happened, what was likely to happen next. She could talk until she passed out if it kept her from those dismal thoughts. It was between breaths I heard an engine—a big one.

"We have to hide."

CHAPTER FOURTEEN
BT

BT BEGAN A controlled slide down the rest of the slope as Michael, Steve, and Lyndsey headed off. He knew his only hope was to hide in one of the machines. He hadn't noticed it at first, as he was trying to keep his footing on his rapid descent, but stones and loose material were raining down on him from above like a cataclysmic storm. The sheer number of zombies running dangerously close to the edge of the pit were knocking all manner of debris free. At first, BT was alright with the occasional pelting, it was when zombies started tumbling down into the pit all around him that he realized how much trouble he was in.

"What the hell?" he asked, shielding his eyes to look up. He'd not been discovered; it was just that some of the zombies were being forced over the edge. Those that fell to the bottom were incapacitated or killed outright. Others, that fell on various parts of the winding roadway only suffered minor injuries or a broken bone or two. They would limp or drag their bad appendage and just keep on going. At first, the zombies began to head back up the slope to their initial pursuit. It was one of the not-quite dead ones that had rolled all the way to the bottom that gave the others a reason to eat in...at a more local venue.

"Oh shit," BT said as he saw the first of the zombies turn to look at him. More than a handful were capable of full sprint and others were being added to the fray. The front end loader was closer but the truck was his preferred destination. It didn't dawn on him that he could get in the big machine and literally bulldoze his way over to the truck.

"This was such a Mike move," he thought, standing midway between the two machines. A hundred yards to the truck, a hundred to the loader, and a fifty yard lead on the zombies now at the bottom of the cauldron with him. "Better not be locked," he said, reaching the truck and stepping up onto the running board. He grabbed at the door handle with too much force, lost his footing and fell to the ground as the door unexpectedly swung open. He landed hard on his side where his rifle was hanging, forcing the air from his lungs. Spitting gravel dust from his lungs, he looked up to see the zombies were closing fast—twenty-five yards, not a foot more.

"Fuck that hurt," he muttered as he forced himself up, grabbed the door handle, swung into the truck and used momentum to pull the door closed behind him. He quickly slammed both doors locked then collapsed on the bench seat to catch his breath. He was looking right up at the dark dome light; the son of a bitch that most certainly had drained the battery because the door had been left slightly open.

"Now what?" he asked, as zombies ran full force up against the large truck. "What would Talbot do?" Then he laughed. "I don't care, because I'd do the damn opposite. That's what." He waited until his chest didn't hurt before he sat up. He pushed back into the seat, surprised to see a zombie peering into the windshield. It had climbed onto the hood to get a better vantage point.

"What the fuck?" he said, scrambling to get his rifle into position. The zombie pushed itself off the hood before BT could shoot it. He peered around. "Can't be more than a dozen, fifteen at most." He couldn't get an accurate count because he couldn't make out all of the activity behind the truck by using only the rearview mirrors. "What are you tricky fucks up to? Time to play," he said as he reached into his pocket for the suppressor he'd brought with him. He unscrewed the muzzle break and placed on the much longer attachment. It wouldn't completely silence the sound like Hollywood portrayed, but it would significantly reduce it. BT hoped it would do its job well enough that no one outside of this pit could hear it.

He unrolled his window, not wanting to damage the only barrier he had between him and the enemy. The closest zombie reached up to get at him, BT blew off most of its skull. Inside the cab of the truck, the expended round was loud enough to make him wince; outside the sound was as flat and stifled as two wooden boards clacking together. Two more zombies died quickly before the rest figured out their food was lethal and hid behind the truck with the rest, silently waiting out their food.

Prey always moves.

BT rolled the window down more, and with some degree of difficulty, tried to fit the firing half of his torso out so that he could kill any zombies that showed themselves. "Like trying to shove a cork up an ant's ass," he said as he pulled himself back in—he was almost certain he heard a "popping" release as he did so. "Dammit." He rolled the window back up. "Well...nothing to lose," he said as he looked at the dangling key fob hanging out of the ignition. He closed his eyes and cranked. So much of nothing happened that he wasn't even sure he'd turned the key. There was no engine whir, no clicking of a solenoid looking for juice, no dim flickering from the dome light or even a light on the instrument panel to give any indication of hope that this truck could potentially start ever again.

"Well, that answers that question." He heard the handle on the passenger side squeal in protest as a zombie tried to open it. BT slid across the seat and quickly grabbed the window handle. He'd no sooner lowered it than a zombie's hand and forearm pushed through. An outstretched finger had narrowly missed poking his eye. Instinctively, BT had grabbed that cold, unnaturally strong flesh. He forced the arm down, snapping the thing's forearm against the door. The resultant sound was louder than the rifle had been. There were no howls of pain, just growls of rage as the zombie was denied a meal. BT rolled up the window as quickly as he'd rolled it down. He trapped the zombie's arm at the breaking point.

"I can't even go into how damn gross this is," BT said as he watched the fingers furl and unfurl in a desperate attempt to get at him. The zombie had stepped onto the running board and was looking directly at him.

"Yeah, this isn't going to work out for us, buddy." BT wanted to get his rifle in the appropriate position to get a shot off, but the angle was tight and he could not get the barrel on the right trajectory as the buttstock kept hitting the ceiling of the cab. With the rifle up against his shoulder, and his right hand holding it tight there with the pistol grip, he rolled the window down a few inches with his left hand. He fired before the zombie had a chance to retreat. A back splash of blood from the close contact killing, sprayed into his face.

"Well, that was pleasant," he said as he wiped his face on a shirt he found on the floorboard that smelled of high school football team, jock strap funk. When he was done, he looked over to the tractor. He was fast; that much he knew. He just couldn't know whether any of the zombies were faster. It would only take one of them to slow him down enough for the others to catch up. One on one was fine; twelve on one? Not so much. He thought that most likely the bulldozer was dead as well. He liked the idea of being able to see 360; in the glass structure although essentially, he would be encased in a fish bowl like the last lobster in a fancy restaurant where you get to choose your entrée.

He slowly opened the door, cursing under his breath as one of the rusted hinges squelched in protest. He could see some shuffling of feet from the zombies but as of yet, none had peered around to see what he was up to. He put the rifle to his shoulder as he moved to get out. Still nothing. He was weighing the pros and cons of flat out turning and running, when one of the zombies peeked around the edge of the tailgate. BT took a shot that whined off the thick metal and buried itself into the dirt some yards away.

"So much for stealth," he said, as he tactically withdrew, keeping his back to the tractor and facing the zombie threat. The zombies didn't take long to circle around the far side of the truck, BT moved quickly away from their shield. "Show yourselves and we can get this over with." As if one of the zombies understood his words, he peered over the hood of the truck; almost as if it was attempting to lure BT to use up his bullets as it ducked back down. The image of a carnival shooting gallery flashed through BT's mind; he smiled. If it had not been for the scraping of rock on rock, BT would not have ever turned to see the line of zombies running full speed down into the pit to come up on his back.

"Tricky fucks," he muttered. Steeling his mind, he started to do the math in his head: how long would he be able to back up this way with the rate the zombies were coming in? If a horde of dead things is charging towards a tractor and a man with a rifle is running towards it from seventy-five feet away while shooting behind him, what are the chances he will beat them to safety? He thought he would have remembered if he had that math question. If he could manage to kill one zombie per bullet and not fuck-up opening the door, he figured he could make it out of here. Even he didn't like those odds, but turned to begin running. Almost immediately he heard the telltale signs of pursuit. He recalculated when he saw their speed; the gap was closing faster than he'd figured. He knew he was going to have to time his entry perfectly; if he fell back, if he slipped up at all, he would not be able to recover. Zombies were just coming around both sides of the dozer as he launched himself upwards using everything he had left. The first third of his boot gripped the top of the tank-like tread; his forward momentum brought the rest of his body up and completely on.

Breathing hard from the exertion, he was reaching for the handle when his left leg was tugged violently backward. With the rifle in his left, he struck backward and down. The aluminum handguard smashed into the zombie's mouth, breaking its teeth into jagged, uneven rows. This somehow gave it a more predatory look, like a shark, but the strike was enough to send the zombie reeling away. BT flung open the tractor door—briefly thankful that it was unlocked. He hopped in, slammed the door behind him and made sure it was locked. He didn't revel in his victory long, as he realized he had put himself in a small, glass enclosure not much bigger than himself. In less than a minute he was completely surrounded by zombies. All of them, for the moment, doing nothing more than staring at him, like they were at the aquarium and he was the sad but prized sea turtle everyone loved to visit.

"Still better than having a conversation with Trip," he said as he caught his breath. He felt that way right up until a few of the zombies began to lick and bite at the glass. "Fuck me," he whispered. Then some began to rap lightly on the structure. "If this is psychological warfare, you guys are winning." BT kept turning to see what they were doing. He knew this monster dirt pusher had to have strong, tempered glass, but that made him feel only marginally better. After all, maybe he was safe for the moment, but he was still trapped in a tight spot. His lack of maneuverability was going to make it difficult to fight his way out of his present predicament.

"Might as well see if anything happens." A ray of hope flooded into his darkening spirits when panel lights turned on as he twisted the key in the ignition. As quickly as those hopes were illuminated, they were blown out when absolutely nothing happened. "NO! I refuse for this to happen!" He turned the ignition again; this time he noticed an orange panel light up. He began to laugh. "I think I just pulled a Talbot. Damn glow plugs." Diesel engines on the majority of heavy machinery use glow plugs, which must be primed and charged up before they are warm enough to start the mini-explosions that crank the powerful engines. It was quite possible the zombies knew he was on to something as well. They bumped up their attack. BT turned lightning quick when he heard the first zombie smash a softball-sized rock against the glass.

With the first strike, there was nothing more than a chipped out star; on the second, fragmented lines began to radiate outward. When BT thought the plugs had warmed enough he turned the key from its three-quarter position to all the way on. There was a hiccup of thick, black smoke, miraculously, the engine sputtered and coughed like a black lung victim before it began its heavy rumbling.

"Yeah!" BT raised his fist into the air; this was punctuated by furious beating against the glass as the zombies realized they might be in danger of losing food. BT found the lever that made the beast go forward; he pressed down on the foot pedal. The large machine vibrated uncontrollably and the motor began to die out. He removed his foot from the pedal and took it out of gear. "Almost stalled it out; I've got a sinking feeling that if this thing dies, it won't ever start again. Damn zombie apocalypse is making a pessimist out of me. I hate when shit like that happens." He pulled down on a lever that showed an image of the engine; there was a delay as the power generator took a moment to accept the command. The dozer shook like a wet dog, a few of the zombies fell off as if they were fleas on the aforementioned canine.

"Now we're cooking with gas!" He put the engine in gear; this time instead of wanting to stall it jumped forward. More zombies were shaken loose or fell from the tracks as their perch began to move. "My turn to play!" He turned the dozer hard to the right and went forward, catching the heel of a zombie that was not quick enough to get out of the way. From his position BT could not hear the bones snap and crunch as the zombie fell over and was mashed into the ground, crushing and grinding every internal organ and bone into fragments. He chased down two more this way before the zombies began to congregate behind the machine where they were relatively safe. So they thought, anyway, until BT found the reverse pedal and took out another half dozen in a similarly grisly fashion. "I'm not sure I should be having this much fun, I'm going to blame it on being around Mike too much," he grinned. Blood erupted like geyser spurts from the intense pressure.

He still had to deal with the zombies that were directly behind him clinging to the machine; at the moment they were just holding on, but eventually they would start the smashing process again and BT did not believe it was going to take much more than five or six good hits before they broke through. BT positioned the tractor where it would have the longest straight run available to him. He wedged the rifle between the pedal and the seat and grabbed the heavy pry bar that was next to it. "I'm going to fuck you up," he said as he swiveled and opened the door. He wrapped his left hand tightly around the assist handle and leaned out. With his right, he swung the metal bar, striking the closest zombie hard enough that its head impacted the glass with enough force to shatter its skull.

"There. You're sufficiently fucked," he told it as it fell away. The second zombie thought maybe it had a chance of getting in close before BT could swing again. She was right and she was wrong. He did not have the momentum to recover from the swing, but he could pull back. He jabbed the zombie in the abdomen and forced her off the structure and onto the tracks where she rode along until it pulled her under the front. The machine gave hardly a shudder from her passing.

"You're next." BT was pointing with the bar. The zombie moved to the far side and tried to wrench open the door. Frustrated, he then began to smash the door handle, which gave way much quicker than the glass. He almost seemed as surprised as BT when he was able to pull the door open. BT swung inside the cab quickly thrusting the pry bar like a spear, breaking through the zombie's chest cavity, completely impaling the fiend and forcing it off the tractor.

"Shit." he said as he looked at the destroyed door. "It was

fun while it lasted." BT turned the dozer and headed for the switchback trail that led up and out.

"Yup, I take back what I said. I'd definitely spend an evening with Trip discussing his fascinating tin foil hat folding techniques rather than this shit," he said as he stared to his left and down the steep embankment. The dozer was wider than the trail in most spots, meaning that half of the track was riding on air. There was not one atom in BT that wanted to experience the sensation of spinning and falling off a cliff in a twelve-ton tractor. Like the pied piper of old, BT led a gaggle of zombies out of the quarry. None approached too closely, falsely fearing that at any moment the machine could be thrown into reverse and run them over. BT himself couldn't imagine the set of circumstances that would compel him to try that. He sweated, swore, and occasionally prayed the entire twenty-minute excursion up the side of the pit. When he finally broke out onto the level surface he congratulated himself on a job well done.

"Ain't nobody could have done it better, baby! That's the law and I laid it down! And who the fuck am I shouting at! Now I have to go and save that cracker's ass." BT had a momentary panic attack as he looked at all the switches and dials until he found the right one. "Three-quarters full. Well ain't that a piece of good news. Although I have no idea what the mileage is on one of these things."

BT watched as it got preternaturally dark due to the murky storm clouds rolling in.

"Looks like you fellows are going to get wet!" BT had stuck his head out the door to address the tailgaters. "Maybe it's time to see some of you off." He pressed a red metal toolbox against the forward pedal before stepping out onto the small plankway atop the tracks. The beating of the tracks on the pavement made for an unsteady shooting platform, but the zombies were close enough he didn't think this would be overly detrimental to his success rate. With a three-round burst, he blew through two of the zombies' knees, each collapsing to the ground before they could pick themselves back up and drag their nearly useless legs behind them.

"Screw the injured reserve—I want you guys to retire…permanently." He raised his aim; his next burst decapitated a zombie. It fell straight to the ground, but still the pursuing zombies followed. BT moved his selector switch from burst to auto. "Time to dance." He emptied the magazine in a few seconds. Half the zombies were either dead or incapacitated.

"More where that came from. Don't go anywhere—I'm going to load another magazine." He was turning to go back into the tractor when the track rolled up the side of an abandoned car. BT lost his grip and pinwheeled his arms as he fought to grab onto something. He watched helplessly as his rifle fell away from him and onto the road. His hand shot out and gripped the last thing available to him before he would have hit the dirt, joining the rifle.

"Please hold," he said as he held on to the bending door handle. "Why they gotta make these things so fucking flimsy?" The zombies, which had looked on the verge of scattering under the leaden assault, were now regrouping when it appeared that a meal would be delivered after all. The locking mechanism sprung free just as BT gripped the edge of the door. "Holy shit," he said as he regained his footing. The dozer jumped all around as the small car was ground down into its original parts. BT straightened the tractor out before it had a chance to dip down into the rapidly approaching culvert. "I'm going to need that gun," he said as he removed the toolbox and began to back up. He could not catch any of the zombies unaware as the heavens opened up and released a torrential downpour of rain. They circled around and followed the tractor from the front.

"Now what?" BT asked as he was looking down at the rifle. The zombies got very curious as to why he had stopped and were keeping all eyes on him. When he opened the door they ran toward him. "Shit shit shit." He pulled the door shut and lurched the tractor forward. The zombies immediately ran to the back. "Well, let's see just how fucked I am. I lost my rifle. It's pouring out, and it's going to get dark soon. Visibility will be close to nothing with these less than street-legal lights, and at some point, I would like to sleep, but since I can't lock either door…. The second I stop, the zombies will come to investigate. I don't know how long the gas will last, and to top off this horrible fucking cake with a cherry, I don't have one iota of a clue as to where Talbot is." BT's mood was souring as rapidly as the rain fell. "I don't even have the lousy pry bar," he mumbled.

He was rapidly approaching the bottom of his well when the dawning of an idea began to brighten his horizon. "Might work...but I'm going to have to do it soon, while I can still see." BT scanned the sides of the roadway until he found what he was looking for. He drove a little past what he hoped was a perfect spot and backed in. There was the cannon fire sound of large branches snapping and the whooshing of leaves as they grudgingly yielded up against the cab then snapped back into place around it. He backed up until he could go no farther. He felt a "buried alive" claustrophobia as he peered out. On one end of the spectrum, he was completely encased in boughs, on the other, his visibility had been reduced to the pinecones directly in front of him. He could barely hear the clawing of the zombies over the thunderstorm as they tried to force their way through the thick, wet growth and tree branches.

"I'm going to find you tomorrow, Talbot. Then I'm going to give you a world of shit because there is no way you are having a worse night than this." His teeth chattered from the chill he felt. Securely embedded within the brush, he shut down the tractor and attempted to find the most comfortable position he could.

"Going to need a good chiropractor after this." And with that, he shut his eyes.

"LINDA, I'M HOME!" Lawrence said as he tossed his work badge onto the kitchen island. It slid halfway across before stopping against a dewdrop covered carton of milk. "Well, that's strange," he said as he looked up from his phone. Grocery bags covered the counter and half the island. It was unlike her to leave anything sitting out. Neat did not even begin to cover her compunction to keep their penthouse suite clean. In fact, "fastidious" even fell a little short. He knew she'd been working on easing-up in preparation for the baby they were getting ready to make, but he thought this was going a little overboard.

"Linda?" He reached for the gun he no longer wore. He might not be a cop any more, but he still had the instincts of one, and something was not quite right here. He heard moaning from down the hallway. He raced down there, heedless of any perceived danger. He turned the corner just in time to see her sit up from the bed and vomit into a small black trashcan that usually resided in the bathroom. Lawrence's relief that she was not the victim of some senseless crime was quickly tempered by how ashen she looked. She wiped the corner of her mouth and waved weakly at him, before crashing back against her pillow. He reached out and grabbed the bucket before she could drop it. He'd smelled his fair share of stomach butter during his time in the precinct; this was different. There was a sickening, cloying scent—as if her organs were liquefying.

"You're burning up," he said, as he placed the back of his hand against her forehead. "We need to get you to the hospital."

"No," she shook her head. "Epidemic. Can't."

"What? I haven't heard anything about that."

After she recovered from her latest expulsion she took a

couple of deep breaths and managed to give him a soft smile. "I'm sure Candy Crush didn't make an announcement."

Lawrence tried to mirror her smile but he'd never been much of an actor; she knew him better than anyone, she'd spot the lie easily. "I'm on level fifty-eight; I don't have time for world events," he said as he stroked the side of her face. "What can I do?"

"I'd love some orange juice. I forgot to buy it while I was out."

"I'll get some. What else?"

"The buck…" She reached out; he quickly handed her the receptacle.

When he got back he checked in on her. She was fast asleep. He turned on the TV to see if he could get any updates. The people in the grocery store had looked concerned, bordering on scared. More than a few had been binge shopping with their entire families, grabbing everything that they could off the shelves—almost as if in preparation for an impending blizzard. He'd always scoffed at those alarmists. There'd yet to be a storm in Denver that had trapped him in his house for more than a day and a half. But some people were so easily led into a panic. This time, though, he was beginning to feel the effects himself. He felt almost foolish when he showed up at the small order line with only a gallon of orange juice when people in front and behind him were dragging multiple carts.

An old lady sneezed two aisles over and she got enough glares that Lawrence thought she might be Typhoid Mary. He paid and walked home as quickly as possible. He'd never liked to drive, and now that he lived in the city, there was no need for it. There wasn't anything he needed, including work, that wasn't within walking distance. Right now though, he would have flown a rocket to get back quicker. Instead of being filled with Christmas cheer, those that were out and about looked wary and protective, not just for themselves, but of the many possessions they were carrying.

"What in the hell is going on?" he asked as Graham, his

doorman greeted him.

"I heard it's a terrorist attack—some kind of bio-weapon," Graham said, glancing nervously up and down the sidewalk and pulling the door closed tight behind them.

"What?" Lawrence turned to look at the man.

"Excuse me for saying this, Mr. Tynes, but you seem to be the only person I've run into today that doesn't know what's going on."

"Linda's sick. I've got to go."

"How sick?" Graham suddenly got very interested.

"Morning sickness," he lied.

"You sure? I didn't think you two were trying for another six months." He followed Lawrence to the elevators. "This is serious, Mr. Tynes. If she's sick, she can't be in here."

"You own this building, Graham?"

"You know I do not, but my family lives here and I will not have them be endangered by your wife or anyone else."

"The only danger you're in, Graham, is from me. Now if you don't stop fucking following me I'm going to grab you by your feet and swing you around like a club and I don't give a shit where your head hits. You got me?"

"I do, Mr. Tynes," Graham said, backing up. "But me and a few others will come up later to see how you're doing."

"You even step on my floor, Graham, and I'll consider it a home invasion. You listening to me?"

There was menace in Graham's normally mild stare. "You just make sure nothing from your home escapes, or I will stop it." Graham tapped a bulge on the side of his hip, hidden under his heavy woolen work coat.

The ding from the elevator broke the uneasy standoff. Lawrence walked in and pressed the button for his floor, never taking his eyes off the man that had been exceedingly civil for all of the three years they'd lived here.

He was having a hard time believing the reports coming in from around the country—he thought perhaps it was the news station pandering to the fear factor. He switched channels to see if he could find less biased versions. If anything, they became more alarmist with every channel change. People were biting others, there were mass attacks and riots in major cities from coast to coast. The National Guard and the Army were being deployed as a measure to contain the civil strife. It sure did look like a bio-attack, like Graham had suggested. He went to his closet and pulled out the large strongbox he'd all but forgotten way in the back. He'd promised Linda that once they had a child he would get rid of it, but for now, he was keeping his old service firearm. Right now the weight of his Desert Eagle fifty cal felt mighty nice in his hand. If Graham and his friends came knocking, he was going to show them the exit one way or the other. Right now, he was going to exercise his sovereign right to defend his home.

He checked the door to make sure it was locked, then checked on Linda, who hadn't stirred for a few hours. He hoped the rest was doing her some benefit and that she just had an early winter cold—not whatever was afflicting the country. He sat back down on the couch and succumbed to the long, strange day. He barely noticed when the television timer expired and the power went off; this was another of Linda's compulsions. She didn't like power to be wasted needlessly and Lawrence had fallen asleep in front of the tube more times than she could count. He told her that sometimes he needed the distraction, that it helped him to not think about some of the things he'd seen on the force.

"Callis don't!" he shouted himself awake from a particularly disturbing reoccurring nightmare that had its roots in the real world. The apartment was dark and quiet, but he was not alone. Someone was silhouetted against the large picture windows that overlooked the city. At first, he feared it was Graham; that he had somehow circumvented his security measures and entered. Then he relaxed when he realized that unless Graham was into see-through nightgowns and had the shape of a Greek Goddess it probably wasn't him.

"You feeling better, hon?" he asked, trying to wipe the

sleep from his eyes. She said nothing. "I got the orange juice. You want some?" he asked, keeping an eye on her. Again she said nothing, although this time, she turned to look in his direction. Whatever cobwebs lurked in his mind were burned away as the reflected city light caught her features. She was an unhealthy bluish color, her eyes as flat and dead as a reptile's, her mouth pulled back in a sneer. He stood quickly.

"Linda?"

She took a tentative step toward him, then another. Lawrence stood, unsure if he should rush towards her or away.

"Say something, honey," he pleaded. A ghostly moan escaped her lips. He looked down to the gun sitting on the couch and quickly dashed his thought, this was his Linda after all. There was nothing they couldn't work through. Hell, if they could survive her abusive, stalking ex-boyfriend, they should be able to get over the flu. Lawrence put up his hands in a defensive gesture. "I need you to say something, Linda."

He remembered something from the TV...someone official looking from the CDC saying that infected people did not behave in their normal fashion and you could test them by attempting to have them communicate. If they could not, assume the worst and extract yourself from the situation. Linda thumped against the back of the couch as she walked into it. She was less than three feet from Lawrence, saying nothing, snapping her teeth wildly. He looked again down to the gun. He knew fundamentally that there was something irreversibly wrong with her, but he was not quite ready to throw the towel in.

"I'm sorry about this," he told her as he grabbed the sofa cushion. He swung hard enough to send her reeling off to the side where she eventually toppled over. He was quick to follow before she could rise up on her own. He grabbed her ankles and dragged her back down the hallway to their bedroom. Her ankles locked under his arm, he once again searched through his closet for supplies from another lifetime and came up with two sets of handcuffs. All the while, Linda was struggling, attempting to twist and turn to sink her teeth into his flesh.

"I'm so sorry," he pleaded again as he lifted her feet-first, like a chicken about to meet its maker. Supporting her by the knees, he swung her up onto the bed. Pressing firmly down on her chest to keep her from sitting up, he was finally able to secure her legs to the footboard before catching her flailing hands. "I'm going to find out what this is, Linda, I promise. And when I do I'll come back for you."

She snapped and snarled as he took her arms and placed them over her head and then secured her wrists to the headboard. The entire time her eyes were locked on his, not in a pleading manner, but rather in a voracious one. That first night, he'd dragged the couch into the bedroom to be with her, staring for long hours, hoping to see some sign of his beloved return. Finally, when he couldn't take it anymore, he'd lain down and turned his back to her. His dreams were riddled with images of Linda chasing him through all manner of buildings, forests, and streets. It was the clicking and clacking of her restraints as she tried to free herself that finally awoke him.

BT screamed out "Linda!" as he bolted upright in his tractor seat. He thought for a moment the female zombie tearing at the lone windshield wiper was her; she grabbed it with her teeth and it would pull back then snap the windshield, the rubberless blade making a very similar sound to handcuffs on an oak headboard. With the sun just beginning to peek through, BT started the engine and tore through the trees, back onto the road. He completely destroyed a row of zombies who were coming into the woods. For the moment, the only zombie he had with him was his new window washer.

CHAPTER FIFTEEN
MIKE JOURNAL ENTRY 11

"WHAT THE FUCK?" I asked my sister as we watched the front end loader approach.

"That's BT," Lyndsey said.

"Plus one." I was pointing to the zombie on the hood. "You see any others?" Zombies weren't known for their lone wolf approach. We walked out onto the road from our hiding spot. At first, it looked as if BT was going to roll on by; he wasn't looking too particularly well. He was close to abreast of us when his head finally turned. The tractor came to a sudden stop, sending his passenger for a short ride down the hood, a bounce off the front blade, and to the ground. A normal person would have been banged up a bit—not so with the zombie. She'd stood and was looking to get back up to her mark before she saw us and had a change of heart.

I was hesitant to shoot her because of the sound, but if the sound of that huge diesel engine wasn't bringing them running then one short report shouldn't either. I neatly drilled her in the forehead. BT shut the engine down and looked out.

"You guys alright?" he asked. "Where's Steve?"

My sister finally broke down as if she'd been waiting for an apparent rescue to allow herself to cry.

"Aw shit, I am so sorry," he said as he came down and

wrapped her up in his arms. Her sobs were muffled into his chest.

"What am I going to tell our son?" she'd asked at one point.

"Huh. A tractor?" I asked, when my sister had finally extracted herself from BT's stomach. She seemed the better for the cry.

"I've had a bad night, Talbot don't give me shit about my ride."

"How come you kept the clinger on? Hood ornament?" I was goading him. I'd looked inside the tractor and had not seen a weapon.

"Oh, you know just wanted a little company for the long haul."

We did quick run-downs of what had happened the previous day, both of us gaining a new level of respect for the other after hearing the harrowing tales of what we'd been through, but now it was time to get back to the house. There was part of me that wanted to go to the school and get a bus, but we'd already been gone for so long that if they needed help, the time saved could make the difference. My sister had wedged herself inside the cab with BT, she sort of looked like packing material as she was pressed up against the glass. I'd initially opted to ride in the bucket. Big mistake, I guess I forgot just how horrible my short-term memory is. Every bump the machine hit made me rock violently back and forth. After smacking my head for the fifth time, I jumped down and went around to the back where I stood on the trailer hitch.

It had given me the idea that maybe we should get some sort of huge trailer, but at a maximum speed of twenty miles per hour, it would take months—or decades to get across the country. We'd be like the first settlers in oxen-drawn wagons.

The way things had started out, I truly expected the house to be under siege. It took long seconds for my brain to stop trying to fabricate a zombie army that wasn't there. I saw a good half dozen rifle barrels pointing at us before they could identify us. Never quite thought about how terrifying it might be to watch a bulldozer head to your stick-built safe-house. I'd got off the tractor and was walking alongside it, hands held up in the air, rifle on my back. We were a couple of hundred yards out when BT cut the engine and we met everyone. Tracy grabbed Lyndsey when my wife had looked to me and I'd shaken my head almost imperceptibly.

There was a lot of discussion about "Now what?" Try as I might I wanted to avoid it all; I'd been the one lobbying to leave and so far we'd gone ten miles and lost two people—and that was lucky. At this rate, we wouldn't make it out of Maine. We'd be playing some sort of macabre racing game called "last man standing" who would last long enough to bury those who lost. I couldn't help but think this was my fault. I was all for going home—licking my wounds, while simultaneously beating myself up. I'd been paying so little attention I hadn't even realized a decision had been made.

"Go for a ride, Mike?" BT asked. "Back to the bus, salvage some supplies—at least some batteries to give us an idea of the size of the storm of shit we're currently swirling around in," he finished when I didn't initially respond.

"Who?" I asked.

"Just you and I. You don't look so good. Figured we'd get some fresh air."

"Yeah, that ought to help."

I'd meant it sincerely, but I think BT thought I was being caustic. Nobody had, and nobody would, blame me for any of this. None of it could be laid at my feet. Nope, my guilt was all self-inflicted. I'd get a reprieve soon enough; didn't make me feel better, though...just worse in a different way.

BT and I were once again loaded up with weapons and ammunition.

"Hurry back, Talbot," Tracy said as she grabbed the back of my neck and pulled me in for a kiss. I noticed my sister give BT an extra long hug. Wasn't sure how I felt about that. It would be weird for me to think about a man I considered to be a brother to actually date my sister. I mean, this wasn't the South. That kind of shit is frowned upon up in Yankee country.

"Do we need to have the talk?!" I shouted to BT. I was standing on a small platform next to the cab as we roared to our destination.

"Huh?"

"My sister! Do we need to have the talk!?"

A dawning realization came to him. "I'm just there for her man, that's all. And who knows, maybe the Talbot line could use a little freshening up." He was smiling; it was good to see that. I had BT kill the tractor when I figured we were about a half mile away from the bus. I wanted something that somewhat resembled a stealthy approach. The bridge was littered with the broken bodies of the zombies we'd stopped. On the far side was a bus that looked like it had been hit by a semi then flipped onto some train tracks where a large freighter had finished off the remaining pile of aluminum junk by strewing it across the countryside.

"It's like they destroyed it on purpose," BT noted.

"Yeah. I don't remember it being that bad, but then again, we were sort of busy at the time."

"I don't think this is such a good idea," BT said as we stood at the foot of the bridge. There were zombie bodies piled half a dozen high in some spots. We'd have a hard time finding a place to step that did not involve putting our feet into a pile of unknown content.

"At a minimum we need those batteries and some water." One step in and I was rewarded with the sound one might get if they rubbed two balloons against each other, only this was way wetter and grosser sounding. So in the end, not really like two balloons, maybe two warm livers? I'd gone maybe ten feet when I heard the same sounds I'd made echoed, as BT followed. Only now there was a narrative lined with curses as he traveled. We were a regular gore a cappella here. I'd stepped into a pile of zombies maybe three deep. I turned to see how BT was faring when I felt an unimaginable pain on my Achilles tendon. I looked down to see a zombie's mouth sticking out from the pile, teeth firmly planted in the back of my boot. He was biting with a crushing force that did not seem capable from a normal human's jaws.

At the time, I wasn't thinking this was an accomplishment on the zombie's part, all that was going through my head was "Get it off!"

BT had seen my distress and was rushing forward to help. I'd just wanted him to shoot the thing but couldn't verbalize it. He turned his weapon and was smashing the biter's forehead into pulp. He'd only missed once, dragging the buttstock straight down my calf, naturally. It was about four blows later when the pincher grip finally loosened and fell away, I'd leaned into BT, not sure if I could support my own weight. If I'd not had the heavy, leather material there in the back, I think the zombie would have crushed the back of my leg; certainly I'd be bit clear through.

"Thanks, man," I said to BT as he helped me to the handrail, where I sat.

"Can you walk?"

"I'm not even going to try and put on a false bravado, man. I can't."

"I'm going to head over and see what I can get. I don't like being here."

"Can't imagine why," I told him as I undid my boot. I needed to take a look at the area the zombie had bit. Through the boot and sock, the bastard had still left a clear outline of his teeth, and it was already bruising into a deep purple. I gingerly touched the area trying to ascertain the extent of the damage. It wasn't like I was a doctor, though, so I could only go by what I saw, which was a relief except for the pain. There was no blood, and no rolled back tissue or tendons. I was gonna go with the assumption I would be alright. If I'd had cloth backing on my boots or sneakers on I'd have been severely hobbled and rushing towards a date with zombieism. I made a mental note to check everyone's footwear when we got back.

"Hey, make sure they're dead before you step on them!" I shouted out needlessly and maybe a little late.

"I'm not you," he answered as he moved over a pretty nasty pile.

"Don't get bit," I mumbled, "because there is no way I can get to you in any sort of hurry." I flexed my ankle and the tendon popped in protest. I cried out in a bit of pain; hadn't meant to.

"Everything alright?" BT had turned quickly.

"Yup—just being a bit of a baby," I answered through gritted teeth. "Don't worry about me coming to eat you any time soon." BT got to the other side and was rummaging around as I sat and rubbed the sore spot wondering if it would be better to put the boot on now, before the swelling, or leave it off. I figured BT could carry me like a damsel in distress. "Naw he'd drop me." I put my boot back on. I finished up and swung over to look at BT who was making a stack of things to bring back. I don't know what made me look back the way we'd come; just a cursory glance, really. And there they were. Two zombies sneaking up on me. They actually froze like we were playing Red Light, Green Light and I'd just busted them moving forward. They'd gotten close—way too close.

"Company!" I shouted to BT as I picked up my rifle. "You're some sneaky bastards but not sneaky enough to fool Michael Talbot." But then again, they were. The reason they'd got so close was because they'd been on the bridge all along. Multiple piles began to move as zombies that had been playing possum began to rise.

"Son of a bitch. I'm in trouble BT!" They were going to be coming from both sides.

"I'm coming man!"

"Don't fucking shoot me!" I warned him. We were basically in a straight line to each other, so the warning worked both ways. The zombies between us would be my biggest threat as I would have to take extra special care with my aim.

I hadn't shot any because they hadn't made a break for me yet and I was trying not to give them the impetus to do so. My first priority was going to be to those blocking the way we had come, if I could dispatch them quickly I could more or less take my time with the others. I could not figure out how I was going to avoid using the river below as my escape avenue. The thought of that was not comforting, especially with an injured flipper.

"Can't imagine that this rifle is making you second guess your options, is it?" I asked. The zombie growled. Figured that was as close to an answer as I was going to get. Drilled him in the Adam's Apple; his head fell to the side and his body followed as he tumbled off the bridge. BT began shooting; I blew off a couple of more rounds. I don't know if it was a ricochet or a bad shot but there was the distinct whine of a bullet careening off a wire right above my head. It was either lead shards or metal shavings that sprinkled in the breeze, sparkling in the sunlight as they fell.

Swiveling back and forth on one leg and acquiring targets was not my preferred method of battle. BT must have sensed he'd gotten close to taking my head off. Instead of getting on the bridge with me, he'd gone down the bank a little ways so he would have safer firing angles. I realized he was shooting at the ones to my left, on the bus side of the bridge, but it is extremely difficult to completely entrust someone with your blindside. However, if I wanted any success of not having to go for a short swim punctuated by a long drowning, that was exactly what I was going to have to do. I heard the thud of a body hitting the ground not more than five feet behind me; I didn't have the time to spare to realize just how close it had been. The only thing saving me was the constriction of the bridge and the piles of dead as the zombies navigated through and around. They were running full tilt and it was terrifying. Looked like a steeplechase as they went over obstacles in an attempt to get at me.

Well-aimed shots were out of the question. Right now it

was a matter of inflicting enough damage to take them out of the fight. A blown out knee cap, shattered hip, broken femur, pulverized pelvis, whatever it took. Occasionally I would luck out and get a head shot when a zombie stumbled and leaned over but that wasn't even my point of preference. Not anymore. It couldn't be. These zombies—though they may be smarter and stronger—these types of injuries seemed to affect them more than their predecessors. Not necessarily a good thing; no brain no pain, was how I used to think of them. Couldn't do that so much, anymore. They got any smarter they'd be able to vote. Next thing you know we've got legislature to stop the violence against zombies, then they'll want affirmative action, then who the fuck knows. For now, it was my job to keep voter registration down.

Instinctively, I knew this magazine was running low. I was going through the math of being able to reload when I was hit from the backside. I let out a loud oomph from the impact. I was forced over—hot, fetid breath blew past my nose as zombie teeth closed shut on air exactly where my lips had been one second before. This was not a delay in shooting I could afford. My landing was surprisingly soft after the crushing blow I'd been delivered. It's amazing how cushy a decaying zombie body can be. Not sure I'd want my new mattress to be made from that material, though. Innards became outtards as me and the zombie that had hit me made a crashing impact with the dead zombie, pushing his vital organs out every hole. Although I guess any organs that are pushed out of you were vital, right?

Entrails landed on my chest and neck; the desire to brush those off was trumped by the gnashing of the zombie's teeth next to me. We were as close to spooning as a couple not in a relationship can be and I was on the wrong side. I was pulling and struggling to get away while she was trying to pull my hair and ask me who my mommy was or something like that. I had to get up and over; it was my only hope. I heard the satisfactory crunch of cartilage as I threw a sharp elbow into her nose. I could hear zombies running in a rush to get in on the dining experience. I had to get up now, or I never would. I used bodies as leverage to pull me free and give me the momentum I needed to stand. Standing and fighting was now completely off the table. I just moved, grabbing the handrail and swinging out. I felt more than one set of fingers break as zombies desperately tried to keep me from leaving too soon.

With hands grabbing fistfuls of my pants and jacket they nearly succeeded in keeping me in their clutches. Sounded like popcorn popping broadcast over a loudspeaker as I twisted all of those digits into misshapen appendages. A zombie zipped past me into the river as I'd inadvertently pulled it off the bridge. I watched part of its descent into the cold water below just as my side impacted the unforgiving steel of the railing and my rifle smacked me in the chin. I don't know if it was the strength of the zombie that kept me from falling or that it had got hung up in my belt, but I seized the opportunity and grabbed at the girder. I was hanging by my fingertips for a second before I could get a better handhold. The one giving me a world class denim wedgie was now half off the bridge and thus was going to be the next problem. If his wrist was bound up in my waistline, when he fell over, his weight was going to be added to my own, and his mouth was going to be somewhere around calf high.

I hooked my arm over the girder just as the zombie fell, my shoulder protested to the point where I thought it was going to pop free from its socket. Here's a lesson kiddies, if you want to fuck someone up in a super unsuspecting way, punch them in their armpit. I had no idea how tender this spot could be. I cried out.

"Hold on!" BT shouted.

I don't know what he thought my options were.

"Reloading!" He felt the need to give me an update.

This was torturous as I tried to shake my piggybacker free while simultaneously keeping my legs from his mouth. He was not overly interested in pulling himself up and taking a bite of my spleen, so much as bobbing and weaving for what was right in front of his face. I don't know what the hell BT was doing but it felt time-wise like he was working on a difficult Sudoku puzzle or something. I shouldn't have complained, bullets started whining all around me as he took hasty shot after hasty shot. Now, I realize he was concerned for my safety, but killing me so that I was no longer in danger was not really a justifiable means to an end.

Then Mr. Klingon and I began to swing as BT finally found his mark and was putting bullets into the zombie. Not sure how this was going to work, though, to effectively neutralize my threat his point of aim would necessarily include me, and that was super unacceptable. Another explosion of a round going off and then the zombie sagged. It seemed to instantly gain a hundred pounds.

"Yes!" BT shouted.

"Yes, what?" I managed to ask, still pinioning my legs so as to not give the zombie anything to latch on to.

"Got him!"

"This zombie? You shot this zombie in the head?" I jiggled the thing around a little to make certain we were talking about the same one.

"Love to chat, but now that you're no longer part of the fare, they're looking to me. Feel free to help me like I just helped you."

I reached up to the bottom of the walkway and hefted myself and a zombie who was very much in need of a dietician. When I was able to put some weight on my legs I was able to unhook my unwanted passenger. Him, I watched splash down into the river with more than a few notes of satisfaction. BT was right; I'd been all but forgotten by the zombies. They were all past my spot on the bridge and quickly making their way to him. If I had been so inclined I could have just walked away, no one the wiser. It would serve the big man right for shooting at me. Unfortunately for me, I would have laid my life down for him. I flipped out my nearly spent magazine and once I was ready, I got into the middle of the bridge and started cutting down zombies. With this much more advantageous pincher movement, we were able to take down the zombies more effectively. It got close for BT only once as he spent more seconds than he should have trying to dry fire. I'd switched my field of focus and was killing the lead zombies that had finally reached land and were making their way to him.

"What the fuck were you thinking?" I asked BT when the last zombie fell.

"You better not be talking about that zombie I shot that was about to eat your ass."

"Eat my ass?"

"Sorry about that, but you know what I mean," he said.

"BT, you were over a hundred feet away hitting a moving target in the head six inches from my ball sack. If you'd missed…"

"But I didn't," he countered.

I mean obviously he didn't, but shit.

"When are you planning on thanking me?" he asked.

"When I'm done with the tremors, I suppose."

"What the fuck was that all about?"

"Good old fashioned ambush, I'm guessing. I wonder if they saw us coming and set this up or they'd been here all along like a spider sitting in her web, just waiting for something to get stuck in it."

"Either way man, I don't like it." His shoulders may have shivered as he said those words. "Get over here, man. We've got some supplies and I don't want to be out here anymore."

"Tell me you're sorry first."

"Fuck you, Mike. Get your not-shot ass over here."

"Close enough."

We packed up some backpacks and were three-quarters of the way back to the house. Neither of us had spoken up to this point, still mostly lost in the battle we'd just waged.

"How's your ankle?" he asked. He stopped the tractor and we got down.

"I'd completely forgotten about it until you mentioned it. Now it hurts like hell. Adrenaline must have finally worn off."

"I'm not carrying you."

"If you loved me you would."

"Guess we're just going to have to test the limits of our relationship," he said as he walked on.

"Harsh man," I told him as I did my best to add an over-exaggerated limp to my walk.

"You're limping on the wrong leg," he told me.

"I am?" I was looking down at my feet trying to figure out which one was betraying me.

"The mere fact that you're confused about it lets me know all I need to. Maybe you should join the zombies in their night classes. Speaking of which..." he started.

"I don't know man...it's happening faster and faster. They're adapting, getting smarter...that ambush? Come on! And, stronger too, I think. That bite was not human."

"These kind of changes would take generations to happen if they procreated."

"Yeah, that's the thing. They have a virus running the show."

"What do you think the evolutionary timeframe is on a deadly strain?" he asked.

"You mean for them to actually die from their own zombieism? Don't know, but whatever it is, I hope I don't live long enough to see two zombies fucking."

"True that," was his response. We fist bumped low on that one.

All looked quiet at the house. I saw a wave from the window upstairs. I think it was Justin. There were a few people on the porch just enjoying some fresh air and to get away from the claustrophobia of being in their tight quarters.

"You're limping, Mike. Are you alright?" It was Tracy come to check on us.

I shrugged my shoulder over to BT. "He tried to shoot me."

"What?" she asked confused.

"Hey, asshole. Why don't you maybe tell her the rest of the story!" he said. He'd stopped walking so he could put his stuff down; I kept going to the porch. Mad Jack was looking back and forth to BT and me. I thought he was going to start hopping around if he got any more agitated.

"Shit, man, just give him the batteries before he spontaneously combusts," BT said.

"First, you try to kill me, then you ruin my fun. Fine." I handed over a box of batteries to MJ who dashed off back into the house.

"Run into a little trouble?" Deneaux asked. She'd pulled a kitchen chair out onto the porch and was smoking a cigarette.

"Got an extra?"

Her eyebrows raised up before she handed one over.

"Mike?" Tracy asked as I'd cupped my hands around the end of the cigarette, while Deneaux lit it. It was obvious to all my hands were shaking. I related what had happened on the bridge and what I felt might be in store for us going forward. I was even going to advocate going back to Ron's when MJ came back out.

"Your brother's house is completely surrounded."

"What?" I asked reaching out to look at the console. "What are they doing? There's nobody even there."

"I think they're making sure it stays that way." Tommy was looking over my shoulder.

"There's a disturbance in the force," Trip said as a heavy cloud of smoke billowed forth from him.

"Okay, Obi-Wan," I said. As usual, I had initially disregarded his comment to only revisit it later and see the validity buried within the haze.

"Scroll back," BT said as ten people tried to stare at the tiny little screen. "Those cars looked parked in a mighty uniform manner."

"I think that's A-1 used car sales," Gary said. "I was just about to buy a sweet Miata when the zombies came. Maybe I could go get it now?" He looked around.

"Yeah, we should be able to stuff ten, maybe twelve people into one of those. Jackass," Deneaux said. Gary appeared to deflate under her words.

"Don't worry, brother. We'll get you that Miata when we get to Washington," I said.

"We're still going?" Tracy asked.

"Hon, I don't know what else to do. We can't go back to Ron's and we certainly can't stay here."

She seemed to understand, but I knew I'd not heard the end of it. Trust me, I was all ears. If someone had a better alternative, hell any kind of alternative, I was listening. The dealership had a couple of cargo vans and a small recreational vehicle; it had been my intention that we should all stay in the same vehicle, but splitting up had merit too. If we ran into mechanical issues we could pig-pile into the other cars until such time as we could secure another ride, rather than just be stranded like last time. Or maybe we could just use these until we could find something else.

"We taking the tractor?" BT asked.

"How far is it, MJ?" I asked.

"Seven miles—give or take a tenth." He was checking the scale.

I was in no mood whatsoever to go out on another run. I was exhausted and scared. My leg hurt. I missed my dog. But I knew our backs were up against it. We'd solved the immediate problem of food and water, but in a few days, we'd be back to square one. Anyway, who the hell else was going to go? I was feeling the weight of the entire troupe resting squarely on my shoulders. I was not comfortable with becoming the de-facto leader.

"You alright man? You're looking a little pasty," BT said.

"Wicked bad gas," I feigned.

He backed up.

"I think I'd like to come," Tommy said.

"No tractor. It's too damn slow and loud. We'll walk." I would have told Tommy to stay behind to keep an eye on everyone, but we were going to need a third driver. If all went right, which I had my doubts about, this should only be about a three-hour jaunt.

"What's the range on these?" BT asked MJ regarding the salvaged walkie-talkies.

"Five miles, depending on the terrain," he answered.

Mad Jack had reluctantly offered up the satellite viewing system. His relief when we'd declined was palpable. I'd rather the people staying behind knew if there was any trouble coming, plus we would be able to stay in contact for most of our walk. And of course, if there was something breakable, odds were I'd find a way to do it. Sure, it wouldn't be my fault, just that I know I'd be in a situation where it would happen. I can't be held responsible if a Yeti swings a tree trunk at me and I have to deflect it with the hand holding the unit. These things happen.

"Can you think of any reason to come with us over staying here?" I asked Tommy off to the side.

"I can't, Mr. T."

Tommy had been sort of our resident psychic, the kid had an inexplicable link to future events. It wasn't quite like a guide book; more like a cautionary tale. But lately, he'd been rooted as much in the present as the rest of us. Well, except maybe for Trip. That guy had no concept of roots; he was more likely to attach himself to high flying objects. I would imagine he had a great view, though. Tommy looked pensive after he spoke, like maybe he had something more he wanted to say but wasn't sure how to proceed...or possibly he didn't know how to verbalize it.

"Say it, Tommy. I can practically see the thought bubble above your head."

He looked at me; there was confusion on his face. Not at my words, but what he was trying to put into words. "When my sister was alive, for whatever reason, I had the ability, to a degree," he quantified, "to see the fates of those that were intertwined with hers. Like somehow it was within my power to attempt to mitigate the damage she was going to cause or suffer, all along her timeline. These visions weren't always clear or relevant; as circumstances would change the outcomes I'd seen before were also altered, and the whole process started over again. That...fluctuation, the diverging paths, the clouded futures, they cropped up way more often once you got involved."

I think he was calling me a monkey wrench in his engine block. Wasn't sure how I was supposed to take that, so I let him continue.

"With my sister's passing, the visions have been getting less detailed, less vivid, less far reaching. All I'm starting to see is the immediate aftermath of an event. Like watching the wake of a vast cruise ship; I know it's coming, but I can only watch the waves until they diminish and are finally still. Mr. T, that wake is fast approaching, and I'm scared."

I grabbed him in a hug. "Welcome to our world," I told him. "I think maybe not knowing the future is slightly less frightening than knowing it."

"I'm losing a sense." He was now crying into my shoulder.

BT was looking over, I waved him off.

When it seemed that Tommy had got it out, I gently pushed him away. "No, Tommy. It's just changing. We're all changing. Come on, let's go for a walk. It'll do you some good, clear your head."

I patted him on the back as we once again headed out.

"Yada yada," I said to Tracy and the kids, hopefully lightening the mood.

"Yeah, dad, we'll keep an eye on things," Travis said.

"Yes I know...you'll be right back," Tracy smiled and gave me a kiss. "Just hurry back this time, will you?"

I took a long look at the tractor as we departed; seemed insane to leave a virtual tank behind, but the noise was too much of a giveaway to us coming. That could have been what sparked the trap from the zombies. That was a lot of assuming on their part, though, wasn't it? That we were the same people that had been there previously, and that we were heading back to our bus. That's a lot of what ifs and a lot of communication on their part to coordinate the attack. But maybe that was just my imagination running wild. They could have been like trolls, just waiting for any poor traveler to cross their bridge. Anyway, the tractor might be safer for the here and now, but not so much for what could happen. I much preferred my zombies to come running into my hail of bullets from a well-protected place rather than getting trapped in a nearly inescapable snare. Although right now, I wasn't exactly in a well-protected area, either.

We'd decided to avoid the bridge on this trip and head back the long way to where the zombies had come and hopefully gone. We'd gone about a quarter mile when I checked in.

"Hey MJ, we still all clear?"

"Don't you think I would have told you otherwise?" he asked.

"Is he being a smart ass?" BT asked. "Because I'll go back and…"

"Not everyone is a Talbot," Tommy said assuaging BT's feelings.

BT calmed down. "Damn good thing, too. Can you imagine this world if everyone ran around like him?" He was pointing at me.

"What the hell man, I haven't even done anything." I was defending myself from an attack brought on from deep left field. "You can both kiss my ass."

I think the duo were getting ready for a good old Talbot smashing. I was saved by Mad Jack's next words.

"There is a small group of zombies about a mile from your location moving in what could be an intersecting path," he said.

"Are they running?" Tommy asked.

"Lightly jogging," Mad Jack said after a pause.

"Do you see any reason other than us, for their trajectory?"

I asked.

"I don't, but I'll keep looking. I'm about to lose my feed."

"We should get going," Tommy said.

"Yeah, I'm not of the same ilk. We sit tight for the forty-five minutes it takes the satellite to come back around. By then the zombies should have passed our rendezvous point." I said.

"How many zombies are we talking about? Maybe we just get rid of them." BT said.

"How about it, MJ?" I asked.

"Seventy-four," he replied quick enough.

"Umm...MJ that's not really a 'small group'."

"It's all relative. It's small compared to what we've been encountering," was MJ's retort.

"I'm just going to kill him." BT's head was shaking back and forth.

Right here didn't seem like such a great locale. We were in someone's pasture—open ground for hundreds of yards in every direction, and for some reason, this place looked like it had been mowed recently; the grass wasn't even to our knees. "The trees ahead or the house behind?" I asked a steaming BT and pondering Tommy.

"Seventy-four Mike. How does anyone call that a small force?"

"We're going to have to move past that, big man. If we started jogging right now we could get back to the house before they ever become a concern. Either that or we hide in the woods and hope they just keep on going."

"What are the odds of that?" BT asked.

"About as good as we could expect," I said.

"So they're coming right for us?" Tommy finished.

"Probably."

BT went down the path I'd been heading without any further prompting from me. "Say they're out here looking for us. If we head back, they'll know where we're at. I vote for the woods."

"So do I," said Tommy.

"I vote for the house. That way, if you guys are wrong, I get to say 'I told you so' right before we die."

"You suck, Talbot," BT said.

It was a pine forest, which had the benefit of the ground being coated in pine needles. If we stayed away from fallen branches and twigs, our footfalls would be nearly silent. The cool thing about a pine forest was the absolute quiet, like the flooring not only dampened sound but absorbed it. Even the wind, which made leaves rustle, giving the illusion of running water, was not a concern here. We found a tree that was massive, had to be pushing seventy years of an undisturbed life, free from home builders and fire starters. We hunkered down behind it, keeping a look-out for the zombie patrol. I used that word because I was convinced that was exactly what it was. I don't know what was tracking us or where and when they had picked up our trail but something was playing a war game with us. I had to wonder if it was someone Deneaux had pissed off; they could have the exact same devices she did. Then I went a step further; maybe she was working in concert with this mysterious force, doing her best to separate me from the group and have me eliminated.

It came down to motive, well not really, Deneaux might kill me for the fun of it. But more likely there would have to be a reason she would do this, some clear and present reward. She could have killed me a dozen times by now since her return, though she would have had a difficult time explaining my death by hand cannon as she held the smoking weapon. No, if she'd made a deal to have me killed, this was the way to do it, sabotage our every move and have me running around on these suicidal half-missions. I mean, we'd basically accomplished nothing but lose our home, my brother, and my sister's husband. I'd been as close as one gets to death several times. We had no vehicle, and so far our plans to get to safety had failed worse than miserably. When we picked her up, no one had wanted her but I'd taken her anyway. I'd told myself to keep an eye on her, and I had. But I'd been so tunnel focused on her current actions, watching for her to pull something overt, that I didn't take into account things she may have already set in motion before she ever got to us. Could be a serious case of paranoia...or not. Her track record wasn't exactly spotless. Shit, the spots on her track record were blemished.

Could have maybe gone in circles a few more times with the Deneaux dilemma, but the thought was cut short as we were joined by zombies. They were jogging, like MJ had said, in more or less a column now as the woods dictated this formation. I know I've said this before, but it bears repeating for those of you not from this locale. I'm sure most of you have been out for a walk in the woods, as it can be a very pleasant endeavor, especially when you're not fleeing for your life from a relentless enemy. The majestic trees and the cool breezes can be invigorating. The wonderful line of sights as you peer into the wild nature of wherever you are—a drink from a cool clear stream, perhaps a picnic table, a berry or two. That's all wonderful, but it in no way describes the deep Maine woods. Here it is an explosion of vegetation, trees, bushes, thorns, wildflowers, saw grasses—all fighting for their small parcel of land to call their own and they stake out their territory with a vengeance. And fucking black flies, which make mosquitoes look like butterflies

A fifteen hundred pound moose could quite literally be within twenty feet of you and you would never see him. Yes, you'd hear the beast pushing through the flora, but you wouldn't see him. That's the Maine woods. We were on a small rise that looked down onto a deer path some thirty feet away. We could just see a piece of the ground they were passing on, maybe no bigger than a standard chalkboard, or whiteboard, for those of you that grew up a little later. So maybe there were seventy-four zombies, according to MJ's calculations. We, however, could only see three at any one time. That left a whole fucking bunch of deadly monsters unaccounted for.

BT raised his rifle up.

"Whatcha doing, pal?" I asked him.

"Want me to write you up a synopsis?" he asked.

"Yeah, as long as somewhere in there it talks about how we have to go running for our lives once you take that shot."

BT looked over his shoulder at me.

"He's probably right," Tommy said, backing me up.

"Really? The man who is generally doused in gasoline and ready to be the first to jump into the fire doesn't want me to shoot?"

"I'm kind of surprised you're in such a rush, buddy."

He thought on that for a moment, his finger alternating between applying more pressure on the trigger and easing up. "This sucks," he said as he lifted his barrel up.

I let out a breath of relief. Fighting in the woods was only cool when you were a Minuteman and you dashed out to the British marching columns, blew a couple of Red Coats away and then melted back in. Not being able to see an enemy until they were right in your face? Well, that loses its appeal pretty quickly. The winds of change or the winds of war, okay, the just plain wind, chose this very moment to pick up. Like a lot of things in life, it started slow enough, I mean, I hardly even noticed it. You would have been hard-pressed to get a kite up in it. But it kept building; I wasn't concerned just yet, even if the wind was to our backs and was pushing our scent to the zombies. They weren't known for picking up trails this way. Nope, I started to get concerned when the branches began to sway.

BT still had eyes on the zombies; Tommy and I were looking upwards. If foul play had a scent, I think we would have been covered in it like unsuspecting shoppers walking through Macy's team of commission-based perfume salesgirls during Christmas.

"We have to go," I said, touching BT's shoulder. An old pine tree not more than ten feet from us crashed down with an explosive fury. It was so violent sounding I thought perhaps we were walking through a minefield.

"Well, we're fucked now. They're looking this way." BT brought his rifle up quickly.

For some reason I could not fathom, he seemed to want this to happen in the worst way. He fired before I could ask him if they were looking at the tree or at us. No escaping it now, we were in the thick of it. I brought my rifle up, sure some of the zombies were still in the patch we could see, and yes, those ones were trying to make a path to us but so were the ones we couldn't see. With two rifles firing we made short work of five, maybe six. Tommy was looking around, if not for the wind, we could have at least heard them coming. I had the feeling we were in some sort of weird weather phenomenon, like a micro-burst where tiny tornado force winds come down and just shred small swaths, although my understanding was they are very short lived. Not this one, though. It seemed to just be getting started.

Large branches were buffeting against each other with enough force to crack them free from their hosts. Looked like some world class slap fighting going on. Bushes were being uprooted, pine needles blew with stinging force whenever they hit exposed skin.

"We have to get out of here!" I screamed trying to be heard over the roar of the wind. If the zombies didn't kill us, the forest would. Tommy had fired off to our left as the first of the zombies made it to us. The zombie's collarbone and part of its ribcage shone a gleaming white as Tommy ripped through its chest, exposing a fair amount of the skeletal frame and musculature. He'd not had a chance to get a second shot off as the zombie had closed the distance too quickly. I then got another demonstration of just how strong the kid was. With his right hand, he punched out. I thought, at first, I'd heard another tree losing its battle with gravity, but it was Tommy's fist pulverizing bone into shattered fragments. Then I realized it was the zombie's skull that Tommy had not only broken but broken clear through.

He had his fist submerged halfway into the brain casing of that zombie, the wind again picked up just in time that I missed most of the squelching sound as he pulled free. Personally, I'd probably have to cut that hand off if it had been mine. There would never be a time where I wouldn't remember where it had been.

"Pull back, pull back! To the field!" The wind had somehow picked up even harder. In less than half a minute we'd made it out of the woods and nearly into another world— one where sunshine and calm dominated. The wind was so tranquil it wasn't even disturbing the grass. After the barreling train sound we'd just left, this was disorientating in its own right. We were only given a moment to stare at each other in wonderment at what had just happened before the zombies began to appear along the tree line we had just emerged from. As soon as the zombies saw us they broke out in a run, there was no hesitation on their part.

We were doing our best to keep containment and appropriate fields of fire and trying not to overlap our shots. We were holding our own, even winning, when the zombies decided to change tactics; they stopped rushing out to meet our bullets. We could catch glimpses of them moving in the woods, but nothing clear enough for shots. They were fanning out to make a much wider offensive line.

"We need to keep backing up," BT said wisely, and that was just what we did. The zombies didn't go for the intimidation factor by revealing themselves first in a great line; they just started bursting forth from the trees. They were savage and fierce looking in their murderous intent. I could almost picture them like early Native Americans, replete in deer skin, carrying tomahawks ready to scalp us for daring to encroach on their land. The ones on the farthest ends of the line did not angle in but kept running straight lines as if maybe they were running a race we weren't aware of. It was Tommy that figured it out first.

"They're going to try to surround us."

They were nearly in position for it to be considered an encirclement right now. Try my ass! I thought sourly. I would have thought that all of the fucking events that led to this very moment were surreal enough, I'd not been ready for a turning up of the dial. There were shouts of men coming from the woods and the percussions of multiple rifles being fired. I was hoping for some long lost military unit stumbling across our position and being in the right spot at the right time to save our asses. What we got instead was fucking Knox. How can shit possibly get shittier? By definition, it is already shit. That's like having a cupcakier cupcake. But that's what just happened. We could hear him issuing orders. As of yet, I did not believe he knew we were out here. Well, he knew someone was out here, just not us.

He was much more efficient tearing through the zombies than we were. As it was, we had to get down into the prone position to keep from becoming victims of friendly fire by the enemy, if there is such a thing. We did our part keeping the zombies from getting close enough to bite us, but it was Knox's forces that did most of the heavy lifting. It did get closer than comfortable a couple of times, pivoting around while you're lying down is not the best battle tactic. BT had sent a zombie spiraling away as it had attempted to land on him as it dove. He'd flipped over and spun at the right moment placing his left foot squarely center mass on the zombie's chest and then heaving him up and away. I'd shot the zombie mid-air like a clay pigeon. You just can't make this stuff up. I mean I guess you could, but no one is going to believe it.

The zombies, seemingly predicting their end was near, were more determined than ever to go out with a mouthful of food. The beauty of the prone position was the ability to get off well-aimed shots, as the recoil was absorbed by all of your mass instead of just your shoulder, making target acquisition much easier. Again, it was just when you had to twist your body that it became awkward, that, and I'd had the luck to place my elbows on rocks shipped in from the Great Barrier

Reef. I mean because they were sharp, you know, like coral. Tommy had reached back with his foot and tripped up a zombie that was about to lay waste to my head, it landed with a jaw-crunching hardness to my immediate left. At last, the Australian rocks had earned their price. I pushed up on my hands and knees and began to slam my stock into the side of its skull and then its mouth when it turned.

When it stilled, I dropped back down, not thinking that perhaps I should have pushed it away, if it had been playing possum it would be able to sink into my shoulder long before I could do anything about it. I was placing my second magazine in when the shooting petered out from its frenetic pace to a smattering...and then silence.

"Hello!" Knox shouted from the woods. We kept silent. "Nothing? Not even a how do you do? Well, that's pretty fucking rude, considering we just saved your asses. Listen, can't we all be friends? This is a messed up world these days, we need as many allies as we can get, and since I have more allies in here than you have out there, I think you should get up so we can discuss this like civilized people!"

"Civilized my ass, I'll bust a cap in him if he shows his punk face," BT said quietly enough, I knew he meant what he said but I could still tell he was nervous.

"Don't make me shoot you before we get proper introductions!" Knox yelled.

I'd tapped Tommy and BT on the shoulder, Knox had his men moving. Surprisingly, they were adopting the same flanking positions as the zombies had.

"Already know who you are asshole!" BT shouted. I was thinking that wasn't the best course of action, but it'd already happened. Now we just had to deal with the repercussions. So this is what it felt like on the other end of the spectrum—watching other people do dumb things, I mean. Huh. I don't think I liked it all that much; might have to reconsider my general actions if we made it out of here.

"I thought I caught a glimpse of your extra largeness. We

have a score to settle me and your group. I lost a lot of good men, and I think some sort of tribute to them is in order, don't you? There's no need for more than a couple of you to die. I'd hate to see anything happen to your main group. We'll bring them in, treat them like red-headed step-children, each and every one of them. I'm afraid though, that you, BT, are going to have to go...and so is your little sidekick buddy."

"Sidekick?" I asked BT.

"Go with it, man."

"They have eyes on us," I said.

Tommy was looking up in a tree. "There he is, he has binoculars and a radio."

"Rifle?" I asked as I swiveled over.

"On his shoulder," he answered.

I'd debated shooting the tree next to him to scare him down, but Knox had already signaled his intention to kill me and take my family, the implication being he knew where they were, as well. This needed to end soon and in our favor so we could get back to them. All of this was going through my head as I lined up the lookout man. At first, I instinctually aimed for his head. He started to scramble when he realized I had a bead on him. I blew a hole about center mass, blowing fragments into his heart, he was dead before he could hit the ground. There was return fire but they were spraying in all directions. Even so, a few rounds got uncomfortably close.

"Cease fire, cease fire!" Knox shouted. "Listen friends! I know there's three of you, I know you just had a firefight with zombies. You're traveling light; can't imagine that you brought more than three or four magazines of ammo on whatever errand you're out here doing. Of that, what do you have, seventy-five rounds or so between you? I have over twenty-five men here with me and thousands of rounds. There's no need to make this messy."

"Wow, you make a great argument," I shouted. "Gee mister, I guess we will just give up with those insurmountable odds."

"What the fuck are you doing, Talbot?" BT asked.

"You started it; I'm just adding flair."

"You're calling that flair?"

"Mr. Knox, if you come out personally, you have my word as a Girl Scout second class that we'll surrender and I'll give you a box of Thin Mints as a bonus."

Nothing for a few seconds, then laughter that echoed through the woods. "You see? That's what's missing with me and my people. Humor. Good old-fashioned sarcastic humor. God, I miss that shit. If I didn't hate you so much I'd let you live and do comedy shows for me every night. And if you had a joke that sucked, I'd stick you with this blade I have...I call him Shorty. We've been through a lot, me and Shorty. Lot of history there," he sighed. "He wouldn't kill you outright; you could fuck up your jokes at least fifty or sixty times. Of course, eventually, he'd wear you down. So you'd have to stay sharp, you know what I mean?"

"This guy is fucking twisted," I said.

"You think?" BT answered sardonically, like maybe I had already forgotten about our earlier encounter.

"You want to know something? I usually wouldn't have said anything, it's a bigger surprise that way. We have night vision. I'm guessing you don't. No moon tonight, either...looks like it's going to stay pretty cloudy. Sure, you can post guards, take turns and all that shit, but you can't watch what you can't see, right? And considering you're out in the middle of a field, we can hit from just about any angle. You'd be amazed at people's faces when you sneak right up on them. I mean 'terrified' is only one adjective and hardly does their expression justice when we capture them, and we will capture you. Oh, I know you're thinking you're going to go out in a blaze of glory, or some shit, or you'll heroically kill each other rather than let us get our hands on you. I get it, and maybe you'll try, but you'll fail. You see, we have medical supplies. Yup, the kind that make you go nightie night real quick. So yeah, my guys are going to shoot you tonight, just with darts instead of bullets. That way, when you wake up, we'll all be by a huge campfire, and we'll be having s'mores, my personal favorite. We secured some marshmallows just last night. A little stale, but over the fire, they should be divine. 'Course, you guys won't. I've been accused of not being a great s'mores sharer."

"Holy shit, man! Are you going to keep yammering? Giving me a fucking headache." I shouted.

"What the fuck are you doing?" BT looked exasperated.

"Really? Are you concerned it's going to get worse for you?" I asked him.

"I am talking!" Knox shouted, apparently he wasn't too keen on being interrupted.

"Keep going, man. I don't want to get in the way of your babbling."

I think Tommy wanted to tell me to shut up, that I was going to get us killed, but we were already heading down that path.

"Spinx. Where was I?" Knox asked.

Presumably, it was Spinx that answered. "S'mores."

"I hate those fucking things," I said loud enough for everyone's benefit. "Gooey fucking mess, shit gets everywhere, more times than not the marshmallow is burned. Who the fuck wants a black marshmallow? I bet you like to burn your marshmallows into fucking ash. Those things taste like old marmite, you ever try that shit? I mean I knew the Brits were a little off-kilter but how is that bitter salty paste a sandwich spread? Sure, crumpets are delicious, then they go and ruin 'em."

"Will you shut the fuck up!" Knox screamed.

"Sure, sure. Go on with your little sad, sadistic fairy tale," I urged.

"Fuck it man, you ruined the moment," Knox replied.

"He gets that a lot," BT added.

"Really man, you're siding with the psychopath right now?" I asked.

"He's right! I'm just agreeing with that one statement…not with his particular stance on the world," he added sheepishly.

"For people that are a few hours away from getting skinned alive, you sure are jovial," Knox said.

"Oh, that's where you were going with that," I said. "Hell of a buildup, I shouldn't have ruined it. That would have been pretty fucking scary, especially if you forced the fucking s'mores on us first."

"What are you doing?" BT asked quietly.

"Look behind you." I heard him shift. "Whoa, how did you know?"

"Been hoping MJ was going to keep an eye on us." The tractor was still pretty far off, but it was going to beat the night. "Tommy over there has been sending a distress signal."

"Wow. I take back all that shit I've been saying about you," BT said. "Well, some of it anyway."

There was activity in the woods. My guess was they were seeing the tractor for the first time.

"You better tell them to leave!" Knox said.

"Yeah, I'm going to tell the people that are going to prevent us from getting skinned alive to stop. Go fuck yourself, Knox."

"We have rocket launchers," he replied calmly enough.

Well, that changed things dramatically. "Tommy, give whoever is driving that tractor a heads up, pretty sure he's full of shit, but we can't risk it."

He began to talk quietly on the radio.

"See Knox, this here is what we call a standoff. We now have as many people as you do and, yeah, we have night vision. Plus, by now my people will be getting into position to take out yours. Things are going to get pretty interesting real soon. I mean, unless of course you just leave."

"Mr. T…it's just a few people on the tractor," Tommy said to me as if maybe I wasn't aware of the present situation.

"It's a bluff, kiddo. Right now we're lying to each other about whose dick is bigger. And really, neither of us wants to whip it out in public so to speak, so it's going to be a matter of who believes the other has the bigger one. You know what I mean?"

"That's the analogy you use? Did you flunk out of fifth grade or something?" BT asked.

"We'll be seeing you real soon, Talbot!" Knox shouted.

"See, I have the bigger dick," I said, happily enough.

"You are the bigger dick, that's for sure," BT replied. We waited until we could no longer hear their departure before we stood, warily.

"Anyone else wondering how he knew your name?" Tommy asked.

"Well shit, I hadn't been. We need to get out of here before he realizes I was full of it."

"What about the cars?" BT asked.

"Don't think it's such a good idea to go back that way," I said. We were on the move. At first, pretty cautious, always checking our sides and back as we left, then we moved to a slight jog to get to the tractor. Deneaux was sitting in the cab, smoking a cigarette. A high-powered rifle with a scope next to her.

"Should have let me get closer. I could have taken a couple of them out."

"Did you hear the part about the rocket launcher?"

"Bullshit." She dropped her smoke and stomped it out.

"Where's everyone else?"

"Heading back, I suppose."

I looked around, to my left were my sons and brother. They waved as they came our way.

"Anyone else?"

"Like who? You realize as a fighting force we're spread pretty thin. Have a lot of non-combatants in the mix."

"Don't even go there, Deneaux. We're not leaving people behind because they can't shoot a gun."

"Your call, dearie, I suppose," she said as she lit another cigarette. "Even if it's the wrong one," she finished in a plume of smoke.

"Since you brought up the subject of unnecessary personnel, you wouldn't happen to know how we keep getting found, would you?"

"How would I?" she answered casually. If I struck even a modicum of truth she'd never show it, and I'd never know. She was in a different league than me when it came to deception. I think her and Satan could have a great sit down regaling each other with stories of complete bullshittery, promising each other all manner of things they would never deliver on and each would probably believe the other would come through.

"Want a ride?" she asked as she started the machine up. A black thick plume arose as she did so, maybe from her, maybe from the tractor.

"Rather walk. The air is clearer."

"Suit yourself." She spun the machine on its tracks. "And you're welcome!" She cackled as she drove on.

"You think she's playing a part in this?" BT asked.

"I don't know, but something's not right. We're definitely being followed. Someone, somewhere, is on to us. Haven't been able to take a shit in a week without someone offering to hand me toilet paper."

"Dude you have seriously got to work on your analogies." BT clapped me on the shoulder. We waited for Travis, Justin, and Gary to catch up and then we went back to the house.

CHAPTER SIXTEEN
MIKE JOURNAL ENTRY 12

WE WAITED TWO full days, no zombies and no Knox. Mad Jack had been keeping an eye on them but when we lost the feed, we lost them, and he'd not been able to pick them up again. My guess was they'd found a place to lay low, like we had. Ron's house was still out of the question. We weren't starving…yet, but we were hungry and everyone was starting to get a little irritable. We had a lot of mouths to feed and dammit if Deneaux hadn't put her cancerous thoughts into my head. Of the twenty-eight of us, really only ten were combat ready and hardened. That made for a lot of people that needed assistance and resources. It wasn't that I was ever going to leave them behind; I just didn't even want the thought of liability to cross my mind. I was not Knox but there was certainly something to be said about leading a fighting force, makes you much more wieldy in a volatile situation. Anything we did had to be thought out with getting the slowest and the most infirm from point A to B as safely as possible.

"Fuck you, Knox." I was standing on the small porch looking out at nothing in particular.

It was BT who heard me. He was looking out at the same expanse. "He's not really there, is he? Because I can't see him."

"I meant in general."

"Just throwing curses to the wind then?"

"Yeah pretty much."

"We can't stay here, Mike."

"Yeah I know."

"The kids are hungry, hell, I'm hungry."

"Have never quite felt as vulnerable as I do now. Cut off from supplies and transportation. We're ripe for the picking. Those zombies head back, the vamps, shit even Knox. One Molotov cocktail and we're done; we won't be able to run from here. All of us, of this, can be undone with a gas filled coke bottle."

"Why the hell are you thinking like that? That's pretty dark, even for you."

"It's not bad enough out there, now we have to deal with a psychotic dictator wannabe who somehow has the ways and means to track us. I can't figure out why he hasn't already exacted justice."

"So you don't think the meet up was a coincidence?"

"Maine is small, brother, but it isn't that small."

"Then why hasn't he attacked here?"

I'm guessing he doesn't want everyone dead. He likes his games. So the bastard is out there, that I know and at some point, he's going to make his move, our only play is to be gone."

"Wherever he is, we still need transportation."

"I know that, BT. So how do we go about it? Do we send out a large force to secure the rides and leave this place undefended or do we go out with a small force that can be easily picked off? Next time he corners us it won't be so close to a rescue and my guess is he will have a response for that anyway."

"We all go."

"How big are your balls?" I asked him, I kept looking.

"Mike, you're making me uncomfortable, I mean at first I figured you were going figurative on me, now I'm wondering if you're leaning to literal."

I shook my head. "No, wait, I definitely don't mean literal. I don't want to see your balls, which I'm sure are the size of grapefruits."

"Ponch, why are you talking about his balls?" Trip was leaning into my ear as if he were going to whisper but was talking at a completely conversational tone.

"Figure of speech, Trip." I leaned back from him.

Trip turned to BT and was leaning over, staring directly at his crotch. "You'd think something that big would bulge out, you must have a great tailor." Trip was reaching out like he wanted to physically inspect what we'd been talking about.

"Get out of here." BT pushed Trip away; if I hadn't been on the other side to catch him, he would have gone flying off the porch.

"They must be sensitive." Trip said as an aside to me. "Anything that big would have to be. Do you think he's embarrassed because he's all balls and no bat?" He started reaching out again.

"You have a death wish?" I asked him as I physically picked him up and out of the way of BT who looked on the verge of sending Trip into the stratosphere without the assistance of drugs. "Stephanie! You need to save your husband!"

She came out onto the porch, she didn't travel too far from him as I'm sure she was used to having to extract him from all manner of issue. She took a quick look at BT and that was all she needed.

"Come on honey, let's see if we can find you some food."

It took BT a few minutes to calm down. "Did you see that man? He was trying to touch my junk! Who does that?"

"Trip, apparently."

"And you just stood there!"

"What the hell did you want me to do? I don't know what kind of deal you two have worked out."

"You're an asshole, Mike."

"Hardly a newsworthy revelation."

"It could work, you know," he said, coming back around to what we had been talking about.

"Yeah it could, so could me becoming a pilot and jetting our asses out of here. There's a possibility of success, just a way bigger potential for failure. We get caught out in the open like that and we'll get slaughtered. We've got three infants and six kids for, fuck's sake."

"We can't stay here, you said it yourself. Those three infants and six kids need to eat. We all do. And I need to hear Trip shut the hell up about his Reuben sandwiches across the States tour."

Trip, of us all, was doing the worst without a constant supply of food. He would go on and on about the different things he'd eaten and where. And for a guy that barely remembered his own name he was very detailed in texture, taste, and presentation of his meals, the latest being the Reuben sandwiches he'd eaten. I had to admit I'd not known there could be so many variations in rye bread.

"The truck. I say we go back for the truck." BT continued.

"Like we haven't had enough bad experiences with dump trucks. Plus, you yourself said it didn't work."

"I'm pretty convinced it's the battery. We take the one from the tractor, switch it out, get everyone in, go a couple of towns over, away from this place and get some real rides."

"And if it's not the battery?" I asked.

"Hell, I don't know man. What if we just wait here until we starve to death?"

"Point taken. I'll get MJ to do extra duty on the sat feed. We'll head out in the morning; maybe get you a sandwich or two—you get so cranky when you haven't had enough to eat."

I told everyone that night what we were up to, no one protested. There really weren't a shitload of substitute ideas thrown around. I could see Deneaux biting her tongue, rare for her but appreciated. I slept that night, barely, not sure if I strung more than five minutes together at any one time.

What I hadn't taken into account the previous evening was whether to take the tractor or just the battery. Obviously, the tractor offered a measure of safety but at the expense of announcing to everyone in the surrounding area that we were on the move. In the end, we took it. I had MJ keep an eye on our perimeter and every time we went off grid, so to speak, we shut her down and took a break. It took way longer than it should have, but I was not going to lead us straight into a trap. It was possible Knox had the same technology and would set something up to hit us during our blind spots.

Then came the fun of the pit, we couldn't send everyone down because we'd basically be in a fishing barrel ripe for the shooting but there were some straggler zombies down there that needed to be dealt with. It was Deneaux that led the charge. I know, I know—it's weird just to write that. She drove the tractor down, crushing everything in her path. BT and Gary followed her to clear away anything that could somehow survive, then most of the rest went after them. Justin, myself, Meredith, and Tiffany hung back as the perimeter guard. Twice I caught Mad Jack looking at his screen like he was a fourteen-year-old boy and he had somehow tapped into the Playboy channel. My heart would quicken and I would make everyone with me get low, convinced we were even now in the crosshairs of a sniper. Neither time amounted to anything though I was tempted to run down that hill and smack him in the head for scaring me.

There were only five shots from inside the hole, Deneaux had been very thorough in her search and destroy mission. Even so, those five blasts echoed loudly out of there as if it were a megaphone. I winced with each and every one. I wondered if Knox had heard it, or possibly more zombies.

"You alright, Mr. Talbot?" Tiffany asked.

So unused to the moniker, I kept on pacing.

"Dad, she's talking to you." Justin put an arm out to stop my earth stomping.

"Huh?"

"Tiffany asked if you were alright."

I looked up from the hole to her to see the concern on her face, she was trying to figure out what had me on edge. "Hey...sorry. And it's just Mike. I get weirded out with Mr. Talbot, that's always how the cops addressed me."

She smiled at that.

"Oh, he's serious." Justin made sure to let her know.

"You've completed your usefulness, why don't you start filling this hole in," I told him. "Changing a battery is a five-minute procedure I'm not sure why it's taking so long, I don't like being out here so long with our d..." I caught myself, not that Justin was going to let it go.

"What dad? What don't you like getting caught out with?"

"He gets caught out with it a lot, apparently, he's a big commando fan." Meredith decided to voice up.

"This is not a conversation we're having. We're surrounded by enemies on all sides and we're discussing my undergarments."

"Or lack thereof," Meredith said as Justin and Tiffany busted out laughing.

I made sure my pacing was a good twenty feet away while they yucked it up. Ten minutes later and they were still working on the damn battery.

"Dad!" Justin called over.

"No more jokes!" I told him.

"No, look down." He was pointing to Mad Jack who appeared to be yelling.

I could hardly hear him. But I didn't need it to be shouted, he was holding the screen up and on a slight breeze his words drifted up so silent as to be a whisper. "Zombies."

"To the mouth of the hole, move!" I told the kids.

All was quiet as we sat on the lip of the access road down. It was pebbles that started rolling down the slopes of the hole that clued me into the number of zombies we were talking about.

"Go now, all of you. Down."

"Dad?"

"No questions, go."

They did, albeit Justin was a little reluctant. I stayed long enough to give them an adequate head start. We weren't going to be able to hold them off; hell, I don't think we'd even be able to delay them much. The only way we could give those down below any extra time would be if we allowed ourselves to be eaten. I wasn't too keen on that option; I was going to keep spinning the wheel until something better came up. The kids were three-quarters down, I was about halfway when I saw BT, Deneaux, and a few others raise their rifles up. Not going to lie, I was happy they were pointing closer to the top. I turned, because let's face it, that's what you do when something is chasing you. This isn't the NFL; I don't have the option of looking at the big screen ahead of me. I stumbled for a couple of steps, but not before I caught enough glimpses of the horde coming our way. Soon enough, bullets started to fly; I was closing in on the kids who were spending way too much time constantly looking over their shoulders.

"Keep running!" I urged.

In between lulls of shooting I could hear Trip shouting. I won't swear on it but I thought I heard him say they needed more time to fit in the flux capacitor. Gary was under the hood of the truck, he also kept looking up the hill to see what was going on and then I could see his arms furiously moving as he was cranking something down or trying to remove something, I was unsure of what his actions signified. It was bad enough that he was still under there. Changing a battery was a ten-minute job, and that's on a bad day. There had to be something wrong. No pressure, but I figured he had about another four to get it done or else.

Tracy, thankfully, was getting everyone into the rear of the dump truck which was no easy feat, given there was no ladder. BT had to leave his post and aid in the effort. He climbed onto the truck and was basically lifting people up by their outstretched arms and depositing them into the bed, handing one to another waiting inside. There was a sharp outcry of pain; Carol had slipped and struck the side of her head on the corner of the truck. She'd told BT in no uncertain terms that she could get up there by herself. The stubborn woman was going to get someone killed as three people rushed to help her back up. Blood streamed down her face, her eyes were threatening to roll back and her legs were wobbly.

Gary's look of panic became more expressive as I, and I guess the zombies, got closer. The kids had finally got down and Justin went over to help his grandmother. Even the unflappable Deneaux kept glancing up as she hurriedly loaded her rifle. Things turned even more askew in a matter of moments, as impatient zombies, unhappy with their place in the conga line decided to take the express route down. Some were spilling off the side of the narrow roadway but even more were taking what should have been suicidal plunges straight down from the rim. I'd mistakenly thought it was large rocks being knocked loose, then there was the resounding cracks of multiple bones snapping as they impacted the ground far below. The entire perimeter of the pit was encircled with zombies who couldn't seem to control themselves enough to not go jumping in. Some were trying to navigate down the impossibly steep sides; they were in the minority. I'd finally made it to the bottom, myself; the zombies that had beat me down there were now crawling, mostly broken, over to the truck. I had a thirty-second head start on those behind.

"Why aren't you in the back?" I asked Porkchop as I was heading to the cab.

He shrugged. It was too late; he was going to have to stay here.

"Gary, get in the truck!" I shouted. Deneaux had got into the passenger seat and was firing, as were multiple guns from the back of the dump truck.

"See if she'll start!" He shouted without looking up.

I didn't hesitate and try to grab him; there wasn't time. I ran around to the far side.

"It's diesel. Deneaux reminded me as I climbed into the seat. Like I'd not heard the words, I cranked the ignition without waiting.

"Diesel, dumbass," she said between shots.

Not sure how many times I said I hated fucking diesel engines in the four seconds it took for the glow plugs to warm up. I started the engine. Gary was propelled off the front of the truck like I'd launched him with an electrical charge and, by the way he swore, that was probably exactly what happened. He stumbled back within inches of the outstretched hands of a zombie that was absolutely sure was finally going to get a happy meal. I'd gripped the door handle and was about to help him up when he righted himself and came running back. He closed the hood just as a roiling black cloud of smoke rose from the twin exhaust pillars.

"Go, go, go!" he shouted as he climbed onto the hood. I had to wait the few seconds it took for him to go up and over the cab and into the back. I knew I was going to make the truck lurch and I'd shake him off like a bad dream if I didn't. Deneaux had pulled in her rifle and rolled up her window as the fastest of the zombies reached the truck.

"Feel free to drive at any time," she said calmly.

"You got it, Miss Daisy." The truck sputtered and spat, coughed a few times, hesitated and jumped into gear. As far as getting a machine rolling, it was about as ungainly as it gets but was still beautiful in its own right. The question now was: how was I possibly going to get out of here? The roadway was packed with commuters; I didn't think I'd be able to force them off without putting us at even more risk.

"I'm dying to see what you do here," Deneaux said as she lit a cigarette. I snatched it from her hand before she could bring it to her mouth. I popped that thing in mine, took two quick drags, killed about half the thing and then handed it back.

"Me too," I said with an exhalation.

"I've always liked you, Michael."

285

"Is this some sort of atonement before we die? Are you trying to make it right? Let's not kid ourselves. Maybe there's some mutual respect for each other's skills, but you and I...we pretty much despise and hate each other. To say otherwise just cheapens our relationship."

"Have it your way. You planning on running straight into the zombies?" She was finishing her cigarette like she had all the time in the world.

"No, I was planning on asking them to move to the side. Sure, I mean, I'll say it as nicely as possible, but if that doesn't work I'll blow the horn."

"That many impacts will destroy the front end—including the radiator, and ultimately the engine will stall. By that point, Michael, not only would we be up shit creek without a paddle, we'll be wading in it, possibly even treading in over our heads."

"Just the way I like it."

"Really, you? The one afraid of sharing another's water bottle would relish the opportunity to swim in a river of feces?"

I couldn't even bluff that I was okay with that. "I'm listening," I said to her. We'd taken out a few zombies as I approached the exit ramp way. I noticed damage already to the hood. Whatever she was getting at, she was right, the truck would not be able to handle that many strikes. But I was pretty sure we did not have the dump truck model with retractable wings. We weren't going to fly out of here.

"You're going to have to back up out of here."

I thought she was joking at first. When I looked over and she wasn't cackling I asked her just how insane she was, as I looked up the narrow, winding and steep roadway.

"I don't really see another way."

She was right and I knew it. I didn't give a shit that it was a woman telling me something. I'm not that egotistical, or even that it was Deneaux; on a fundamental level, I couldn't stand her but right is right, and she'd done well for herself for a long, long time. I brought the truck to a stop, to the complaints and questions of those in the back.

"You're going to have to watch the side," I told her. Just so happens she was on the sheer side. I was going to have to do this without the aid of a rearview mirror or even being able to turn over my right shoulder and out the rear windshield.

"What the fuck are you doing, Talbot?" This from BT. A middle school drop-out could have figured it out. I was heading at a decent clip to the ramp, ass backward. "I don't like this idea!" He let me know in no uncertain terms.

"Yeah, me fucking neither!" I yelled back. The real beauty (still trying to figure out how to use a sarcastic slant as I write) was that the truck had to stay at a particular speed as I went backward or it would start to buck and threaten to stall out. It was somewhere between first and second gear speed, going straight forward. I was not going to be able to crawl my way up.

"You might want to move a little farther your way," Deneaux said as the truck jostled violently. I was off to an auspicious start, the passenger wheels having already slipped off the path. That was all fine and dandy when we were six inches high, but was really going to suck when we were up sixty feet. I jerked the wheel hard my way...maybe seeing if we could climb the wall vertically. There were more cries of panic from the passengers. This was not going to be a fun ride for any involved, especially those bouncing around inside a steel box. We thumped back down as I brought the wheels back onto the path. The hits were jarring, as I was mowing down zombies and it got no better as they were run over. I could barely make out anything of substance from the side view mirror as it and I were jostled. The problem was, we were out of tune, so the image was even more blurred.

I was going to need to stick my head out of the window as I went. The problem there was the zombies trailing. They were easily keeping pace and even now jumping up on the hood and running board doing their best to get inside to the chewy center.

"BT, keep them off the front!"

"What about the ones behind?"

"There're hundreds of them...nothing you can do! I need to see where we're going!"

Bullets started whining down the front of the truck; the ones to my side were killed or hindered. The ones on the hood were going to be yet another problem. They couldn't be shot down without the risk of putting a hole in a pretty vital spot in the hood.

"What don't I have to do?" Deneaux sighed as she started firing through the windshield.

"Holy fuck, woman! How about a little heads up?"

I rolled the window down farther and stuck my head out. I was stretching my body as much as I could and still reach the gas pedal. Unfortunately, the dump part of the truck was further obscuring my vision.

"Deneaux, you're going to have to step on the gas!"

"How many things do you believe me capable of?" she asked. "I cannot reach the pedal and keep an eye on the side."

"Fuck." The frustration and fear was mounting within me. "Porkchop, you're up."

"No way, Mr. Talbot."

"All you need to do is step on the gas. I need you, kid." It seemed to take hours before he got the necessary nerve to step down, and when he did, he stomped like he was trying to drive a tent stake into rock hard soil. I pulled my foot away, to keep it from being sandwiched by Porkchop's particularly heavy-footed approach, the truck heaved backward. I almost scraped my head against the rock wall. I was now leaning far out of the truck, my right hand on the steering wheel and my left on the door frame holding on for dear life.

"Your way, Michael!" There was more panic in Deneaux's voice then I can ever remember hearing.

I wanted to ask her where she thought I was going to get that extra space, I was already within a few inches of the wall but I wisely figured this wasn't a good time to argue the point.

"Ease up a little Porkchop!" The truck went from seemingly flying to sputtering. My perch was already precarious and when he pulled up I started whacking my head against the side of the truck as we sputtered along. "Gas! Gas, Porkchop!!" The kid had never driven before in his life and he was most certainly not going to learn on this jaunt. I felt us careen, lurch, and was terrified we would roll.

"Turn coming up!" Deneaux warned. It had to go off to the left because it was completely blind to me. Basically looked like we were going to go flying off the side. Must have been twenty feet high by now. Maybe those of us in the cab would survive a spill, but those in back would be thrown free like steaks tossed into a lion's cage, into the waiting teeth of the horde or just crushed into the ground like olives being pressed for oil. I cut it too soon; it was the screams from the back that clued me in to my mistake before I could process it. The normal knee jerk reaction is to over compensate and pull the wheel back hard the other way; I fought every instinct I had in regards to that. I eased back down the side of the slope, the truck jostling even more. More rounds were being fired, some in front, some in back; that was not something I could spare even a modicum of attention for. Maybe next time I'll rethink that stance; I felt a hand rake down the back of my head before falling away.

"You can thank me later!" It was BT, leaning over.

"Freaking out right now, man!" I yelled back without turning up to look at him.

"Doing fine, buddy!"

"Yeah...now I know I'm fucked."

"Buddy's here?" I could hear Trip somewhere back there. "That dude makes the best Rice Krispie treats. There's lime rice, pulled pork, salsa..."

"That's a fucking burrito you stone head," BT told him. The rest of their conversation, if it happened, faded as I needed all of my concentration focused on trying to keep us on a path not much more than six inches wider than the truck.

"Turn harder!" Deneaux shouted. "Wheel off!"

"Fuck, fuck."

"Two wheels!"

One more and we were done. My body was pulled at unnatural angles, my back and neck ached. My ribs were being twisted out of shape along with my spine, I was getting a severe case of vertigo as I kept looking over my shoulder and none of that mattered. I needed to keep a truck, that felt like it was in a clothes dryer, being driven by a kid with a lead foot, from falling off a rock strewn precipice. Just another day at the office. I'm not going to even try to guess how I kept that truck on the ledge. Physics-wise I'm sure we should have been heading down using the express lane. Maybe it was the combined willpower of us all that nudged us back; not sure, don't care. If I stopped to wonder why I lived every time I should be dead, I'd be about four or five years back from my present position. When I say it like that, it doesn't sound quite as bad.

"Another turn!"

This one I could see as it was heading out. Instead of turning too soon, I waited too late. The rear end of the truck slammed into the wall with a bone-jarring crunch. There was an increase in gunfire for a reason I could not discern. The roadway was littered with dead, destroyed zombies. There was a remote part of me that feared that we would slip off the edge on their blood and guts. The sheer volume of bodies was staggering. There was a loud squeal of metal on rock as I turned the wheel enough to force us off the wall. The truck began to slow, I thought Porkchop was actually learning how to finesse the gas a little bit. Not sure why I was so optimistic. Then we started slowing some more, then a little more.

"Porkchop—more gas!"

"I haven't let up," he wailed back.

"Deneaux, are we out of gas?"

I hadn't at any point even thought to check out that fairly

important piece of information. Although in retrospect, what would it have mattered? Our bed was most definitely made and we were going to have to lie in it whether it had bedbugs, clowns hiding under it, cum stains...well, preferably none of the above, but in any case, we were in it now.

"Plenty!" she called out.

All I could figure were mechanical issues, then BT shouted.

"Mike, we have bulkers, they're trying to hold us back!"

Trying? I thought. They were doing a pretty damn good job. We were as close to stalling out as one can be and still be moving.

"Kill them! Fucking kill them all!"

I know he wanted to tell me "What the fuck did I think they were trying to do" but he didn't.

It sounded like everyone that had a gun was blowing holes in zombies. The truck bucked one final time and then did stall. "Move, Porkchop!" I dove back in and sat. Not only were we rolling back down, but we were also being pushed to the edge by the press of the bulkers.

I cranked the ignition. Isn't the definition of insanity doing the same thing repeatedly and expecting differing results?

"Diesel engine, Michael," Deneaux said.

"Fucking diesel!" If the inventor of that engine had been anywhere near I would have given him a piece of my mind. I waited for the glaciers to recede, or for the glow plugs to warm up, then proceeded to flood the engine. We got a whir of engine noise and nothing more. "FUCK!" I slammed my hand against the dashboard.

Deneaux was peeking out her window while simultaneously, and I think unconsciously, sliding my way. I fought with the wheel to keep it turned to the safety of the wall, the bulkers had other ideas. How the fuck they were managing to move a twelve-ton truck like it was a Tonka toy was beyond me. I waited again for the glow plugs to ignite, this time laying off the gas. The engine came to life. I put the stick in forward and slammed into the zombies in front of us. I wanted to give a little distance between the bulkers and our ass end.

"Get ready, Porkchop."

"I really don't like driving," he told me.

"Yeah, me neither." I didn't even try to completely stop before I forced that fucker into reverse, sheering through gear teeth as I did so. We lurched backward as I built up some speed to hit the fat bastards with. There was an extremely satisfying crunch as I won the war between steel and flesh. The truck bumped upwards as I went up and over the first of them.

"Yeah! Hit them!" BT was shouting. "Keep going!"

"It's on you Porkchop." I didn't even give him the chance to protest, as I again went out the window.

"Gonna make it!" BT was giving updates.

What was left of the windshield exploded outward, Deneaux was almost firing across her chest to keep the zombies from grabbing a hold of me. If they got me, they got me, I couldn't spare the time to look at how close they were. Let's just say I could hear the bullets whizzing by my ear, like a persistent deer fly. Porkchop was crying, Deneaux was shouting, BT was screaming encouragement. Me? I think I was laughing. I could be mistaken, there was just so much going on I couldn't even begin to fathom being normal at the moment, my mind was stretched as far as was capable, maybe it snapped right there and then, might have been the only fucking thing that saved our asses.

I cannot even recall the moment we were no longer climbing the hill but rather were out on level ground. I suppose it didn't matter because we were still in a hell of a jam. When I realized there was no longer a wall on my side I was in the process of pulling my head in when we hit our largest obstacle. Could have been a wall of bulkers or a building. Porkchop, who had been on the edge of his seat pushing the gas, now found himself pushed down into the pedal compartment.

"Straight Michael, do not move that wheel," Deneaux said calm enough but she was as pale as the wrapper of her cigarette. We weren't just hugging the edge, we were riding it. I could not turn the truck to angle us out of there or my front tire would have dipped down and taken the rest of the vehicle with it. I locked my arms, not even daring to move my head to look for fear that I would subconsciously turn the truck to my gaze. I could see the pit in the periphery of my vision and that was enough. We were surrounded by zombies on three sides and Porkchop was wedged down on the gas, we were picking up speed as we jostled.

"You need to move, Porkchop." Poor kid was just about upside down, his face mashed up against the gas pedal and his ass presented to me.

"Stuck," was his muffled response. "Need help!"

"Deneaux help him." I don't want to move, she was transfixed by the potential for devastation to our immediate right.

"Deneaux!"

"I was unaware of the extent of my aversion to heights."

On one end, it was nice to see that she shared something with us lowly humans. But of all the times she chose to show her weaknesses, this wasn't the best.

"Help the kid! Help Porkchop up. We keep building speed and I'm not going to be able to keep this truck on the straight and narrow."

"Yes, yes..." But she was still looking out the window. Maybe some part of her knew that if we rolled down that canyon wall, and she died, she'd be that much closer to her final destination. She moved closer to me, grabbed Porkchop by the collar and waistband and strained as she tried to extract him from the floorboard. "Maybe if you laid off the cake," she puffed.

"I'm big boned," came the muffled excuse.

"Yes, yes, you're just husky. That's what all mothers tell their children to make them feel better about being fat."

"What the fuck, Deneaux? I said get him out, not drive him into therapy." I couldn't tell specifically what she was doing, but by the way Porkchop was squealing and the way Deneaux was gritting her teeth I'd have to say she was pinching the hell out of him. This had the unfortunate consequence of making the kid rock back and forth on the pedals. I bounced my head off the steering wheel the first time he slammed the brakes.

"Come on Lardy, get your ass up!"

"My name is Porkchop!" he cried out. He finally popped out of that hole like a champagne cork.

"Works every time," Deneaux said as she looked at her claw-like hand.

Porkchop was furiously rubbing his ass, fat tears streaked down his face. He tried to push as close to me as he could without being in my lap. The truck bucked as I regained control of the foot pedals.

"Need an update, Deneaux." I was sweating profusely, I was afraid my hands were going to slip with how slick they were.

"I did not know you had the capability to hover," she was gripping the door tightly. "From my angle I cannot see wheels on terra firma."

"Wonderful." We were a butterfly kiss from being pushed over and I had at least another hundred yards before the pit finally curved away from us. I'm not proud of this, but I shut my eyes. No, I wasn't going all use the force-y, I was just trying to keep from doing what I so naturally wanted to do, which was look to my left. Unlike Deneaux's, my fear of heights is well documented and there's no telling what I would have done if I only saw air and the occasional eagle flying by. Much like Porkchop's wedged-in body I also kept the gas shoved to the floor, there was no room or option for finesse. We would brute force our way out of this or we wouldn't.

Five seconds...no more than ten, before someone shouted: "Clear!" I think I re-lived every highlight and lowlight twice in that time period. I braked and opened my eyes at the same time. When I got her stopped, I shoved it into first. By the time I got it up to third, the zombies were nearly back upon us, I was turning away and they were chasing. I was bathed in enough sweat that if someone were to gaze upon me they would think I'd just climbed out of a pool. Nobody said anything for a few miles, each of us attempting to move past this latest chapter in our lives. No one had been hurt, but there would be a lot of sleepless nights to come, rehashing this one in our memory. After a bit, I got the wherewithal to look at the gas which was sitting comfortably at a half. Next I started to figure out where we were and where we should be going. I had been driving just to drive, basically like I was on auto-pilot.

"You did alright, Michael." Deneaux was attempting to act like this hadn't ruffled those feathers of hers. The way the cigarette jiggled in her hand betrayed her composure. "I didn't mean anything by the things I said," Deneaux was talking to Porkchop, who was still sniffling. "I was afraid and was trying to anger you into moving faster."

I wasn't liking this humanistic Deneaux, it was like watching a reptile try out emotions. Unnatural. I drove in the neighborhood of ten miles farther before I felt we had sufficient distance on the zombies. I wanted... no, I needed to hold Tracy and check on how everyone was doing. I'd not been expecting the amount of pain when I moved from that seat. I had been clutching every muscle in my body to the point where my bones hurt. It took a few minutes before I could stand straight up. There was a myriad of injuries from those in the back, contusions, bumps, bruises, fat lips, bleeding heads, very bad moods.

"Want me to crack your back?" BT asked my hunched over form.

"I'll be alright in a minute. Help everyone down; we'll take five."

Trip was one of the first down. "Ponch, do you realize there's an infinite number of alternate realities where we didn't make it out of there? Glad this wasn't one of them." Then he walked away.

"Yeah, thanks for that," I told him. He couldn't hear me

over the crinkling of the chips package he was opening.

Tracy said nothing as she hugged me, just hugged me. One lone sob escaped my mouth as I buried my face into her shoulder. "It's okay, we're okay," she said softly. We were given space as I did my best to recollect the pieces of me that were cracked or had broken off.

"How about we don't do that again?" she said.

"I'm good with that," my muffled words came through her hair. "How the fuck are you so rock solid right now?"

"I never looked."

"Smart woman. I've always said that." I finally felt solid enough that I wasn't going to just start bawling uncontrollably from the release of stress. It was funny how everyone was finding other inane things to do. Gary was actually counting change in his pocket.

"What are you doing with change?" BT asked.

"You never know when we might come across a working vending machine and I would kill for a Cran-Apple drink."

"You know we can just bust them open right?"

"Not the same," he replied.

"They stopped their pursuit," Mad Jack said, starting up the sat-tracker.

"What we need to know is why they keep showing up like that," Travis said, and I had to agree. It inspired confidence in me to see the next generation of leader asking the questions that needed asking.

"Augusta—we're heading to Augusta," I said. I was relatively certain my voice wouldn't waver or crack. Knox was still out there, and last we knew his stronghold was in Bangor. I could not afford another run in with a lunatic at this exact moment.

"You mind if someone else drives?" BT asked in all seriousness. "You look a little tapped."

"I'm good with that," I told him truthfully.

"I'll do it," Tommy said. Deneaux stayed in the passenger seat; no surprise Porkchop climbed into the back with the rest of us. The damage to the rear end was more extensive than I could have imagined. The tailgate was pummeled in like the hammer of Thor had struck. The bed of the truck was actually creased down. The tail lights were distant memories, the trailer hitch was hanging askew and the air brake canister wasn't looking too particularly well. We were going to need a newer, more fitting ride. I wanted to close my eyes and sleep away this nightmare, but even on a regular roadway, the back of this truck was only suitable for gravel.

We had to take the long way to skirt Belfast, which was still a hotbed of zombie activity. I didn't pay much attention to what MJ was saying. I was doing my best to not have my teeth rattle out of my head. He was saying something about it looking more like an occupation than an invasion. There were entirely too many implications down that line of reasoning. We could run circles trying to figure it out and still nothing would change. Right now I didn't care, they could have the town. Although, now I was wishing that MJ had completed his fission bomb. We'd been in the truck for nearly an hour and I'd had my limit, American drug traffickers held in a Thailand prison were treated far better than we were. I would rather walk and was about to tell Tommy to pull over so I could, just as he was pulling into Lemmy's Used Car Emporium.

Emporium might have been a bit of a stretch...shit, flea market might have been pushing it. These were the cars that were traded in from those crazy radio ads from dealerships that offered money for any car that you pushed, pulled, or dragged in. Yeah, this was those cars. There were a plethora of Ford Taurus's, the dreaded Chevy two-doors, and generic sedans. Right now that Chrysler minivan with the sliding door looked like Angels on high had hand-crafted it. I gave the truck the middle finger as BT helped me out.

"Quarter tank of gas," Tommy said as he came out to talk to us.

"We keeping this thing?" BT asked.

"Man, you need to get your slip and slide checked out, that

thing's not safe for kids." Trip said to me, as his wife massaged the small of his back. Speaking of kids, we'd done our best to ensure their safety by everyone pretty much pretending to be blocks of shipping styrofoam, packing them in tight. Good for them—not so much for us. Nobody ever opened the box and complained about broken packing foam. Deneaux was exiting the small building, a fistful of keys in her hands.

"Talbot, this helpful Deneaux thing is starting to weird me out."

"Enjoy it while you can. It won't last," I told BT.

"That makes it better." He went over to grab some of the keys.

I was in no particular rush to get behind the wheel of a car anytime soon. Want to know the odds of the first car we got started being that minivan? About a hundred percent. After some loud squealing from loose belts, she sounded much like the washing machine she was. Had to give it to Lemmy, either he was or he employed a hell of a mechanic. I wouldn't have bet that ten percent of those junkers would have started. We actually got our pick. Gary, who was a decent mechanic, looked them over. We checked tires, fluids, and gas before we settled on six of them. I was not thrilled; in my morose frame of mind that was six opportunities for things to go wrong. It severely sucked to live in that house of pessimism; I'm not going to say I'd been Ollie Optimistic my entire life, but I wasn't usually waiting for shit to go bad either, and I found myself doing that more and more. At least I couldn't be blamed. The world was skewed severely against good and didn't seem to be on the upswing just yet.

If there was this much bad, didn't it stand to reason that there had to be some good? Maybe the settlement in Washington State was hoarding it. Made getting there even more paramount.

"We taking the truck?" BT asked again. I was sitting in the car my wife had picked out, it was a reasonable facsimile of a Jeep, albeit a foreign wannabe. Tracy and Stephanie had seen to the division of passengers in cars. Trip had loaded into the seat behind mine and began to play the drums on my headrest.

"I'm always so charged up right before a show. I'm going to have to puke soon."

I turned, making sure to avoid his blur of beating hands. "What are you talking about?"

"Peyote man, if you don't puke you can get really sick."

"Sounds just like how I would want to start my trip. Nothing says 'good time' like a good puking."

"See! You know!" He stopped drumming long enough to point to his nose, like all of a sudden we were playing charades and I'd hit the answer on the head.

"John, let's go!" It was Stephanie, thankfully arguing him into another car.

"Gonna miss you."

"Who is that Goddess?" he asked looking over to his wife.

"I don't know, man, but if you play your cards right, you might get lucky."

"You think?" he asked me with a twinkle in his eye. "You really think she's a cupcake vendor?"

"Get out." I pointed with my finger as I let my head sag.

"Hell yeah I'm getting out! The most beautiful woman in the world is offering me unlimited snack cakes. I'm all about that." He'd got out of the car and poked his head back in. "I'll see if she has a friend, man." And then he walked off with his wife.

We had Tracy, myself, Nicole, Wesley, Sty, Ryan, and Angel in our ride, with the animals in the cargo area. Henry looked at Patches the way I look at Deneaux, especially in those tight quarters. We all had to take one for the team eventually; he was up. I think he was going for chemical warfare to keep her away. We did our best to keep fighters in each car. Again, not thrilled; we were already spread thin in that department. Our strength came from our unity.

We'd left the truck. I voted to keep it, use it as a battering ram if...I mean when it became necessary. It was getting gas

for the pig that proved its undoing—that and the thing couldn't
go much past fifty. We got back on the road and had been
driving close to two hours. We took a pre-scheduled stop to
change some diapers, scope out some gas, and get an eye in
the sky report from Mad Jack.

"Portland is a no go," were the first words out of his mouth.

I'd hoped he was being dramatic; surely zombies can't
have the entire city. Wrong. The main highways, I-95 and 295
were out of the question; zombies lined the roadway like a
gauntlet. We decided to backtrack to the zombie-free zone of
Brunswick and pick up the much slower route 202, a two lane
divided highway, common in this part of the country. These
roads sucked because of their vulnerability to ambush. They
were narrow and windy and offered few ways off in the event
of an emergency. Plus you couldn't really throttle up the
engine on them. It was tough to tell if the obstacles were there
to thwart our efforts to leave or if they were there to make us
stay. When I rethought my thought I realized I'd just said the
same thing.

We needed to raid a store, plain and simple. Gas was a
must, but so were the staples humans needed to survive.
Stopping, however, was inherently more dangerous than
moving. If I made it to Seattle without having an aneurysm,
I'd feel pretty lucky. MJ found a small, secluded local store
that wasn't much bigger than a double-stacked trailer, in fact,
it might have been; there's no accounting for Maine Redneck
ingenuity. No zombies and no people as far as we could spy;
it was worth a go. We rolled up to it with two cars. The other
four hung back. Trip was first out.

"Smell that?"

"Your feet?" I asked him.

"The sweet, sweet smell of Twinkie wrappers."

"Just hold on for a second—I'll go check it out." I could
not help but think back to the store that had been a zombie trap
and a human lure. I knocked on the door, if it was the
aforementioned trap, I wanted the zombies to come to me

rather than relive the nightmare of seeing captive humans being slowly eaten alive. Nothing. I pulled on the handle, it was locked. I was actually kind of happy about that, meant maybe there was something left inside.

"Locked," I called back to BT, trying not to be too loud.

"Hold on." He rooted around in his car until he got the tire iron. He was just coming back when I heard movement above me.

"Tell your friend to stop moving."

I looked up to see maybe the largest bore I'd ever had the misfortune to stare down. Fifty cal, ten gauge maybe, I don't know, pretty sure it would make everything above my shoulders look like spaghetti with one shot. Not sure how BT missed this, but he was still coming.

I turned slowly, letting my rifle fall to its sling and raising my hands. "BT you might want to hold up man!"

He was confused only for a moment as he caught sight of the gargantuan gun. Got to admit I was pretty impressed when three rifles on our side were trained on the man that got the drop on me. Of course, it would be too late for me, but I'd be avenged. It was tense and it only got more tense as nothing was said on either side. It was quiet, like I was sitting on the back porch during a lazy summer night, quiet. It was the cries of a wet and hungry Wesley that broke the détente.

"That a baby?" It was the distinctive voice of a female this time. I did not look up, not wanting to see that barrel again.

"That's my grandson, ma'am," I answered.

"Are you Christian people?" she asked.

"I was baptized, if that's what you're asking. Haven't been practicing much lately."

"There's always time for the Lord's Prayer," she admonished me.

"Yes, ma'am."

"Talbot?" BT asked, he couldn't hear our exchange.

"She's thinking I should join a monastery," I told him. That got a laugh from my gunman.

"Oh don't I know it," the man said, "she's been saying I drink and swear too much, though I haven't had a drink in ten years. What are you doing here?" He got serious right quick.

"We're trying to leave the state. We heard there's a settlement in Seattle and we want to get there," I told him honestly. Amazing the power of truth detection bullet lead has.

"We'll get to this 'settlement' and whether it actually exists, more specifically later. First, what are you doing here?" he asked.

"We need supplies. We ran into a horde of zombies larger than anything we've encountered so far and we needed to vacate before we could grab our things. We have infants and children."

"Oh, my," the female said. I couldn't see her, but I imagined she had put her hand to her throat in an expressive manner.

"What's his story?" the man asked, motioning toward BT.

"You talking size or color? He gets pretty riled up if we start down the race road."

"I don't give a goddamn about his color."

"Vincent, that will be quite enough with the expletives."

"If you're referring to size, I think it's a growth hormone experiment gone awry."

"Son, are you alright in the head?" Vincent asked.

"Sir, have you ever had a tank turret aimed at your head? It tends to make you act a little crazy," I told him.

"Vincent, stop pointing at him."

"Harriet, in case you haven't noticed they have more guns pointing at us than I do them. He's my only leverage."

It was my goal to head this one off at the pass. I turned slightly to my group. "Please, guns down."

"That was the only thing saving your life, son," Vincent said as I heard the hammer pull back. I was not about to look back over my shoulder in wonder at the man that was about to murder me. I was on the move, mid-dive as a matter of fact, when I heard the staccato burst of an M-16, not the thunderous expulsion of the large caliber round I had been expecting. I never felt the burst of pain I'd been waiting for either. I got up, trying to figure out what exactly had just happened. Vincent and Harriet were dead, he had been thrown back through the window and was draped over the sill. A large part of Harriet's brain was lying on the concrete next to me.

Deneaux was off to the side, the barrel of her weapon still smoking. "What?" she asked. "He had every intention of shooting you. Again, I saved your life. I figured when we joined back up that you would be the one doing all the heavy lifting. Had I known it would be my shoulders supporting, I may have chosen my path more wisely."

"What the fuck, Deneaux? You couldn't possibly have known he was going to shoot!" BT was pissed.

"You're a smart man, Lawrence, as is your friend Michael. Great instincts most of the time. But you have your weak points, too, blinders even. Look at the ground beneath Michael's feet. The discoloration—and if that's not enough, look at the bullet hole divots in the concrete. You're not the first person to show up here."

"And how do you know they weren't fighting off zombies?" he asked.

"They weren't good people." She put her gun down and lit a cigarette. "My guess is they killed the original owner and took the place over."

"Oh please, do tell us how you came up with that theory, Mrs. Sherlock."

"Look at the sign." She pointed, took a drag then pointed again.

"What the fuck is that going to prove?" BT was hot.

"Just do it."

He did, as did I. BT was not doing his best to contain the white hot anger threatening to bubble up. "Convenience Store. Big deal. What the hell does that mean?" he asked.

"Sometimes I don't know why I bother. Whose convenience store is it?"

I was looking at the sign. "Joel's...it was Joel's," I answered.

"They could have bought it off Joel," BT said weakly.

"Harriet had a piece on you, Lawrence, and they had just given each other a nod. That giant gun was cocked and in Michael's face. If not for me, your friend would be dead and you would be bleeding out. I shudder to think what they would have done with the women and children. Now be a dear and check inside, I'm getting low on cigarettes."

"Did you see her gun?" BT asked me.

I shrugged in response. "I couldn't see much beyond the tunnel of a barrel he was pointing at me."

"You can't do that! You can't just kill people!" Tracy had come out of the car, and she was heading right for Deneaux, that finger of doom was out in full force.

Deneaux had not even turned to look. I'd been married to Tracy long enough to know that ignoring her was not an option.

"Bitch, I'm talking to you!" Tracy yelled.

"Oh-oh," was all I managed. BT intercepted the fiery redhead before she could make contact. Deneaux would only suffer so much.

"Put me down, BT! She has to know that you can't just butcher people!"

BT was looking over at me. "On your own," I mouthed, that was what he got for interfering.

"Talbot!" BT yelled as he tried to restrain a writhing Tracy.

"Everyone just take a second! Please. BT, put my wife down. I cannot believe I am going to have to defend you," I said as I looked over to a smiling Deneaux. "Listen, you know she's already saved my ass a couple of times. Let's just give her the benefit of the doubt on this until we can prove otherwise."

"Benefit of the doubt? Is that how you're going to justify murder? And what if you find out that woman did not have a gun? Then what, Mike?"

"Tracy, hold on. He basically told me straight up that he was going to kill me. I didn't see Harriet's gun, but Vincent had pulled the hammer back on his rifle which seemed like it was inches from my nose. I didn't take a dive for nothing. I believed he would likely do as he threatened; that was why I was trying to get out of the way."

The anger that Tracy had threatening to boil over was being shifted to me. It did not dissipate as one would hope, just redirected. I wouldn't doubt if my wife was feeling a bit of betrayal as I shielded Deneaux from her assault. I turned to fire on the door locking mechanism, figuring it should be sufficiently loud enough to distract Tracy. I don't know what I was hoping to find when I kicked in the door. Something that would unequivocally prove my stance. Maybe chained up puppies, starving or beaten bunny rabbits. Not that I wanted to see those things, but maybe I needed to. There was nothing. Well, except for some dried blood stains and shelving which had all been pushed over to the walls. I scanned the room quickly but there really wasn't any place to hide, even the cash register station had been pushed flush with the wall. Looked like maybe Harriet and Vincent liked to come down here and dance every Saturday night or something.

That thought was not making me feel any better, imagining them trying to remember a better time in their life, so they came down here and did a little line-dancing. "Yeah, keep it up Talbot. Keep going down this road. Works wonders for your psyche. Hey, maybe it's cleared down here because they run a field hospital for orphans. Yeah, that's what the fuck is going on."

"Who you talking to?" BT had come in.

"What's left of my brain, I guess."

"So just a memo then?"

"Basically."

"You ready to go upstairs?"

"No," I told him truthfully.

"What if she doesn't have a gun, Mike?"

"I don't know, BT. I just don't fucking know. Tracy will lose her shit and I'm already treading water right now by siding with Deneaux."

"It's not just that, Mike. She could have murdered those people if they had been perfectly cordial. Have you seen her? She's leaning against that car, smoking up a storm like nothing out of line happened. She's the coldest person I've ever met, period. I knew serial killers, hit men even, that showed more emotion for their victims. If she killed them in cold blood, we can't have her in our group. I don't trust her Mike. Shit, even if she did save us like she says, I still don't trust her."

"I don't either but, look, that hammer was pulled back. In one second I might have been permanently air-conditioned, man. Those people were total strangers. Maybe we should see how little we should actually trust her before we kick her out. You cool with that?"

"You realize, like, less than a month ago you said, and I quote: 'if I ever see that demented crazy bitch again I am going to put a bullet in her brain casing,' unquote."

"I'd appreciate if you didn't use my own words against me. My wife does that all the time."

"She has a right to; it's because you say crazy shit."

"Can we get this done?" I was showing him the door.

"Why do I have to go first?"

"Well, I'm figuring if they have a Claymore mine you can shield me from it."

"I'll shield it with your face." He quite literally picked me up by the scruff of the neck and opened the door, holding me in front of him like a medieval shield.

"You're an asshole," I told him when nothing exploded and we were looking up a steep staircase absolutely coated with potato chip and other snack bags.

He put me down. "You ever stop to think that maybe if you kept that trap of yours shut every so often, that those around you wouldn't feel the need to harness their inner asshole?"

"Nope. Never crossed my mind." I went up the stairs. "Holy fucking potato chip bags, this must be their early warning alarm system."

"Or they were just fucking slobs."

"There's that." I could barely hear myself as I crunched down on all manner of cellophane material. "Fuck me," I said when I got upstairs. The place was absolutely choked with food. The only piece of furniture I could see was a twin bed and even that was partially encased. Harriet and Vincent had been busy pulling all their stockpile up here. Must have had calves like pro football players after all that exercise.

"This will at least solve our food problems," BT said as he somehow shouldered his way past me. I was just about embedded into the wall as he did so.

"Don't let me get in your way," I muffled out.

"Son of a bitch." He'd made his way over to the prone form of Harriet. I didn't need to see her exposed skull to realize what he was seeing. "She had a rifle. Loaded and the safety was off. Would have been a lot easier getting rid of that witch if that wasn't the case."

I wisely said nothing. I hate to admit it, even to myself, but I don't think I would have got rid of Deneaux, even if Harriet had been holding a rosary.

BT pulled Vincent's body out of the window. "She was right," he said to Tracy, showing her the rifle.

"Of course I was, dearie," I heard Deneaux call up to him. "I don't need a formal apology; a simple thanks will suffice."

"You're lucky I don't just shoot you," BT told her.

"That's not an acceptable way to thank someone for saving their life." I couldn't see Deneaux, but I knew she was smiling up at him.

"What exactly did Vincent say?" BT asked pulling his head in from the window.

"He said he was going to shoot me or something like that."

"Not something like that. What exactly did he say?"

"BT, you know I'm not good with remembering stuff

exactly and I was a little under duress. You saw me diving, I definitely thought my life was in danger." As I said the words it sparked the memory. "Wait, wait...he said something like 'That was the only thing saving your life' when I'd asked everyone to put their guns down and then he cocked the hammer."

"You sure about that?"

"That, I'm a hundred percent sure about. That's a noise that gets kind of burned deep into the folds. BT, I'm not completely convinced he was going to fire, or if she was, but I was at the point where I thought it was a distinct possibility."

BT wiped his face with a meaty hand. "Let's just get some people up here, there's a lot of food to grab."

I laid the couple out and grabbed some blankets off the bed to cover them up before anyone could join the working detail. It was not lost on me that Deneaux did not come up and help. I can't believe that it had anything to do with guilt or that she didn't want to see her handiwork. I was pretty sure it was more about not doing menial labor.

With most of us working, it only took about an hour to grab everything we could fit or that was worth taking. On one hand, it was great having Trip. He ate his weight in food that hour making it that many fewer trips we had to do up and down those stairs. On the other, it was a pain in the ass working around him, as he was constantly eating and moving at a quarter speed as he did so.

We were just about done; Trip was leaning up against my car. He was eating a jar of ham hocks, whatever the fuck those are—smelled pretty ripe.

"Mike, she's not supposed to be here." He'd stopped eating, a ham hock caught between the lip of the bottle he was holding and his mouth. He was staring off into space. I cannot even begin to convey how unsettling it was for him to call me Mike. I had a feeling who he was talking about, but I had to make sure before he slipped back down.

"Deneaux?" I prodded.

"She's changing everything. People that are supposed to die are being saved and those that should live are being killed. She is single-handedly destroying this timeline."

My mouth was open, a thousand and two questions at the tip of my tongue. Suddenly John became Trip again.

"Ham hocks? Oh crap! I'm a vegetarian!" He seemed genuinely distressed as he ate three more before putting the lid back on and the bottle in the car. "Ron't rell Rephanie," he chewed.

"Vegetarian my ass. I've watched you eat raw frozen hot dogs."

"Those weren't popsicles?"

I left him there with his blank look as he tried to figure out what exactly he'd eaten. I noticed he reached back in the car and spun the top off his definitely not-vegetarian snack.

"What the hell good is it having a Spirit Guide that's always getting lost?" I asked no one. I sought out the only one that could help. "Tommy, any news on the psychic hotline?"

"I haven't heard from Dianne Warwick, if that's what you're referring to."

"Too bad. Maybe she'd know what the hell is going on here." I explained to him what Trip had just said.

"Oh," was Tommy's response, though he looked like he had a whole lot more going on in that head of his.

"Oh? Spill it, kid."

"You know that since my link to Eliza was snapped I've not had the same view of the unseen."

I nodded.

"Right after the Demense building, and even more so. But since she showed up at your brother's, it has gotten worse, significantly worse."

"You mean your ability to divine?"

"My perception of things that could happen has been severely hampered. If what Trip says is right, that could be the explanation. I can't see what hasn't already been written."

That gave me chills right up and down my spine. Deneaux

was in our midst and she was a great agent for change, but just who exactly was she working for? There was safe money you could bet, for what team she played. But that would be as obvious as sending an older white guy with a crew cut into a Pink Floyd tailgate party to buy bags of maryjane. Yeah, no one would see that narc coming from a mile away. Maybe he could sound more authentic by asking where he could obtain some blotter-type acid, the kind that really makes your mind go loopy. The dipshit that sold to him deserved to be busted. You could probably see the outline of the badge hanging under his shirt. Deneaux was that obvious, or so it seemed. Would the bad team really make their intentions that discernible? And at this point, who exactly was the bad team?

My best bet was to ask the source. Even if she did know, which I doubted, she wouldn't have any reason to tell me the truth. My life was complicated enough. I just marched right up to her face.

"Deneaux, why are you here?" I asked bluntly.

She eyed me through a haze of smoke. "I would imagine you are not referring to this exact spot, correct?"

"Correct."

"I'm not sure, Michael." She took a long drag from her smoke. "I was positive you had died in the destruction of the Demense building."

"No thanks to you."

"Are we going to rehash that? I was doing my best to have you killed. That's no secret."

"What's changed?"

"I have. I have had a change of heart."

"The question begs, why?"

"When I saw you and Tommy leave the building, I decided there and then I was going to go the complete opposite way that you had. I was on my way to the West Coast, as a matter of fact."

"That's when you came across those men?"

"It is. Though, technically, they came across me. I was

sleeping at a truck stop. I had no other options; you were the only person that I could think of that would help."

"Pretty big risk you took there."

"Everything we do is a risk, especially now."

"So, a slight twist in fate has put us back together."

"It would seem so," she answered. "Perhaps, Michael, this is the way it was supposed to be all along. We are survivors, you and I. Maybe we go about it differently, but in the end, we will not allow anything or anyone to interfere with our continued existence."

"That statement rings true enough, though we both know my self-preservation extends far beyond my own skin."

"It is a flaw you will overcome eventually."

"Why did you kill Harriet and Vincent?"

"Weren't they about to kill you and BT?"

"I'm not sure."

"Then it's a good thing I am here. I've been playing this game far longer than you. Little Miss Christian up there? Yeah, anything but. She would have put holes in the both of you and thought less about it than I did."

"How can you be so sure?"

"While you all were getting the food, I took a little walk to the back of the building. There are over thirty bodies, not zombies, mind you, that I believe were standing in the exact spot you were when Bonnie and Claude up there sent them packing."

I believed her so much so I didn't even bother going to check. BT did, though, when I told him.

"Son of a bitch," was all he said when he came back. He was wiping his mouth with a rag. He looked pretty pallid.

We left, I was sitting next to a seething Tracy, she was still pissed off about Deneaux's actions and now maybe more pissed that she was going to have to apologize for her outburst. I wisely said nothing. I did not so much as look in her general direction, she was actively seeking for something to turn her ire on and I was determined to make sure that wasn't me.

Maybe Deneaux was right; maybe I was more into self-preservation than I cared to admit.

We got out of Maine without having to make another stop. I couldn't tell if I was relieved or not. It would be nice to not have to think about all that had gone wrong, though there was a deep sadness for those left behind. We did have to make a fuel stop in New Hampshire, but we decided to stay away from gas stations. It was Gary that said we should go to a dealership and siphon some tanks. It just so happened we ended up at Bournival Jeep dealership, I looked at my fifteen-year-old cheap knock-off and made up my mind right there: I was going to upgrade. Screw the roll-over loan amount and the twenty-one percent interest. My wife deserved a new one after what I'd done to hers. And plus, it did wonders for dampening her level of hostility. We topped off what needed topping and headed out. Mad Jack had suggested grabbing a trailer and some drums and filling them with gas, but I wasn't too keen on the notion of rolling around with our own bombs. We'd just have to stop again, multiple times, in fact. Things were bound to happen, there was no way around it. We'd be vigilant, we'd stay as safe as we could. We were finally on the road to Etna Station.

EPILOGUE ONE

"I CAN SAVE them, Michael, I can save them all," her voice came over loud and clear on the radio.

"What do you want, Deneaux?" Michael's grip nearly cracked the microphone in his hand.

"Just a promise—just one small promise and they'll all be safe. You can do that Michael, can you not?"

"Tell me what you want." He did his best to contain his anger.

"You will bite me."

Michael understood the implications of this. Deneaux the Immoral wanted to be Deneaux the Immortal. She could make Eliza look like a cartoon character in comparison. Were the lives of his friends and family worth unleashing this creature onto the world, with her own set of twisted rules?

"You're taking an awfully long time to give me an answer. My window of opportunity won't be open forever. Yes or no?"

"You can't possibly understand what you are asking of me, Deneaux. What you are asking of yourself. You realize what happens to your soul, don't you?"

"Soul?" She started laughing. "What am I going to do with that hole ridden dirty sheet?"

Mike heard a distant scream come over the radio.

"That was your beautiful wife, Michael. Do you want me

to save her? Yes or no?"

"FUCK!" he screamed. "Do it! Save her. Save them all!"

"Promise me first."

"I promise! I fucking promise! Just do it."

Mike knew in his heart he'd damned himself and he'd damned them all. "What have I done?" He held the microphone to his head. Deneaux had left her side on; he could hear her shots and the cries of surprise from the people holding his loved ones captive. His only hope now was that Deneaux would succeed in saving them and then as they retreated to a safer place she would trip and fall onto a land mine. All of his problems solved.

No, he was not going to be able to leave this one up to providence. He would honor his promise and so much more, Deneaux had sealed her fate when she'd presented this crossroads. He knew which road he was going to take.

EPILOGUE TWO

IGGY WANDERED, EATING the near-deads when necessary but preferring human meat above all others. Near-deads had hunted him mercilessly until he had turned the tables—instead of running, he'd attacked. He'd savagely ripped through throats, torn heads free from bodies, laid torsos open. At first he'd just been trying to stop them from chasing, but when he'd bitten through the arm of one of his pursuers he'd decided they were good enough to eat. He had been supplementing his diet by hunting them ever since his escape. The humans, though, they were what he wanted. Human flesh was the cake, the icing, and the cherry upon it. He stripped meat clean from their bones, savoring every morsel. Just the previous week he had come across a group of five that he had stalked, killed, and eaten. He'd eaten heartily, but now the ravenous hunger pangs were back.

"Holy shit, Bob. I think that there's a Bigfoot!" Dave exclaimed as he stood up quickly, spilling his hot coffee over his brother's lap.

"Jesus, Dave! You jackass. That shit is hot!" Bob stood abruptly and was brushing the liquid from his crotch.

"What do you think Bigfoot tastes like?" Dave was bringing his rifle up.

"Give me the binoculars, you dumbass. Gretchen just got

these pants clean. She's gonna be pissed."

"Not if we bring back enough food to feed everyone for a week," Dave replied.

"Holy shit," Bob said as he zeroed in on what Dave had seen. "It's not a yeti...of that I'm glad."

"What? Why?"

"Because I'm sick of eating canned beans and I would have had to shoot it. But hell, if we'd stumbled upon one just a few years earlier we'd be millionaires. Television shows would want our story, museums, scientists...everybody would want a piece of that animal. We could sell it to the highest bidder. What we've got down there is a gorilla. Yeah, it's a big one, but just an animal that escaped from a zoo or something."

"What's gorilla taste like?" Dave asked.

"How the hell would I know? It's not like they have the McApe down at the burger joint. I don't give a shit anyway. It's still got to be better than beans and our families deserve some real meat."

Dave was wiping drool from his mouth as his brother-in-law spoke; just thinking about having the meat roasting over an open fire was causing him to salivate. "Don't miss."

Bob braced his rifle up against a tree. "Don't move, you magnificent feast." He took a deep breath and squeezed the trigger. Birds flew up from nearby trees as the great beast went down.

"You got it, you got it! Dave was jumping around.

Bob was feeling pretty good about himself, he estimated the shot to be somewhere in the three-hundred-yard range, and considering he'd never fired a rifle before the zombie apocalypse, he thought that a huge victory.

Iggy heard the loud report of the gunshot and watched as a tuft of grass ten feet away was blown up into the air. An ancient, primordial part of him demanded that he run away from the danger. The newer, more lethal part knew exactly what to do. He fell over as if the bullet had hit him; he would wait for his prey to come to him.

"Is it dead?" Dave had his revolver out.

"One shot, one kill!" Bob boasted as they got closer. "That thing is stone cold!"

"Wow, he smells like he's been dead for a while." Dave had put his firearm away and was fanning his face.

"How do we dress out a gorilla?" Bob asked. He had to admit the smell of the beast was ripe, but he figured it was just dirty after he'd escaped or been abandoned by his handlers.

"I don't know, dumbass. Just peel off the hair and scrape out the innards. We worked at a cereal processing plant. The hardest thing I'd ever done was use a can opener...before the zombies came, that is."

"Help me roll him over." Bob had lightly kicked at the gorilla's side. Both men were bent over, Bob at Iggy's shoulder and Dave at his hip.

"I think he moved!" Dave jumped back in alarm.

"I killed it," Bob said, but he felt a niggling of fear run through him as he touched the gorilla's arm, though he didn't want his brother-in-law to know that. He pulled Iggy over so the gorilla was on its back. Iggy's eyelids opened; the pale gray eyes burned with intense hatred and great yearning. They locked onto Bob's terrified face. The man tried to back away but Iggy was too quick. He sat up and grabbed the man's head, snapping it violently to the left, cracking his vertebrae. Left on his own, Bob would eventually succumb to his injuries; right now he was a paraplegic witness to the horrible events about to happen.

"Bob! He's alive!" Dave turned and made an attempt to escape. Iggy got onto all fours and in two strides he leaped and landed on Dave, breaking three of the man's ribs and a femur as he slammed him to the ground. Iggy dipped his head down and tore into the screaming man's thigh, pulling up a long section of meat. Bob watched in horror as his sister's husband was eaten one piece at a time. Dave had stopped crying out after the third bite; the convulsions stopped after the fifth. Heavy tears fell from Bob's eyes as he watched the monster gorilla finish, stand, and turn in his direction. His screams ripped through the day like Iggy did through his genitals.

EPILOGUE THREE

INDIAN HILL HAS always been a special place for me. A place of discovery, of imagination and even solace. At times, it has even been a place for healing. Jennifer, the girl I had thought I was going to spend the rest of my life with, had just broken up with me. At fifteen, that's torturous; it's unfathomable at that age to think there could possibly be worse things in life. Ah, to be that naïve again. I'd waited until my mother had gone out to do errands to raid her liquor cabinet. Then, I grabbed a bottle of gin. Soon there would be two things in my life I did not like, one was Jennifer, and the other was gin.

I'd cut through Rusty's territory, not giving a shit if the neighborhood bully showed or not. He didn't. I crossed Plimpton Avenue and then the trestle, half hoping a commuter train would come barreling around the corner. Something, anything, that could take that savage stabbing pain from my heart.

"Kenny fucking Addison. She broke up with me to go out with that fucking geek!" I shouted from atop the bridge. I actually liked Kenny, we played football together. He was a pretty big kid, offensive lineman. Didn't mean I wasn't going to try and hurt him out on the practice field, though. In the end, I didn't have to. He hadn't even known about Jennifer's crush on him and when she'd approached him, he'd flat out refused, knowing that she had been dating me. After that, she'd come back to see if we could get back together, but by then I associated her with gin flavored vomit and I wanted nothing to do with either.

I was taking large swigs from that bottle as I headed up the hill, wincing with each and every one. I climbed up the Great Tree and sat nestled in her boughs while I took heavy pulls from that bottle and whined a constant "why me?" By the time I was ready to come down, I more fell out than actually climbed. I landed with a heavy thud on the ground, a small cloud of dust rising up.

"Huh! Didn't spill a drop!" I said, holding the bottle triumphantly high. The Great Tree stood alone in a vast field. Off to my right was a large hill with a huge rope swing and at the top was where we had lit many a bonfire; that was my next destination. I was looking forward to the exhilarating rush of air as I used the swing to sweep out over the hill. I'd no sooner stepped out of the field and into the woods when a spiking chill ran up my back.

"What the fuck?" I asked as I looked around. You know that feeling you have when you absolutely know someone is looking at you? Yeah, that's what I had. I spun to look back the way I'd come. Really, the only place to hide in that direction was the Great Tree. Whoever was watching me was in these woods. At least there are lines of sight in Massachusetts woods. Yes, it is a sea of pine trees and nothing else; someone, or some thing would have a difficult time completely sneaking up on me, though that did little to ease the anxiety that was taking root in my body.

"Come the fuck out," I said as bravely as the gin could make me. Two drinks later and still nothing moved. I couldn't shake the feeling, however, even after two more swallows of the caustic alcohol. "Who drinks this shit?" I asked looking at the bottle. I was still peering at the older Scottish man adorning the label when a blur skirted across my periphery vision. I just caught the back of something impossibly large, greenish...or slightly brown. I don't know if it was the liquid courage that was flowing through my bloodstream, but instead of running away I walked towards it.

This shouldn't be considered flirting with danger; this was flaunting my arrogant ass at it. Whatever it was, was huge, and I was armed only with a half bottle of cheap booze and a bad disposition. I'd not caught another glimpse of the beast as I climbed the hill. All of that changed when I got to the top.

"Paul?" I asked. It was my best friend who had moved away just that summer. Well, it was and it wasn't. He was older and in a uniform, as were the many men around him. They all had rifles and appeared to be getting ready for a battle. A knot formed in my throat when I caught sight again of what I had been following. The beast was huge. He was also carrying a weapon, though he was not firing at the humans, and they were not firing upon him. I was trying to piece all of this puzzle together when I nearly swallowed my own Adam's apple. You think that is an impossibility until you nearly choke on the fucking thing.

I, or at least a very reasonable facsimile of me, perhaps a few years older looking, had gone up to the beast as casually as if we were drinking buddies. I started talking to it. Well, at least my mouth was working, yet I could hear no sound; nothing from any of the dozens of people walking around me, either.

"What the fuck is happening here?" I could clearly see them, but I was certain I was not part of their reality. I know that sounds bizarre, but more than a few had walked within inches of me and had not acknowledged my presence. "Whoa, who's the hottie?" I asked as a red-headed, camouflage-clad woman came right up to "future me". We exchanged a few words and a brief kiss. I learned all I needed to from that brief encounter, they...err...we were in love.

"Guess Jennifer is out of the picture by this time." I took another long swig, the world tilted severely on its axis, or more likely I did. All manner of food I'd taken in for the last few hours made its triumphant return. By the time I pushed up from the ground and away from my steaming pile of vomit, the vision, if it had ever been there at all, was gone. I never told anybody about my experience, and it wasn't until years later after I'd married her that I had a dream about that day. It was then I realized camo-hottie had been a younger Tracy. It seemed that no matter what shit-fest I found myself in, I would always have this beautiful, strong woman by my side to help me navigate through. "Fuck you, Jennifer. Oh yeah, Kenny says fuck you, too."

About The Author

Visit Mark at www.marktufo.com

Zombie Fallout trailer

https://youtu.be/FUQEUWy-v5o

For the most current updates join Mark Tufo's
newsletter

http://www.marktufo.com/contact.html

Also By Mark Tufo

Zombie Fallout Series book 1 currently free

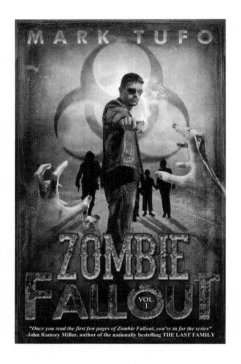

Lycan Fallout Series

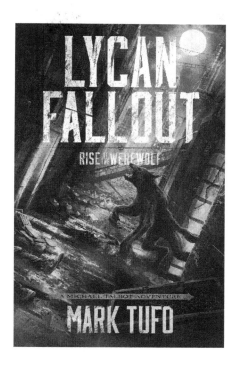

Indian Hill Series

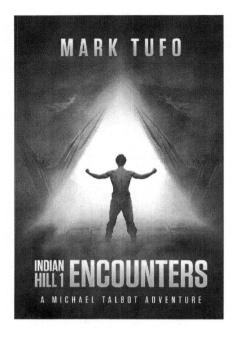

The Book Of Riley Series

Also By Devil Dog Press

www.devildogpress.com

Burkheart Witch Saga By Christine Sutton

The Hollowing By Travis Tufo

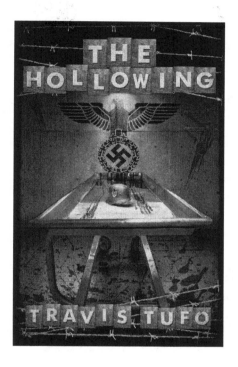

Humanity's Hope By Greg P. Ferrell

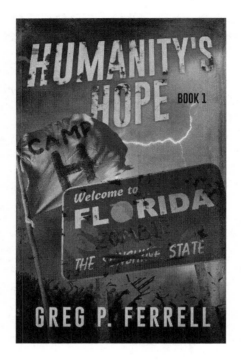

Revelations: Cast In Blood by Christine Sutton, Jaime Johnesee & Lisa Lane

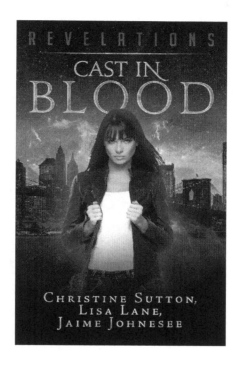

Made in the USA
Middletown, DE
27 July 2017